PRAISE FOR JU[

T0282065

THE RECALL PARADOX

"Stunning and complex, *The Recall Paradox* cracks open the vast world introduced in the first book with interwoven histories, fascinating new characters, shifting relationships, and chilling revelations. The story hits the gas pedal on page one and just keeps climbing. This was truly a satisfying reading experience; I couldn't put either of these books down."

—FRANCESCA PADILLA, AUTHOR OF CRITICALLY
ACCLAIMED *WHAT'S COMING TO ME*

"*The Recall Paradox* hooked me from page one and refused to let me go until I finished. Like *The Memory Index*, this sequel is at once a thrilling dystopian adventure and a beautiful meditation on grief, memory, and humanity."

—NICOLE ZELNIKER, FORWARD INDIE BOOK AWARD
FINALIST AND AUTHOR OF *UNTIL WE FALL*

"*The Recall Paradox* is a mind-bending, action-packed, and heartfelt novel that merges sentimentality with science, challenges the connection between history and memory, and reinforces the importance of self-discovery and friendship. Vaca has delivered more than a book; this sequel is a warning to protect everything you know and love before they are rewritten."

—NATHAN ELIAS, AUTHOR OF *COIL QUAKE RIFT*

"*The Recall Paradox* starts with a bang and never lets off the gas. This trippy, thought-provoking thrill ride is full of mystery and heart. Julian R. Vaca created a world in which memory is in constant flux and then filled it with a cast of indelible characters who are impossible to forget."

—ROB RUFUS, ALA/YALSA ALEX AWARD–WINNING AUTHOR

THE MEMORY INDEX

- One of Bustle's Most Anticipated Books of August 2022
- One of SCRIBD's Best Books of August 2022
- One of Book Riot's Books to Add to Your TBR – August 2022
- A Nashville Scene Summer 2022 Reading Pick

". . . Fun and engaging, evoking the spirit of '80s action/adventure movies, and the characters are intriguing, their personal development nearly as compelling as the main storyline. Thrilling worldbuilding plus a creative tangle of mysteries mark this debut."

—*Kirkus Reviews*

"Vaca's mind-bending, 1987-set debut centers on a quartet of teens attempting to uncover the secrets behind Memory Killer, a disease afflicting humankind that renders people unable to retain a large portion of their memories without artificial aid . . . Via expansive worldbuilding and complex characters, Vaca adeptly combines a mysterious disease, corporate malfeasance, a sprinkling of romance, and good old-fashioned teen sleuthing to deliver an absorbing adventure."

—*Publishers Weekly*

"This speculative YA story is heavy on '80s nostalgia, making it an atmospheric read with elements of adventure and mystery."

—*Scribd*

"An exciting sci-fi premise with loads of opportunity for world-bending consequences that speak to the loss of privacy and proliferation of data mining that dog us today . . . Vaca capitalizes on opportunities to surprise us. He also creates a rich atmosphere that's dotted with cultural touchstones . . . a heady sci-fi tale with heart."

—*Nashville Scene*

"Vaca . . . tackles real-world issues of racism, capitalism, politics, and the exploitation of youth by those in power . . . *The Memory Index* actively examines its own reality . . . Vaca's storytelling is immersive, opening with a high-speed car chase reminiscent of something out of a *Fast & Furious* or *Mission Impossible* movie."

—*Chapter 16*

"A clever and empathetic work of speculative fiction that examines the power and fragility of memory, recommended for general purchase. Cinematic writing, teen sleuthing, and a nostalgic setting make this book a great recommendation to fans of *Stranger Things*."

—*School Library Journal*

"A brutally smart story with intrigue and mystery at every step, *The Memory Index* is a gripping, addictive read. Set in a deeply twisted and immersive world with an engaging cast of characters, *The Memory Index* will have readers racing through the pages to find out what happens next."

—FRANCESCA FLORES, AUTHOR OF *DIAMOND CITY*

"Remember this name: Julian Vaca. *The Memory Index* is a brilliant debut. A novel concept, fascinating characters, and a stirring plot add up to an unforgettable story that promises to be just the first of many by a wildly talented author."

—ANDREW MARANISS, *NEW YORK TIMES* BESTSELLING AUTHOR

"Vaca's debut is a thrilling and often unsettling examination of the elusive nature of memory and truth. *The Memory Index* will leave you breathlessly turning pages until its satisfying conclusion."

—JONATHAN EVISON, *NEW YORK TIMES* BESTSELLING AUTHOR OF *SMALL WORLD*

"A thrill ride from beginning to end! I don't need artificial recall to confirm . . . *The Memory Index* is an unforgettable read. Vaca delivers a poignant and visionary novel reminiscent of retro science fiction. He's one to watch."

—CAROLINE GEORGE, AUTHOR OF *THE SUMMER WE FORGOT*

"*The Memory Index* is a cross between John Green, Neal Stephenson, and Philip K. Dick. Vaca has developed his terrifying premise into a suspenseful tale filled with a visceral sense of nostalgia—plus plenty of '80s references. Readers will be ready for more before they even finish the epilogue."

–ELIZABETH FOSCUE, AUTHOR OF *PEST*

"A fascinating sci-fi premise explored by an endearing cast of characters, set against a nostalgic '80s backdrop. An engaging, fast read that kept me guessing. I can't wait for the sequel!"

—LAUREN THOMAN, AUTHOR OF *I'LL STOP THE WORLD*

ALSO BY JULIAN R. VACA

The Memory Index

THE RECALL PARADOX

a novel

JULIAN R. VACA

THOMAS NELSON
Since 1798

Published in Nashville, Tennessee, by Thomas Nelson. Thomas Nelson is a registered trademark of HarperCollins Christian Publishing, Inc.

Thomas Nelson titles may be purchased in bulk for educational, business, fundraising, or sales promotional use. For information, please email SpecialMarkets@ThomasNelson.com.

ISBN 978-0-8407-0115-2 (trade paper)
ISBN 978-0-8407-0142-8 (e-book)
ISBN 978-0-8407-0143-5 (downloadable audio)

Library of Congress Cataloging-in-Publication Data

CIP data is available upon request.

Printed in the United States of America

23 24 25 26 27 LBC 5 4 3 2 1

To my dearest friend, Tama Powers McCoy,
for keeping the window open

Tomorrow belongs to those who can hear it coming.

—DAVID BOWIE

PROLOGUE

October 22, 1987

Alana Khan stared at the yellow honey-locust trees that lined Wheeler Avenue, wondering why her surroundings always seemed so enchanting—so beautiful—right before her world turned violent.

"The calm before the storm." She turned to Zayne Olson, who sat beside her in the passenger seat of the utility van. "Gimme! Gimme! Gimme!" by ABBA played on the tape deck. "Has there ever been a more apt cliché?"

Zayne procured an inhaler from his windbreaker, sucked in a sharp breath through the mouthpiece, then exhaled deliberately after ten seconds. "I hate clichés."

Alana smiled. *Don't we all?*

She exited the utility van shortly after six, alert and resolute. "On my signal," she told Zayne before shutting the door. He nodded and then disappeared into the back of the vehicle. Alana turned her attention toward the looming Tudor-style home at the corner of Twenty-Fourth Street and Wheeler. At dusk, the Ransom residence appeared almost wistful—its wide lawn and waist-high shrubs awash in waning light and crisscross shadows.

Homes shouldn't look sad. She slipped her hands into her

trench-coat pockets as she walked up the winding footpath toward the front door. *Homes should look . . . homey.*

She rapped on the door with its vintage brass knocker. A moment later, a short man in a green flannel shirt answered. His white hair was unkempt. He smelled of whiskey and deep regret.

"Kendall Ransom?"

"Yes?" the man said, his mouth lingering open. Alana sniffed. That was most *definitely* bourbon. Good. That should make executing the plan easier.

"I'm Detective Forsite." She flashed her badge. "I'm so sorry to trouble you at this hour, but we have reason to believe someone may be planning an attempt on your life."

"I . . . what?"

"I'm afraid it's true. We've been in contact with your employer, Memory Frontier, and have already conducted a thorough search of your offices."

Mr. Ransom swore.

"With your permission," Alana continued, urgent yet controlled, "I'd like to check the premises of your home. I'm also going to have one of my officers stationed across the street around the clock, and for your safety I'd urge you to stay with family for a couple of nights. Do you have family nearby, Mr. Ransom?"

Mr. Ransom swallowed.

"May I come in?"

"Er, yes, please." He stepped aside, his complexion florid and his eyes wide. Alana walked into the foyer and he shut the door. "This way." When he turned his back, Alana reached for the switch on the wall and flipped the porch light on and off, on and off. She did this twice, quickly and discreetly, before following Mr. Ransom down the arched hallway and into the living room.

"Are you the only one home?" She surveyed the tall ceiling and plaster walls, which showcased expensive-looking art. Abstract stuff, really, and Alana eyed it ambivalently. She couldn't understand why people spent so much money on oil paint splatters, pretty as they may be. It felt irresponsible.

"It's just me, yes."

Alana circled the living room, scoping out the interior. Two leather love seats. A bulky coffee table, upon which sat an empty glass, a decanter, and a magazine. A few floor lamps. An empty fireplace. A record player in the corner. The room looked and smelled just as it had in her vision, down to the faint scent of duck sauce.

"Kitchen's through here." Mr. Ransom cleared his throat as they walked into the next room. "So what is this all about?"

Alana noted the bamboo bowl of fake fruit on the island, as well as the half-empty Chinese take-out boxes. "It's the Memory Ghosts, I'm afraid."

"The terrorists?!"

"I'm sure you've heard they attacked a Memory and Cognition Enforcement vehicle in Chicago."

"*Horrendous* . . . and with homemade explosives, yes?"

"Molotov cocktails. Those poor MACE agents." Alana pursed her lips, selling her disgust. "We believe the terrorists have set their sights on Memory Frontier leadership."

Mr. Ransom shuddered. "Why? Why would they come for *me*? I sit in conference rooms all day. I'm no threat to them!"

"Calm down, Mr. Ransom," Alana pleaded. "We're one step ahead of them. You needn't worry."

Mr. Ransom leaned against the island to steady his breathing.

"How many points of entrance are on the main floor?" she asked, then watched as he counted on his fingers.

"Four. There's the front door, the french doors in the dining room, the side door in the laundry room, and the french doors in the primary."

"And you keep your doors locked at all times?"

"At all times. I have a home alarm system too."

"Wonderful. The primary?"

"On the other side of the house." He led her back into the living room, and his breath caught in his throat in a watery choke. The living room had been rearranged. The love seats now faced each other, not the hearth, which held a small crackling fire. Two of the floor lamps had been replaced with potted ficus plants—their stems swaying slightly from having just been moved—and where the coffee table had once sat there was an oriental rug.

"Mr. Ransom?" Alana placed a hand on his quivering shoulder. "Is everything all right?"

"This isn't . . ." His voice was small, far off. He glanced about the living room, looking panicked and fretful. "Something's wrong."

"Something's *wrong?*"

"Yes!" he thundered, shaking off her hand.

"I don't understand."

"Those aren't mine!" He wagged a finger in the direction of the plants. "I *hate* indoor plants! And that rug . . . my couches . . . what the *hell* is going on?"

"Sir, calm down, please." Alana lowered her voice, then posed the inevitable question: "Are you misremembering?"

Mr. Ransom's eyes darted toward her, and where there had been disorientation there was now only fear. Giant orbs of pitch-black fear. Suddenly, it looked as though Mr. Ransom wasn't sure—about any of it. Alana could tell by the way the fear spread from his eyes to his forehead, where beads of sweat began to form. Then that fear spread down to his hands, which he wrung intensely.

Excellent.

"Here, let's check your primary," Alana offered. Without remark, Mr. Ransom padded out of the living room and down the hall with Alana in tow. Cautiously, he opened the door, revealing a four-poster bed, an armchair, and—

"My drapes . . . Where are my drapes?" Mr. Ransom breathed, crossing the wide bedroom toward the floor-to-ceiling windows, which faced east. "And what are these hideous things?" He brushed his fingertips across the white silk curtains, then recoiled. He appeared utterly gobsmacked.

Alana suppressed a grin. "Sir, you look out of sorts. Is everything—?"

A high-pitched alarm screeched throughout the home.

Alana flinched and was reaching for the handgun holstered to her waist when she smelled smoke. Lots of it.

It was the fire alarm.

Now Alana was the one who panicked. *No . . .*

They both sprang into action, darting from the primary bedroom and racing back into the living room. White and gray smoke billowed out of the fireplace and rose toward the ceiling in dense clouds. Mr. Ransom fled into the kitchen and returned with a fire extinguisher.

"I never use the fireplace!" he shouted between coughing fits, blasting the logs in the hearth with his fire extinguisher. "I keep the damper closed! I *always* keep it closed! I never would have started a fire!"

Alana's heart raced. How could she have missed that? It wasn't like her to be this sloppy and—

Through the shrill fire alarm, Alana managed to hear the buzzing in her trench coat. She pulled out her boxy cell phone and answered. "This is Detective Forsite."

"Abort the plan." Mr. Lear's voice was thick and grave. "Our safe houses have been compromised. I'm paging Zayne with my coordinates now."

"But, sir—"

"Alexander Lochamire's agents have successfully knifed Malcolm Heckman's memories."

Alana swore into the receiver, thinking back to their last Transference on the 405. Had Lochamire really managed to access Malcolm's memory of that reckless chase?

"This changes everything. Leave at once."

"Yes, sir." She slipped the cell phone into her trench-coat pocket, and that's when she became painfully aware of the silence. The fire alarm had stopped. Mr. Ransom wasn't shooting carbon dioxide into the fireplace. He wasn't even coughing anymore. She turned to face him and found that he was pointing a silver revolver at her chest with shaky hands.

"You're not a detective." His voice trembled. "You . . . you think I'm crazy?"

Alana held out her hands slowly. "Sir, please lower that firearm."

"Who are you? Who do you work for? I could shoot you right now, you know, since you're in my home!"

"I wish you wouldn't."

"Your cognition wheel." Mr. Ransom's eyes narrowed as he studied the tattoo on Alana's right palm. "It's a four-quarter mark."

"It is."

"That . . . that is *impossible*. No one has the four-quarter mark."

"I do."

Mr. Ransom pulled the hammer back with his thumb and slowly wrapped a finger around the trigger. "I'm going to shoot you *right now* if you don't tell me who the hell you are!"

Alana dropped her hands to her sides. "My name is—"

Her phone buzzed again.

Mr. Ransom pulled the trigger.

His aim was erratic, and the bullet whizzed past Alana's head and punctured the wall above a painting. Alana dove behind one of the love seats, unholstering her own pistol and clasping it tight. She wasted no time, shouting, "Drop your weapon!"

Instead, she heard the sound of footfalls scampering away,

followed by the opening and slamming of a door beyond the kitchen. Alana whipped around the couch, holding her pistol in a modified weaver stance.

Mr. Ransom was gone.

A moment later, Zayne appeared in the hallway, clutching an empty crate and panting heavily. "You . . . okay?"

Alana rushed past him toward the front door. "We've got a runner! Come on!"

"What about my props? Those curtains are expensi—!"

"Leave it!"

Alana flung open the door with Zayne at her heels, and as soon as they stepped out into the twilight, a black Buick zoomed down the driveway toward Wheeler Avenue. Alana and Zayne bolted toward their utility van.

"You think he saw the plants swaying? I practically threw them in place." Zayne struggled to keep up with her. "And I *barely* made it out of the living room in time. I'm surprised he didn't see—"

"That's a moot point, Zayne, seeing as our target is fleeing!"

When Mr. Ransom turned onto the street, he rolled down the passenger window and shot in their direction.

Alana heard the bullet zip between her and Zayne, who yelped and threw himself onto the grass.

"Were you hit?" She turned back toward Zayne. He lay in the fetal position, peeking up from behind his empty crate.

"No!"

"Then let's move. C'mon!"

❖ ❖ ❖

Alana shut the driver's-side door and jammed the key into the ignition. Zayne fastened his seatbelt as the van lurched forward. He tossed the crate into the back of the van, where boxes were organized in tight rows on makeshift shelves. It was Zayne's expansive prop collection: various throw rugs, desk lamps, couch cushions, and random art trinkets fit for the most pretentious of mantelpieces. Just enough decor and bric-a-brac to alter and scramble someone's setting a noticeable amount, and Zayne was an efficient Scrambler.

Most of the time.

"I'm sorry about the damper," he said as Alana zoomed down the street toward Mr. Ransom's rapidly vanishing headlights. "I was moving as fast as I could. If you had bought me an extra minute, I could've checked—"

"You're right. It's my fault." She ran a stop sign, gaining on the '87 Buick GNX. "Though not because I didn't buy you enough time. In my vision, I clearly missed the damper."

Zayne's voice softened considerably. "Look, how were you supposed to catch every single detail?"

"I'm the one with the visions, remember?" She eased off the gas slightly and took a sharp turn onto another residential street. "It's my job to log all the details. And if I had emphasized that the fireplace was empty, you would've been more careful."

Zayne clutched the handle above the passenger window as Alana neared seventy miles per hour. "You knew things were going to go south, didn't you?"

"What do you mean?"

"Before you went in. You said it felt like the calm before the storm."

Alana shrugged. "It just always feels like that, doesn't it? There— he's headed for the interstate."

Their target swerved onto the shoulder and flew past the stalled queue of evening commuters, clipping a few side mirrors before disappearing.

"I'd hate to be Mr. Ransom's insurance provider." Zayne reached into his windbreaker and pulled out his pager. "What's your plan when we catch up to him, anyway?"

Alana opened her mouth to answer, but she could tell Zayne was now fixated on his pager. "Alana? Why did Mr. Lear send me this address?"

She ignored the question and followed the path taken by Mr. Ransom—up the shoulder, around the idle cars, and onto the interstate.

"Alana."

"He wants us to abort the plan. But things changed when our target opened fire."

"Things *changed*? Alana, we're not law enforcement. You could've been killed back there. *I* could've been killed!" Once more Zayne produced his inhaler and sucked in the medication through a hasty breath. "Plus he's no good to us all freaked out like this!" He exhaled. "Scrambling isn't meant to make the target *defensive* . . . it's meant to make them *defenseless*."

"Well, we're past that point, aren't we? And anyway, we *need* those blueprints!"

"I'm telling you he is no good to us in this state of mind. We're wasting our time!"

Alana swerved across a lane and onto the shoulder, narrowly missing a motorcyclist, who shouted over his shoulder at her. She put the van in Park and balled her hands into two fists, punching the steering wheel over and over until her fingers went numb. She reached back and pulled her black hair into a ponytail just to give her hands something else to do.

Once composed, Alana licked her lips and put the van back in gear. "Now what was that address Mr. Lear sent over?"

❖ ❖ ❖

Across town, in the basement of an abandoned halfway house in a middle-class neighborhood, Philip Lear blinked his eyes open and sat up. He removed the receivers from his temples and set them on the table beside the bulky, first-generation Restorey. The scene from his memory tape lingered like the sting from a cut.

"I'll never understand why you, of all people, feel the need to use artificial recall." Irene Porter stood from her stool and brought Mr. Lear a glass of water. The basement was dimly lit and cramped; the square windows near the low ceiling admitted only a fraction of the diffused moonlight.

Mr. Lear ejected the memory tape and slipped it into its case. "I suppose it's a lot like returning to an old book. I don't *have* to, but then, some books demand rereading."

"I'm gonna take your word for it."

Mr. Lear smiled and took a sip. "Once the Task is complete, you'll understand."

Irene nodded as if she agreed, even though he suspected she didn't.

Mr. Lear shifted in his seat. "Alana? Zayne?"

"Almost here. Gemma's en route too."

"Good." He held his right hand in his lap, fingering the four-quarter mark with a contemplative gaze. Irene regarded the cognition wheel on her dark brown skin—a circular tattoo with three colored quadrants etched into her palm.

"You've never asked why my cognition wheel has four quadrants." Mr. Lear smiled at Irene.

"That's because I know why."

"Oh?" He chuckled at that.

"Sure. It means you have a special ability. It's why Gemma and Alana have ones, too, but Zayne, Emilia, and Malcolm don't."

"Well, now that's an interesting theory."

"What I can't figure out, though, is *your* special ability." Irene eyed Mr. Lear suspiciously.

An urgent rapping from above stirred Mr. Lear and Irene into action. He stood and dragged the small end table toward the wall while she climbed the creaky stairs to unlock the door for the others.

Mr. Lear got to his knees, his joints moaning, and carefully rolled up the floral rug like a giant map. On the cement floor, written in smeared chalk, was a series of numbers and equations.

At the top of the stairs, Gemma Morris appeared. She was a retired neuroscientist, an elderly woman who never left home without her clutch purse. She was Mr. Lear's Listener. Then there was Zayne Olson, a young man in his late twenties who obsessed over antiquities and artifacts. He was Mr. Lear's Scrambler. And finally there was Alana Khan, also in her twenties. Alana was a bright epidemiologist and Mr. Lear's Seer.

"Good evening," said Mr. Lear, rising to his feet. Everyone moved into a circle around the scribblings on the floor, and it was a long while before anyone spoke. Irene—the youngest of the group, barely nineteen—eventually returned to the basement, offering glasses of water. Only Gemma accepted; the rest politely declined. Irene retreated to the stairs and plopped down onto the bottom step.

"Joshua Cohen was arrested." Mr. Lear sighed. "As you know, the congressman was critical to the Task. This is a major setback, and Alexander Lochamire's camp is sure to spin it in Memory Frontier's favor."

Alana gritted her teeth. "With the congressman *and* Malcolm in police custody, our numbers are thinning."

"Indeed." Mr. Lear looked about the group. "And now that Alexander has found agents capable of knifing, there's no telling what other information he will glean. The Task just got harder."

"My oh my." Gemma clasped the glass of water with her veiny

hands. "So Mr. Lochamire's done it. He's figured out how to enter someone's memory. But who has he recruited to knife?"

"There's no telling," Mr. Lear replied. "I suspect they're highly capable agents, especially if they managed to intercept one of our messages during a Transference."

The group nodded solemnly.

After a while, Alana whispered, "I screwed up tonight's plan. We really could have used those blueprints from Kendall Ransom's safe, and now all we've done is scared him and put him on high alert. This will inevitably get back to Alexander." She cursed and broke the circle, walking toward one of the windows and looking up at the sky, adding, "I'm sorry."

"You two did your best," Mr. Lear assured her.

"Which wasn't good enough," Zayne said, chagrined, gripping his inhaler at his side. He gasped as a thought occurred to him. "If Malcolm's memories were knifed, does that mean MACE agents could be on their way here at this very moment?"

Mr. Lear shook his head. "Remember: I don't disclose *every* safe house to all of you. Malcolm was never aware of this one; we are safe here."

"For now." Alana absently adjusted her ponytail as she rejoined the circle.

"This is our next move, is it?" Gemma asked gently, staring down at the white-chalk equations. The numbers were gibberish to all but those five in the basement—a tight-knit collective of men and women who sought to expose Alexander Lochamire's dark secrets and who understood the coded message. Should their memories of that evening ever be knifed, the code would be impossible to decipher.

"It'll never work," said Zayne, his eyes flying across the numbers over and over, as if he couldn't believe what he was reading. "And it's *insane*."

"I like it," said Gemma, a hint of laughter at the edge of her throat. "Mr. Lear, you sure are full of surprises, aren't you? My oh my."

Mr. Lear smiled despite himself.

Alana stroked her chin. "It's risky . . . no doubt about that . . . but I like it."

"Really, guys?" Zayne scoffed. "Am I the only voice of reason here?"

"Every outfit needs one," Irene remarked from the stairs, raising her glass and winking at Zayne.

"Aren't you supposed to be waiting outside?" Zayne snapped.

"Hey, cool, Zayne's in charge, everyone." Irene stood. "Mr. Lear, your services are no longer required. Zayne's gonna steer the ship now."

"That's enough, you two." Mr. Lear shot them both a look. "Zayne's right to be skeptical. We need every potential move heavily scrutinized. Time's running out, and we must be certain we're thinking through our strategies."

Zayne folded his arms across his chest as if to say *I told you so*, but his smug expression melted away as Mr. Lear continued: "That said, I've considered countless other scenarios, yet I keep coming back to this one. I strongly believe it's our best shot at leaking the truth to the world and bringing down the Memory Frontier empire for good."

"We still have to vote," Zayne said. His last-ditch effort.

"Wonderful idea, my dear," said Gemma, her tone neither sarcastic nor condescending. "Those opposed?"

Zayne raised his hand confidently but with reddened cheeks.

Gemma continued, "And those in favor?" Hers, Mr. Lear's, and Alana's rose into the air. "Three to one, then."

Mr. Lear looked around the room. He was proud of this lot, proud of their honesty and bravery and shared commitment to seeing the Task through. Zayne would come around, as he always did, and when such a time arrived, the Memory Ghosts would be in a position to finally put a stop to the madness.

"There's one other thing of note." Mr. Lear walked to his chair and sat, resting his hands on his belly. "I believe we're on the precipice of a succession. Alexander's daughter, one Brenda Sanders, appears to be involved in matters relating to Memory Frontier now."

Gemma closed her eyes and placed an index finger on the nape of her neck. "Ah. You spoke on the phone with her earlier."

Mr. Lear gave a nod. "If Alexander's health continues to deteriorate, I suspect she'll be handed the proverbial crown."

"Can you warn us before you go and read someone's thoughts?" Zayne used his inhaler and then pocketed it. "It freaks me out, Gemma."

Gemma kept her eyes closed but turned and pointed her face at Zayne. She flared her nostrils. "My boy, those are some dreadfully disturbing thoughts."

"Ha-*ha*." Zayne rolled his eyes. Mr. Lear and Irene chuckled; even Alana let out gentle laughter. Gemma opened her kind eyes and smiled sweetly.

"This Brenda Sanders," Alana asked, slipping her hands into her trench-coat pockets. "What do you know of her?"

Mr. Lear tilted his head back and stared at the exposed plumbing in the ceiling. Sure, he knew *plenty* about Alexander's daughter—his estranged goddaughter who, at one time, was like a true daughter to him—but he stuck to the salient parts: "Dr. Sanders is a respected cognitive psychologist. Recently married. She's only been working for her father for the past few years and is currently teaching at Foxtail Academy."

Gemma shifted her weight. "She's overseeing that mysterious trial of his?"

"It's possible. I have some theories." Mr. Lear crossed his legs.

"Well, I think you all should take the rest of the evening to yourselves. Tomorrow we begin our Hail Mary."

Everyone agreed, and then, one by one, they quietly filed up the stairs and left. Once again, only Mr. Lear and Irene Porter occupied the musty basement. Mr. Lear nodded toward the floor. Irene grabbed the small broom from behind the stairs and—careful not to glance at the cryptic message—swept away the chalk scribblings.

When she finished, Mr. Lear thanked her and asked, "Are you ready for your assignment?"

Irene leaned the broom against the wall and folded her arms across her chest. "Only if you tell me what this Hail Mary plan is."

Mr. Lear flashed her his usual grin, the one he always gave her when she asked to be more involved. "You know I can't do that. It's too risky, especially now that we know Alexander has agents who can knife."

"Yeah, yeah." Irene flipped her hand.

"Besides, I have a very important assignment for you."

"If you tell me to take out the trash, so *help* me."

Mr. Lear's grin broadened and his eyes twinkled.

1

FREYA IZQUIERDO

A Few Days Earlier

As I climb into Dean Mendelsohn's rental, invigorated about the answers that lie ahead, I'm met with intense panic.

It's sort of like this: Sometimes, in the dense darkness just before dawn, when everything outside my window is just as still and quiet as everything inside my bedroom, I wake up and forget where I am. Two things happen then, and in this order: (1) I anxiously look about the shadowy room, and (2) I spot my foster sister, Nicole, sleeping soundly in her bed. Then I remember: I am a student at Foxtail Academy in Tennessee, but right now I am a foster kid on fall break, at home in California. In those predawn moments of forgetting where I am, seeing Nicole anchors me to reality, and I'm able to fall back asleep, if only for a little while.

But the panic I feel right now in Dean Mendelsohn's car is

17

different from the one that sometimes visits me before daybreak. It's not that I forget *where* I am but rather *why* I'm going where I am going, as in, *After all this time, am I really ready to face the answers about Dad's mysterious death?*

Of course I am. This shouldn't even be a question. But panic cares little about logic. Panic can't be reasoned with. It comes and goes as it pleases, and sometimes I need a life preserver to cling to so I don't drown in it.

I wish Fletcher were here, holding my hand from the back seat of the dean's rental. I can weather this on my own, sure, but I *want* him here.

"Are you still dizzy?" The dean's voice, soft and cautious, cuts through the silence.

I can't talk about this right now. If I do, I'll be forced to dwell on my latest vision . . . the one of Fletcher lying motionless in—

No. Stop, Freya. Not now . . . not yet.

I distract myself by fishing out the voucher from my back pocket. Dean Mendelsohn gave it to me just before we left, and it grants me a cognition wheel upgrade. I stare at the words on the piece of paper, trying to decide how I feel about becoming a recollector . . . an elitist. Part of me despises the thought—if the two-quarter mark was good enough for my dad, it's good enough for me. But the other part of me wonders what kinds of doors this could open.

There's definitely a lot to consider.

"Where are you taking me?" I ask, putting the voucher back in my pocket.

"We're almost there." He glances at the digital clock above the speedometer. "He agreed to meet us at Shoreline Aquatic Park."

He? I shrug this off, figuring *he* is either some social worker or private investigator Dean Mendelsohn hired to find answers about my dad. But the question sits with me like a pesky fly that quickly becomes intolerable, and so I ask, "Who is *he?*"

The dean sighs. "I'm sure this is all very . . . complicated. I spoke with your foster parents ahead of time, and they agreed you should take as much time as you need."

He's not answering my question. Why isn't he answering my question?

"Okay. Fine. But who is *he*?"

The dean scrunches his eyebrows together. What isn't he telling me?

"Freya, I . . . I'm confused."

"That makes two of us."

"We're going to see your father."

"You mean we're going to see *about* my father."

"Huh?"

"We're going to see *about* my father since, you know, he's dead."

"Dead."

"Yes, dead, as in no longer alive. You said you had answers about his death."

"I said I could get you the answers you sought, as in the answers to his whereabouts."

This is quickly becoming one of the most confounding and frustrating conversations I've had in a long time, and I once lived in a foster home with not one but three six-year-olds.

"Freya?"

"Dean Mendelsohn."

"Who, um, told you that your father died?"

My frustration rises to an angry boil, and I just might snap. *Who told me?* Really? What is Dean Mendelsohn implying—that my dad staged his death and then, from the shadows, just let me fall into the state's fractured foster system so he could watch from afar as I popped from one foster home to the next for over two years?

Before I can push back, the dean rolls to a stop in an empty parking lot, and I see a lone figure sitting on a bench beneath some palm trees, his back to the car. The man, backlit by the twilit sky, turns toward us.

"Do you . . . do you want me to come with you?"

Dean Mendelsohn's words are garbled, like he's speaking underwater, but instead of replying I unfasten my seatbelt, get out of the car, and walk toward the approaching stranger—all the blood in my body rushing to my head.

The tall stranger and I meet on the lawn.

The man has a sad, tired face. It's the kind of haggard face a lonely person wears, a person who lives a sequestered life.

"Hey, *mija*." His voice is as tired as his eyes.

This man is clearly not my dad. And yet . . . and yet his eyes . . . the shape of his nose and ears . . . the way his chin curves up, like it's trying to get away from his face . . .

"You're *not* my father," I say defiantly, but then I gasp and all sound and smell and sense of where I'm standing evaporates.

Memories of my childhood crash into me, a tropical storm rushing a fortress, threatening to crush me into fine powder. The water washes the dirt off the photographs in my mind. Now I see the gallery of my past with newfound clarity: This man, this coward who stands before me, left me when my mother died, forcing my older *brother* to raise me. All this time I had been misremembering my brother's identity. Because he raised and cared for me, because he was more than I ever could have asked for in a dad, my subconscious skewed some details and rewrote my past.

No . . . it can't be . . .

Hot tears materialize in the corners of my eyes.

"We got a lot to catch up on," the man says, his frail voice quivering.

2

FLETCHER COHEN

Fletcher watched in horror as three MACE agents escorted his father out of their home, across the lawn, and into the back of a hulking armored vehicle. It all happened so quickly that Fletcher didn't even know what was going on until his father was out of sight.

Reporters were everywhere.

The neighbors watched from their stoops.

And Fletcher's mother openly wept on her son's shoulder.

The Cohen family attorney, Quentin Thorne—a tall man whose hands were mottled with liver spots—exchanged quick words with one of the MACE agents before joining Fletcher and his mother on the porch.

"Here's what we know." Quentin always seemed to start his conversations with what he or others knew. "There's evidence tying your father to the Memory Ghosts, who were allegedly plotting a coordinated attack on multiple MACE field offices up and down the coast. Right now, the charges are domestic terrorism."

That's impossible, Fletcher thought, only he said, "Maybe let's talk about this later." His mother needed to get inside, away from the flashing cameras and snooping neighbors.

"I'm headed to the station with your father," Quentin said, and then to Fletcher's mother, "I'll call later this evening with an update."

Fletcher's mother nodded feebly, then he led her inside and shut the door and deadbolted it.

He recalled that evening when he came home and witnessed his father meeting in secret with a woman he'd never seen before. Suddenly this all felt a lot less impossible, and all he wanted to do was hop on his motorcycle and go see Freya.

3

FREYA IZQUIERDO

"You're a coward," I say, tears pouring out of me at an embarrassing rate.

He nods, and I'm annoyed with his agreement.

Before he gets the chance to say anything, I yell, "So why now?"

"Why now?"

"Why come out of hiding?"

He glances past me at the dean, who's still sitting in the driver's seat of his rental, pretending to read some book.

Of course. I'm so stupid. He's only here because the dean forced him to be here.

"Did he pay you?"

"What?" The stranger shifts his weight. "*Mija—*"

"Did Dean Mendelsohn pay you to come here and see me?"

There's a long beat; the stranger runs a hand through his shaggy hair. I catch sight of his two-quarter mark and decide right then that *degenerate* has been an appropriate descriptor only once, and I'm staring it square in the face.

"He said he'd make some calls, get me a clean record and whatnot."

And whatnot. Am I really this man's daughter?

My breathing starts to quicken; my body tells me this "conversation" has run its course. I take the cue and turn on my heel.

"Wait," the stranger calls. I almost don't, but his tone has shifted, so out of curiosity I loiter for a second. "Don't you wanna know about your *mamá?*"

I decide that's it, that's enough, that's about all the earth-shattering news I can handle for one night. See, my mom died giving birth to me, and this I know to be true. I can think back to those moments in our apartment when my *brother* . . . when Ramon would talk of her big and bright light, of her stubbornness, of the way she'd sing over the skillet like she was "serenading dinner"—her ceremonial routines, as Ramon put it. He'd talk about her death with sadness, then would hug me and say the world couldn't handle all the big and bright light that she had to offer, and so she was called home.

My mother's name was Theresa, and Ramon said it meant "to harvest," and I remember him saying that every harvest must come to an end. He told me it was now his purpose, his calling, to protect and hold me close just as our mother had protected and held him.

So I don't care what this stranger thinks he knows about my mother. Ramon already told me everything I need to know, and between that and my pictures of her in my photo album, I don't want hollow words from some stranger in a park.

"Take me home, please," I say when I get back to the car. Tears run down my flushed cheeks in rivulets. I wipe them off with a flick of my hands.

Dean Mendelsohn starts the engine without saying a word. We pull out of the parking lot wordlessly, and I watch the silhouette of the man who is my father but is *not* my dad vanish into the night.

4

FLETCHER COHEN

Quentin Thorne phoned an hour later. Fletcher's mother assured her son she was of sound mind and could take it from there, so he retreated to his bedroom. Muscle memory led him to his knees so he could retrieve his *Raiders of the Lost Ark* lunchbox.

Fletcher cursed. He'd left it in his dorm room on campus.

Great. He stayed on the floor with his back against his bed, trying not to think about the implications of his congressman father being charged with domestic terrorism.

But he was hopeless against the fearful thoughts, which circled Fletcher like vultures:

Is Dad going away for life?

Just what is his involvement with the Memory Ghosts?

Is that young woman he met with connected to all of this?

Are Mom and I going to have to move out?

Will she want to move to Oregon to be closer to her parents?

And what does this mean for me and Freya?

"Get a grip, Fletcher," he said, leaning his head back and closing his eyes. He pushed away these disturbing thoughts and, with much effort, replaced them with a single thought of hopefulness . . . one he wanted to be true so badly he chanted it in his heart over and over until he thought he might cry right there on his bedroom floor.

What if they have the wrong guy?

❖ ❖ ❖

Fletcher barely slept that night. He did have the presence of mind to slip on his Reflector receivers at some point after ten, but from that point on he slipped in and out of half sleep, and it wasn't until the first bits of sunlight seeped through his blinds that he realized just how long a night it had been.

The kitchen was empty. Fletcher found his mother's Restorey on the island with the receivers unspooled. Beside this, a note:

I'm taking your father's Restorey and his memory tapes to the station. He's never missed his window before. I hope nothing happens. I love you.

I hope nothing happens, Fletcher thought, picturing his exhausted mother hunched over the island, penning many meanings through those four cursive words. He pictured her getting into her car and driving to the station, putting on a brave face, and pushing through the sea of reporters, who had likely staked out all night. Fletcher wondered if she'd be permitted to see his father, or if that wasn't allowed. He imagined her handing over his father's Restorey and bag of memory tapes to someone who assured her they would deliver them to Joshua Cohen's cell, and that hearing the word *cell* would finally do her in again, and the weeping would return.

❖ ❖ ❖

Fletcher flipped on the TV.

"... *which they're calling one of the greatest scandals in recent American politics—*"

Fletcher flipped off the TV.

I can't do this by myself, he decided, marching to his bathroom and splashing water on his face.

5

FREYA IZQUIERDO

I skip breakfast the next morning, and thankfully no one in the house needs an explanation. Nicole gives me my space, as do Joaquín and María, who spend most of their time out in the backyard anyway. And so, like many times before, I'm left to my ineluctable thoughts.

How could I have misremembered such an important person in my life? I lie facedown on my bed, feeling beyond overwhelmed. I'm so racked by last night's discovery that I can't focus on which part overwhelms me the most: how sacrificial my brother was, giving up his life to raise me, or the fact that my actual father is still alive, meaning I'm not the orphan I believed myself to be these past two years. And what was that he said? About wanting to know my mom? As if he can tell me something—*anything*—that Ramon hasn't already!

I still feel parentless. I turn onto my back, my entire body leaden, and stare at the popcorn ceiling. And what's more? I'm no closer to discovering the truth behind my brother's suspicious death in that Memory Frontier factory. *¡Maldita sea!* I feel back at square one.

I swing my feet off the bed, traipse across my room, and grab my photo album from its hiding spot behind the boombox. I collapse onto the carpet and flip it open.

My family stares up at me. In one photograph, my teenage brother holds his bat, decked out in his baseball uniform, smiling reservedly; in another, my beautiful mother stands over a steamy pot of pozole in a cramped kitchen, her flowing black hair tied behind her back; and in another, my father . . . the stranger from the park . . . leans expressionless against a vintage car under the beating sun. He's young in the photograph, his eyes deep pools of brown. He looks so similar to Ramon, or I suppose Ramon looks so similar to him. I've looked through this photo album countless times! How could I just . . . *mix up* my brother's and father's identities?

The photo album feels incredibly heavy in my lap, and the faces in the photographs become those of strangers, not *mi familia*. I am an impostor, holding the pictures of someone else's loved ones.

I crawl back into bed. I grab my pillow and cover my face, hoping to find some quiet in the dark but knowing I'll never be able to silence these questions that trail me like monsters in the dark.

Sooner or later, I'll have to open my eyes and confront the monsters again.

❖ ❖ ❖

A soft, cautious knock at my door prompts me to slide my photo album under my comforter.

"Come in," I say, removing the pillow and sitting up. The door cracks open, and my weary heart skips a beat. I leap out of my twin-size bed and throw my arms around Fletcher before he even enters the bedroom.

"Hey." I close my eyes. As I firmly hold him—take in his scent, feel his chest rising against mine as he breathes—my mind is filled with the images of my last vision. I'm in the snow, the mysterious mansion looms in the distance . . . Fletcher's lying in my arms, motionless . . . he's *so* bruised . . . he's *so* still . . . and he's dressed in the jumpsuits we wear for memory knifing . . .

Stop! I try to banish the haunting pictures, but the more I try not to think about them, the more I end up thinking about them.

Fletcher's here . . . he's safe . . . he—

"Hey, hey." Fletcher pulls back from our embrace, holding me by the shoulders, looking deep into my watery eyes. I'm shivering. Head to toe. Even my teeth are chattering.

As if I've just been sitting in the snow.

"Freya, what's wrong?"

"Nothing, I just . . ." What do I say? The truth? That last night I had a prophetic vision of him lying unconscious in my arms . . . maybe *dead*?

"You're freezing." He pulls me closer toward him. *Get ahold of yourself, Freya!* I let him hold me, and just when it seems the tremors won't stop, he lightly tilts my chin up and draws my gaze to his. He blinks, then kisses me on the lips.

Instantly, my body goes calm against his, and an exhilarating warmth trickles down from my mouth, through my body, and to my feet. I feel light-headed, almost weightless—like I'm soaring through the flashing neon colors of a memory knife—and my stomach flips in circles.

We eventually break away, and I lead him into the bedroom and shut the door. "I'm fine now that you're here. I just . . . I had the worst night."

"I may have you beat."

"Oh?" We sit across from each other on the carpet, and as we do, I'm able to read his face. Everything clicks. *His father . . . the premonition I had in Malcolm Heckman's memory . . .*

"My dad's facing some pretty serious charges."

"I'm so sorry, Fletcher."

"Yeah, me too. Me too."

"How's your mom?"

"Hanging in there. I think."

"I can't imagine . . ."

"I know."

I stroke his arm. "Stay here as long as you need."

"I think . . . I kind of need some air."

"What'd you have in mind?"

6

FLETCHER COHEN

Fletcher sped down the street on his Ducati with Freya on the pillion, her long arms wrapped around his waist. He drove south toward Laguna Beach, eventually merging onto the Pacific Coast Highway. With no real destination in mind, he zoomed past cars and then turned up a residential street, and it wasn't until Freya lightly squeezed his ribs that he realized how fast he was driving.

He pulled off the road and parked the motorcycle, panting.

"Fletcher."

"I . . . I'm fine."

"You're not, and that's okay."

"I *am*, I just . . ." He dismounted and began to pace back and forth on the sidewalk. "What's his problem? Like, how selfish do you have to be . . . how *deranged* do you have to be to get caught up in that? He's a congressman, Freya. A *congressman*! Did he really think he wouldn't get caught? And what about me and Mom, huh? He's *so* selfish."

Freya listened quietly, watching as Fletcher worked through his thoughts, and in that moment—in the midst of Fletcher's desperate cries—a look of realization passed through her eyes.

"When we knifed Malcolm Heckman's memory . . . ," she began, dismounting and joining Fletcher on the sidewalk. She took one of his hands and held it in hers, forcing him to slow down. "We perceived a lot of information about Malcolm . . . all kinds of context that was baked into his memory. Remember?"

"Yeah."

"I . . . I didn't perceive any kind of evil motivation on Malcolm's part. Not once."

"What do you mean?"

"We supposedly entered the memory of a terrorist, right? Don't you think that experience would have been laced with—I dunno, like, evil undertones? Some kind of unsettling, disturbing energy tied to Malcolm's goal?"

"I dunno, maybe."

"The first thing we perceived when we dropped into his memory was that sense of anxiety, remember? It nearly knocked us off our feet. But Malcolm's anxiousness never felt—how do I put this?—like the kind of anxiety one might experience if they're trying to get away with murder."

Fletcher shook his head. "I dunno, Freya. I was just focused on manifesting my motorcycle and then staying on Malcolm's tail."

"We should ask the others—"

"Why?"

"I—"

"Like, why would that matter? So what? Who cares how Malcolm did or didn't feel?"

"It matters because what Malcolm was carrying was eventually delivered to your father. And if it wasn't evil—"

"How do you know that?"

Freya stopped short. She was holding something back, and Fletcher slowly withdrew his hand. "Freya?"

"Here, let's sit." She led Fletcher to a nearby bench. "I never got the chance to tell you, but when I was alone in Malcolm's memory . . . shortly after you'd safely ejected . . . I had another premonition."

"You did?"

Freya nodded. Then, carefully, she continued, "But because I was in Malcolm's memory, the premonition had to do with him, not me. And I saw a . . . a flash-forward of him in a car outside your house in Manhattan Beach. The young woman he was with—her name was Alana, I think—she was there to hand-deliver a message to your father."

Fletcher leaned back on the bench, dumbstruck.

"I should've told you sooner, I just hadn't found the right time. I'm sorry."

Fletcher took Freya's hand back. "You have *nothing* to be sorry for. You didn't ask for these premonitions."

"No, I didn't."

"Okay, so back to Malcolm's memory. What's the big deal about us not perceiving the sinister intent of his goal? He was probably so focused on not being caught that he didn't have time to think or stress about anything else."

"Maybe." Freya turned, staring out toward the glistening coast, clearly formulating a plan. "Unless . . ."

"Unless what?"

"The address that Malcolm was carrying . . . Dean Mendelsohn said it was the address of a MACE precinct that the Memory Ghosts were planning to attack, right?"

"Right."

"Maybe we should swing by."

"'Swing by'?"

"C'mon," she said, standing. "I still have the address memorized."

7

FREYA IZQUIERDO

Fletcher rolls to a stop in front of the empty storefront. We're inland, just outside Riverside, and this address led us to a strip mall off the freeway. More specifically, it led us to a vacant space sandwiched between a Laundromat and a Greek restaurant. In other words, it couldn't be farther from a MACE field office if it tried.

"You're positive this is the address?"

"Yes." I hop off his motorcycle and cross the parking lot. I walk to the glass door, cup my hands, and peer inside. About as empty as I'd expect a vacant storefront to be. There are a couple of chairs inside, lots of dust on the floor, and what appears to be an upside-down jack-in-the-box toy. Fletcher joins me and gazes through the bay windows. "This was the address at the bottom of that document Malcolm handed over to Alana. I'm sure of it."

"This doesn't make any sense."

"No. It doesn't."

A frightening possibility begins to materialize in my mind. *Dean Mendelsohn lied to us. The Memory Ghosts never were going to target a MACE field office.* And if that *is* the case, what is this place, and why is it significant?

"Freya." Fletcher's tone is sharp. He nods toward the window, and at first I think he's trying to get me to see something inside, but then I realize he's looking at the glass's reflection: past the parking lot, beside a payphone on the sidewalk, a man watches us. His posture is tense, and I can tell he's trying to be discreet. But with our backs toward him, he's begun to stare at us openly.

"Has he been there the whole time?" I whisper back.

"I'm not sure. Let's get out of here."

We turn around, and the man—who wears a baseball cap, hoodie, and sunglasses—nonchalantly redirects his attention toward something in the sky. We get back on Fletcher's motorcycle and peel off.

The man, whoever he was, was staking out that strip mall. There's no doubt in my mind.

What's going on here?

"We need to meet up with the others," I say into Fletcher's ear at the first red light.

He nods and says, "Took the words out of my mouth."

8

FLETCHER COHEN

Chase Hall and Ollie Trang met them at the closest In-N-Out Burger, where Chase wrapped Fletcher in a sympathetic bear hug. "I saw the news this morning. Dude . . . how you holding up?"

Ollie lightly batted Chase away. "Quit hogging him," she said, giving Fletcher an even bigger hug.

"Guys, I'm—It's fine. I'm fine."

Ollie pulled away and gave Fletcher a doubtful look.

Chase wore a forest-green bomber jacket, and his wavy blond hair fell past his ears messily. Ollie had donned a pair of her favorite acid-wash jeans and a faded MTV sweatshirt.

"I *am* fine," Fletcher insisted. As he sized up his best friends, he actually believed himself. A lot had transpired since their dinner together the night before, and Fletcher was grateful to have their support. "C'mon, let's eat. Freya and I have something to tell you."

The four walked into the burger joint, ordered, then found a spot in the corner opposite the register. In low voices, Fletcher and Freya took turns detailing Freya's observation about Malcolm's memory . . . what she described as "a lack of malicious intent" when they knifed and were perceiving details and context. They told Chase and Ollie about what they'd found (or rather, didn't find) when they'd gone to the address that was supposed to be a MACE field office.

"Hold up," Chase said, pushing his animal-style fries aside. "You're saying the address Freya swiped from Malcolm's memory was to some dinky office?"

Freya and Fletcher nodded.

"Dean Mendelsohn said the Memory Ghosts were plotting a major attack," Fletcher reminded the group. "That our mission was about saving lives. But there's not a MACE field office within a twenty-mile radius of that strip mall. We checked the Yellow Pages."

Ollie slurped her strawberry milkshake. "Are you implying that the dean lied about the whole mission?"

"Freya." Chase leaned back, sighing. "Is it possible you're . . . you're misremembering the address?"

"No," she said firmly. "In Malcolm's memory, I recited that address over and over again and inscribed it on my heart. There was no way I was forgetting that address and potentially blowing my deal with the dean."

"Speaking of which," Fletcher said, turning toward her. "Has he reached out to you yet to keep his end of the bargain?"

Freya took a drink of her Coke. "Yes, but . . ." She trailed off, and no one pried. Ollie did, however, reach across the table and squeeze her friend's forearm, as if to say, *We're here when you're ready to talk about it.*

The table fell silent. After a while, the restaurant started getting busier and noisier.

After finishing his burger, Chase spoke up. "I guess with as much lying as Dean Mendelsohn and Memory Frontier do, it shouldn't come as a shock if they lied about this too."

"But if we didn't knife to stop a terrorist attack," Ollie said, shaking her head, "then why? What's so important about that address?"

"There's one more thing." Fletcher lowered his voice. "Freya and I are pretty sure someone's staking out that strip mall and keeping an eye on the vacant store."

Chase flattened his bangs with his hands, sighing dramatically. "Ugh. Guys. Our fall break is shot. *Shot!* We're supposed to be vacationing right now. Does that mean nothing to you? *Va-ca-tion-ing.*"

"As always," Freya said dryly, "your priorities are in perfect order. *¡Bien hecho!*"

"Dr. Sanders said we'd earned this break, remember?" Chase continued, grabbing a pinch of Freya's french fries and tossing them into his mouth. "Is nothing sacred to you guys?"

"So what's our plan?" Ollie asked, sitting up and then adding out of the corner of her mouth, "That's me ignoring you, Chase, just to be clear."

"*Crystal,*" Chase said, swiping Ollie's milkshake and taking a drink.

"For starters," Freya said, looking them each in the eye, "we can't let Dean Mendelsohn know that *we* know the truth about that address."

No disagreements.

"Since we have a few more days until we have to go back to Foxtail," she continued, "I propose we do some digging on the Memory Ghosts."

Fletcher shifted awkwardly in his seat. With his father now allegedly linked to the terrorist group, Fletcher desperately wanted the Memory Ghosts to be the harmless, petition-peddling protesters he'd always believed them to be. Yet Dean Mendelsohn had the four convinced that the Memory Ghosts were havoc-wreaking bad actors thirsty for the blood of MACE agents.

So if the wool had been pulled over their eyes, why *did* the dean—and, beyond him, Memory Frontier, Alexander Lochamire, and Dr. Sanders—need them to knife Malcolm Heckman's memory and acquire that address?

"Hey, so we should probably leave." Chase nodded toward the windows. Fletcher shrugged off his thoughts and glanced up, noticing not one but *four* news vans pulling into the parking lot. He heard the anchor's voice from earlier that morning play back in his head.

One of the greatest scandals in recent American politics . . .

Like wolves with insatiable appetites, the reporters had managed to track down Fletcher, and it was most certainly time to leave.

"In and out, am I right?" Chase said, then they all darted for the exit.

9

FREYA IZQUIERDO

Chase plops down on his haunches in the sand, a burst of cool sea breeze tousling his hair. "If I *were* to agree to help you guys research the Memory Ghosts, where would we even start?"

Ollie sits down next to him, crisscross, and wastes no time chiding him.

"What?" Chase throws up his hands as Fletcher and I sit down across from them on the beach. "One of us has to defend the sanctity of our vacation."

Fletcher gazes at the ocean, squinting against the hot sunlight that reflects off the water. I take one of his hands and clasp it in mine and say, "We could start at the library." Chase moans, but I continue. "Use those microfilm readers to dig up every newspaper article we can find about the Memory Ghosts."

Ollie sighs. "I thought about that too. The problem is that

whatever we find in the newspapers will only be what the journalists know . . . surface-y stuff."

Chase and I nod.

"This is gonna be tricky." Chase straightens and begins counting with his fingers: "For starters, the Memory Ghosts have a kind of scattershot collection of identities—some fly airplanes over Foxtail with cryptic messages, some vandalize property in a mall while wearing stolen MACE gear, and others attack MACE vehicles. They're all over the place. Then there's the matter of their intent. Just what exactly *is* their end goal? Dean Mendelsohn said they're terrorists, but since he lied about the MACE field office, we have to take that with a grain of salt."

I flash him a half smile.

Chase frowns. "What?"

"Sanctity of vacation?" I cock an eyebrow.

Chase gives me a face that says, *Touché.*

"Oh!" Ollie snaps. "The manifesto. Didn't the dean say the Memory Ghosts mailed their official manifesto to . . . ?" She trails off, frowning. "Never mind. Grain of salt."

We all nod. Fletcher, who hasn't said a word since we arrived at the beach, finally turns from the ocean view to face us. His expression is somber. "We have to search through my father's things."

A silence sets in, and I feel Fletcher's palm grow cold in my hand. For a while it's just the waves and the seagulls and the cars at our backs.

"Fletcher," Ollie says delicately, leaning in. "Wasn't most of your father's important stuff confiscated by the authorities after his arrest?"

Fletcher shakes his head. "There's a hidden door in my parents' walk-in closet. It's behind their shoe rack. Mom always said it's for her jewelry and family heirlooms. I'm betting there's more than antiques in that hidden room."

"We don't have to do this." I stroke his hand. "We'll find another way to track down info on—"

"No." Fletcher meets my eyes. "My dad is a direct link to the Ghosts. Chances are, he's our best shot at getting to the truth behind these terror . . . behind *them*. Plus, who knows? Maybe we'll be able to clear his name."

No one says anything.

Ollie pulls her windswept hair into a ponytail. "So does that mean you've accepted that he's really one of them? That he wasn't framed or something?"

I take this one. "There's something else I haven't told you guys yet." I tell Ollie and Chase about my vision in Malcolm's memory—the one where I saw a young woman named Alana delivering the manila envelope to Fletcher's father outside their home.

"You had a vision inside a memory?" Chase looks back and forth between Fletcher and Ollie, like he's saying, *You guys heard that, too, right?* "And the vision was about Malcolm, not you?"

I draw my lips into a straight line, suddenly feeling *very* embarrassed.

"Has that ever happened before?" Ollie looks concerned, kind of scared actually.

Great. Now I've disturbed my best friends beyond repair. Way to go, Freya.

"You guys are missing the point." Fletcher gently squeezes my hand. "Freya had a vision that ties my father to Malcolm Heckman and the Ghosts. As hard a pill as that is to swallow, at least I know where my father stands. And that wouldn't be possible if not for Freya."

Chase's and Ollie's expressions soften.

Fletcher sighs. "Now we just have to learn everything we can about the Memory Ghosts, figure out why the dean lied to us, and keep a low profile."

"Sounds easy enough." Ollie lowers her voice. "I mean, the four of us *did* just memory knife a few days ago. There's nothing we can't do!"

❖ ❖ ❖

On the walk back to the parking lot, I start to worry that digging through Fletcher's father's things isn't the best idea. Fletcher is pretty raw right now. Is he really ready to face whatever secrets are holed up in his parents' hidden room?

I'm struck by the universe's cruel timing: Fletcher and I were *both* hit with disturbing revelations about our fathers on the same night. Mine's a liar and a coward; Fletcher's might be a deeply troubled criminal.

What a world, what a world . . .

"That work for you, Freya?"

I nearly flinch and look up as Fletcher watches me expectantly.

"Sorry . . . I . . . so what's the plan?"

Fletcher chuckles. "I was saying that since my mom's spending most of the morning tomorrow at our attorney's office, you guys should come over then."

"Right, yeah." I tuck a few strands of loose hair behind my ears. "That's perfect."

We mount his Ducati together, and a second later Chase pulls up beside us in his gray Honda Prelude. Ollie sits in the passenger seat, and both windows are rolled down with Jefferson Starship's "Jane" blasting from the stereo.

"Looks like the band's back together." Chase spreads his arms, nearly smacking Ollie. "We're a Great Dane away from being the Scooby-Doo gang, am I right?"

Ollie shoves his arm away. "A band has to be *broken up* before it can get back together, you—"

Chase howls and peels out of the parking lot. That is, as much as a hand-me-down Prelude can peel out.

❖ ❖ ❖

Back in my room later that afternoon, I find my foster sister, Nicole, on her bed reading.

"Hey," she says, not looking up from her book.

"Hi." I trot over to our shared dresser and fish for some clean clothes, deciding a midday shower is what I need to clear my head. The quiet. The hot water. The steam. It always does the trick. I'm heading for the door when Nicole asks, "What's that, by the way?"

I turn around and find her—still refusing to emerge from behind her V. C. Andrews novel—pointing at something on my desk. I chuckle and walk over to where she's pointing and see the blue voucher that Dean Mendelsohn gave me the night before.

I fold it up and toss it into one of the drawers. "It's nothing."

"Hmm." Nicole turns a page. "Didn't look like nothing."

"Ah. So you *do* know what it is."

"Well, sure, but I wanted to give you the chance to tell me. It'd be rude if I started talking about your voucher for a three-quarter mark without giving you the chance first."

"Rude as opposed to, say, going through my stuff."

"You left it out in the open." She turns another page. *Is she really reading while talking to me?* "You were begging me to inspect it."

"Begging you. Really?" I roll my eyes.

"Mhmm. So are you gonna get it?"

"Get what?"

"The three-quarter mark." Another page turns. "Doy."

"Look, can we not talk with you hiding behind your book? If you're going to go through my stuff, the least you can do is look me in the eye—"

Nicole lays the book open across her chest, revealing her face. She's not wearing her glasses, and both her eyes are filled with a cold, milky grayness.

Memory Killer. *I am such an idiot.*

"They still gray?" she asks, blinking softly.

I nod.

"Awesome." She pulls the book up and tents it over her face. With her voice now partially muffled, she says, hands clenched at her sides, "This has been happening a lot lately . . . feels like more than it should."

I toss my change of clothes onto my bed and sit at her feet. "How'd you know it was happening right now?"

"Saw my reflection in María's stupid mirror clock in the dining room. Came in here to wait it out."

"And what makes you think your Memory Killer attacks are happening more frequently?"

"When school started a couple of months ago, it felt like a classmate was giving me the look-away at least once every period." She sighs. "I know we all do it—the not-so-subtle, turn-your-head-in-a-forced-casual-way thing—but it gets really old when it happens to you *that* much."

Sitting there on Nicole's bed, hearing my foster sister's melancholic words, I realize how difficult the last nine weeks must have been for her. She and I have never been super close, and yet we've shared the same cramped bedroom for almost a year, had a lot of the same classes together at Victory, and often ate lunch together at our lockers.

Obviously, that all changed when I went to Foxtail Academy. And while I was making new friends in Ollie, Fletcher, and Chase, benefiting from a change of scenery, and basking in the school's many amenities, Nicole was suddenly without her foster sister and stuck here in Long Beach.

A bud of guilt begins to blossom in the pit of my stomach.

"I'm sorry."

Nicole pulls her book off her face and blinks her eyes open. They're back to their beautiful, sharp-blue selves. "Don't be. Happens to all of us, you know? I'm sure it's just—"

"No, I mean, I'm sorry I just left you . . . for Foxtail. I'm sorry I didn't, I dunno, write. And I'm sorry that Memory Killer attacks have been happening to you so frequently. That's awful."

She smiles demurely. "You didn't abandon me, Freya. I have other friends."

"Oh, of course, I just meant—"

"I know what you meant." She reaches down and squeezes my forearm, her smile spreading. "Thanks."

I smile back.

"By the way, you have *tons* to fill me in on." Nicole slips her glasses back on, swings her feet around, and sits beside me. "What's the strange, secretive tech you're trialing for Memory Frontier—that little pager you slept with last night? How's boarding-school life? Do classes suck as much there as they do here? And is motorcycle dude your boyfriend? He's definitely got a dreamy George Michael thing going on. Oh! And how did it go yesterday after dinner, meeting your dad?"

My dad . . . meeting my dad.

Before I received that bombshell news, I'd dedicated unremitting attention to learning the truth behind Dad's—er, my brother's—violent death at the factory. Now, for the first time in, well, *ever*, it's the last thing I want to think about. I need time to process all of that . . . that my actual dad is still alive, Ramon is the one who was killed, and—

"Sorry." Nicole pushes up her glasses. "I didn't mean to pry."

"No, it's just . . ." A thought occurs to me. "What do you know about my story? Like, why I've been in foster care for a couple of years."

She shrugs. "I never asked. And you never offered much. Took that as a hint. It's just as well. We're all in here because we're parentless. That means different things to different kids."

Boy does it. *Dios ayúdame.*

"I guess I do have a lot to fill you in on." I stand, collect my change of clothes, and head for the door. "But first, a shower."

I pause on the threshold, thinking, then turn back to Nicole. "You know what? I think I *will* get that cognition wheel upgrade."

"Yeah? You'll be a recollector then."

I nod. "Think of all the trouble we could get into if I no longer require a handler to go certain places."

Nicole's face drops. "I really don't want to get arrested again. Once was enough for me."

I wink at her and leave for the bathroom.

10

FLETCHER COHEN

Fletcher rolled off the couch around 9:00 a.m. to someone knocking at the front door. He'd fallen asleep in front of the TV, which was playing the music video for "Vacation" by the Go-Go's. He shut it off with the remote, pulled the Reflector receivers off his temples, and tossed the tiny device onto an end table.

Midyawn, he opened the front door to a guy in a navy jumpsuit standing on the step. A rat-shaped patch below the collar read Foscue Pest Control.

"Morning, sir," the tech said awkwardly, picking up his large sprayer. "Just here for your routine—"

"Yeah, okay, fine." Fletcher turned, leaving the door open, and made for the kitchen. He set to work brewing a pot of coffee as the pest control technician silently sprayed the foyer and the living room and then disappeared down the hall toward the bedrooms.

A few minutes later, Freya, Chase, and Ollie appeared at the edge of the foyer—scanning the living room, looking apprehensive.

"Fletcher?" Freya called out.

"In here, guys." He waved them over to the long island that separated the two rooms.

They collectively sighed in relief, and Ollie scolded, "Do you always leave your front door open like a maniac?"

Fletcher smiled, amused, and poured four mugs of steamy coffee. "Pest control's here."

Freya, Chase, and Ollie shuffled up to the island, receiving their mugs with thanks. Fletcher leaned forward and pecked Freya on the lips as Ollie looked about the expansive Cohen house and whistled.

"You did all right for yourself, Fletch," she said, swinging in a full circle on her stool. "This place is nice."

"With my gray clunker parked in your driveway, there's a preeeetty good chance the neighborhood association's gonna fine you." Chase raised his mug. "If they do, just forward it to me. I'll make sure the parentals take care of it." He took a sip of the coffee and immediately winced. "Ugh, is that motor oil? Got any creamer?"

Fletcher stifled a laugh. "In the fridge."

"*Gracias, amigo.*"

"What's a neighborhood association?" Freya asked, cupping the warm mug in her hands. She wore hoop earrings, and her jet-black hair was in a taut high bun. She had a snug-fit hoodie and high-waisted jeans, and Fletcher marveled at how beautiful she looked in her casual clothes.

He became painfully aware of his holey T-shirt and gym shorts.

Ollie sipped her coffee. "Neighborhood associations are . . . you know what? You're better off not knowing."

Freya shrugged. Chase returned to his stool with a bottle of liquor he'd apparently found in one of the cupboards.

"That's not creamer, dude."

Chase unscrewed the top. "Maybe not to you." He turned to the girls. "Anyone else need a little hair of the dog?"

Ollie rolled her eyes and Freya leaned in closer to Fletcher, who still stood in the kitchen on the other side of the island. "How'd you sleep?"

"Oh, you know." He took a drink of his black coffee. "Barely at all."

"I'm worried about you."

"Don't be. I'm sure each day this will all get . . . easier."

"Maybe." Freya watched the steam rising from her mug, thinking. "Just don't forget that you're grieving, and grieving doesn't necessarily get easier over time. It just . . . evolves."

"Freya's right," Ollie chimed in. "You need to take care of yourself. You need to process this with, I dunno, a professional."

Fletcher shook his head. "Are you guys saying I need to see a therapist or something?"

Chase shrugged. "At the very least, maybe a guidance counselor."

"That reminds me." Fletcher turned, grabbed an open envelope that sat atop a small pile of mail, and pulled the letter out. He held it up for his friends to see the Foxtail Academy letterhead. "You guys get this too?"

Ollie and Chase groaned, but Freya perked up. "At breakfast, my foster parents told me I had some mail, but I didn't bother to check it before I left the house. What is it?"

"The dreaded college conversation," Ollie said, sounding winded.

"Mr. Williams is scheduling one-on-one time with all the seniors so he can regale us with college success stories." Chase glanced down at his mug. "If we're gonna talk about college, I'm going to need this to be stronger."

Fletcher set down his letter and stared at it. "At least you guys will have a shot at getting into the college or university you apply to."

"Huh?" Freya tilted her head. "What are you talking about?"

"You think any university's going to admit the son of a terrorist?" Fletcher crumpled the letter and tossed it into the kitchen wastebasket. "Think again. No one's gonna want that kind of bad press. Honestly, I'm half expecting to return to Foxtail with all my bags packed and a letter of expulsion waiting on my pillow."

"Stop that, Fletcher," Freya said, though her tone was subdued. "Foxtail is *not* kicking you out. As bad as this sounds, you're too valuable to the dean and Memory Frontier now that you're a proven memory knifer. And any university would be lucky to have you apply, let alone accept your enrollment. You'll see."

Fletcher threw on a fake smile, but before he could reply, the pest control technician reappeared in the hallway. "All finished up, sir! Already sprayed the perimeter of the house, so you're all set."

Fletcher nodded. The tech pulled an inhaler out of his jumpsuit pocket, took a sharp breath of the medicine, then showed himself out.

"Did that dude just call you *sir*?" Chase snorted. "Wild times indeed!"

Fletcher chuckled. "How about we pause all this talk and go break into my parents' hidden room already?"

Fletcher led his friends down the hallway, past his and the guest bedrooms, and into the primary. He felt his face go cold at the sight of his parents' king-size bed: one side had clearly been slept on, while the other was perfectly made. There was even a small mound of tissues on the carpet beside his mother's side of the bed.

She cried herself to sleep. Fletcher shivered. *I should have checked on her in the middle of the night . . .*

His eyes lingered on the scene briefly, and his stomach pricked at the sight of the framed photographs on the end table near his mother's side. A wedding portrait. A picture of Fletcher in grade school. A black-and-white ultrasound of his sister, Josephina.

Half of my and Mom's world has been ripped from us. Fletcher set his jaw. *It's downright unfair.*

He looked away, crossed the bedroom toward the walk-in closet, and flipped on the light.

His breath caught in his throat: the hideaway door was ajar, and through the opening Fletcher and his friends could see all kinds of upturned boxes and random items spilled about the floor.

11

FREYA IZQUIERDO

"Let's not jump to conclusions," Ollie says, though her voice is rising with apprehension. "Maybe your mom was looking for something in a hurry . . . you know, before she left this morning?"

Fletcher shakes his head and moves toward the hidden room, pulling the hideaway door open all the way. He swears loudly and runs his hands through his wavy hair. "My mom wouldn't leave this mess." He gets to his knees and starts shuffling the papers and small boxes around. "I don't care how upset she is . . . she just *wouldn't*."

I leave Ollie and Chase in the closet doorway and join Fletcher on the floor, scooping up documents and organizing them into small piles.

"Someone must've broken in while I was sleeping." He holds up one of his mother's necklaces, a beautiful, glittering piece of jewelry that probably costs more than Chase's Prelude. "Look—they left my mom's valuables. Whoever did this was looking for something specific. They *knew* this room was here."

"Dude. Fletcher." Chase comes up behind us, peering into the hidden room. "That pest control tech . . . did you have eyes on him while he was back here spraying?"

"You guys showed up right after he did." Fletcher carefully deposits his mother's necklace into a small metal box. "Besides, he wasn't back here that long."

"Unless your dad," Chase persists, "or someone who works for your dad, sent him here to grab something."

Chase actually makes a pretty good point. That technician *was* carrying a large sprayer. It could have been a fake sprayer, a container for storing or hiding something. And the person, like Fletcher already said, would need knowledge of the hidden room in order to be able to access it—and access it so quickly.

"This is unbelievable." Fletcher rises to his feet, sounding and looking overwhelmed.

"Maybe we should look through some of this stuff anyway," Ollie suggests, kneeling beside me. "There's a good chance we'll still find something about the Ghosts."

"I dunno, maybe." Fletcher doesn't sound convinced. And frankly, I'm not so sure either. I highly doubt that whoever turned this room upside down left anything remotely incriminating behind.

But the four of us quietly riffle through Fletcher's parents' things anyway. We go through the motions, half searching, half cleaning up the mess. We find social security cards, passports, some tax documents, a living will—the sort of things one might store in a family safe. As for intriguing information about the Memory Ghosts and Congressman Joshua Cohen's role in their schemes? *Nada.*

"This could not have been a bigger waste of time." Fletcher slams the hideaway door shut, and when he does, a small book on the top row of the shoe rack is jostled. It falls to the ground, along with a pair of high heels.

I reach down and pick up the book, an ancient-looking hardback titled *The Listener, The Scrambler, The Seer, & The Task*. No author is attributed to the book, and when I crack it open, I see why. It's a hollow book.

Fletcher, Ollie, and Chase lean in around me, and we all silently stare at the lone, unlabeled memory tape inside the book.

"So . . ." Chase tousles his moppy hair. "*That's* pretty weird."

❖ ❖ ❖

The four of us relocate to Fletcher's backyard, where we sit on a lush patio sectional by the pool—huddled around the ancient memory tape.

"As far as memory tapes go, this thing looks old." Ollie picks it up gingerly and turns it side to side. "It reminds me of the memory tapes my grandparents used, back when I was like eleven. Could be a first-gen tape . . . it's *so* heavy!"

"Why would your old man keep a decade-old memory tape?" Chase asks, flipping his bangs out of his eyes.

"That's the sixty-four-thousand-dollar question, isn't it?" Fletcher takes the memory tape from Ollie and inspects it. "Whatever memory it holds, my dad clearly didn't want to chance forgetting it."

"You know"—I watch Fletcher, choosing my words very carefully—"it could be your *mom's* memory tape."

The group falls quiet. Ollie slowly nods. "The hollow book *was* hidden behind her pumps."

Fletcher sets the memory tape onto the glass table. "You're right, Freya."

"Regardless of whose it is," Chase says, "what I don't get is why they didn't store it in the hidden room. If you're gonna go through the trouble of hiding something in a hollow book, you might as well take the extra precaution and keep it with your other hidden stuff. Right? Is that not weird to you guys?"

"Not any weirder than a book called *The Listener, The Sailor, The Seer, & The Map*," Ollie says, crossing her legs. "Or whatever the heck it's called."

"Yeah." I chuckle. "We need to look up that title in the library when we get back to Foxtail."

"Why bother?" Fletcher slaps his knees, stands, and begins to pace beside the pool. "It's probably some random antique my mom found at a swap meet."

"I dunno, man." Chase shrugs. "No offense, but your folks don't strike me as the swap meet type."

Fletcher blinks. "What's that supposed to mean?"

"A hollow book isn't something you just stumble upon," Chase clarifies. "It's something you seek out when you're trying to conceal something, like an ancient memory tape."

"Fine," Fletcher concedes. "But the memory on that tape is probably . . . I dunno . . . something dumb, like when I took my first steps. *That's* why it wasn't in the hidden room, which means it has nothing to do with my dad and the Memory Ghosts. This morning was a total bust."

I hate seeing him like this. At this point, I wish we *had* found something substantial or incriminating. The not knowing almost feels worse.

A plan formulates in my mind. "Fletcher," I say delicately. "At this point, we don't know for certain it's your mom's tape, but there's a way we *can* be certain."

"I'm not asking her outright." Fletcher stops pacing and puts his hands on his hips. "I don't want to risk upsetting her if the memory on that tape is—"

"No," Ollie cuts in. "I think Freya means we could take the memory tape back to campus and use the dean's tech so you can knife it."

12

FLETCHER COHEN

Fletcher laughed. At first, it was forced laughter, but then it quickly spiraled into the atonal laughter of a delirious, sleep-deprived seventeen-year-old. Before he knew it, Freya, Chase, and Ollie were staring at him as if *he* was the crazy one.

He paused to catch his breath, then said, "You're really suggesting that we knife this memory tape?"

"Not *we*." Freya straightened. "*You*, Fletcher."

"Let's say that this *is* my mom's personal memory," Fletcher said, bewildered. "Do you have any idea how weird and invasive that'd be? *Knifing* my own mother's memory?"

"More invasive than rummaging through your parents' belongings?" Chase raised his eyebrows. "Plus, like Freya said, we don't know that it's your mom's memory tape. What if it *is* your dad's, and it has critical information on it? What if the memory on the tape proves the Ghosts *aren't* terrorists . . . proves your dad is innocent?"

"What if, what if, what if." Fletcher sounded like he might laugh some more.

"I'm confused." Ollie stood, her tone razor-sharp. "Isn't this what you wanted, Fletcher? For us to help you?"

I don't know what *I want*, he silently mused, leaning his head back. "Sorry. I . . . maybe we should just take five. I'm starving."

Before anyone could reply, the sliding glass door partially opened, and Fletcher's mother stuck her head outside. Her sandy-blonde hair was pulled back in an attempted ponytail, but loose locks fell across her oval face. Her green eyes, usually alight with enthusiasm for the day, appeared tired and dull, and the minimal eyeliner she wore was smeared.

"Oh, hey, hon." She mustered a feeble smile. "Didn't realize you had friends over."

"Hey, Mom." Fletcher stood aside. "This is Chase, Ollie, and Freya. Everyone, this is my mom." They all waved, and Ollie had the presence of mind to pick up the memory tape and slip it to Chase, who wedged it between two throw pillows. Freya, meanwhile, stood, joined Fletcher's side, and reached out a hand to his mother—who still hadn't joined them on the patio.

"I'm Lila Cohen." She accepted Freya's gesture. "But don't any of you *dare* call me Misses. Lila will do just fine, thank you."

"I'm really sorry to hear about your husband," Freya said gently. "How are you?"

"Right now?" Fletcher's mother looked to the sky as if the answer might be written in the clouds. "Hungry."

Chase and Ollie joined them and flanked Freya and Fletcher. "We should probably go," Chase said, glancing at Ollie and Freya.

"Why?" Lila opened the sliding door all the way. "So an exhausted, depressed woman can sulk with her son? Nonsense. You're eating with us."

Freya smiled.

"I can always eat, Mrs. C!" Chase actually patted his belly.

"How are you with a grill?" Lila raised an eyebrow. "I prepped shish kebab earlier this week and I'm in no mood to grill it myself."

Chase chuckled, but when he realized Fletcher's mother wasn't joking, he paled. "I, um—"

"Good. And what did I say about calling me Misses?"

13

FREYA IZQUIERDO

Chase, as it turns out, is a perfectly capable grill master.

He mans the grill, sporting Lila's "Hot Stuff Coming Thru" apron like a champ. Ollie is on standby, prepping the patio table with plates and silverware, and Fletcher and I sit with his mother on the sectional.

"Have you seen him yet?" Fletcher asks of his father, watching his mother for any facial movement that might offer a subtle clue.

"I haven't, no." She sounds neither bitter nor hurt. She doesn't even sound indifferent. Just . . . matter-of-fact. "Quentin said he'll be transferred to a federal prison unless he can work out some way to get him sent to the Fold instead."

"I . . . the Fold?" Fletcher narrows his eyes. "Why?"

"Well, for one thing, it beats prison." Lila crosses her legs. "If Quentin can somehow prove your father's been under duress, that his involvement with the Memory Ghosts was not only minimal but against his will . . . perhaps he can avoid incarceration. For now, anyway. At the Fold, I imagine they'd run a bunch of tests and, well, buy us time. It's a long shot, but it's something."

I can't help but feel a pang of resentment at the possibility of a congressman managing to dodge prison because of some clever lawyering. I'm holding out hope that Joshua Cohen is innocent, especially for Fletcher and his mother's sakes. Yet I'm certain if this were someone like, say, my foster parent Joaquín, he'd be in federal prison like *that* and already facing a daunting sentence.

For some, innocent until proven guilty is just a nice idea.

"Is that true?" Fletcher leans in. "That Dad was somehow coerced into helping them?"

Lila bites her lip, her expression distant. "I don't know, hon. I mean it when I say I only know what you know."

My heart sinks. If Fletcher is devastated by all of this, his poor mother must be reeling. You think you know your spouse—your life partner, the father of your child—only to find out he's actually harboring unspeakable secrets.

I just can't imagine what they're going through . . .

Except that I kind of can. For years I misremembered my past . . . I thought my dad was laying down his dreams to raise me. Only, my dad was actually Ramon, my brother. My *real* father? *Un cobarde.* He's been lying since the moment I was born, when he decided to abandon me and Ramon and—

"Freya?"

I look down. Fletcher has gently grabbed hold of my hand, and he interlaces our fingers.

"Mom was asking what you think about Foxtail so far."

Oh. Right. Foxtail.

"Although," Lila says, her face suddenly filling with color, "now I'm more curious about *this!*" She gestures toward our hands, and

I feel my neck grow hot. "What are your intentions with my son, Freya?"

"Mom, no, *please* no jokes."

"O-oh . . . u-um . . ." Am I stammering? *Have you forgotten how to string a complete sentence together, Freya?*

"Relax, my dear." Lila smiles, and thankfully it feels wholly genuine. "The fact that you're sitting right here at my son's side despite all the gossip and headlines speaks volumes. He's beyond lucky to have you as his girlfriend."

Girlfriend? I can tell Fletcher's starting to panic. So I figure I might as well have a little fun. "She's right, you know. You're *beyond* lucky."

Fletcher chuckles, but not nervously . . . *playfully.* "Guess I am, huh?"

"You carnivores ready for your lamb or what?" Chase crosses the patio and sets a serving plate of steamy shish kebab on the table. "If you don't hurry, Ollie's gonna scarf it all."

"No, but I *will* skewer you," Ollie snaps, stabbing one of the unused skewers into the air like a dagger.

Lila rises to her feet. "It smells wonderful, Chase, thank you. And look! You managed not to burn my house down either."

We all laugh as we take our seats at the table, and Fletcher steals a kiss on my neck when no one's looking. I feel gooseflesh spread down my back at the touch of his lips, and as we both sit down and load up our plates, I decide that *girlfriend* has a really nice ring to it.

"By the way, Mom." Fletcher pulls a bell pepper off his skewer and tosses it into his mouth. "Pest control stopped by this morning while you were meeting with Quentin."

"Huh." Lila pours herself a glass of lemonade. "Weird. They already serviced our house this month."

Fletcher shoots us all a worried glance. "Yeah. Weird."

❖ ❖ ❖

The next morning, Joaquín drives me to our county repository so I can redeem the voucher Dean Mendelsohn gave me for an upgraded cognition wheel. I'm not keen on sitting through the painful tattoo process again, but I figure the discomfort just might be worth it in the short term. If Memory Frontier is still a year away from deploying the Reflector to the public, having recollector clearance between now and then could prove very beneficial.

The way I see it, this is all about function—not status.

So, okay, fine. Give me the three-quarter mark. Let me use this dumb tattoo for my benefit. Let me use it to find info on Ramon's death.

"You want me to go in with you?" Joaquín asks after he parks his car.

"I'm good, thanks." I unfasten my seatbelt.

"This is good, you know." Joaquín rests his hands on the steering wheel, beaming. "You . . . a recollector. And to think just two months ago María and I were picking you up from a police station. Look how far you've come!"

If he only knew what I'd been through the past few weeks . . . the truth behind what Memory Frontier is doing at Foxtail Academy. I hold my tongue, smile, and reach for the door handle. But Joaquín's not finished.

"Freya, do you think you could talk to Nicole?"

"We talk every day."

He laughs uncomfortably, shifting in his seat. "Right. Of course. What I mean is, could you talk to her about her decision to skip her artificial recall windows?"

I clutch the door handle anxiously. *Why would Nicole do that?*

"Oh, sorry, I . . ." Joaquín glances away. "I only guessed you two had talked about it."

Her abnormally frequent Memory Killer attacks, I realize with a chill. *That must be why they're happening.*

"Freya?"

"I'll talk to her," I say, and he turns to meet my eyes. I gasp and avert my gaze. Memory Killer, as if sentient—as if sensing we're talking about it—is feeding off some random memory of Joaquín's.

He pulls the rearview mirror toward his face and checks his reflection. *"Maldita sea."*

"I should go." I open the passenger door, but before I step outside, I say, "I'm sorry." I mean to add *for freaking out,* but the straightforward apology will more than suffice. Because the truth is, I'm feeling sorry—feeling guilty—about a lot of things right now. Sorry for how I treated my foster parents all those months with my proclivity for breaking rules; sorry that Nicole is scaring them with this inexplicable urge to skip artificial recall; sorry that I have access to a Reflector already and they do not.

For all the lies Memory Frontier has spun about the true intent of Foxtail Academy and the Reflector trial, I can't deny how incredible it's been not having to lug around my Restorey and memory tapes, not having to plan entire days around artificial recall. And most important, not having to worry about unexpected Memory Killer strikes—and the discoloration of my eyes that comes with them.

The Reflector, clichés be damned, has been life changing.

I wave to Joaquín through the windshield and then make my way up the steps toward the repository. As I walk, rubbing my arms against a cool October breeze, I realize something. By the time we knifed Malcolm Heckman's memory tape, the four of us had been transitioned off our Restoreys and using Reflectors for *weeks*—over two months, even with the boys having skipped the first week of the trial. And yet Memory Killer still attacked Fletcher. I can still see his cold, colorless eyes as he lay on the ground, breaths away from being trapped in a memory loop.

But the Memory Frontier spokesman . . . Marshall, I think his name was? He said the technology in Reflectors had off-the-charts results in containing Memory Killer. That early testing had shown this was breakthrough technology.

So why was Fletcher still attacked like that? Was it because we were memory knifing, and his defenses were down?

That has to be why, I decide. I store these thoughts away and head into the building to get my tattoo.

In the cramped, windowless waiting room, I check in with the receptionist. After I hand her my voucher, she writes a few things on a clipboard and then tersely orders me to sit until my name is called.

"Imagine being a degen," says a teenage girl, who's maybe my age, sitting one row over. I glance her way, unsure if she's talking to me. She flips through a magazine lazily, and her handler (a scrubs-wearing older guy with a five o'clock shadow) appears to be asleep. The girl meets my eyes. "Having to work in a stuffy repository all day . . . watching countless sixteen-year-olds shuffle through and get their recollector branding . . . knowing that *you'll* always be a degen . . . like a hopeless serf enslaved to the elite. How utterly depressing."

I glance back at the receptionist, who is now wearing headphones. She's probably playing mood-matching music to help her remember the task she's currently doing.

"Maybe things will change one day," I say, leaning back in my chair, thinking about Memory Frontier's Reflector and how, a year from now, the release of the technology is going to eliminate the need for cognition wheels.

"Maybe." The girl tosses her magazine onto the table, disturbing her handler. He grunts in his sleep. "Maybe brandings have always been around. Maybe brandings will never go away."

I slip my hands into my pockets and look the other way, remaining quiet for a time. Eventually, the girl's name is called, and she follows a uniformed man through the door beside the receptionist. In the quiet, I turn my thoughts to my visions. I've been avoiding confronting a troubling reality for some time: switching to a Reflector did not eliminate my premonitions, which I had long thought were fragmented memories.

Now not only do I have to figure out some way to protect Fletcher from that disturbing fate he meets in my latest vision, but I have to work extra hard to understand where the visions are coming from—and why they're happening in the first place. As much as I'd like to keep my interactions with Dr. Sanders to a minimum, she's likely my best shot at learning what's wrong with me.

I sigh and glance about the waiting room, noticing on the table a super-old issue of *Bop* magazine that the girl was reading. The band Talk Talk is featured on the cover with the headline LET'S TALK TALK ABOUT THE NEW SINGLE "IT'S MY LIFE"!

The song title gives me pause, and I slowly formulate a theory.

What if I could control my *ability*? What if there were a way to summon premonitions instead of fearfully wondering when they might strike? Could I take control and harness these visions . . . use them to my advantage?

The longer I meditate on it, the faster my heart beats. Could this work? Have I been thinking about this all wrong?

Maybe my visions aren't a curse but a gift.

14

FLETCHER COHEN

On the evening before they were set to return to Foxtail Academy, Fletcher and Freya sat on the patio of Gloria's Ice Cream & Soda Shoppe. Manhattan Beach Boulevard was bustling with evening shoppers, joggers, and dog walkers. Palm trees were as ubiquitous as the smell of salt water that hung in the air.

This world existed within a big, shiny bubble that even plague-like memory loss couldn't penetrate. Here, avoidance, not ignorance, was bliss. Sweet, bountiful, overindulgent avoidance.

Sometimes I feel like this place is Pompeii, Fletcher's mother would say from time to time. *Knowing Vesuvius is going to erupt but ordering a glass of Domaine Leroy anyway.*

Regardless, Fletcher tried to savor it all—the dessert on the table, the distant sound of the ocean, Freya's intoxicating smile—because as soon as he and his mother received an update about his father, things would change.

"How's your cognition wheel healing?" he asked, staring at the transparent adhesive patch wrapped around her right palm.

"Fine, I think. It's still pretty sore."

"Man . . . I don't think I'm ready for you to have recollector status. It's gonna get to your head *so* fast."

Freya scowled across the table at him. "That's not funny. In fact, it's the opposite of funny."

"So, what, unfunny?"

"*Very* unfunny."

Fletcher smiled innocently, taking a long drink of his malt. After a moment or two, he said, "I think I should stay back here with my mom, in Manhattan Beach."

Freya set down her spoon. She looked unsurprised. "I think that's a good idea."

"You do?" Her agreement hurt a little, even though he'd suggested it.

"Sure. If that's what you want to do," she said. "But what does your *mom* want? Have you asked her?"

Fletcher looked out at the street, now paying scant attention to his malt. *She wouldn't want me to put my life on pause.* He sighed inwardly.

Freya reached across the table and held his hand. "At school, you'll have classes to distract you. You'll have your friends. You'll have . . . me."

"No, I know." He gave a flimsy nod. "Plus, I've given it some thought, and I think I *do* want to try to knife that memory tape we found in my parents' closet."

"Yeah?"

"Could be nothing, could be something." Fletcher shrugged. "But between that and anything else we can secretly research about the Memory Ghosts, maybe we *can* find out why Dean Mendelsohn lied about the knifing mission."

"And clear your father's name," Freya added, squeezing Fletcher's hand.

"Yes." He conjured a smile. "Either way, it'll be a good distraction."

"I've always said I make a good distraction."

Fletcher laughed. "'Good'? Adequate at best."

She lightly kicked him under the table, a sparkle in her eyes. He leaned across the table and kissed her, then they sat in a comfortable silence, a silence that drowned out the chatter from the sidewalk, the din from the surrounding storefronts and busy street—a silence that covered them like sea breeze.

"I need to tell you something," Freya eventually said, pushing her half-eaten sundae aside. "This week, two things happened, and I've been avoiding dealing with them as much as I can. But if the last couple of months have taught me anything, it's that I don't have to face my problems alone anymore."

"You can tell me anything, Freya," he said, as if she needed to be reassured.

"I know that." Slowly, she withdrew her hand, then she told him about her recent vision, the one involving a bruised and unconscious Fletcher. And then, before she could even catch her breath, she told him about meeting her father, about remembering that she'd actually been raised by her brother, Ramon—that *he* was the one who had died in that factory explosion two and a half years ago.

Fletcher leaned back in his chair when Freya finished. He was shell-shocked.

"What's wrong with me, Fletcher?" she said, her voice quivering. "Why do I get these premonitions? How could I have misremembered my own past . . . someone so critical to my childhood? How could I be so . . . so *weak*?"

Fletcher stood up, dragged his chair around the table beside Freya, and held her. He didn't have the answers, but he could sense that Freya didn't need answers right now.

She needed to be held.

So hold her Fletcher did, forehead to forehead, and hot tears spilled out of her and onto his lap.

❖ ❖ ❖

Later, after Freya had composed herself, after Fletcher had paid for their desserts and they collected their things, the streetlights overhead flashed rhythmically. Curfew for degens. Fletcher saw Freya tense as they approached the parking meter. He took her wrist and held up her hand, as if to remind her of her newly minted cognition wheel.

"Oh. Right." Her tone was thick with guilt, not relief. "Guess I don't have to worry about curfew violations anymore . . ."

Fletcher watched her curiously as she trailed off, her eyes suddenly widening with excitement. He asked, "What is it?"

"Are underage recollectors able to access public records?"

"Not sure what the restrictions are for minors." Fletcher shrugged. "We could go to the city clerk's office tomorrow and find out. Although, if we do, we probably shouldn't mention my name. Might get us kicked out."

Freya tapped her chin, appearing to only half listen. "My father said the dean was going to help him get a clean slate. Makes me wonder if there's anything public on my father."

"You mean like a criminal record?"

Freya blinked.

Fletcher mounted his Ducati, and she climbed on behind him. "You know, there was an amendment to the Public Records Act not too long ago. My dad talked about it all the time, how it required the state to include detailed information about one's status as a degen or recollector."

"I remember seeing that on the news." They put on their helmets. "I'm thinking I should pay a visit to Long Beach City Hall tomorrow before our flight."

"Good idea." Fletcher fired up the motorcycle and they were off.

15

FREYA IZQUIERDO

Before sunup the next morning, I'm dressed, out the door, and pacing in the driveway, waiting for Fletcher to pick me up. Long Beach City Hall opens in fifteen minutes, and our return flight to Nashville isn't until 2:00 p.m. This should give me plenty of time.

In the quiet of dawn, I grow increasingly anxious about what I might find at the city clerk's office. It sounds silly, maybe even callous, but things were simpler when I was just investigating the cause of my "father's" death. With my *actual* father back in the picture, there is so much more to unpack. And even if I ultimately decide never to speak to my father again, I can't avoid processing the implications of his return.

So why not do a little digging into his past?

I hear Fletcher's motorcycle before I see it. He turns down my street and coasts to a stop beside my mailbox. He hands me my helmet and says, "You know—and sorry if this isn't my place—but wouldn't it be easier to get answers if you just talked to him?"

I slip on the bulky helmet. "Easier, except for the fact that I can't trust a thing he says."

"Point taken."

I hop on and squeeze Fletcher's torso, indicating that I'm ready. He revs the Ducati before peeling away.

❖ ❖ ❖

The outside of Long Beach City Hall is a striking contrast to Manhattan Beach, where Fletcher and I spent our evening yesterday. Here, the street and front entryway are crowded with throngs of protesters who wave painted signs and chant angrily.

Fletcher parks across the street and we dismount. "Mom said these protests have been on the rise in the past couple months."

I squint at the signs as we jog across the pedestrian crossing. One sign in particular seems to summarize what the protesters are calling for: STEP UP OR SECEDE!

"They don't think the federal government's doing enough to hold Alexander Lochamire and Memory Frontier accountable," Fletcher yells over the shouting as we approach the crowd. "And apparently Foxtail Academy's existence is just kerosene on the fire."

"These people think protesting the *city* is going to make a difference? Shouldn't they be at the doorstep of the Capitol instead?"

"Oh, they're at the Capitol too." He leads me into the sea of protesters, and we have to zigzag our way to the glass doors. "Soon they'll be everywhere."

❖ ❖ ❖

Fletcher, convinced he'll be recognized and that his presence will hinder me, waits in the lobby. I follow the long marble hallway to the city clerk's office and let myself in. Opposite the door is a rectangular pane of glass, behind which sits a thirtysomething man at a desk. Shocked to find no one in line, I steel myself and approach him.

"Hi, hello."

Without responding, he slides open the window.

"Oh, right." I clear my throat. "Hi."

He reaches into a desk drawer, procures a cognition wheel reader, and sets it on the counter. The clerk watches me with a bored expression. I swallow, then delicately place my right palm on the reader. The skin with my fresh tattoo smarts, but after a few seconds there's a soft *ding!* and I withdraw my hand.

I expected my first moment receiving recollector clearance to feel emotional. Or, if not emotional, certainly different. For years I've been denied entrance, access, and privilege at every turn.

But that? That was painfully anticlimactic.

"How can I help you." He says this with no inquiring inflection in his voice.

"I was hoping to access . . . er, criminal records . . . my father's, that is."

He hands me a clipboard with a questionnaire. I fill out every field to the best of my knowledge, leaving only a handful of the questions blank. After I hand it back to him, he gets up and moves about the large filing cabinets at the other end of the room. Figuring this could take a while, I retreat to the plastic chairs lining the side wall. Before I can even sit down, he calls out to me.

"There's no criminal record under that name on file."

"I . . . *really?*" I find that hard to believe. Did I spell his name wrong? Surely that can't be it; minors' cognition wheels have identification information that's paired with parents—living or deceased.

Unless the dean already worked his magic and had my dad's criminal record expunged . . .

"Will there be anything else." Again, it's more statement than question. The clerk doesn't wait for my reply before returning to his paperwork.

I sigh and turn to leave when an idea pops into my head.

"Actually, yes, there is something else." I smile across the counter. "Or rather, some*one* else."

❖ ❖ ❖

Fletcher stands as I reenter the lobby. "So? How'd it go?"

"Well, there wasn't a criminal record on my dad."

"Usually that's *good* news." Fletcher smirks.

I see his point. We head toward the exit. "But they had something on Ramon, my brother."

"Oh wow."

We both loiter near the doors, and I can hear the protesters' muted shouting. "Yeah. So get this: Apparently, the week before my brother died, there was an incident at the factory. He got into an altercation with a coworker. The police came and ended up arresting his coworker. Memory Frontier never pressed charges against my brother, though, and he returned to work the next day."

"Did the report say what the fight was about?"

I shake my head. "I'm still convinced the answers are at the factory where my brother died."

Fletcher nods grimly.

"I will find out who killed Ramon, even if it takes me my lifetime."

❖ ❖ ❖

After our long flight to Tennessee, Fletcher, Ollie, Chase, and I are slightly dazed but filled with a sort of collective determination on our bus ride back to Foxtail Academy. At the back of the lumbering vehicle, we discuss in hushed voices our plan of attack: First, we need to find a time when we know for sure Dean Mendelsohn and his staff won't be at the facility in the woods. Then we'll have to figure out how to safely administer the sedative so Fletcher can knife the memory tape. Next, we'll scour the facility for clues—clues about the Memory Ghosts and the real reason Memory Frontier and the dean had us knife Malcolm Heckman's memory for that address.

"And somewhere along the way," Ollie says, zipping up her hoodie and shutting her eyes, "we need to maintain decent GPAs and apply to colleges."

"The rest of senior year is gonna rock," Chase says dryly.

"By the way." Fletcher turns in the seat and faces me, lowering his voice. "I'd rather not knife that memory tape alone. I was kinda hoping you'd join me."

The thought had crossed my mind. After what almost happened to Fletcher the last time we memory knifed . . . well, it's just too risky knifing alone. From now on, if we must do it, it has to be done in pairs—at a minimum.

"Of course," I tell him. "If you want me to join you, I'll be there with you."

"I *need* you to join me," he clarifies, and then he trains his soft I-see-down-into-your-soul gaze on me, and it feels like I'll never be needed the way Fletcher needs me at this moment.

When the bus eventually rolls onto campus, it's nearly 6:00 p.m., and the four of us grab our things and sluggishly file off, bringing up the rear. Outside, the cold air shocks me to attention, and I regret not wearing more layers. Apparently, I'm not the only one; my classmates all groan, almost in unison, as they disperse at a jog toward the dorms.

Ollie and I tell the boys we'll meet up with them in half an hour for dinner at the Foxhole, and as she and I walk briskly toward our room, the familiar views of Foxtail bring me sudden warmth. The weak autumn sunlight washes the expansive campus in beiges. There's the massive auditorium, the scattered stand-alone buildings that make up our classrooms, and the glass architectural wonder that is the library, which separates the girls' and boys' dormitories—two L-shaped buildings that border the dark woods.

My time at Foxtail Academy has been very strange thus far, and yet I actually missed this place. I missed the grounds. I missed the Southern-inspired meals in the dining hall. The senior lounge. Juniper Lake. And most of all, I've missed our secret spot in the forest at the lake's edge.

"Good to be back, isn't it?" Ollie says when we finally reach our door.

"Yeah," I agree, and then we spill inside our dorm room and bask in the central heating.

Ollie and I take our trays of steamy brisket, sautéed carrots, and rolls and spot Fletcher and Chase at a table near the vending machines. We head over to join them, and along the way we pass Adam McCauley, one of the school prefects and Ollie's biggest fan.

"Hey, Adam, good break?" she asks as we pause beside his table.

Adam all but flinches. He looks up from his food, glances around the table at his friends, confused, then tries to play it cool but fails miserably. "Yeah? I mean, did you . . . ?"

Ollie's smile fades. "Yeah. Great." And then she marches off without warning, forcing me to practically sprint to catch up. I almost lose my roll.

"Well, *he's* acting weird," she says as we plop down beside Fletcher and Chase.

"Guys." Chase slurps his Coke. "If you're talking about Fletcher, he's sitting *right* here."

"She's talking about Adam," I say.

"What did he do?" Fletcher asks, rolling his eyes at his roommate.

"He acted like Mr. Cool in front of his friends," Ollie explains, exasperated. "Like he didn't even recognize me. If he thinks Ollie Trang plays games, he's got another thing coming." And then she tears into her brisket like a wild animal.

"Wait . . . you like *like* Adam?" Fletcher looks to me for help, but I just shrug and take a bite.

"I don't *dislike* him." Ollie cocks an eyebrow. "At least, I didn't before he pretended not to remember me."

Fletcher sets down his fork. "I'm confused. So you didn't like him before, but you didn't dislike him either, only now you *do* dislike him?"

Now Ollie's the one who turns to me for help. So, naturally, I take another bite of my dinner and motion to my mouth, like I wouldn't *possibly* dare speak while chewing.

"I got you, Ol. Men these days lack a certain . . . class." Chase leans his head back slightly and belches.

"I'll drink to that." Ollie takes a long swig.

"Yeah, well, I kinda wish people didn't recognize *me*," Fletcher mutters, moving the food around on his plate with his fork.

I start to notice the sporadic whispers. The quick, subtle looks from our classmates. Suddenly, it seems as if a quarter of the dining hall is throwing discreet glances at our table.

Of course, I think, scolding myself for not being sensitive to this immediately: *They're staring at Congressman Joshua Cohen's son . . . Fletcher, whose dad was all over the news for being linked to the Memory Ghosts.*

16

FLETCHER COHEN

The gang's secret spot on the banks of Juniper Lake—deep in the woods, nearly a fifteen-minute trek off campus—brought Fletcher needed relief from his classmates' unwanted stares.

"Looks like I'm gonna be spending a lot of time here," Fletcher said defeatedly, pulling himself up onto the fallen tree—their make-shift bench. "Guess it's a good thing we didn't end up having to change hideouts, huh?" Even though they were a good distance from the Foxhole, Fletcher still felt a tad exposed now that the trees were nearly bare. He fidgeted with the drawstrings on his jacket as Freya sat beside him.

"This is the part where I tell you not to worry about what everyone thinks." Freya inched closer to Fletcher until their legs were touching. "But I know me saying that won't change how you feel right now."

Chase and Ollie nodded.

"Freya's right." Chase climbed up onto the mossy tree and stared out at the undisturbed lake. "But I'd take it a step further . . . I say let yourself be pissed off right now."

"Chase—"

"No, I'm serious." Chase's uncharacteristically firm tone quieted his friends. "Those kids don't know what the hell they're even whispering about. They don't know what the four of us just went through . . . what *you're* going through, Fletcher. So be pissed off. Just don't *stay* pissed off. Tomorrow, when classes resume, we gotta stay focused. We gotta start figuring out how we're going to execute Operation: Expose Those MF Lies."

Ollie snorted. *"Memory Frontier* lies?"

Chase drew his lips into a disappointed line. "No. Those mother—"

He couldn't even finish the expletive before the rest of them were laughing, their breathing expelling misty clouds into the cold air. After their laughter tapered off, no one spoke for a long time, until at last Ollie begrudgingly suggested they head back to the dorms before curfew.

"Guys," Freya said right before they paired off for the boys' and girls' dormitories, "Halloween is in one week."

They all stopped in place despite the cold.

Freya rubbed her arms. "If there's an attack on a MACE field office, like the dean said there would be when he recruited us, it will be all over the news."

Ollie shook her head. "Soon we'll know if we prevented that bombing . . ."

". . . or if it was never going to happen in the first place," Fletcher said, completing her thought. They said nothing more as they stalked off to the dorms.

❖ ❖ ❖

80

After an evening of fitful sleep, Fletcher woke up, tossed his Reflector aside, showered, and got dressed. In the dining hall, he and the gang scarfed breakfast and then sprinted through the dreary October wind toward the classrooms.

First and second period moved along at a torturously slow pace. To make matters worse, Fletcher continued to draw not-so-subtle glances and stares from his peers, and he did his absolute best not to let it stoke his anger.

But when an unfamiliar voice called out to him on the grounds as he walked back to his dorm room before lunch, Fletcher snapped.

"Yeah?" He rounded on the poor woman, who fumbled the stack of books she was lugging. "You doing some article for the school newspaper? Need a quote from the son of a terrorist?"

The woman stammered, "I-I . . . d-does Foxtail have a school newspaper?"

Fletcher narrowed his eyes and sized up the staffer: She had deep brown skin, a petite frame, and a voluminous Afro of black hair. She appeared to be in her early twenties and wore a heavy jacket over her Foxtail polo, as well as pressed khakis and a pair of ratty Chuck Taylors. The ID clipped to her jacket read ASSISTANT LIBRARIAN.

"I'm Irene." She reached out to shake his hand and nearly lost everything she was holding. "Irene . . . *Porter.*" She whispered her last name, like it was some kind of secret she wasn't supposed to divulge.

Fletcher shook her hand and noted, curiously, that her ID didn't have her name—or photo—printed on it. A new hire?

"Did you need something?" He looked around, hoping to spot Freya or Chase or Ollie. He needed reinforcements. "Directions to a classroom, or . . . ?"

"Nah." She flipped her hand, *again* almost dropping her precariously stacked books. "Been trying to find you all morning, but you know . . . training. Anyway. You got a minute to chat in the common room?"

"Um . . ."

"Great!" Her obliviousness agitated him. She turned toward the common room, but Fletcher reached out and lightly took her arm.

"Hey, look, I'm not trying to be rude, but—"

"Most people who are rude don't try to be," Irene said. "They just *are*."

"Er, okay. What I mean is, I should probably get going. I need to—"

"Don't you want to know why your dad's being set up?"

Fletcher nearly choked on his spit.

She doubled down. "Completely innocent. As are the Memory Ghosts"—she dropped her voice considerably at that—"the *real* Ghosts, that is. Not the wannabes on the news. C'mon. I've got a *lot* to tell you, and I'd very much prefer not to miss lunch!"

17

FREYA IZQUIERDO

At lunch, Chase and Ollie complain about the weird behavior of our teachers and some of our classmates.

". . . treating us like, well, like strangers," Ollie was saying, annoyed.

"Mr. McDonough actually handed me a syllabus in AP lit." Chase shakes his head. "It's like, *dude*, I know I phoned it in first quarter, but did you really forget I was in your class?"

"Maybe they *did* forget about us," I offer, only half listening. *Where the heck is Fletcher?* "I mean, we did miss a good chunk of first quarter holed up in the dean's"—I drop my voice to a whisper—"*facility*." I think about the mantra we created before fall break. Forgotten but Not Forgetful. Feels eerily prophetic now . . .

"Speaking of which." Ollie consults her day planner, which is lying open in her lap. "I'm so behind on my reading I'll have to pull a few all-nighters if I hope to catch up."

"This blows." Chase slides his tray of half-eaten casserole

aside. "The dean recruits us to help save the day but doesn't give us the courtesy of writing us exemptions. Someone should talk to him. Where's Fletcher? Fletcher should *so* talk to him and set this right."

Yes. Where *is* Fletcher? Before my curiosity can grow too much, Mr. Williams—Foxtail Academy's bubbly, mustachioed counselor—bounds toward our table looking as cheerful as ever in his Members Only jacket.

"Mr. Williams, thank *heavens*," Chase says dramatically. "Please tell me you come bearing exemptions for us."

"I'm afraid not, Mr."—he consults his clipboard—"Mr. Hall! I was reviewing my list this morning and realized that I somehow managed to forget meeting with you three individually before fall break to discuss college applications."

Ollie, Chase, and I exchange a look. Did Dean Mendelsohn and Dr. Sanders really not tell him why we missed a portion of first quarter? The dean was adamant that our knifing mission was top secret. So then, what explanation *did* he give to the Foxtail faculty? What reason . . . what lie . . . did he offer for our mysterious absences?

Mr. Williams checks his clipboard again, squinting. "Let's see . . . Freya Izquierdo? I sure do hope I'm pronouncing that correctly!"

"Er, yeah, that's me." *He's acting like we've never met . . .*

"*¡Muy bueno!*" He flashes his pearly whites in an impossibly large grin. "Anyway, sorry to steal you away from Mr. Herschel Jones's famous casserole, but we should probably go on and meet now. Might make you tardy for"—another glance at the clipboard—"Algebra II, but I've already cleared it with Ms. Schneck."

"Oh, sure," I say. *Why is he acting so weird? It really* is *as if the faculty has forgotten us.*

Ollie offers to take my tray for me. I tell her thanks, gather my textbooks, and follow Mr. Williams as he snakes around the cafeteria tables toward the exit. Outside, we walk in stride toward the admissions building, wherein lie the faculty offices. In the light of day, I observe just how bare and cold the trees are. They stand fraily against the gray autumn sky.

"Mr. Williams?"

"That's my name." He slips his clipboard under his arm and zips up his jacket. "And all that business about not wearing it out!"

"Right." I clear my throat. "Do you . . . do you not remember me? Or our conversations?"

Mr. Williams frowns. "I'm so sorry, Freya. Foxtail Academy boasts a roster of nearly five hundred students, almost a hundred of which are seniors—like yourself. As convenient as it'd be for me to blame Memory Killer, the more likely explanation is that I am *terribly* busy. Who knew the inaugural year of a boarding school would be this much work!"

Is he serious? Has he completely forgotten about our conversation on the bus *and* the one we had outside the library? Normally, I'd be inclined to believe that he *did* simply forget those moments—he's a degen and hasn't begun using a Reflector yet. Memory Killer has scourged humanity for so long that it's sadly common for people to forget not only certain conversations but the person with whom they had the conversations. This really shouldn't shock me that much.

And yet . . .

And yet Ollie and Chase were just talking about how many people around campus seem to have forgotten us four. I start to realize just how odd this is. I can buy one person forgetting us, even several, but this many? Something's definitely up.

"I hope I haven't upset you, Freya." He leads me up the steps toward the entrance, and before we walk inside the admissions building, I see Fletcher emerging from the common room beside the boys' dormitories. I'm far enough away that he likely doesn't see me with Mr. Williams, but it doesn't matter. The next second a young woman I don't recognize emerges too. They both glance around, like they're checking to see if anyone's around, and then quickly disappear across campus.

Who was that?

18

FLETCHER COHEN

Fletcher immediately spotted Chase and Ollie at their go-to table near the vending machines, but where was Freya? They needed to convene immediately; Fletcher was even willing to skip third period if that was what it took.

"This way," he said to Irene, leading her through the busy dining hall toward his friends. A quick glance at the clock above the food lines informed Fletcher only fifteen minutes of lunch remained.

"There you are." Ollie shut her day planner and set it on top of her textbooks. "Who's this?"

"Irene," she said, before Fletcher could even open his mouth. Then, sounding almost reverent, she whispered to Fletcher, "They did it too?"

"Did what?" Chase planted his chin on his fists, smiling. "Chase Hall, by the way. And whatever it is I did that has you so impressed, I'm willing to do it again for you." He punctuated this with a wink.

"Where's Freya?" Fletcher looked around the Foxhole. "The four of us need to take Irene to our spot *right now* . . . you're not going to believe what she knows. But we have to hurry."

"You just missed her," Ollie said. "Mr. Williams towed her away to discuss colleges. *Blech.* Is everything all right?"

"Everything is *not* all right." What terrible timing. Fletcher had half a mind to race over to the admissions building and see if he could—

"Ah, Ms. Trang . . . Mr. Hall . . . Mr. Cohen." Dean Mendelsohn approached their table, a steamy mug of coffee in his left hand. In his right he cupped two cylindrical pills, which he tossed into his mouth and washed down with a swig of coffee. "I'm afraid I need to borrow you for a moment."

"Oh goody, someone who actually remembers us." Ollie rose to her feet, collecting her things.

Dean Mendelsohn bristled at Ollie's comment but steeled himself and continued, "Where's Ms. Izquierdo?"

"Getting the ol' college pitch from Mr. Williams." Chase, too, stood. Fletcher felt his palms sweating. This *had* to be the absolute worst timing!

"That won't do." The dean shook his head. "I'll send Dr. Sanders to fetch her at once."

At the mention of Dr. Sanders, Irene stiffened beside Fletcher. Though her face remained expressionless, he could sense how tense she'd grown. Dean Mendelsohn apparently sensed it, too, as he fixed his attention on her.

"You're one of our new hires." He looked her up and down disinterestedly but shook her hand all the same.

"I'm making my rounds." Irene smiled wanly. "Tracking down overdue books."

"Don't let us keep you," the dean grunted. He gestured for Fletcher, Chase, and Ollie to follow him.

"You coming?" Chase asked, noticing that Fletcher was lingering beside Irene.

"I . . ." He watched as the dean led Ollie through one of the Foxhole's side exits. They paused at the threshold, waiting for Fletcher and Chase to catch up.

"Sorry." Fletcher flashed Irene a worried glance and added in a whisper, "We'll come find you after third period." Then he and Chase crossed the dining hall to join Dean Mendelsohn, who led them across the chilly grounds and toward the woods that bordered the faculty housing.

❖ ❖ ❖

While it had been only a week, if that, since Fletcher and his friends last stood in Dean Mendelsohn's high-ceilinged facility—the epicenter of Memory Frontier's clandestine operations—the imposing bunker's interior still managed to impress. Opposite the entrance, rows of desks and computers stood cluttered in front of a wide wall, upon which hung a large dry-erase board. Adjacent to this wall, and beneath hanging tube lights, was a collection of cots. Fletcher shivered at the sight . . . that cramped corner of the expansive facility had been his "home" for weeks as he and the others had undergone their memory knife training. Across the way, an unmarked door led to a kitchen, another to a shared bathroom, and two more into tiny dressing rooms.

In the middle of the huge facility was the dean's towering Restorey—a nearly seven-foot-tall open reel-to-reel tape machine with dials, knobs, buttons, and myriad switches. Fletcher could only guess at the functions of the switchboard-like control panel.

Currently, no memory tape was threaded into the Restorey's reels. The computers and desks were unmanned. The facility was empty save for the dean, Fletcher, Chase, and Ollie.

I hate this place even more when it's quiet. Fletcher's hands ran cold.

"Welcome back, everyone." Beside the Restorey, Dean Mendelsohn turned and faced the three, then gulped down the rest of his coffee. "I hope your fall break was . . . pleasant."

Fletcher, Chase, and Ollie stood where the reclined chairs were usually stationed. At the moment, the chairs had been collapsed and were stored against the wall.

"You didn't write us exemptions for class." Chase set his book bag on the ground and folded his arms.

"Oh, didn't I?" The dean sniffed.

Ollie took a step forward. "Do you have any idea how behind we are?"

But Fletcher wasn't nearly as concerned about classes and required reading as his friends were. Not only was he still processing all that Irene Porter had just revealed to him about his father and the Memory Ghosts, but the implications of her wild claims completely reframed everything the dean and Memory Frontier were doing in this very bunker. Fletcher would have to find some way to vet Irene's claims and verify her credibility, but he was very hopeful that—

The sliding door behind Fletcher, Chase, and Ollie ground open, and Dr. Sanders and Freya walked in.

"As I was saying," Dean Mendelsohn continued, nodding to Freya as she fell into line beside Fletcher. "You'll have to bear with me. I'll get your past-assignment exemptions sorted by end of day."

"You've had all week," Ollie said, scowling.

The dean sighed. "Yes, well, after you four completed that successful knifing of Malcolm Heckman's memory, Dr. Sanders and I were quite busy. We divided our time between DC and Memory Frontier headquarters, enduring meeting after mindless meeting. You see, your being able to intercept that message—and so efficiently—has gotten the attention of high-ranking government officials and top brass at Memory Front—"

"*Efficiently?*" Freya broke out of line and took a few steps toward the dean and Dr. Sanders, who half stood, half sat on the edge of one of the desks just beyond the Restorey. "You *do* remember that Fletcher was almost pulled into a memory loop, right? If I hadn't gotten lucky, he'd still be stuck in there!"

Just like your son is still stuck in one, Fletcher reflected. The hairs on his neck rose at the horrifying thought.

"Why did you even bring us back here?" Freya quelled her temper, breathing steadily through her nose. "Haven't you punished us enough? We did what you asked us to do! Now leave us alone . . . let us finish the Reflector trial along with our classmates, let us resume classes so we can graduate next spring and never have to think about this godforsaken place again."

"I'm afraid it's no longer that simple." Dr. Sanders smoothed her pinstripe skirt and joined the dean beside the Restorey. Fletcher's chest burned hot with outrage. *When was any of this simple?* Before he could demand this aloud, Freya took another step.

"Why don't our classmates remember us?"

Fletcher walked to Freya and stood at her right, and soon Chase and Ollie flanked her on the left. The four quietly matched one another's resolve.

Freya repeated the question, calmer this time. It was an enraged kind of calm.

The dean appeared to be getting ready to reply when the kitchen door flung open unexpectedly. "Higher Love" by Steve Winwood loudly spilled into the facility, reverberating off the high ceiling. A man appeared in the doorway—tall, lanky, with greasy brown hair pulled into a ponytail. He wore an untucked aloha shirt and slacks. The second he realized he was not alone, he gave a shrill gasp and practically fell back into the kitchen—clicking off the stereo a moment later.

"Yikes! Guess we got carried away in there, huh?" The lanky man laughed to himself as he strolled up to the dean and gave him a side hug. "I requisitioned that stereo from the supply closet, Rusty. Hope you don't mind!"

The dean shut his eyes and set his jaw. Dr. Sanders inched away, looking equally annoyed.

The man dropped his hand and set his sights on Fletcher and his friends. "And you must be our champions. Boy, have I heard a lot about you four this week. A *lot*. Let me first say how honored I am to be here, standing in your midst—the world's first memory knifers— wow. This is a lot to take in!"

Chase's posture went lax. "Happy to sign autographs—"

"And you are?" Ollie interrupted, eyeing the man apprehensively.

"Oh! My deepest apologies." He tugged at the hem of his shirt and straightened. "I'm Dr. Gilbert Grondahl. I've been appointed by the administration to oversee your training!"

Fletcher glared at Dean Mendelsohn and Dr. Sanders. "We don't need to be trained. We already completed Memory Frontier's mission." *Which was a total lie.* Irene Porter's words were still fresh in his mind. "The four of us are never going to knife for Memory Frontier again. Ever."

Dr. Grondahl frowned. "I see. Well, regarding that last part, I do hope I'm able to persuade you otherwise."

We'll see about that. Fletcher gritted his teeth.

"And regarding your training . . . once more, I apologize! I should clarify." Dr. Grondahl whistled. The next instant, four teenagers— two girls, two boys, all appearing the same age as Fletcher and his friends—marched out of the kitchen. They wore freshly laundered jumpsuits—the very jumpsuits Fletcher, Freya, Chase, and Ollie wore every time they knifed.

"You four will be training our new recruits!" Dr. Grondahl beamed, holding out his bony arm toward the four stone-faced kids who now stood—feet shoulder-width apart—in front of the Restorey. "Exciting, isn't it?"

19

FREYA IZQUIERDO

"I hope you know what you're doing," Fletcher whispers in my ear as we stand near the cots. He, Ollie, Chase, and I have changed into matching jumpsuits, and we're currently loitering in the shadows while the dean's team sets up eight reclining chairs in a half circle beside the Restorey.

"Yeah, Freya." Ollie comes up beside us. "This feels like a shoot-first-ask-questions-later kinda deal. What's the plan?"

"I'm thinking," I say, which isn't a lie. In fact, I have so many thoughts that they're careening into each other with endless possibilities. After Dr. Grondahl announced that he'd been tasked with overseeing the training of these "recruits," Dean Mendelsohn told us that—should we accept—we'd be spending our daily free period in the facility. We'd mentor the new kids, running through drills and memory knifing exercises and showing them the ropes. Without a second's hesitation, I had spoken up for the group and told the dean and Dr. Sanders that we'd do it. They were shocked, of course, as were Fletcher, Ollie, and Chase.

But I trusted my gut, because I realized as the dean was talking that he'd simplified something for us.

"Go through the motions," I tell my friends, keeping my voice above a whisper. "Play the part. This gives us access to the facility and to the dean's Restorey. And when the moment's right, we can turn this place upside down for clues, and Fletcher can knife that memory tape he found."

Chase whistles low. "You're right. We were gonna have to figure out some way to break in, but the dean left the key under the mat for us."

"That's a terrible analogy." Ollie ruffles her hair distractedly. "And anyway, I don't have a good feeling about this, Freya. Being under the dean's nose like this seems riskier than just breaking in one night."

Fletcher taps his foot, and I can tell he's weighing everything. "I think I'm with Ollie on this one. This is pretty risky. Plus, I still haven't told you guys what Irene told me."

Irene? The girl he met with in the common room? "What's up?"

"Not here." Fletcher glances over his shoulder at the new recruits. They're talking with Dr. Sanders and Dr. Grondahl, who's laughing and moving his hands in wild gestures. Behind them, a crew of scientists have begun to take up their posts at the computers. Dean Mendelsohn threads a tape into the Restorey, and two nurses in scrubs begin to prep the IV bags. "Suffice it to say, if Irene's telling the truth—which I kinda think she is—well, it changes everything."

"I wonder—could you be vaguer?" Chase rubs his chin.

I ignore him and zero in on Fletcher's words. "So you're saying this is a mistake? As much as I hate everything it stands for, it's our best shot at—"

"I don't know if it's a mistake." Fletcher shuts his eyes for a moment. Now I *really* want to know who this Irene is and what she possibly could have said to put Fletcher so out of sorts. "Let's just get through this afternoon and reconvene with Irene before dinner."

Ollie nods. "Sounds like a plan to me."

"Yeah," Chase adds, though he suddenly looks glum. "Sure."

I remain quiet, feeling an unexpected sting in my stomach. A pinprick of frustration. I had assumed they'd be on board with this plan, rushed and uncertain as it may be. We literally just agreed on the bus yesterday that sneaking back into the facility was paramount.

But now a total stranger has Fletcher second-guessing everything.

I need a quick distraction. I take a moment to size up the new kids, who all look vaguely familiar. While I recognize them from around campus, I'm certain we've never spoken. One of the girls is tall and athletic with shoulder-length blonde hair. It appears bleached, because her eyebrows are a dark shade of brown—nearly black. She has high cheekbones, a pointy chin, and a confident gaze.

If there's a leader of their pack, this girl's definitely it.

The other girl is tan, short, and lean, with a head of brown permed hair. She has stud earrings in both lobes, a lip piercing, and she exudes an I'd-rather-be-anywhere-else-on-the-planet kind of attitude. I immediately like her. This girl is flanked by the boys. One appears very mousy. He has shaggy red hair, square glasses, and a round freckled face. The other boy stands at intense attention, his muscled arms folded behind his back. He's pale-skinned, broad-shouldered, and expressionless. A true soldier if ever there was one.

"You all ready?" Dr. Sanders's cautious words bring my thoughts to a halt. She holds out her hand and gestures for us to follow her to the chairs. The other four recline first, then the nurses affix the electrode stickers to various places on their heads.

It's so strange seeing other people my age lying there in such vulnerable positions. They have no idea the terrifying, mind-altering experience that awaits them.

My palms start to sweat.

"Freya, my dear, how'd you rest over fall break?" Dr. Sanders says this out of the corner of her mouth, her way of asking if I had any visions. It makes me wonder if she's told the dean about my secret. I go to answer her but am briefly distracted by a burst blood vessel in her right eye. I hadn't noticed it on the walk over. The blood is crimson, thick as dye, and encroaches on her iris like spilled ink.

She catches me staring and averts her gaze.

"Good," I lie. "Filled with peaceful, dreamless sleep." Now's not the time to tell her my visions are actually premonitions or that my most recent one involved an unconscious Fletcher—

I gasp and freeze.

My premonition . . . in it, Fletcher was wearing a jumpsuit!

"Freya?" Dean Mendelsohn walks over, rolling up the sleeves of his shirt. "Everything all right?" Both he and Dr. Sanders study me.

"This memory we're about to knife. Where does it take place?"

The dean and Dr. Sanders swap a glance.

"In a library," Dean Mendelsohn replies.

Dr. Sanders holds my arm. "What's wrong?"

"And in this memory, is there snow? Do you . . . do you go outside in the snow?"

The dean grunts. "I hate the snow. I avoid it at all costs. But to answer your question, no. This particular memory doesn't involve snow. In fact, far as I can recall, only a handful of my memory tapes do."

"You'll tell me if it does?" At this point, Fletcher, Ollie, and Chase are staring at me from their chairs.

Dean Mendelsohn arches an eyebrow. "I . . . of course. Sure. I'll tell you beforehand." He pauses, his expression growing more concerned. Before he can say anything else, though, Dr. Grondahl lopes over—humming idly to himself.

"We good here? Not getting cold feet, are we?"

I brush past them and take my chair at the end of the half circle. One of the nurses has just finished hooking up Fletcher's electrode stickers, so she sets to work on mine.

"Freya . . ." Fletcher watches me intently.

"I'm sorry I suggested we go through with this." I blink back tears that burn behind my eyelids. "I was trying to help. I thought this was our best move. Now I'm not so sure."

Before Fletcher can reply, the dean takes up position beside the tall Restorey and briefs us.

20

FLETCHER COHEN

"What you four did before fall break was heroic." Dean Mendelsohn gave Fletcher and his friends a quick nod of appreciation. "And I know I said that mission would be all that's required of you." *Not a single one of us is surprised that you lied*, Fletcher thought bitterly, darkening his stare at the dean. "But thanks to the address Freya was able to seize from Malcolm Heckman's memory, along with her description of his accomplices, we've been able to apprehend another key player in this war."

Fletcher's chest tightened. Was Dean Mendelsohn referring to his father? Were they going to be knifing his memory tapes at some point? If so, wasn't that some kind of conflict of interest? Fletcher met the dean's gaze. The older man was poker-faced. Regardless, before the dean could elaborate, Dr. Grondahl walked right over to the dean and patted him on the back. Dean Mendelsohn turned so red in the cheeks Fletcher thought he might combust.

"Rusty's right! This Emilia Vanguard we apprehended is currently in forced stasis at the Fold, and we've determined that she is another integral runner for the Ghosts!" He rubbed his hands together. "Her memories are actively being scanned because we have new intel that indicates she was carrying a *critical* message for the Ghosts."

Ollie propped herself up awkwardly, the wires from the electrode stickers draping down the sides of her face. "Why are we going through all the trouble of training fresh blood then?" She glanced at the four recruits, who still had not said a word to Fletcher and his friends. "No offense. You guys seem lovely."

"Well, now, isn't that a great question, Ollie?" Dean Mendelsohn said through gritted teeth. Fletcher noted the dean's look of restraint, of wanting to say so much more but forcibly holding his tongue. It was the kind of look a person wore when they'd been forced to plead the fifth.

We're in the middle of some political tug-of-war, Fletcher realized.

Dr. Sanders smiled ruefully. "I can field that one, Miss Trang. While you four have certainly proven capable of knifing, the powers that be are growing restless. And understandably so. The elusive Memory Ghosts are planning something *big*. The president and his cabinet want as many agents on this mission as possible. Strength in numbers, as it were."

Agents. Fletcher hated that word. Its nonchalant use implied an order to all this madness. There was no order. There were only lies. Heaping piles of lies.

"The administration is working hard to stamp out these terrorists." Dr. Grondahl grabbed a remote off one of the desks and powered up the giant projector. On the wall behind the scientists, a massive image appeared: it was a formal-looking crest with the acronym AMK prominently featured. "By foiling the Ghosts and their plans, you're actually laying the groundwork for an all-new counterterrorist initiative. This is history in the making!"

"What does that stand for?" Fletcher nodded toward the letters. "'AMK'?"

Dr. Grondahl pointed the remote at Fletcher. "*So* glad you asked, young man. Alliance of Memory Knifers. The AMK will soon work directly with MACE, the FBI, and perhaps one day the CIA. You all are true pioneers."

Fletcher banished the temptation to yell. He steadied his voice to the best of his ability and said, "You're planning to memory knife *more?*" He knew he shouldn't be so surprised. And yet hearing it out loud—seeing it formalized with an actual government logo—disturbed him.

This was wrong. It was all so . . . wrong. Fletcher looked from the dean to Dr. Sanders. She cleared her throat. "I may understand *and* hate this decision in equal measures, but it wasn't my call."

Dean Mendelsohn looked like he was going to say more, but instead he motioned for Dr. Grondahl to step aside so they could begin. Dr. Grondahl shuttled off toward the rows of computers with Dr. Sanders, a bounce in his gait.

"Let the training," the dean intoned, shooting Dr. Grondahl a caustic glare, "begin."

The neon lights descended upon Fletcher's mind. They consumed him, *pulled* him, until he was one with them. The neon lights shifted, burning like a flameless fire, penetrating his shut eyelids with a tearing, expanding brightness.

Fletcher chanced a peek into the swirling, colorful void. In the falling up, in the space between spaces where there were only neon lights, Fletcher saw Freya.

Her long black hair floated around her face, fanning out in a wispy crown—like she was descending through water. Her eyelids fluttered, but only just, as if she was peaceful in this terrible ante-chamber of the mind. Her arms lolled at her sides, graceful, somehow undisturbed, and slowly her lips parted.

Fletcher realized something in that split-second breath of observation: he was being tugged into the memory by the neon lights; Freya was *riding* the neon lights.

He was a prisoner.

She was a passenger.

They were both weightless, but only Fletcher was helpless.

And then the "ride" was over, quicker than the angry sting of a stove-top burn. Floor-to-ceiling shelves materialized, as did the spines of countless books. Floor lamps slid into place; a wide table was assembled as if by invisible, proficient hands; windows were cut into the walls. Outside, the gloaming faded into the blurry, warbling edges of Dean Mendelsohn's memory.

Fletcher exhaled, looking about the stuffy, cramped study. Freya, Chase, and Ollie were there, and beyond them two of the four "recruits" stood on shaky feet with their quavering mouths hanging open in rapt disbelief. The other two—the tall, muscled boy and the girl with the lip piercing—were nowhere in sight.

A college-aged Dean Mendelsohn sat in the corner, poring over a tattered textbook by lamplight.

Freya met Fletcher's gaze and said, her voice appearing in his mind like mist expelled from a spray bottle, *Okay . . . so now what?*

21

FREYA IZQUIERDO

We should probably go over there and, you know, break the ice, Chase says of the other two, who are pacing around the study near the shelves, taking it all in.

The red-haired kid with glasses slips his hands into his jump-suit pockets leisurely, strolling about the room like a bright-eyed and bushy-tailed kid on a field trip to the museum. Between him and the girl, he seems more approachable.

I nod to Chase and lead my friends across the study.

I'm Freya, I tell the kid, who jumps, then beams at us.

I know who you are! He extends his hand and shakes mine; his touch generates a tingly sensation. He waves to Fletcher, Ollie, and Chase. *Isn't this just so amazing? Feels like . . . magic, doesn't it? Not real magic, of course, but magical in the way that record players work. I've dis-assembled many record players and rebuilt them, and it still seems magical to me . . . like all of this!*

Yeah. Chase blinks. *Magical.*

I'm Rhett, by the way, Rhett Villa. It's a pleasure to meet you guys!

Ollie clears her throat. *Charmed, I'm sure.*

Well, since you two made it here, guess that means you passed the first test and your friends didn't. Fletcher glances over at the young dean, who crosses his leg and turns a page, engrossed in his textbook.

Oh yeah, Sade and I passed that first test yesterday! Rhett pushes up his glasses. *So sad about that poor woman's goldfish.*

I narrow my eyes. *You guys have already knifed?*

Rhett nods, his shaggy bangs falling across his lenses. *Twice yesterday and once this morning! We just met those other two kids this afternoon. Guess Dr. Grondahl wanted to see if he could squeeze more recruits into the mix.* And then, with the ease of someone opening an umbrella, Rhett manifests a digital watch on his freckled wrist and sets a timer. *We probably only have a few minutes, so we should get started.*

I'm unable to suppress my surprise. *You . . . you already know how to manifest?*

Before Rhett can reply to my rhetorical question, the girl walks over and faces us at the center of the room. There's a fearlessness to her gaze, like she once stared unblinkingly into the eye of a great storm.

I gulp.

She is the first to speak. *Right. Are we getting started, or . . . ?* She speaks with a heavy South African accent; her consonants are punchy, pronounced, like the clank of hammer against nails.

Ollie folds her arms across her chest. *I'm sorry . . . And you are?*

Sade van der Merwe, she replies, flashing a predatorial scowl. *You're Hoa Trang, though for whatever reason you go by Ollie. This accessory on your hip*—she cocks a brown eyebrow at Chase—*is Christopher Hall . . .*

Chase props his arm on Ollie's shoulder coolly. *Pleasure's all mine, Miss Sade.*

And this is Fletcher Cohen, son of Joshua Cohen . . . embattled congressman. Sade shifts her weight, letting a few awkward moments tick by. I can practically feel Fletcher steeling himself beside me. *Now that we're all good and acquainted, can we get started?*

Fletcher shakes his head. *Just where exactly do you suggest we start, Sade?* He says her name as if it's an insult. *Being that you two are already familiar with knifing and can apparently manifest, I'm not exactly sure what "training" you require.*

Rhett tilts his head, confused, then turns to me. *You're going to show us how you pulled Fletcher out of a memory loop.*

22

FLETCHER COHEN

Fletcher could feel his neck reddening, a strange and delayed sensation while memory knifing. It *felt* the way an afterimage *looks*. He ground his teeth. *What did you say?*

Sade rubbed the bridge of her pointy nose irritably. She stalked away, visibly gathering her thoughts. *Did you or did you not rescue Fletcher from a memory loop, Freya?*

I . . . yes . . .

Good. Sade put her hands on her hips. *Now teach us how to do that.*

Yo, Chase said, shaking his head and holding up his hands. *I didn't sign up for this. None of us did.*

And yet here you are. Sade narrowed her eyes into slits. *Do you not hear how reluctant, how* scared, *you four sound?*

Freya clenched her fists. *You don't know anything about us.*

I know that it took some convincing to get you to knife—both initially and today. And I know that you still don't recognize how much power you have. We're here, us six, not Dr. Sanders, Dr. Grondahl, or the dean. I know how scared you are because I can see it all over your faces.

There's strength in relinquishing power, Fletcher said curtly.

Maybe. Sade eyed Fletcher, slowly looking him up and down, then snickered. *But there's a difference between relinquishing power and denying it outright.*

Rhett perked up. *Um, guys?*

So what do you want us to do? Ollie's tone was cold as metal. *Hold a seance, summon Memory Killer, and then have Freya deliver a lesson behind a podium?*

Rhett again, more urgent: *Guys . . .*

Well, now, that'd be a start, wouldn't it? Sade chuckled. *It would definitely be more productive than—*

Guys!

Everyone turned to Rhett.

What?

He glanced at his wristwatch. *The dean's memory is about to end.*

Sade walked over and sat on the edge of one of the tables. *Wonderful. That means this was a total bust.*

I . . . Freya glanced at her friends, then back to Rhett. *How do you know that?*

Rhett cupped his ear. *There's a faint whooshing sound at the close of every knife . . . it sounds like wind passing through a keyhole.*

Chase snort-laughed. *Yeah, okay, whatever you—*

Rhett smiled wanly as Dean Mendelsohn's memory collapsed in on itself and expelled the six, shooting them violently through the turbulent, all-consuming neon lights.

23

FREYA IZQUIERDO

"I'm sorry, but that is *not* how I intend to spend my free periods the rest of the semester!" Chase says as we race through the woods back to campus. Dry leaves and twigs crunch beneath our shoes. It's cold. I'm still slightly dizzy. And the air smells faintly of standing water and woodsmoke.

We have only a few minutes before Memory Theory with Dr. Sanders starts—our last class of the day. Moments ago, after the six of us slowly regained consciousness in the dean's facility, Fletcher and I all but lambasted Dean Mendelsohn.

Did he *really* expect us to knife until Memory Killer seized one of us? Yes, I'd somehow managed to save Fletcher the last time that happened, but that was nothing short of a miracle! My body was trembling with adrenaline in Malcolm Heckman's memory, and the fear of losing Fletcher to a memory loop spurred me to act in desperation.

What if I couldn't duplicate what I'd done to save Fletcher? What if someone got hurt . . . what if someone got trapped in a memory loop—like Daniel, the dean's son?

"This changes everything," Ollie says between breaths, clutching her textbooks to her chest. "This is way too risky. I don't want any part in this."

I nod.

"It's strange," says Fletcher beside me, his voice distant. "Sade and Rhett seemed to be so much more comfortable knifing than we are—and after only two days at it."

Chase grunts in agreement. "That Rhett kid did, that's for sure. He gives me the creeps."

We emerge from the woods behind the faculty housing and pick up the pace once the classrooms come into view.

Fletcher tugs the collar of his denim jacket absently. "And Sade . . . what did you guys think about what she said?"

"Cool accent aside," Chase says seriously, "she *also* gives me the creeps."

I try to read Fletcher's face as we jog-walk to class, but it's impossible. "What do *you* think?"

Fletcher shrugs. "I hate that facility. I hate all the lies. I hate that the government is planning to use memory knifing to carry out special operations. And I *hate* what Memory Frontier is up to, especially after meeting and talking with Irene. But . . ." He sets his jaw. "But Sade was right about one thing."

"Which part?"

"Memory knifing—there's power in it. And since none of the adults can do it—namely, the dean—it gives us an incredible advantage."

There's something lurking behind Fletcher's words. I can sense it. An idea, a plan. I just hope he lets me in on it before he does something impetuous.

The classroom is quiet and still when we enter and take our desks at the back. Dr. Sanders (who apparently left the facility when we were knifing) gives us a knowing glance. Then she gestures toward the dry-erase board, which has a fresh reading assignment written in red.

❖ ❖ ❖

There's a vacant table in the corner of the senior lounge. After we grab our dinner trays, we slump down and scarf the baked chicken, fried okra, and greens. Then Fletcher sets off to find this mysterious Irene Porter. A few moments later, he reappears at the top of the stairs with her.

She wears the uniform of a Foxtail staffer: a polo, khakis, and sneakers. She lugs a tote bag bulging with books. She smiles widely as Fletcher drags a fifth chair to our table.

"Hi again!" Irene says to Ollie and Chase, and then to me with a scintillating expression, "You must be Freya. I can't tell you guys how cool it is to finally be meeting you."

You're the second person to feel this way, I reflect, thinking back to the eccentric Dr. Grondahl.

"Tell them, Irene," Fletcher urges, leaning in. Ollie, Chase, and I do likewise.

She scoots her chair forward and whispers, her voice brimming with excitement: "Everything you've been told is a lie. The Memory Ghosts are not petition-peddling protesters propagating conspiracies—"

"Say that five times fast, Peter Piper," Chase cuts in with a snicker.

Irene clears her throat and continues: "The Ghosts are not violent, anarchical demonstrators. Those are impostors who have adopted their name, but they are no more Ghosts than a fish is a bird. And the Ghosts are *not* terrorists bent on pulverizing MACE, as Memory Frontier—or the government—would have you believe."

"I'm sorry," I say, gently cutting her off. "And I mean this as politely as possible, but how the hell do you know all this, and why should we believe you?"

Irene's smile turns to a crooked smirk, a mischievous spirit about her wild eyes. "Philip Lear's my great-uncle. He sent me here to find you."

Philip Lear . . . I absently pleat the hem of my sweatshirt, thinking. *I feel like I should know who that—*

"Wait." Ollie perks up. "Philip Lear? As in the cofounder of Memory Frontier?"

"I thought he was excommunicated from the company," Chase says. "What's"—he pauses as a group of bubbly girls leave their table, pass us, and make for the coffee bar—"what's he got to do with all this?"

"Come to think of it . . ." I stare at the ceiling for a moment, visualizing the picture I saw in the dean's facility a few weeks ago when he was briefing us on Malcolm Heckman. "I'm pretty sure Dean Mendelsohn and Dr. Sanders have a photo of your great-uncle pinned to their wall of suspects."

Irene gives us a grave look. "Alexander Lochamire is trying to do everything he can to silence my great-uncle, including lying to the FBI and telling them he's a terrorist." Irene swears under her breath. She blows a dangling curl from her Afro out of her eyes and continues, now sullen, "My great-uncle formed the Ghosts in an attempt to expose Memory Frontier's dark secrets. He's a good man. He's trying to right his wrongs."

"And just what are these dark secrets?" Ollie asks cautiously.

Irene pulls back, slouching in her chair. "He . . . won't tell me. Not yet, at least."

"Why?"

"He thinks it's too risky. He thinks my knowing the truth could jeopardize my safety."

"And sending you to Foxtail Academy, a boarding school funded by the company that's trying to silence him, *isn't* jeopardizing your safety?" I suppress a chuckle, glancing from Fletcher to Chase and Ollie, then back to Irene. "I'm sorry, but I just don't see what Mr. Lear gains by secretly sending you here without needed information."

"He will tell me," she replies simply. "He'll tell all of us. When the timing's right."

Before I can press her on that, Chase raises his hand. "I still don't understand *why* your great-uncle sent you here."

"Initially, to spy on Dr. Sanders. But learning about you four and your ability to knife was a revelation." Just like that, Irene is spirited again. "We believe you could *dramatically* increase the odds of helping the Ghosts succeed."

Chase scrunches his eyebrows together. "Really? But how are we going to—"

"Hang on." I drop my voice. "*How* did Mr. Lear find out we knifed? Does he have a mole working at Memory Frontier?"

"You guys told him." Irene snort-laughs. "Well, indirectly, that is."

Fletcher sighs. "Yeah, so apparently that pest control tech is one of Mr. Lear's guys."

"Zayne Olson." Irene rolls her eyes. "He can be *such* a drag sometimes. But he's good at what he does, gotta give him that. Anyway, he was sent to grab something from Fletcher's house and overheard you guys talking about knifing."

My ears burn red-hot. *How could we have been so careless?*

Chase and Ollie swap worried looks. I bet they're both thinking the same thing I am: What if the wrong person had overheard us? Someone dangerous, someone who wanted to harm us?

We *have* to be more careful.

Irene senses the anxiety hanging in the air. "Don't worry. Your secret's safe. If you hadn't said anything when Zayne was there, my great-uncle might never have learned who Memory Frontier enlisted to knife. The Memory Ghosts may not have found you in time."

I lean back, my head swimming. If Irene is telling the truth, and that's a pretty huge *if*, the implications are massive. Like these "dark secrets" that Alexander Lochamire and his company are harboring—does it all somehow play into my brother's death? Was Ramon silenced for learning something he wasn't supposed to, for learning about the secrets? And what does it have to do with Memory Killer's relation to artificial recall? I think back to what my brother witnessed on the bus the day he was killed, the elderly man who was stricken with Memory Killer *while* he used artificial recall.

Even though I didn't see what Ramon saw, the image of the elderly man's gray eyes fluttering while he was tethered to his Restorey was enough to startle my brother. I may have misremembered Ramon's identity, but I'll *never* forget the quiver in his voice when he called me.

That phone call haunts me to this day—for more than one reason.

I turn my thoughts toward Dr. Sanders. If what Irene says is true, I can no longer confide in my teacher about my premonitions. I have lost my best shot at discovering the genesis of my ability and whether it can be controlled. I'll have to be extra guarded around her and the dean.

Irene's claims have a far-reaching ripple effect.

I feel nauseous.

"It's a lot to take in, I know, like being told up is *actually* down." Irene looks us each in the eyes before standing.

"Something like that," I mumble to myself, watching as she scoops up her tote.

"Take the night to process everything I've told you." She half waves. "I'll come find you guys at breakfast tomorrow to pitch you next steps."

When she's out of earshot, Fletcher turns to me.

"Before you say anything," he pleads, and it feels like he's talking to just me, "the address. The one the dean had us extract from Malcolm Heckman's memory."

Right. Dean Mendelsohn said it was a MACE field office, but as Fletcher and I saw with our own eyes, it wasn't. So just what is the significance of that location to Memory Frontier?

"At this juncture, it may be impossible to prove the credibility of Irene's claims." Now Fletcher looks Ollie and Chase in the eyes too. "But what we *can* prove is that the dean and Dr. Sanders lied."

"So what do we do?" My voice has a faraway quality. It sounds foreign to my own ears. Everyone shakes their head.

Eventually, Chase says, "We distract ourselves with some chess pie."

24

FLETCHER COHEN

The epidermis—one's outermost layer of skin—is nothing more than dead cells and, in point of fact, detects very little feeling. Fletcher had read that before. He believed it now. By lamplight, he picked at a pesky splinter with a needle on loan from Ollie, finding it strange that he felt nothing when he expected to feel something. The flimsy shard of wood was burrowed beneath his skin just above his cognition wheel; he was *finally* managing to fish out the splinter, his tongue clamped between his teeth, his eyes sharply narrowed.

Fletcher sat at his desk in their dorm room while Daryl Hall's "Dreamtime" played on the boombox. Chase lounged on the couch, half working on homework, half listening to the music, wholly absorbed with the day's recent developments.

"The way I see it, man," Chase said, flipping his textbook shut and tossing it onto the coffee table, "we have two options."

"Oh?" Fletcher set the needle down and attempted to pull the splinter out the rest of the way with his left thumb and index finger—nature's true pliers. *Almost there . . .*

"Option one: we believe what Irene says and help the Memory Ghosts." Chase stood and walked over to the window. Outside, the nighttime was blue and black; it was the kind of naked, lightless evening that foretold a cold winter. "Option two: we get the hell out of Foxtail Academy and live like nomads, off the grid and off of Memory Frontier's radar."

Fletcher snickered. "You wouldn't last two seconds without running water."

Chase grunted, but he didn't disagree. Out loud, anyway.

"Besides," Fletcher said, at last getting a good enough pinch on the splinter's tip and carefully extracting it, "I'm of no help to my parents on the run." He exhaled through his nose, holding the tiny splinter up to his eye and studying it under the light. He flicked it into the wastebasket under the desk.

"Valid point." Chase turned and leaned against the wall, facing his roommate. "Which means . . . ?"

Fletcher sighed. "I think we *have* to believe Irene. I've played out all kinds of scenarios in my head since dinner, and I keep coming back to the lies."

"Sadly, that doesn't narrow it down. Could you be more specific?"

"How Memory Frontier lied about the true intent of the Reflector trial," Fletcher said, folding his arms. "Then how the dean lied about the risks involved in memory knifing. He lied about the address we knifed. He lied when he said we'd only be needed for one mission. And come to think of it, he also lied when he said he'd get us assignment exemptions for Q1."

"Fair enough." Chase shrugged. "Although, based on his interactions with Dr. Grondahl, it sounds like the dean's not fully to blame for this new knifing assignment." Chase mustered an exaggerated look of surprise. "Who would've thunk the higher-ups would want us to memory knife again after they found out it was possible? Shocker!"

"The fact remains that Memory Frontier and Dean Mendelsohn lie." Fletcher glanced out the window, which at this point merely reflected the dorm lights and furniture. "And let's not forget the dean tried to recruit me to spy on my classmates."

Chase blew the bangs out of his eyes. "All good points. Plus . . ."

"What?"

"Well, we kind of glossed over how Dr. Sanders and Memory Frontier managed to steal Malcolm Heckman's memories in the first place. How they're managing to do it again, to this Emilia Vanguard."

Memory indexing, Fletcher thought, troubled. *Dr. Sanders all but admitted it was happening when we asked her and the dean how they managed to seize that memory of Malcolm's.*

"Is . . . is *that* the dark secret Irene referenced?" Chase sounded uneasy, like he was processing being diagnosed with a terrible illness. "Is that what her great-uncle and the Ghosts are trying to expose?"

"I guess it's possible."

A hooded face appeared on the other side of their window. Chase shrieked, but Fletcher's eyes adjusted to the shadowed face almost immediately.

"Freya!" He popped open the window, removed the screen, and helped her climb inside.

"Okay, look," Chase said, panting as Fletcher closed the window. "I'm all for these late-night romantic escapades, but we need to lay down some ground rules."

"You peed yourself, didn't you? Admit it." Freya flipped her hood back coolly and slid into Fletcher's arms. The skin on her forehead was so chilly that it slightly jolted Fletcher. He pulled her in tight, embracing the cold, grateful this was something he could feel.

"Not dignifying that." Chase crossed the room to the bathroom, adding, "And I'm just brushing my teeth!"

"He definitely peed himself," Freya whispered after Chase shut the door.

Fletcher smiled into Freya's hair; she smelled of the outdoors, of dry leaves and crisp air. Loose strands escaped her high bun, tickling his nose.

"What are you doing here? If one of the prefects—"

"I'll tell them to take it up with the dean," Freya said, breaking away.

Fletcher smiled. "Good point." He raised his eyebrows. "I think we've earned more than a few get-out-of-jail-free cards."

They sat down on the couch. "I'm worried, Fletcher."

"Doesn't feel like we have much of a choice, does it?" He held her hand, staring at their reflection on the TV screen. They both looked more tired than any seventeen-year-old had any business looking, the kind of tired forged in hardship and wrought with pain.

"I don't think I *ever* had a choice," Freya whispered. "The dean gave me no choice when he dangled that carrot over my head. He never should have manipulated me like that, and I never should have taken the bait. You were right. Now I've dragged you guys into this mess and I don't know how we're supposed to get out."

"Hey, whoa." Fletcher wrapped his arm around her, pulling himself closer. "We made our choices. We decided to stick with you. Don't for a second blame yourself or—"

"If we had never agreed to memory knife for the dean, your dad would still be a free man." Freya shook her head. "Haven't you thought about that?"

"Maybe. But I'm choosing to believe that what Irene says about the Ghosts is true, which means my dad's imprisoned because he was secretly fighting for the truth. I think that's pretty cool."

"But, Fletcher, *I* put him there."

"Indirectly," Fletcher insisted. "And anyway, if we do help Mr. Lear and the Memory Ghosts, he'll be free again soon."

Freya covered her face with her hands and said into her palms, "I don't know, I'm still wary of trusting Irene outright."

"Okay, well, give me one reason we *shouldn't*."

"Her great-uncle sent a stranger into your home to steal something from your parents' closet!"

"But he might have been looking for something to help my dad. If Dad's working with the Ghosts, he likely told them where the hideaway door is. How else did that pest control tech, er, *Zayne*, find it in the first place?"

Freya sighed.

"Plus, Irene's risking a *lot* spilling all this to us," Fletcher added. "What's to stop us from going to Dean Mendelsohn and telling him the great-niece of public enemy number one just introduced herself to us, that she openly admitted to being here to—"

"Okay, okay, I see your point." Freya crossed her legs. "I just needed to work through all of this out loud."

They sat in silence for a moment. The shower turned on in the bathroom.

"I still can't believe Memory Frontier wiped our classmates' memories," Freya said after a while.

"What?"

"Fletcher, it's the only explanation. No one seems to remember us." Freya fidgeted with one of the buttons on Fletcher's jacket. "I had two personal conversations with Mr. Williams, neither of which he remembers."

"I mean, it could just be Memory Kill—"

"No." Freya closed her eyes. "Adam McCauley? All our teachers except Dr. Sanders? It's too big a coincidence. This place has taught me to reject the idea of coincidences."

Another period of silence. The shower turned off, and a few moments later Chase emerged in gym shorts and a baggy T-shirt. His wet hair fell across his face. "So?" he said, drying his hair and tossing the towel back into the bathroom. "You guys solve all our problems or just make out?"

Freya smiled. "That reminds me." She turned Fletcher's face toward hers and kissed him as though they were the only two in the room.

When they finished, Chase glowered at them. "You two are insatiable."

❖ ❖ ❖

The next morning, it was cold. Fletcher emerged from underneath his bedsheets, his teeth all but chattering. Slowly, he removed the Reflector receivers from his temples and crawled down the bunk bed ladder. The baseboard heater hummed and rattled, but when Fletcher inspected it, he found that it radiated almost no heat. He yawned, made a mental note to notify one of the campus staffers, and turned around.

His heart stuttered in his chest.

On the top bunk, a faceless form floated just a few inches above his mattress. Though to call it a *form* was being generous. It was more or less billions of dazzling particles that, connected, formed the outline of a person.

The form floated there, unmoving.

Fletcher swallowed.

A few breathless seconds ticked by.

Then the form seemed to beckon Fletcher.

Fletcher obeyed without even realizing what he was doing. He climbed the ladder. He hunched over the form on his mattress, his back grazing the ceiling. Defying gravity with ease, Fletcher bent his knees, leaned backward, and gracefully lifted his bare feet— first the left one, then the right. Now Fletcher hovered in the air beside the pulsating outline, and he willed himself to float toward the particles until his entire body filled the space and he was jolted from the experience—sweaty, hair tangled, but awake.

A vague sensation of dreaming floated away from him.

The heater purred softly, in perfect working condition.

Fletcher removed his Reflector receivers, yawned, and pulled himself out of bed, only to find the sheets soaked in sweat.

25

FREYA IZQUIERDO

At breakfast that morning, Fletcher, Chase, and I agree to trust Irene. For my part, it ultimately comes down to two things: (1) A few weeks ago, Dr. Sanders essentially admitted that Memory Frontier was using indexing to scour the Ghosts' memories, and (2) all memories of us clearly have been erased from our classmates' and teachers' minds. Obviously, this does not sit well with me. If Memory Frontier and its cogs (namely, the dean and Dr. Sanders) can do this with such ease, what other nefarious things are they capable of?

Chase is hesitant, and he *does* raise some good points. For example, what if Irene is actually doing Memory Frontier's bidding, luring us into some elaborate trap? After some discussion, though, Fletcher manages to sway him.

Fletcher's reasoning for trusting Irene is clear: it gives him a path to proving his father's innocence.

As for Ollie, well, she finally agrees, though only because she intends to keep us four intact, not because she is willing to trust Irene. Not yet, at least.

"This is terrific news. My great-uncle will be so pleased," Irene whispers at our table after breakfast. "For now, keep working with the dean and Dr. Sanders. Keep up appearances. I'll bring you guys word from Uncle Philip soon." And then she bounds off toward the library like it's nothing, like she hasn't just pulled four strangers into a complicated web of conspiracies and intrigue.

So the four of us agree to do just that, to keep up appearances.

After our first two periods and lunch, the four of us march through the biting wind. The twisted woods behind the faculty housing bid us welcome as we head toward the bunker, which looks as dreadful as ever as it eventually comes into view beyond the skeletal trees.

"I hope we made the right choice," Ollie whispers, linking her arm with mine.

I tell her I hope so too.

"Well, well," Sade van der Merwe says as we enter the bunker. She and Rhett walk out of the kitchen and meet us beside the looming Restorey. "Howzit? I'm a little surprised to see you, to be completely honest."

Chase snorts, pocketing his hands. "Yeah, well, *we're* a little surprised to see you too."

Sade and Rhett blink, their expressions blank.

"Yeah, so," Chase adds, desperately trying to play it cool, "howz *that*?"

An uncomfortable moment passes through the facility. Blessedly, it doesn't last long. Dean Mendelsohn and Dr. Sanders walk to us from the computer stations with an ever-bubbly Dr. Grondahl in tow.

"Ah, you made it!" says Dr. Grondahl before either the dean or Dr. Sanders can get a word in. "Must admit I had my doubts that you'd return."

"Yes, well." Fletcher clears his throat. "If helping you means putting more of the Memory Ghosts behind bars, then sign us up."

Wow, I think. *He's playing the part well . . .*

"Good." Dr. Sanders's eyes fall on me, and I sense a hint of scrutiny behind her stare . . . maybe suspicion? She's likely wondering why we one-eightied so quickly after having *just* castigated Dean Mendelsohn. Yesterday we were vehemently opposed to tempting Memory Killer while knifing. Now we're back, ready to roll up our sleeves.

I swallow and go to avert my eyes, but before I do, I notice Dr. Sanders now has a burst blood vessel in her left eye. Or . . . was it always in her left eye, and maybe it just hasn't healed yet? Either way, the blood-red cloudiness unsettles me.

"Get changed," the dean instructs us, interrupting my thoughts. "We have work to do."

❖ ❖ ❖

The new cadence of our schedule, a hard and taxing regimen, leaves my body depleted at the end of every grueling day. The cycle is brutal. We wake up, have breakfast in the Foxhole with the rest of our classmates, power through our first two periods, scarf lunch and cram in some reading for lit, then spend our free period in the bunker memory knifing with Sade and Rhett. We round out our afternoons in Memory Theory.

A part of me figured Dr. Sanders would go easy on us. We did agree to be Memory Frontier's long-term knifing agents, after all.

. But no.

If anything, her lectures seem more intense than usual.

In class on Wednesday, she paces the length of the dry-erase board. She wears dress pants, a loose-fitting blouse, and a fanciful scarf draped over her shoulders. "In thinking through the basic framework of our consciousness and how we store explicit memories, we can separate memory storage into two categories— episodic and semantic. The former, of course, pertains to you as an individual, like what you ate for dinner, where you went for fall break, or how old you were when you learned how to ride a bicycle. The latter deals in facts independent of you, such as Ronald Reagan is the fortieth president, there are twenty-four hours in a day, or that humans are actually paralyzed in certain stages of sleep."

That last fact gives me goose bumps. I take notes as she continues, "Curiously, Memory Killer seems most drawn to episodic memories. Of course, those aren't the only kinds of memories that are at risk"—I think of scholastic gaps, which are vulnerable aspects of our schooling that are imprinted on memory tapes and relearned through artificial recall—"but, well, in a 1985 poll, we found that upwards of 75 percent of the average person's memory tapes relate to episodic memories."

I set down my pencil, reflecting on my own memory tapes over the years. Come to think of it, it *does* seem like most of my at-risk memories have to do with my personal life. Conversations with my brother, Ramon, at the park. Scenes of us at the beach, racing to build elaborate sandcastles before the tide came in. Watching him burn dinner in the kitchen while belting along to Rubén Blades's "Sin Tu Cariño," and—

My heart sinks. If so many of these memories were stored on tapes, how did I manage to misremember Ramon's identity? Am I really that weak?

The bell rings, cutting off my thoughts. I grab my things and shuffle out of the classroom with my peers.

❖ ❖ ❖

By the time study period rolls around on Thursday, all I want to do is sleep. In fact, I'd be happy to hibernate straight through the weekend. And since we spend study period in our dorms, I'm thinking I might actually nap the time away.

The problem is, I can't shut off my brain.

All I can do is think about memory knifing with Sade and Rhett. Each day has been the same. Fletcher, Ollie, Chase, and I get dressed in our jumpsuits and then knife a different memory. And each time, the same thing happens: We all appear in Dean Mendelsohn's memory, gather around in a wide circle, and I tell them how I managed to prevent Fletcher from slipping into a memory loop. I tell them about our shared memory, how he and I had fixated on a landmark—the crepe myrtle beside Juniper Lake—and how the tree had managed to *ground* Fletcher. Next, Sade and Rhett ask me a bunch of questions, and then we just wait around anxiously . . . wait for Memory Killer to strike one of us.

Almost a week and it hasn't happened yet.

I'm not complaining.

Earlier today, Rhett asked a troubling question in the dean's memory. We were hiking through Redwood National Park. It was midday. The mammoth old-growth trees dwarfed us, reaching up toward the blue sky like mossy skyscrapers. When we arrived in this particular memory, slabs of bark and fragments of branches shot through the air, assembling the redwoods in quick succession. Their formation was punctuated by a ghostly low-hanging mist, which appeared out of nowhere and fell *up* from the ground. It hung in the air like wispy smoke, rolling over the greenery and diffusing the sunlight.

It was breathtaking.

A late-forties dean appeared next, clasping a walking stick. He leisurely led his son, Daniel (who was only eight in this memory), up a crooked path. The six of us followed closely, and I periodically glanced over my shoulder, eyeing the edge of the memory scene—an enormous, pulsating curtain that closed in on everything in step with Dean Mendelsohn's gait.

What happens if Memory Killer seizes us all at the same time? Rhett asked, walking up beside me.

I . . . don't know, I replied honestly. It was a good question, one that caused immediate panic.

Wow. Rhett shrugged, slipping his hands into his jumpsuit pockets. *I'm surprised you hadn't considered that possibility before.*

To be fair, I never really intended to make knifing a hobby.

Rhett nodded. *You divorced yourself from knifing, but knifing didn't sign the papers.*

I . . . that's a weird way to put it.

Sorry. My mom says things like that. A lot. After I mentally checked out of soccer my sophomore year, she said, "You divorced yourself from the team, Rhett, but marriages are a holy covenant, even the loveless ones. So get your ass back on field!" I hate soccer.

I wasn't sure if I was supposed to laugh at that, but thankfully, Rhett chuckled and lightly nudged me. (When his elbow grazed my ribs, the sensation felt . . . unnatural, a faint vibration that went down to my bones.)

Your parents are split up? I asked carefully.

No. Rhett frowned, then he added sarcastically, *Happily married for nineteen years. Ask me again, though, when they're empty nesters in a few years.*

Oh. I'm sorry.

That's probably some subconscious thing she's doing, isn't it? Using the word divorce *all willy-nilly like that?*

Maybe.

Yeah. Maybe.

Rhett and I walked in silence for a moment, trailing everyone else in pairs: the dean and his son, Fletcher and Sade, and Ollie and Chase. The mist was everywhere. I tried imagining what the redwoods smelled like.

Rhett sighed. *The subconscious terrifies me.*

How so?

Well, so there's the conscious, subconscious, and unconscious, right?

I nodded.

He said, *The unconscious is kinda like Memory Killer—it's where past events or whatever go to die. Like the first word you learned how to spell. No one remembers that. Then there's being conscious. That's where we have the most control, isn't it? It's where we have the most agency.*

I nodded again, ducking underneath a massive log that was leaning precariously against the hill to our right. I moved through the triangular passage, and when I came out on the other side, Rhett continued.

But the subconscious . . . I dunno . . . sometimes it feels like our minds have minds of their own. Ever think of it that way?

I told him no, I hadn't.

Back home, in Indianapolis, I drive the same route home from school every single day. I pick up my brother Tommy from Covington Middle, hit the interstate, and fifteen minutes later we pull into our neighborhood. More often than not, when my brother and I walk in the front door, I'm smacked with the realization that I don't remember driving. It's so strange, and it's more than just muscle memory, you know? It's like I just checked out and my subconscious took the wheel.

I saw his point. And truth be told, it kind of freaked me out. Not really sure why.

Anywaaay, he said, drawing out the word, *regardless of how vulnerable our minds are, they're also the most powerful weapons in the world.*

Weapons *is kind of a strong word, isn't it?*

Rhett kept quiet the rest of that walk. Strangely, I could sense how intensely he was listening to our surroundings. It's hard to explain, but it's as if he was quietly *probing* Dean Mendelsohn's memory as we hiked through the woods.

I'm pondering that experience when Ollie bursts into our dorm room. She rubs her hands together and blows into them, warming herself.

"If this is fall, I do *not* want to know what winter's like."

I grunt, sliding off my shoes.

"We need to do something fun."

"Sleeping's fun."

Ollie gives me a look. "Ha. No. This week is kicking our asses. We've worked hard, so it's time to play hard. Halloween's Saturday."

"Ollie."

"Don't *Ollie* me. You'll thank me later, trust me."

I pull my scrunchie out and run my hand through my hair, sinking deeper into the couch. "Ugh. Why do I get the feeling I *won't* be thanking you later?"

"Just put your sneakers back on and—"

A knock at our door. Ollie groans and answers it.

"Hey, sorry, this a good time?" Irene pokes her head in.

"Er, yeah." Ollie opens the door all the way and Irene steps in.

"Hey." I slide to the far side of the couch so she can sit, which she does with a long exhale, and Ollie plops down on the edge of our coffee table, facing us.

"Just spoke with Uncle Philip." There's no pep in Irene's voice. Only a dry coldness, like the one that hangs outside our dorm windows. "He said Lochamire captured someone else."

I sigh, nodding. "Emilia Vanguard. Apparently, she was a runner for the Ghosts?"

"Yeah. A total badass too."

"We're training these new kids." Ollie crosses her legs. "Looks like the mission is going to be intercepting another message. We'll be knifing Emilia's memories."

Irene takes a beat, assuming a quietly inquisitive look, her brown eyes bouncing from Ollie to me. Then, "He'll want to know that, my great-uncle, along with anything else you guys think is pertinent. He wants to meet with you. This weekend. He's flying in to Nashville tomorrow."

Wow, I think. *That feels awfully risky on his part . . . though I guess not riskier than sending his great-niece into the belly of the beast.*

"I'm driving to Nashville to meet him." Irene stands. "I'll come find you guys in the Foxhole on Saturday, and we'll go from there."

She excuses herself and disappears through the door. Ollie locks it.

Wordlessly, she crosses the bedroom, climbs the bunk bed ladder, and lies on her side. Her expression is distant, almost catatonic. She makes no more mention of doing something "fun."

We sit in silence.

I think about the implications of meeting Philip Lear, the mysterious man behind the Memory Ghosts. If we meet with him this weekend, there will officially be no turning back. We'll have exposed ourselves to the man who's trying to bring down Memory Frontier—either joining a noble cause or placing a huge target on our backs.

Did we bite off more than we can chew?

I doze off with the lights on.

26

FLETCHER COHEN

Friday was cold and dreary, as if winter was getting grossly impatient with fall. It was also the day before Halloween.

"Couple of people are talking about going to a college party in Clarksville tomorrow," Chase said that afternoon after classes concluded. The four ordered coffee in the senior lounge. Hot drinks in hand, the friends walked to the couches. "At Austin Peay."

"I'm in." Ollie raised her latte toward the ceiling. "Let's just hope this"—she lowered her voice, glancing about the senior lounge—"this meeting with Mr. Lear doesn't go too long."

Fletcher chuckled. "You guys wanna party after meeting with the man who claims to know earth-shattering secrets about Memory Frontier?"

"Hey, we're teenagers with needs." Chase slurped his drink. "And right now, those needs are going unmet."

"You poor thing." Freya arched an eyebrow.

"It's settled, then." Chase clanked his drink against Ollie's. "The only challenge will be convincing Irene to drop us off at the party, since she's driving and—"

Chase swallowed the rest of his words, staring past his friends. Fletcher, Freya, and Ollie followed his eyeline and spotted Sade at the top of the stairs. After spending one week together, Fletcher and his friends had grown accustomed to seeing her in her jumpsuit. But today she wore neon-green joggers and a gray jacket, which didn't appear to offer adequate warmth against the cold. Sade also didn't appear the type who minded the cold.

She scanned the senior lounge until her eyes fell on Fletcher and his friends. She smirked and strode toward them, and as she did, Fletcher wondered if it marked the first time he'd seen her on campus.

"You guys look like you enjoy this place." Sade absently pulled her long bleached-blonde hair to one side.

"I feel like I should be offended at that," Chase said, squinting.

"Foxtail Academy isn't some magical institution with magical amenities." She looked around the senior lounge, which was dotted with fall decor. Arrangements of pumpkins and gourds. Strings of red, yellow, and orange leaves lined the coffee bar. There was even a pair of large cornstalks flanking the entrance. Fletcher and his friends found it charming; but there was a kind of loathing in Sade's eyes. "You ever wonder why Lochamire and Memory Frontier chose a *boarding school* to trial the Reflectors?"

Fletcher sat up. "So they could audition teens for knifing."

"That's part of the reason, sure. But if that were the *only* reason, why not just recruit in secret? Why erect a multimillion-dollar school with tons of press and fanfare?"

Fletcher and his friends remained silent.

"For the pageantry." Sade shook her head. "On the other side of this, the student body will be Alexander Lochamire's success story. We'll be living proof that the Reflectors and the evolution of

Memory Frontier's technology are the future—*his* future. Foxtail Academy is a hugely expensive marketing ploy."

Fletcher found himself nodding. *It makes total sense. We're being used in so many ways.*

"I suppose it'll only be for a few more weeks," Sade said. "After we complete this mission, Dr. Grondahl's confident the remaining terrorists will be smoked out, finally putting to rest their dangerous anarchical efforts. Then I'm leaving this place for good."

"Wait." Ollie tilted her head. "A few more *weeks?*"

"Mhmm. Sounds like they're pretty close to isolating the memory we need to knife from this Emilia Vanguard. Dr. Grondahl thinks it could be as early as after Thanksgiving."

So the ticking clock begins, Fletcher thought, sipping his coffee.

Sade flared her nostrils as if she had caught a whiff of something pungent, then she was gone.

"Okay, so Sade found us just to kill the mood?" Ollie sniffed. "Anyway. About this college party . . ."

"You guys sort that out," Fletcher said, standing. "I'm gonna call my mom."

Freya reached out and grabbed his hand. "Want some company?"

"Nah, I'm good." Fletcher conjured his most convincing smile. "I won't be long."

Fletcher dialed his home number from the payphone behind the admissions office. The plastic receiver was ice cold against his right ear. He slipped his free hand into his armpit to keep warm.

The phone rang only twice.

"Hello?" His mother sounded exhausted.

"Hey, Mom, it's me."

"Fletcher? Everything okay?"

"Yeah, of course. Wanted to check in. How are you and Dad?"

She sighed into the receiver. "I finally spoke to him on the phone this week. He's maintaining his innocence, hon, but he won't outright deny that he's linked to those terrorists. Quentin thinks the Memory Ghosts might've brainwashed him." Her tone shifted at that last sentence; it was thick with anger, the kind reserved for injustice.

"So, what, he dances around the question when you ask if he's involved?"

"More or less." Another sigh. "Quentin's deeply concerned that your father might not be of sound mind. Frankly, so am I." She cleared her throat, abruptly cutting herself off. "Don't you worry, hon. We'll get this sorted. How's school? How's the trial going?"

Oh, it's a trial all right. "Fine."

"You allowed to tell me about this mysterious technology yet?"

If you only knew. "It'll just bore you. And anyway, you only half answered my question."

"Huh?"

"I asked how *you* and Dad are. So how are *you*?"

She paused, collecting her thoughts. But her voice didn't quaver. Not even a little. "I'm managing. I love your father. I believe he's innocent, I *really* do, and I'm trying to remain optimistic. Sometimes optimism feels foolish, but optimism always leads to hopefulness, and remaining hopeful is *never* foolish. At least that's the way I see it."

Fletcher felt the sting of approaching tears. He blinked them back and, before he could stop himself, muttered, "Dad *is* innocent. And I'm gonna prove it."

She didn't press him on that. Likely she believed them to be the desperate words of a son on the precipice of losing his father. "I love you."

"I love you too." Fletcher hung up the phone and turned around to find Sade standing a few feet from him, hugging herself against the morning wind. She licked her pink lips, which appeared chapped. Her pale skin seemed to glow in the late-morning sunlight.

Neither of them spoke for a few seconds; they silently regarded one another. Until she said, "It must be hard to do what you're doing."

Fletcher steeled himself. "What are you talking about?"

"You're helping us fight the Ghosts, but your father's on the wrong side of the war."

Fletcher took a step forward. "What makes you think you know anything about my family?"

Sade flashed her customary smirk. "Call it intuition."

Fletcher held her stare, then marched past her, lightly bumping her shoulder as he passed. When he'd taken only a few steps, though, she said, "Both my parents were beaten to death when I was a child."

Fletcher froze, unsure if he'd heard her correctly. Slowly, he spun back around.

She continued, "They were closely aligned with Steve Biko, a South African activist who made headlines in the seventies. He vocally opposed apartheid, the segregation that still has a stronghold over my homeland. Biko was eventually murdered in 1977, as were some of his closest allies, which included my parents. I was seven."

"I . . . I'm sorry."

Fletcher wasn't sure what else to say. Sade looked uncharacteristically vulnerable; gone was her condescending disposition. Indeed, her hazel eyes had grown soft, her lips drawn into a half frown.

A gust of wind passed between them, tousling her hair like weak branches on a tree.

"Why did you tell me that? About your parents?"

Sade shrugged. "I'm proud of the stand they took. But that doesn't mean I don't resent them for dying." Her tone was fragile, like a cracked vessel that was one drop away from shattering. "I love them, and I'm angry. All at once. Something tells me you know what that's like."

Fletcher didn't reply.

"We're not so different. War can be such an affecting force, especially when it claims our family." Sade closed her eyes, took a slow breath, then opened them.

"When did the dean recruit you and Rhett?"

"During fall break. Rhett and I were among a handful of students who stayed on campus."

Fletcher nodded. *Of course. Losing her parents, and in such dramatic fashion . . . grief has probably rent her to pieces.* If Dr. Sanders's theory was true—that loss and grief are at the heart of one's ability to memory knife—then someone like Sade van der Merwe was the ideal candidate. Dr. Sanders likely pored over the Foxtail student records in search of students affected by profound grief.

So what was Rhett's grief story?

"It's cold out here. You should get inside." Sade turned to leave but added, "See you Monday."

Fletcher watched her go. She appeared almost ghostlike as she vanished toward the girls' dormitories. And while he stood there, shivering in the biting wind, reflecting on his conversation with Sade, he wondered what Chase's grief story was.

Freya had shared a little bit of Ollie's one day over break, but he'd yet to learn the full story of Chase's cousin—a loss Ollie had alluded to at the school dance.

Few go untouched by grief, he mused as he retreated to the warmth. *And Chase, beneath his class-clown exterior, is no exception.*

27

FREYA IZQUIERDO

After lunch on Saturday, the four of us cram into Irene Porter's black Taurus. Fletcher sits in the passenger seat, and Ollie and I flank Chase in the back. Ollie wedges her bulging JanSport backpack between her shoulder and the window to use as a pillow. (When I asked her why she needed to bring her backpack, she merely winked and then fist-bumped Chase, who giggled.)

The rest of the drive is long and quiet, devoid of small talk or music. There's plenty to discuss, sure, but I think we share a collective hesitation to converse openly around Irene. She is, after all, still a stranger.

Nearly an hour after leaving campus, Irene says, "I'm sure you guys have a *ton* of questions for Uncle Philip. But we get only one hour with him and he has a lot to cover."

"Bummer," Chase says, frowning. "And here I was hoping we'd have time to shoot the breeze."

Irene merges onto a main road, which is lined with abandoned fast-food restaurants and shuttered businesses that boasted five-minute oil changes. Debris and waste litter the sidewalks and parking lots. The aftermath of riots and looting. Through the air vents, I smell the heavy scent of gasoline and burned rubber. It agitates my nose, and I manage to stave off a sneeze.

We pass an empty car dealership. Someone has spray-painted YOU FORGOT ABOUT US across the once-colorful, now faded signage. Beside this, a holey American flag waves at half-mast just above the Tennessee state flag.

The effects of Memory Killer have been unkind to this corner of the South.

Irene doesn't tell us where we're headed. After a while, she turns into a neighborhood off the main road. It's hilly. The trees are naked, and the greasy-gray sky emphasizes their nakedness. We pull into a drive-way at the end of a long cul-de-sac. The house is brick and the shutters are vine-covered. The brown grass in the front yard is ankle-high. A rusted riding lawn mower sits beside the porch, its tires deflated.

The tires aren't the only thing robbed of air. Past the abandoned mower, in the front yard next door, three makeshift grave markers poke out of the dirt. The crosses appear to be constructed of old fence planks. Instantly, I start to wonder who's buried in the ground. The crosses are small . . . have some parents laid their children to rest?

I force down a lump in my throat and get out of the car, fixing my attention on the house where we're parked. From the outside, it appears vacant, like every other house on this street.

"C'mon." Irene leads us up the cement steps, and after opening the creaky storm door, she knocks. I hold my breath as Fletcher clasps my hand, and I suddenly feel very anxious about this whole thing.

It's as if I didn't fully grasp the weight of our decision to trust Irene until this very moment.

Whatever happens when we step over the threshold, there's no turning back. We'll have exposed ourselves to the Memory Ghosts, the very group Dean Mendelsohn led us to believe was public enemy number one. This choice *will* have consequences.

There's a faint clicking sound as the door unlocks. Then it opens.

28

FLETCHER COHEN

The woman who answered the door was vaguely familiar to Fletcher. She was young, likely only a few years older than him. Black hair pulled back into a ponytail. Light brown skin. Dark eyes that pierced with knowledge and understanding, the sort of gaze a person gives when they've had to surmount a lot of obstacles.

"Ah, Irene, you're early." The young woman sized up the group, and when she made eye contact with Fletcher, it all clicked.

This is Alana Khan. His mouth dried. *The woman I caught meeting in secret with my father.*

"This way." Alana led them inside and shut the door, then deadbolted it. The house's interior was mostly plundered and abandoned, mirroring the run-down neighborhood and the cold town. The living room had a ratty couch and smelled of must. The kitchen linoleum curled like parchment paper with burnt edges.

Irene, Fletcher, and his friends followed Alana past the island and through another door, which led into the adjoining garage.

A circle of metal folding chairs surrounded a kerosene heater, which thrummed like an idling pickup. Fletcher recognized Zayne Olson, who had worn a pest control jumpsuit the last time he'd seen him. He currently wore slacks and a fleece pullover. He was sitting cross-legged beside an elderly woman with heavy lipstick, vibrant white hair, and an expensive-looking clutch purse. She beamed at Fletcher and his friends as they entered.

Beyond Zayne and the elderly woman, a man stood with his back to them, jotting something in a journal. The man was round and of small stature, and he wore a beige suit with a matching fedora. Upon hearing the newcomers enter, he turned, revealing a bright paisley tie.

"Ah, welcome, Special Ones." He closed his journal and set it down on the dryer. Mr. Lear appeared to be in his sixties, with brown-and-gray hair that poked out from beneath the brim of his beige hat. He removed this and held it over his heart. "I am so thankful you agreed to meet. Please, have a seat. There's much to discuss."

Fletcher exchanged a look with the others, then took one of the chairs across from Zayne and the older woman. Freya, Chase, and Ollie did likewise, and Irene and Alana bookended them.

"Where to start?" Mr. Lear put his fedora back on, sighed the longest sigh Fletcher had ever heard, then whispered, "I suppose at the beginning, yes?"

INTERLUDE

FEBRUARY 1972

I believe I've solved it, Alexander wrote in his letter, feeling out of his depth but absolutely certain that his closest friend would manage—as he always did—to keep him afloat. *I need to talk, face-to-face. Obviously, this would require you to come back to San Francisco for a time. I can make the arrangements.*

The arrangements were made. A few days later, Philip Lear arrived on the stone steps of Alexander's tall, cobalt-blue Edwardian home. It was evening, and the chill that hung in the air was the unforgiving kind.

"This way, in my study," Alexander said when Philip had only barely set down his luggage in the foyer. They walked together, two men in their fifties nearing the end of their storied careers, an uncertain future stretching out before them.

Alexander slammed the door to his study and sat behind his desk. Inside, the octagonal room smelled of stale coffee and tobacco. The spines of countless books stared down at Philip as he took a seat across from his friend.

"Coffee?"

Philip politely declined. "Alex, what is this about?"

Alexander sipped from his ceramic mug. The coffee was

cold; his fifth cup of the day. "'No problem is insoluble.' Do you remember who said that?"

Philip nodded. Of course he remembered, but his friend's question was not rhetorical.

"Who said it, Philip?" Alexander asked, leaning forward, the lamplight accentuating the bags under his tired eyes.

"You did," said Philip. "Our second semester at Cornell. It was our first research assignment together in discrete mathematics. I felt like we'd hit a wall, yet you insisted that no problem is insoluble."

Alexander closed his heavy eyes and nodded, the muscles around his chapped lips quivering. "Yes. That *was* me." For the first time that night, Philip observed just how frail his friend looked . . . emaciated even. His concern grew.

He looks like he's aged decades *since last I saw him.*

"Memories are life's connective tissue."

Philip cocked his head. "I . . . what?"

Alexander opened his eyes. They were alien, eyes that did not belong to Alexander Lochamire despite inhabiting Alexander Lochamire's skull. Philip could swear his friend's eyes were slightly discolored—though it was too dark in the study to be sure.

"And once that connective tissue deteriorates," Alexander continued grimly, "once a man's memories depart from him and drift to sea, what is his life but a lost ship devoid of passengers?"

"You need to see a doctor."

"But failing connective tissue can be repaired."

Is he even listening to me? Philip wondered.

"And I believe our waning abilities to remember can be repaired too."

"That's . . ."

"Impossible?" Alexander smiled, though it was an empty smile, the crooked smile of a mask. "No problem is insoluble . . . not even the seemingly impossible ones, old friend."

❖ ❖ ❖

Alexander shuffled the pages and folders and books off his desk and then unfurled a large drawing, placing four empty mugs at each corner to keep the crude diagram from rolling in on itself.

Philip leaned forward and inspected Alexander's rushed drawing, which depicted a crescent moon–shaped device with tendrils of wires sprouting out of one side like the wild roots of an upturned tree: thicker at the base and then thinning out.

The contraption looked like something pulled straight from the cover of an Arthur C. Clarke novel, some rendering of a futuristic piece of hardware that could only exist in a work of science fiction.

"What is this?" Philip asked.

"The solution."

"Okay. But *what* is it?"

"Schematics for a reader, a reader that will scan the human consciousness for autobiographical memories and then archive them. If this technology can be properly constructed, I believe it will grant us an agency over our memories such as we've never experienced before. And I want you to help me perfect it."

"This is what you've been laboring over for months?" Philip leaned in closer, his eyes scanning the blueprints intensely. "This design . . . the processing power alone would take—"

"I've already built a prototype."

"You . . . you have?"

"Would you like to see it?"

At that moment, Philip Lear noticed the uncharacteristic stillness of the Lochamire home. Where was the incessant yapping of the Pomeranian, Lou Ottens? Where was the soft lull of the TV from the living room, where Mrs. Lochamire could always be found—without exception—working through her sudoku puzzles in an easy chair? And where was their daughter, Brenda, who (last Philip had heard) was staying with her parents while she completed her master's degree? Up to this point, Philip had paid scant attention to his familiar surroundings, and only now was he beginning to notice the unfamiliar absence of things.

The house itself seemed to have stopped breathing.

"Would you like to see it?"

"Where is Lettie?" Philip asked of Alexander's wife.

Outside the study, the grandfather clock tolled, signaling the top of the hour—as if reassuring Philip that the house was not completely devoid of energy. Not yet, at least.

Alexander explained that she had left, but that it was for her own good, and would he just hurry up and answer the question already?

"Yes. I would like to see your prototype."

The garage was a mess. Every surface was littered with disassembled electronic devices and index cards covered with barely legible scribblings. Mounds of crumpled paper rose everywhere, great mountains of discarded thoughts and ideas. The helmet stood proudly before these paper mountains. It rested precariously on an ironing board, Alexander's makeshift table, and Philip was now certain that his friend of many years had gone certifiably mad.

The helmet was large and bulky and looked similar to its diagram; Philip would give Alexander that. It was a Frankenstein's monster of a contraption, complete with oversized screws, shoddy welding, and an exposed motherboard.

Philip approached the helmet like an explosives specialist approaching a bomb. His eyes fell on the many wires, which draped off the ironing board, snaked across the unkempt floor, and plugged into an open reel-to-reel tape machine.

"Would you like to give it a try?"

Philip flinched, as if he'd forgotten Alexander was there. "I'd rather not."

"The world is changing," Alexander said, circling the helmet, a proud creator regarding his creation. "It's dying, really. Brilliant minds like ours are humanity's only chance."

"This will never work. The human brain is far more complex and advanced than we'll ever know. Capturing memories and then . . . What was it you said—*archiving* them? It simply can't be done."

Alexander said nothing. Instead, he pulled an unlabeled VHS tape out of his inner blazer pocket. At least, Philip *thought* it was a VHS tape. Alexander set it beside the helmet on the ironing board.

"You are right," Alexander said, and Philip found that he could not take his eyes off the tape. He could not stop himself from speculating as to what was on it. "Our brains are wonderfully advanced things, more powerful than any computer we could conceive of. What if there was a way to tap into that power?"

"I don't follow."

"What if the human brain possesses the processing power to make technology like a memory reader possible?" He pointed to the tape on the ironing board. "What if it's possible to pinpoint our fading memories and then imprint them onto tapes, ensuring we could relearn them and never lose them?"

"So by harnessing the energy in the human brain, you power the technology in your . . . your helmet . . . which in effect scans the human consciousness for fading memories?"

"Our brains are precious vessels filled with electrical synapses. Think of this MeReader as a flywheel that collects energy and momentum and then relies on that conserved energy and momentum to function."

"*MeReader?*"

Alexander put his synthetic smile back on. "Do you like it? It's short for *memory reader*. I thought it a bit simplistic at first, but then, all the great descriptors are, aren't they?"

"I have many concerns, least of which is whether *MeReader* is a great descriptor."

"Don't you see? The human brain, the very thing that deteriorates with age and succumbs to memory loss, is the key to *fighting* memory loss."

"Yes, fine, but at what cost?"

"That's where you come in. I need someone with your experience and expertise to lead a team of scientists, which I've already assembled. I need your sharp eye and steady hand to oversee testing and analysis before we can move into production."

"You're serious."

"*Dead.*" The word sounded cold on Alexander Lochamire's tongue, and Philip felt a chill run down his spine as he realized this ambitious technology was going to be fast-tracked with or without his involvement.

And so, Philip Lear felt as though he had no choice. Someone needed to remain close, to help shepherd the engineering and testing and ensure that any risks were identified and addressed before it was too late.

"What's on that tape, Alexander?" Philip asked, nodding at the ironing board.

He picked it back up and ran his fingertips along its sides. "The first memory I'll never forget."

29

FREYA IZQUIERDO

Mr. Lear pauses, gingerly loosening his tie and then taking the last empty seat, between the elderly woman and Zayne Olson. Outside, a gust of wind rattles the garage door.

"What happened next?" I ask, leaning forward in my seat.

Mr. Lear nods. "First, some context: The company Alexander and I cofounded in 1962, Hart Industries, garnered us more success than we ever could have dreamed. We eventually sold our biometric technology a decade later for a large fortune. Ten years can feel like a lifetime." Mr. Lear removes his fedora and places it on his knee. "It can also vanish in a blink.

"The money was truly staggering. As such, when Alexander conceived of his idea for the MeReader in '72, the prototypes were self-funded, and in the span of thirteen months they were well into production.

"During this time, our nation was rattled by the Watergate

scandal. Distrust of the government permeated the country, creating waves of unrest and unease. Introducing this technology and the guarantee of unparalleled agency over our memories offered a kind of hope, a kind of healing, when people seemed to need it most. The MeReader, Restoreys, and cyclical use of memory tapes were met with widespread acceptance. And by 1977, the world had embraced artificial recall. A couple of years later, an intergovernmental alliance was formed, which elevated Memory Frontier's prominence and granted the company command over humankind's battle with memory loss."

"Wait a sec," Chase interrupted, holding up a hand. "Countries can't agree on a *single thing*. There are literal wars over religion. I realize Memory Killer was—or *is*—a doomsday-level threat, but I have a hard time buying *that's* what united the world around the campfire for a round of 'Kumbaya.'"

"I never said there was unity." Mr. Lear's voice sharpens, stilling the room. "Indeed, Memory Frontier made more than one unilateral decision, and—"

"Memory indexing," I say, realizing the truth. Everyone's eyes fall on me. "That's it, isn't it? *That's* how Alexander Lochamire was able to get buy-in from world leaders."

Mr. Lear gives me a grave look.

I continue, "Artificial recall was billed as this life-changing, *lifesaving* technology, but it also gave Memory Frontier access to everyone's memories . . . to everyone's secrets."

Ollie shakes her head. She pats around her jeans pockets like she's checking for cigarettes. "No, no. Dr. Sanders called indexing a 'fringe feature.' She said it was utilized only to help them narrow the search for Malcolm Heckman's memory. Remember?"

She's not convincing any of us and, by the look of her strained face, not even herself.

Mr. Lear stares at his fedora, fingering the brim of the hat absently. "One of the great tragedies of humankind is that we weaponize that which was intended for good."

Beside me, Fletcher's fingers coil into fists.

"I'm not saying Alexander's intentions with artificial recall were heinous from the outset." Mr. Lear sighs, his voice tapering off into a mumble. "But he's a businessman in every sense of the word."

"He capitalized on Memory Killer," Fletcher says through gritted teeth.

Mr. Lear meets his eyes. He opens his mouth to respond, pauses, then clears his throat. "I'll say this: Alexander Lochamire isn't a hero; he's an opportunist. That, my friends, is a terribly important distinction."

"My dad could be facing a lifetime behind bars because of his involvement in all this!" Fletcher stands up, knocking back his chair, which topples over and clangs against the cold concrete. "Why haven't you gone to the press? Why haven't you told them about indexing?"

"It's not that simple." Alana crosses her legs, fixing her attention on Fletcher. "The world has been programmed to rely on artificial recall. It's a way of life now. It's defined a generation. And with Memory Frontier set to release their newest tech next year, promising a significant victory in Lochamire's self-proclaimed 'battle against memory loss,' well, let's just say it'll take more than the wild claims of a former employee to expose Memory Frontier's lies."

"But you're not just *any* former employee," Fletcher insists, pointing at Mr. Lear. "You *cofounded* this company. Aren't there documents or evidence of some kind that you can leak?"

"Yes. There is evidence." Mr. Lear puts his hat back on and stands. He walks over to the wall behind the washer and dryer and flicks on a projector that I hadn't noticed before. Instantly, a massive blueprint appears and covers the garage door. It's difficult to decipher at first, but the longer I stare, the clearer the image becomes:

two brackets face away from one another, representing four wings joined at the center by a long hall. We're looking at a hospital floor.

But it's not just any hospital.

"This," Mr. Lear says, striding around the chairs toward the garage door, the corners of the projected blueprint spilling across his back as he walks, "is the Fold. It's the flagship hospital, the one erected nearly ten years ago in Alden, Nevada. As you know, the Fold is a system of hospitals with a presence in every state. Alden is home to HQ."

I glance at Ollie, wondering if this blueprint is triggering anguish. She spent time at the Fold, undergoing tests and enduring intense monitoring when artificial recall disinterred traumatic memories of her father.

Mr. Lear continues, "This building is more secure than a federal prison, complete with twenty-four-hour surveillance and armed guards. But the security is not in place to protect its patients. It's to safeguard what's being housed in the basement."

I swallow what feels like a fist-sized lump. "And that is . . . what, exactly?"

"The evidence," Mr. Lear replies simply. "The secrets that will unravel all of Memory Frontier's lies."

"Okay, but *what* is it?" Fletcher asks impatiently. "And why has Alexander just allowed this evidence to exist in the first place? What's stopping him from destroying it?"

Irene stares at her sneakers, wearing an expression of annoyance. *This is the part that he refuses to tell his great-niece, which means . . .*

"I will tell you all this in due time." Mr. Lear slides his hands into his coat pockets. "I realize how cryptic this all sounds—"

Chase snorts. "I'm not sure you do, King Lear."

Mr. Lear ignores the remark. "But you must trust that my withholding certain details is in your best interest . . . that it's for your protection."

"Fine." Fletcher rights his chair and sits down slowly. "So is that your big plan then? You guys break into the Fold, steal whatever's in the basement, and reveal it to the world?"

"Actually . . ." Mr. Lear looks at Zayne, Alana, and the elderly woman, then back to Fletcher. "That's where you four come in."

"You want us to help you break into the Fold?" Ollie shoots me a look that says, *You're hearing this, too, right?*

Mr. Lear takes his seat again. "After my team gets you past security and into the basement, I need your help cracking the safe and extracting the evidence."

"The closest I've ever been to safe-cracking is when I watched *Thief*," Chase says, chuckling, before gesturing at me and Fletcher. "So unless these two moonlight as bank robbers, I don't think—"

"The safe is a memory tape," Mr. Lear clarifies.

Of course it is.

He softens his voice and says, "You four have been through so much already. I can only imagine the emotional whiplash you're experiencing having *just* knifed for Memory Frontier. But it's clear you are a gifted lot, and having your help could very well end this madness once and for all."

I shake my head. The déjà vu is laughable! If we agree to help the Memory Ghosts, we'll have gone from being the dean's puppets to Mr. Lear's—all in the span of a couple months. I'm so sick of having no control over my life. Whether it's my premonitions, misremembering Ramon's identity, being forced to confront the fact that my dad's still alive, or being pulled *back* into Memory Frontier's knifing mission, I'm just so sick of being a puppet time and time—

"You will not be puppets."

I flinch, then look around the garage slowly and find the elderly woman smiling in my direction, her eyes closed. Eventually, she opens her eyes, and her smile broadens. Then she stands, sets her clutch purse in her chair, and hobbles around the kerosene heater toward me. She leans down near my face, though she's so short she doesn't have to bend much, and I inch backward.

I chuckle uncomfortably. "Um, can I help you?" I glance at Fletcher out of the corner of my eye.

"My oh my," she says, her soft gaze falling from my eyes to my hand. "May I?" Without waiting for me to reply, she reaches forward and takes my left hand, cradling it in her leathery palms. She squints, and then her smile widens even more.

"What is it, Gemma?" Mr. Lear asks, unable to downplay the budding curiosity in his tone. I hear Zayne take a sharp breath through his inhaler.

Gemma meets my eyes again and holds my stare as she says, "This one can remember the future."

30

FLETCHER COHEN

It was well beyond dusk—long after the sky had blackened and the air had chilled—when Irene pulled into the apartment complex where the college party was underway. The low pulse of bassy music thrummed in the distance. A faulty streetlight flickered overhead.

Irene pulled into a spot marked VISITOR and put the car in Park. She glanced at Freya, Chase, and Ollie through the rearview mirror, then at Fletcher.

"So, um, how are you guys doing?" Irene turned off the engine.

Fletcher unfastened his seatbelt. *You mean after being pushed around by people who just want our skills for their agendas? Peachy.*

"Just . . . processing," he mumbled.

"And crashing a college party *always* helps me process," Chase added, following Ollie out of the car. She slung her backpack over one shoulder as Freya got out next. Irene, however, remained in the driver's seat. "You coming?"

"Parties aren't really my thing," she replied after cracking the window. "I'll just meet you guys back here in a couple hours."

They nodded, thanked her for the ride, and shuffled down the sidewalk toward the music. The path was bordered by waist-high shrubs, which were encased in decorative polyester cobwebs. As they got closer to the buildings, Fletcher saw a variety of jack-o'-lanterns outside people's front doors. Decorations—including witches, cauldrons, and black cats—swayed in the evening breeze like teetering bowling pins.

"You doing okay?" Fletcher whispered to Freya, who zipped up her hoodie and then linked her arm with his.

"That's a complicated question that requires an even more complicated answer." She sighed, watching her breath turn to a misty cloud. "I *so badly* want to trust Gemma and Mr. Lear—I want to believe they can help me and provide answers about my visions—but these days, with all the back-and-forth, it feels like the only person I can really trust is you."

"We heard that," Ollie called back to them.

Freya sniffed. "You know what I mean."

"Mhmm." Ollie sounded annoyed.

As they approached the loud music, Fletcher tried to organize his thoughts. At the meeting's close, Mr. Lear had told them all to give his proposition some serious consideration, and that he'd be in touch soon.

In the meantime, he'd added, shutting off the projector in the garage, *continue to work alongside Memory Frontier. Though I would also ask you to consider sharing any pertinent information you discover with Irene so she can relay it to me. This would help us remain one step ahead of Alexander.*

So by Fletcher's count, he and his friends would be carrying *three* burdens: the burden of training Dr. Grondahl's recruits, the burden of knifing Emilia Vanguard's memory, *and* the burden of secretly working with the Memory Ghosts to bring down Alexander Lochamire.

And they were expected to do all this while projecting convincing loyalty to Memory Frontier and the dean.

Fletcher grimaced, feeling a migraine coming on.

Before they'd left the garage, Mr. Lear and Gemma pulled Freya aside. They claimed to have answers about Freya's "gifts," as Mr. Lear put it, and Gemma's ability to read Freya's thoughts was proof of that.

Or so they said.

"You're positive Gemma knew what you were thinking?" Fletcher asked as they turned a corner, approaching a wide courtyard at the center of four apartment buildings. The loud music reverberated from the third-story breezeway of the far building. They saw a small gathering of costumed college students mingling and drinking from red plastic cups. "Like . . . is it possible she guessed at something *close* to what you were thinking?"

"It was that word, *puppets*." Freya shook her head. "I remember sitting there, feeling like we were puppets in all this. First the dean's, now Mr. Lear's. And then Gemma used that same word. Either that's one lucky guess, or she *did* manage to read my thoughts."

"Just when I thought things couldn't get more bizarre."

"Right?"

"All right, guys, look," Chase said as he and Ollie stopped in the middle of the grassy courtyard and turned around. "You're right. Things *did* just get more bizarre. But you know what? We're going to worry about that tomorrow."

"Yeah, tomorrow." Ollie swung her backpack around and started to unzip it. "Tonight? Tonight we're gonna clear our heads. We deserve this. We *need* this."

"I dunno," Fletcher said, glancing past his friends at the breezeway. "We're gonna stand out like sore thumbs. We didn't even bring costumes."

"Didn't we, Fletcher?" Ollie procured a white bedsheet and handed it to Chase, who theatrically whipped it like a matador before throwing it over himself. There were two crude holes cut into the sheet, which Chase lined up with his eyes.

"Boo," he deadpanned.

"You've got to be kidding me." Fletcher rolled his eyes as Ollie divvied out two more bedsheets to him and Freya, who couldn't suppress a giggle. She threw the sheet over herself at the same time Ollie did, leaving only Fletcher costumeless.

"These are spook-tacular, Ollie," Freya said, her giggles intensifying.

"I'm surrounded by nerds." Fletcher regarded the balled-up bedsheet in his hands.

"And don't you *ever* forget that," Ollie said, jabbing him in the chest through her sheet. "Now get dressed or you'll be denied entrance to the party."

"You don't know that," Fletcher grumbled, slipping under his bedsheet and lining up the holes over his eyes.

"At least you make a really hot ghost," Freya said, nuzzling her nose into the side of his covered face.

"Yes," Chase snickered. "I've always said Fletcher's hottest with a bag over his head."

"Is this the first that Freya's hearing about your feelings for her boyfriend?" Ollie asked, slipping on her backpack. It gave her a slight hunch under the sheet.

Chase spun on his heels and led them across the courtyard toward the stairwell. "Fletch knows how I feel, and that's all that matters!"

They laughed and climbed the stairs, pulling up their sheets so as not to trip on the hems. When they reached the third floor, Bobby "Boris" Pickett crooned "Monster Mash" through the speakers, and Fletcher started to let himself relax. Perhaps Ollie was right. Perhaps they did need a night of fun, a night where they could let loose and forget their troubles. So much had happened in just a few short months; so much had been required of them. What was the harm in making a choice for themselves? What was the harm in choosing to spend the evening like normal teenagers?

"Thanks, Ol," Fletcher said as they approached the apartment. Flashing lights and raucous laughter spilled out into the breezeway, filling the air with a kind of tangible excitement. It seemed to warm Fletcher down to his bones.

"You're welcome! The costumes weren't hard to fashion. In fact, with a little help, I bet Chase could've made 'em."

Chase groaned. "Boooo."

"And to clarify," Ollie whispered. "We're not dressed as Memory Ghosts; we're just *ghost* ghosts. You know. The haunting kind."

"*Ghost* ghosts," Freya repeated, and Fletcher heard her smile. "I like that." And the four of them entered the loud apartment single file, where they were immediately offered drinks by a guy decked out as the zombie Michael Jackson from "Thriller."

31

FREYA IZQUIERDO

Generally speaking, my first college party is hugely underwhelming. At first, anyway. There's a lot of drinking. Clusters of college kids are crammed in the living room, in the hallway, in the kitchen, on the balcony, and mostly they just laugh and talk. There's no dancing. There's no real activity beyond racing to finish a drink so you can move on to the next one. And the drinks never seem to run out.

"It's like this apartment is built on top of a well from which endless libations spring forth!" Chase shouts with glee under his ghost costume.

"I think he needs to be cut off," I mumble to Ollie, who laughs. She guides Chase toward the kitchen, and they both squeeze past an astronaut and a girl in a toga and start raiding the cabinets for food. Fletcher and I move toward a corner of the living room, one that's farthest from the speakers.

We clank our red plastic cups together through the bedsheets and then sip.

"This is a momentous occasion, you know," Fletcher yells over the blaring music.

"Oh yeah?"

"It's our first party together as boyfriend and girlfriend."

"Oh, Fletch," I say dramatically, sighing. "There's really no easy way to say this, but, well, I don't date spirits. Tried once, but it felt like making out with air."

"I'm glaring at you underneath this thing."

I laugh and take another drink. "Boyfriend and girlfriend, huh? Usually, one of us has to ask the other one out to make it official."

Fletcher swears, then blinks through his eye holes. "Right. Sorry. I'm not . . . I should've—"

"I'm teasing!" I say, though it *does* get me thinking. I take another drink and say, "Why do you want to be my boyfriend?"

His shoulders sag a little as his body relaxes. "Oh, that's easy. Things have just been so incredibly unstable since we arrived at school in August. You know? It's like we've lived these two condensed, chaotic lifetimes—one before we found Dean Mendelsohn's bunker and one after. And things haven't slowed down since. With my dad now—" He cuts himself off, and I hear him take a swig. "Let's just say things are crazy unstable right now. But when I'm with you, Freya, I feel this real sense of stability . . . this security. I dunno. I've always thought that when I date a girl, I need to be a protector. It's different with you, though. You're a constant, an anchor. You help me believe things are going to be okay."

I smile, then feel hot tears tingling at the edges of my eyes. I compose myself, then say, "Fine. Guess that's a good reason."

Fletcher chuckles. He pulls me toward his body and plants his lips against mine. Even through two layers of bedsheets, his warm kiss manages to flush my cheeks. The sensation is kind of magnetic; the imprint of his mouth in the fabric makes me want him more.

"That should've felt weird," I say after we break away. "But it didn't. Also, props for being able to find my lips when they're covered."

"I've studied your face so long—the curve of your chin, the distance from your eyes to your nose to your mouth—that I could draw a map."

"How many beers have you had, Fletcher Cohen?"

"Apparently, not enough."

I blink and an hour's passed.

Fletcher and I pass the time laughing and talking underneath our ridiculous costumes, unable to keep our hands off each other. His green eyes, which are outlined by the two holes in the bedsheet, have an affecting way about them. I just *can't* look away; thankfully, he doesn't seem to mind staring into mine, either.

Someone cuts off the overhead lights. Now only strands of Christmas lights that hang haphazardly across the walls provide light. Toto's "Africa" fills the apartment, Bobby Kimball's bright and soaring vocals filling the laughter-soaked air. A few people sing along. I hear Chase and Ollie loudly cutting up, making friends with people who have no idea they're still in high school.

Things may get worse, I think as I reach out from underneath my bedsheet and grab Fletcher's hand. *But we'll always have this night together.*

We stumble across the apartment grounds as we make our way back to the parking lot, laughing so loudly I'm *certain* we're going to wake the entire complex. We ball up our ghost costumes and hand them to Ollie, who tries but fails to get all of them back into her JanSport. Eventually, she resorts to putting her bedsheet back on, and then we're laughing even louder.

A group of four or five college guys, who all wear the same fighter pilot jumpsuit worn by Tom Cruise in *Top Gun*, walk past us as they head toward the party. I hear them freeze in their tracks behind us.

"Guys, it's Casper the Friendly Ghost!" one of them shouts.

We stop and turn toward the Maverick wannabes. They each have a flask, brandishing it proudly like it's a part of their costume. "Why are you guys bailing?"

These guys are pretty intoxicated, making us seem sober and levelheaded.

"She turns back into a human at the strike of midnight," Chase says, hiccupping. "So we . . . we wanted to leave . . . with enough time to get her back."

The Mavericks laugh. "This dude's *hilarious.*"

"What are *you* supposed to be?" one of the guys says, pointing at me. "F-Frida? That Mexican wh-who painted? You forgot the unibrow!"

Fletcher takes a step forward, but I pull him back by the wrist. "We should go."

One of the guys mumbles something I can't hear, and then they're all talking raucously and heading off to find the party.

Fletcher, Ollie, and Chase are quiet the rest of the walk back to Irene's car. Before we climb in, I say, "Well. Now we have a new barometer for drunkenness: zero to Cruise."

I get a pity laugh from Ollie and Chase, but Fletcher meets my eyes. Before he can say anything, though, I mouth, *Just leave it,* and then get in the car.

❖ ❖ ❖

Monday afternoon, Dean Mendelsohn gathers us around the open reel-to-reel tape machine in his bunker. Sade and Rhett are still wearing civilian clothes, and I can tell they're starting to loosen up around us.

Sade even smiles at me. Well, her version of a smile: she purses her lips, and the edges of her mouth flick up ever so slightly, punctuating her dimples.

I'll take it, I guess.

The dean folds his arms across his chest. "Saturday, as you know, was Halloween."

"Man . . ." Chase clicks his tongue. "If this is about us not inviting you to come trick-or-treating with us, that's my bad, Dean M."

Dean Mendelsohn blinks. "As I was saying, with Halloween having come and gone, I'm pleased to report that our mission was a success. No attack was leveled against a MACE field office. You helped us thwart the Memory Ghosts' plans. So, well done."

Behind him, the men and women stationed at the computers stand and clap, and I see Dr. Sanders and Dr. Grondahl among them, beaming in our direction.

Fletcher, Ollie, Chase, and I look at one another, obviously wondering how the hell we're supposed to fake a halfway believable response.

Thankfully, the moment's fleeting. The dean signals for quiet, and the facility hushes almost at once. "Unfortunately, our threat hasn't been completely neutralized. The Memory Ghosts are still out there, plotting their next move."

Yeah, and we might be helping them . . . right under your nose. I look away from Dean Mendelsohn and find that Rhett is staring at me, smiling. He blushes and turns.

"Over the weekend," the dean continues, "our team managed to identify a significant date. One year ago this month, Emilia Vanguard was involved in what the Ghosts call a Transference. This is essentially an elaborate, high-risk event that the Ghosts coordinate in an effort to make memory knifing difficult."

Ollie raises an eyebrow at me. She was right. She called it: that's why Malcolm Heckman and his fellow Ghosts engaged in that daring chase on the 405.

"Turns out," Dr. Grondahl says, his voice swimming with excitement as he joins the dean beside the giant Restorey, "this Emilia Vanguard matches the description of a young woman who engaged in a hyper-daring stunt, which included reckless driving, scaling the side of a cliff, and—here's the best part—leaping through the air into the cabin of a helicopter. A *helicopter*! Can you believe that?"

Great. I picture me and my friends climbing a jagged cliff and attempting the feat of jumping into a helicopter after Emilia. None of that sounds fun. But Mr. Lear *did* insist we keep up appearances. I guess when Fletcher, Ollie, Chase, and I knife that memory, we'll just have to find some way to throw the mission.

"This knifing mission is going to push you to your physical limits," Dean Mendelsohn says, and I realize that Sade, who looks the most physically fit, is likely the only one actually capable of trailing Emilia and completing the mission. "As such, we'll be running through training exercises and—"

"*Ahem.*" The voice is soft, so soft, in fact, that it takes me a second to realize Dr. Grondahl is the one who spoke. "May I, Rusty?"

The facility falls into a weighty silence, the kind you can inhale like a scent. The dean and Dr. Sanders look at one another briefly, a million unspoken words passing between them. Dr. Grondahl steps forward with his too-big grin.

"Who here knows how to fly a helicopter?" I half expect Rhett to raise his hand. But, of course, we're all just teenagers. Ordinarily, I'd have expected Chase to offer some quip; he still looks stunned that Dr. Grondahl had the nerve to cut off the dean.

"Well, I've got *wonderful* news." Dr. Grondahl pulls out a folded piece of paper from the breast pocket of his Hawaiian shirt. "I have in my hand formal authorization—" He drops the piece of paper and mumbles an expletive as he bends down to pick it up. "This is an authorization, signed by the president, to train two of you how to pilot a helicopter. Since you're all still minors, this is a *very* big deal. The two of you who volunteer will spend Thanksgiving break learning how to fly so that you can each manifest a helicopter while knifing Emilia's memory, which is officially scheduled for the Monday after break. Exciting, isn't it?"

"Is one week really enough time for two of us to learn?" Ollie asks, sounding as skeptical as I feel. "Plus, one week's worth of memories flying a helicopter doesn't seem like nearly enough for us to be able to manifest one. Dean Mendelsohn said—"

"Thirty hours of training on helicopter operations will be plenty, Ms. Trang, on both fronts." Dr. Grondahl opens the piece of paper and scans it as if referencing a script. "Now. Do I have my two volunteers? Come on, now, don't be shy!"

Sade raises her hand without much delay. No shock there. I fold my arms, waiting for Rhett to inevitably raise his hand, too, when Chase mutters beside me, "I'll do it."

You will? I jerk my head back and eye him.

He shrugs. "How many seventeen-year-old actors have 'helicopter-pilot training' on their résumés?" I give him a skeptical stare.

"This is excellent!" Dr. Grondahl gives them a thumbs-up. "I'll make the arrangements." He bounds toward the exit, his ponytail bouncing with each step.

"Well then," Dean Mendelsohn grumps. "Enjoy your free period. No knifing today."

❖ ❖ ❖

"Well, *that* was weird," Ollie says as she and I race through the stabbing cold toward our dorm room.

"Which part?" I jam my freezing hands, which feel like hard rocks, under my armpits. "Chase volunteering, or Dr. Grondahl usurping the dean's throne?"

"Heh. Both, I guess." Ollie kicks a pebble off the sidewalk as the girls' dormitories come into view. "The dean must be really annoyed to cancel our knifing exercise for the day."

"Feels like it was a total power play."

"How do you mean?"

"Dr. Grondahl threw a wrench into his plans, right? So to show he still retains power, Dean Mendelsohn gave us our free period back."

"Huh. I guess that—"

The rest of Ollie's sentence evaporates on her breath. I follow her eyeline and see that she's watching one of our classmates jog away from our dorm. I recognize her immediately, the outline of her Afro and small frame.

Wait. It's not a classmate. It's—

"Irene?"

"Yeah," I say, watching as she disappears around the corner. I mean to call out to her, but I figure if she needs to talk to us about something urgent, she'll just come back later. Plus, the cold's unbearable.

As soon as I open the door, I spot a white envelope addressed to me in cursive on the carpet.

So Irene stopped by to drop this off. I pick up the envelope after Ollie slips into the room. I shut the door, sit on the couch, and pull out the letter:

Dearest Freya Izquierdo,

I hope you don't mind me writing to you like this, but I felt it both urgent and necessary to extend to you an invitation. I would love for you to stay with me during your school's next holiday at November's end. I realize that's asking you to trust me a great deal, given that we've only met once! But I get the sense that you're tired, Freya. Tired of wrestling with these burning questions about your gift. And make no mistake, it is a gift. I'd be honored if you would give me the opportunity to help you understand your potential and, beyond that, how to harness your gift. You see, clarity is like being handed a lantern in the dark. Sure, you could fumble around yourself, and you might eventually get to where you're going, but my oh my—the time and frustration it spares you when someone just hands you a lantern!

Please do consider my invitation, Freya. I have a lantern that I'd love to hand you.

Yours,

Gemma Morris

32

FLETCHER COHEN

"So are we officially doing this, or . . . ?" Fletcher finished off his orange juice and stacked the cup on top of his empty breakfast plate.

Ollie poked at her eggs; she'd barely eaten. Freya, too, seemed to have no appetite. By contrast, the Foxhole was alive and well that Tuesday morning, the usual din of banter and laughter bouncing off the high ceiling.

Chase, who'd already gotten seconds, finished off his last bite of waffles. "Yeah, I mean, how can we *not* at this point. Right? We're in too deep."

Everyone at the table nodded.

"Then it's decided," Fletcher whispered. "In what may go down as the world's most ridiculous one-eighty ever, the Forgotten Four are officially working with the Memory Ghosts."

"Great. Now that that's settled"—Ollie turned to Chase, one

eyebrow cocked—"would you care to explain to us why you volunteered to spend Thanksgiving break with"—she coughed into her fist, building up the drama—"with Dr. Grondahl, aka Ponytail, and Sade from Hades so you can *learn how to pilot a helicopter?*"

"*Sade from Hades?*" Chase snorted. "*Ponytail?*"

"It's not my best work, no." Ollie reached across the table and jabbed Chase in the arm with her index finger. "But quit deflecting and answer the question."

"Look, I dunno." Chase flipped his bangs out of his eyes absently. "No one else raised their hand. Figured I'd rather spend Thanksgiving break doing something cool than being stuck at home."

"Fine." Ollie stood and grabbed her tray, leaning toward Chase and lowering her voice. "Don't tell us the truth, Christopher Hall." And then she stormed off to discard her tray near the kitchen.

"Yikes." Freya smirked. "She busted out your first name. Means you're in trouble."

"Gee. You don't say." Chase grabbed his own tray and left the table.

"Hey, so there's something I want to talk to you about," Freya said once the coast was clear.

"Oh?" Fletcher was only half listening; he was scanning the dining hall for Irene so he could wave her over and tell her they'd officially decided to help her great-uncle.

"Yeah." Freya pulled Gemma's letter out of her pocket and slid it across the table.

"What's this?" Fletcher opened it but kept his eyes on Freya. She didn't answer; she merely gestured for him to read. So he did.

When he finished, he folded the letter and handed it back. "Wow."

"Yeah. Wow." Freya slipped it back into her pocket. "What should I do?"

"I mean, I know this woman sort of, like, read your thoughts," Fletcher said, dropping his voice. "But she's a complete stranger."

"So is Mr. Lear," Freya countered. "And so is Irene. Yet we *just* agreed to help them. Plus, how did Gemma know about my visions? She looked at me and just knew? That doesn't strike you as—?"

Fletcher grinned.

"What?"

"You've already made up your mind, haven't you?" Fletcher sighed. "You're going to write back. You're going to accept her invitation to, what? To train you?"

"No, I haven't made up my mind." Freya broke eye contact and fingered the zipper on her jacket. "But would that be so bad? Getting 'training' from someone who understands my gift?"

Fletcher winced at her mention of *gift*.

Freya met his eyes again. "What, you don't think it's a gift?"

"I never said that, Freya."

"You didn't have to."

"I just want you to be careful is all." Fletcher wanted to take her hands in his, but she kept them hidden under the table, like she was guarding herself. "What if I came with you?"

While her expression softened, her tone remained firm. "If I do this, *I* need to do this."

"I was afraid you'd say that."

Freya doubled down. "I believe Gemma has what I so badly wanted Dr. Sanders to have: answers."

Fletcher wanted to argue more, but what was the point? *Who am I to stand in the way? This could be Freya's best shot at learning about her premonitions.*

"When you're deep in thought," Freya said, pulling her hands out of her lap and taking Fletcher's, "you let your mouth hang open ever so slightly, like you're midword."

He flushed and looked away. "Flirting to distract me? That's an evil tactic."

"*Evil's* kinda harsh. I thought it was smart." She half stood and leaned over the table, kissing him on the indent between his chin and bottom lip.

"Oh, hey, sorry to interrupt," Irene said, absently adjusting the ID clipped to her Foxtail polo.

Fletcher withdrew his hands and threw on a smile. "What's up?"

"I just thought I'd check in. See if you guys had decided."

Chase and Ollie returned to the table, and Fletcher and Freya gathered their things and stood.

Fletcher looked at each of his friends briefly before telling Irene, his voice even, "We're in."

After the first two periods ticked by, Mr. Williams cornered Fletcher as he walked across the chilly grounds toward the dining hall.

"Mr. Cohen!" He waved with one hand and clasped a clipboard in the other, jogging across the sidewalk. A man on a mission.

"Your hour of reckoning has come," Chase mumbled to Fletcher, then he and Ollie and Freya made a beeline for the dining hall.

"I hate you guys," Fletcher called after them, and Freya turned and mouthed, *Sorry*, before disappearing inside with their friends.

"How goes it?" Mr. Williams asked, panting.

"It goes." *Let's get this over with.*

Mr. Williams pushed his aviators up his nose and scanned the document on his clipboard. "Need to book some time with you to discuss college applications and—"

"*Listen.*" Fletcher reached out and gently lowered Mr. Williams's clipboard. "I really don't want to waste your time. I don't think college is in the cards for me."

"Oh?"

"Yeah, well, with everything going on with my dad . . ." Fletcher looked around. His classmates flowed across campus toward the Foxhole, talking and laughing loudly, and when they passed by, a noticeable number of Fletcher's peers gawked at him. "Let's just say I'm not keen on amassing a pile of rejection letters."

"I see." Mr. Williams tucked the clipboard under his arm. "So let me get this straight. Regardless of your father's guilt or innocence, you're letting *his* legacy dictate what *you* do or don't do after high school?"

Fletcher opened his mouth, but Mr. Williams wasn't finished. "And—sorry, I want to make sure I'm understanding you correctly— not only are you letting it dictate your choices, but you're also letting it scare you with what-ifs?"

"I'm just saying—"

"*What if* you get a bunch of rejection letters?" Mr. Williams's voice was rising. "*What if* no admissions committee grants you acceptance because of who your father is? Well, let's play that game, Fletcher. *What if* you never apply?"

Fletcher was stunned, speechless. He hadn't expected the usually jovial senior counselor to get this worked up. "Um."

Mr. Williams sighed and removed his sunglasses. His eyes were a deep gray. "Look, it's in my literal job description to ensure that you and your classmates are set up for success after graduating. Things just aren't as simple as collecting your diploma and then jumping into the real world, even for a recollector. In the uncertain age of Memory Killer, you have to have a plan."

Fletcher held his stare. "Plans can change."

"Sure." Mr. Williams put his sunglasses back on and made a note on his document. "But you gotta have a plan before it can change."

Fletcher held his tongue. He wanted to argue further, to say that just because he wasn't going to apply for colleges didn't mean he didn't have a plan. But there was a heavy sense of finality in Mr. Williams's tone.

"I have you down for 6:30 p.m. on the Tuesday after Thanksgiving break. This should give you ample time to prepare a shortlist of universities." Mr. Williams opened the door to the Foxhole for Fletcher. "I hope to see you then!"

❖ ❖ ❖

In the bunker that afternoon, the lights dimmed as Fletcher, his friends, and Sade and Rhett lay back in their chairs and waited for the nurses to apply the necessary sedative to their IV bags.

This marked the sixth time the six of them would be knifing together, and Fletcher feared their inevitable encounter with Memory Killer was drawing near.

"Memory Killer's unpredictability has certainly made this training exercise difficult." Dean Mendelsohn began threading a memory tape into the Restorey, his back to the group. "But Dr. Sanders and I have a promising theory that should help us lure Memory Killer out of the shadows."

"And that is?" Fletcher hoped he sounded more intrigued than nervous.

"Fear," Dr. Sanders replied, walking over from the computer stations. She consulted her leather-bound journal. Interestingly, Fletcher noted a subtle change to Dr. Sanders's cadence as she continued speaking. The rhythm to her words sounded . . . off. Almost as if someone were doing a poor impression of Dr. Sanders: "Fletcher, when Memory Killer overtook you in Malcolm Heckman's memory, you were in physical pain, and the edges of the memory were closing in on you like great waves. You were *very* distressed and disoriented, and that led to fear. Did it not?"

Fletcher couldn't deny that. He'd felt as if he'd broken multiple bones—as if blood was actually spilling out onto the ground and pooling around him, even though none of it was real. Even though it was all just happening in his head. But the pain felt real. It was a wonder he didn't black out and eject from Malcolm's memory.

Instead, his body began to fade before Freya's eyes as Memory Killer seized his mind.

Fletcher had to admit their theory made sense: a heightened sense of fear could trigger Memory Killer while they were knifing because the rules of Memory Killer—whatever those actually were—didn't seem to apply when they knifed.

"So you're gonna make us knife a memory that'll spook us?" Ollie propped herself up on her elbows.

"More or less." Dean Mendelsohn finished threading the memory tape and turned to face them. "In the early days of MACE, we'd run our agents through rigorous drills and tests to measure their physical and mental abilities. They had to pass these tests before being allowed to work in the field."

"Great." Chase dipped his chin down and eyed the dean. "So we're gonna knife a memory of you watching your agents perform one of these drills. Right?"

Dean Mendelsohn ignored him and continued, "I designed these drills myself, and as a best practice, I always subjected myself to them first. I had to be certain they could be completed."

Fletcher could feel his heart laboring in his chest. *Awesome. This should be fun.*

"You gonna at least tell us what to expect?" Freya asked. Fletcher watched her wipe her sweaty hands across her jumpsuit pants.

The dean sighed. "That might defeat the purpose. If we're to test this theory of ours, we need you six to experience actual, genuine fear."

Fletcher closed his eyes and exhaled through his nose. *This drill could be anything, literally anything, and something tells me it's gonna feel like one of those Tarzan assault courses from the movies.*

"Are there any further questions before we begin?" Dean Mendelsohn hooked his thumbs on his suspenders, looking like he enjoyed the idea of thrusting six minors into some intense, formidable drill meant for adults.

No one said a word.

Dr. Sanders finished writing on her clipboard, coughed into her arm, then about-faced and made for the computers.

"Good." The dean flipped on the Restorey; the buttons and levers lit up. "Let us begin."

33

FREYA IZQUIERDO

Ribbons of neon light fluctuate and burst like a great star exploding into existence over and over again—its heat and presence a consuming force of nature. The familiar passageway into Dean Mendelsohn's memory tape is both an outburst of energy and infalling energy; the neon lights draw us up and then down into . . .

. . . nighttime.

Dense rain hits black asphalt in ninety-degree weather, then rises as steam. Fletcher and Ollie and Chase appear, followed by Sade and Rhett. I don't so much feel and smell the warm summer rain as I perceive it. It drenches my hair and rolls down my back . . . or so I think. I hold my left hand up to my face and see the rivulets of raindrops hovering mere millimeters above my skin. The raindrops roll down my wrist and jumpsuit sleeve and off my elbow, where gravity pulls them toward the pavement. And even though the raindrops don't contact my hair, skin, or jumpsuit, I look and feel drenched—as if my brain can't handle me standing in the pouring rain and not getting soaked.

The rain isn't touching you because you weren't here when the memory was formed, Rhett says, coming up beside me.

At first, it doesn't look like the rainfall is interacting with his body the same way it is with mine, but upon closer examination, I can see how it's tumbling around him like he's encased in an invisible force field. *It can't fall through us*, he continues. *See?* He laughs, then opens his mouth and tilts his head back. I watch as the raindrops bounce off an unseen mouthguard and roll down his cheeks—never once falling into his mouth or brushing the skin on his face.

No offense, kid, Chase says, *but this ain't exactly the time to sing in the rain.*

Chase is right. Sade puts her hands on her soaking-wet hips. *Anyone spot Dean Mendelsohn yet?* She scans the empty parking lot. I observe a few streetlights behind her. They emit off-yellow, rain-dotted glows.

There, nine o'clock! Rhett exclaims. We follow his gaze and spot a gray two-door sedan parked maybe fifty yards away. The headlights are off.

Chase! Fletcher shouts.

I'm on it. Chase holds out his hands. Ollie, Fletcher, and I back off, and a moment later Chase manifests his car. The hubcaps and muffler are still sliding into place when Sade manifests a vehicle too. It's an off-white, European-looking sedan with foreign plates. Fletcher hops into the passenger seat of Chase's car, and before Ollie and I slide into the back row, I shout over to Rhett: *Don't forget what we talked about! If Memory Killer attacks either of you, it's up to the other person to* anchor *you with a shared memory. Focus on a fixed object or landmark . . . somewhere you've* collectively *spent time! Recall together—share the memory.*

Rhett gives me a thumbs-up before clambering into Sade's car. I sigh before getting in the back seat and slamming the door shut. I gasp. I'm completely dry, and so are Ollie and Fletcher and Chase.

Just when you think these memory knifings can't get any trippier, Ollie says, turning her hands in front of her face.

I don't like how he's just sitting there, Fletcher whispers, staring past the windshield wipers at Dean Mendelsohn's car. *What's he doing, anyway?*

Waiting, of course, Chase replies. He puts his car in gear and drives forward, turning in a wide berth and slowing to a stop behind the dean. Sade does likewise, and now both of our vehicles idle in the rain beneath a streetlight. Waiting.

The rainfall pounds.

My breathing starts to hasten.

And then, all at once, it happens.

A black pickup truck with a ripped, nondescript, weather-torn flag affixed to its tailgate comes barreling onto the scene. It zooms across the wet pavement, hydroplaning for a brief moment before course-correcting and shooting off in the opposite direction.

The dean flicks on his headlights and accelerates in pursuit, and Chase follows.

I click in my seatbelt out of habit and glance out the back window; Sade quickly closes in on us.

Please be careful, Chase! Ollie shouts, clutching the back of his headrest.

Nah, Ol, I thought I'd be reckless! He means to sound sarcastic, but I hear an edge to his voice.

Ahead, Dean Mendelsohn swerves hard left, nearly spinning out of control, and Chase cranks his steering wheel and compensates with the brakes. I hold my breath, feeling the distinct sensation of hydroplaning—of our driver having no control over his vehicle—and then, like that, Chase manages to right the car.

Anyone else thinking maybe Chase shouldn't be driving? Fletcher clasps the handle over his door with one hand, and with the other he leans against the glove box. *You know . . . given his track record with driving while memory knifing?*

An excellent point, Fletcher. I can't tell whether Ollie's about to laugh or cry (or both).

Trust me, friends: years of video gaming has prepared me for this moment, Chase shouts over the whooshing windshield wipers and drumming rainfall. *I am your champion!*

I grind my teeth. How Chase is managing to keep his sights on the dean's car through all this rain in the semiblackness of night is truly impressive, though I know it's mostly dumb luck.

And one's luck eventually runs out. Always.

Suddenly, our ride gets bumpy, and when I glance out my hazy window, I see we've merged onto a gravel road. Just when I start to wonder where this memory takes place, it informs me that we're on a long strip of unfinished interstate.

A second after that realization enters my head, a hulking heavy-duty truck—complete with concrete mixer—appears seemingly out of nowhere and flies past the dean at a hair-raising speed. Dean Mendelsohn's car screeches and swerves, causing Chase to react. He curses and manages to alter his path, avoiding ramming into the dean by inches. The cement truck, which only narrowly missed exploding into Dean Mendelsohn's car, disappears into the rainy night. After only a breath, the pursuit is back on, and we're speeding after the dean and the pickup.

Well, surely that *did the trick,* Ollie says, leaning over the center console and glancing at her reflection in the rearview mirror. Her eyes haven't grayed. Neither have mine, Fletcher's, or Chase's.

It's going to take more than that, I'm afraid, I say.

More than almost getting crushed by a truck-sized battering ram? Chase grips his steering wheel, his focus intent on the road.

I glance over my shoulder again. Sade is still on our tail, but then I notice a shadowy figure bringing up the rear. I squint. At first, I think it's an optical illusion, a trick of the flickering headlights, but then I notice the rainfall hitting—

Sade jerks out of the way at the last second, creating a path for the mammoth cement truck, which has doubled back and is racing toward Chase's car. In seconds it will slam into us, propelling us into the air where we'll spin, side over side, before crashing violently into the ground.

I close my eyes and brace for the terrifying impact.

34

FLETCHER COHEN

Chase shouted. It was a guttural shout, a kind of tribal war cry laced with both terror and determination. Then, that very same second, Chase yanked the steering wheel left without checking his blind spot. The vehicle slid off the gravel and onto an uneven shoulder. Chase didn't brake. He kept his foot on the pedal and navigated the rough, bumpy terrain with only the headlights as his guide.

The cement truck rushed past them *right* where Chase's car had been a moment earlier. And just before it closed in on the dean's car, he, too, maneuvered out of the way.

This cannot just be a training exercise, Freya said from the back seat.

Fletcher nodded. *It's like the dean has a death wish.* The four watched as the rain-drenched cement truck flew past the pickup with the flag and then disappeared. It was clear the massive cement truck had no intention of ramming into the pickup; its target was Dean Mendelsohn's car.

Chase checked his right-side mirror before pulling his car back onto the gravel road. Sade sped up and fell into line beside Fletcher, rolling down her window in a panic and motioning for Fletcher to lower the passenger window. He did, letting in a frenetic flurry of wind and rain.

It's happening! Sade shouted through the rain, her eyes darting back and forth between the road and Fletcher. *It's happening to Rhett!*

Oh no. Fletcher turned to Chase. *Pull as close as you can to Sade's car. I need to get over there and take the steering wheel so Sade can help Rhett before he fades away.*

Fletcher, that's insane! Ollie turned on Chase next. *Just pull the car over and—*

He can't, Freya said. *At the speed Dean Mendelsohn's driving, we'd lose sight of him in seconds. Then we'd all be ejected—except for Rhett.*

Chase and Ollie swore, and without wasting another second, he merged his car closer to Sade's until only a foot or so separated the two vehicles. Quickly but carefully, Fletcher stood on the passenger seat and, hunched over, gripped the sides of the door and prepared to leap into the back seat of the—

Chase, look out! Freya screamed. He jerked his car left and avoided a concrete median. Fletcher flew backward, smacking his shoulder against the center console.

Dammit. Fletcher righted himself, nursing his arm.

Dude, you okay? Chase was breathing heavily, visibly shaken from nearly crashing into the barrier.

Yeah, fine. Fletcher got back into position as Chase eased his car toward Sade's again. Fletcher glanced at Freya in the back seat and whispered, *I hope you're watching, because this might be the most badass thing I ever do. Ever.*

Freya smiled despite the fear that was clearly flooding her system. *Be careful.*

Fletcher smiled back. *Nah, I was gonna be reckless.*

Chase gasped. *That's my line!* And then Fletcher leapt through the passenger window and into the rain, appearing weightless as he flew the handful of feet between Chase's car and Sade's. He was airborne for maybe two seconds, if that, but time slowed down into measured, even breaths.

And then Fletcher collided into the side of Sade's car, dangling out of the open rear window on the driver's side. He'd expected his torso to slip on the door, but it was completely dry despite looking sleek and soaked. Fletcher's heart raced as he climbed into the back seat and assessed the situation.

Inside the cab, it was emergency room–level chaos.

Rhett was panting, his wide eyes gray as storm clouds. Sade was shouting out of the side of her mouth while she drove, urging him to breathe and stay calm. Fletcher stifled a gasp. Rhett's skin was changing, turning transparent. "Fading" seemed an inadequate descriptor now.

Rhett Villa was deteriorating, like wispy embers rising in the air.

Fletcher kicked into action. *Sade, keep your foot on the pedal, but move toward Rhett so I can take over the wheel.* Sade obeyed, forcing Fletcher to lean over the headrest awkwardly and grip the steering wheel. Now that Sade could give Rhett her full attention, she grabbed at his dissolving outline and spoke with confidence.

It's like Freya said. Sade's voice was deep and controlled. *We have to recall the memory together, Rhett. Our morning walks during fall break, in the woods behind the bunker. Think about that rusted antique cultivator we found!*

Fletcher kept his eyes on the road, feeling as if perspiration was dripping from his hands as he steered the car across the drenched road. *When does this chase end?*

Sade persisted. *Think, Rhett. The cultivator . . . do you see it?*

Yeah. Rhett's voice was frail. *I'm recalling the second time we found it, when I climbed up into the seat and then fell off.*

Good, good! Me too.

This interaction was followed by a brief silence. Just whishing wiper blades and roaring rainfall. Fletcher weaved around a discarded traffic cone, almost slamming into Chase, but he steadied his direction. Ahead, the dean was closing in on the pickup at last. But what then? What would happen if the dean reached the flag? Would that mark the end of the drill or signal the next phase?

The brief silence in the cab turned into an extended one.

Fletcher was too afraid to take his eyes off the road. Not because he might crash but because of what he might see in the passenger seat beside Sade.

Or, rather, *wouldn't* see.

Just when Fletcher was beginning to fear the worst, he heard Sade cackle with laughter. Gradually, the laughter intensified, and then it was followed—blessedly—by Rhett's laughter.

Could someone please tell me what the hell is going on? Fletcher steered the car right as the road took a gradual bend east, toward what appeared to be an overpass.

See for yourself, Sade replied, taking the steering wheel back without warning. Fletcher collapsed into the back seat, his neck and forearms throbbing fiercely. He turned to Rhett. The kid had regained his true form, and all color had returned to his hazel eyes. He ran his hands through his shaggy hair, looking like he might cry.

You did it, Sade, he said, his voice cracking.

Sade nodded once, making brief eye contact with Fletcher in the rearview mirror before her expression switched from elation back to its usual brooding.

You guys did good, Fletcher said. He took a long, deep breath and then inched toward the passenger door. *See you on the other side.* He opened the door to the intense rainfall and manifested his Ducati on the road. With his mind, Fletcher pushed the manifestation ahead of Sade's car so that when the assembly finished, it rolled backward beside the passenger door. He timed his leap so that he mounted the motorcycle the second it completed assembly. He swerved a bit, but—with the throttle fully open—Fletcher climbed to near top speed and fell into line ahead of Sade and Chase.

As he approached the dean's car, something menacing came into view.

Is that a . . . ? Fletcher leaned over his handlebars and squinted. He had spotted a looming tower crane perched atop an overpass. Of course, the crane wasn't just perched there. It was in motion.

When Fletcher finally saw the gigantic wrecking ball careening toward him, it was too late.

35

FREYA IZQUIERDO

I mean to scream, but only air escapes my throat. The wrecking ball collides with Fletcher's Ducati and the motorcycle explodes in a dazzling display of fire and smoke. Chase dodges the blinding explosion and the wrecking ball, which is unaffected by the impact.

This is a memory, I remind myself. When this moment happened in real time, the wrecking ball never smashed into Fletcher and his motorcycle. It just kept swinging after missing its target—Dean Mendelsohn.

I turn and watch as the motorcycle's fiery wreckage rolls across the gravel like tumbleweeds before being sucked past the edges of the memory, where Fletcher is ejected back to the facility.

He's okay, I say out loud.

Ollie squeezes my knee before climbing over the center console and sliding into the passenger seat. She fastens her seatbelt. *I'm promoting myself to copilot, and I suggest we pull over and let ourselves get ejected.*

Chase lets out a shrill laugh, then quickly wipes his forehead with the back of his hand. *We've made it this far. Plus, I really don't want to lose to Sade.*

This isn't a game, Chase. Ollie looks back at me for reinforcement. *Tell him, Freya.*

I'm all for ejecting now, especially since Rhett's okay. I mean, why else would Fletcher have manifested his motorcycle and left Sade's car? Right?

Everyone's quiet. We're only underneath the overpass for one or two seconds, but during this window the rain stops beating against the roof of Chase's car. The silence is calming, comforting—an audible reassurance that things will get better—and then it's gone.

Chase clears his throat. *Sade and Rhett?*

Ollie glances at the side mirror. *They dodged the wrecking ball too. Emerging from the overpass now. Closing in on us.*

Rainfall continues to pour across the windshield in buckets. The dean zigzags across the road, closing the gap between himself and the pickup with the whipping flag.

Almost there. We're almost *caught up.*

But then what? Does the dean reach out of his window and pull the flag off the tailgate, signaling the end of this intense drill?

I hang on to the back of Ollie's seat, feeling like I should be bracing for another deadly obstacle. But for the first time since this chaotic race began, I see the glowing red of the pickup's brake lights.

What's happening? I ask, leaning forward to get a better look.

The dean begins to slow down, and so does Chase. Now we're all cruising at a modest sixty miles per hour in a mini procession: the pickup at the head, followed by Dean Mendelsohn, us, and Sade and Rhett at the rear.

The dean designed this drill, Ollie reminds us, tucking her hair behind her ears anxiously. *He's probably anticipating the next phase of—*

A booming, splashing *whoosh!* across the gravel road ushers in a fleet of fifty speeding pickup trucks. Chase's car actually teeters in the dizzying mad dash as the pickups race by. Every single truck is identical to the first one—though the flags are different colors. Some are deep red; others are purple or faded orange.

I panic. *You guys are seeing this, too, right?* I wonder if I'm witnessing some anomalous defect brought on by our memory knifing.

Oh, we're seeing this, Ollie mutters.

As the fleet hurtles through the rain past the dean, I lose sight of the first pickup—Dean Mendelsohn's initial target—and I realize I can't recall the color of its flag.

The dean's an evil genius! Chase smacks the steering wheel, and I watch the trucks accelerate through a dangerous choreography of shifting formations. *It's a moving cipher or puzzle . . . look! See?*

We watch as the pickups maintain a steady speed, never once eclipsing sixty miles per hour. When Dean Mendelsohn swerves toward the far left, four pickup trucks with purple flags emerge from the center, swoop back around in a wide U-turn, and encircle the dean. Now he's only five rows back from the middle of the moving formation.

This is . . . this is nuts! Ollie straightens in the passenger seat so she can see better. *When would a MACE agent ever be faced with something remotely close to this in the field?*

He's training his agents to multitask, to problem-solve on their feet. Chase looks like he's in a state of reverie. *Don't you see?*

I see that you look impressed with this insanity! I scoff from the back seat.

Hey, why can't I appreciate a work of art? Make no mistake . . . this is art.

Couldn't they just, I dunno, learn to play chess instead? I roll my eyes. It's no wonder MACE agents are so militaristic. If this whole drill is representative of their physical and psychological training, it makes sense why they're callous and aggressive.

The dean is pushing toward the center of the formation when, at the last second, he swerves back to the left. In response, four or five pickups with orange flags break formation, double back, and form a new back row.

Isn't he basically cheating? I ask, shaking my head. *He's the one who created this stupid drill.*

Maybe. Chase scratches his chin, taking one hand off the wheel for the first time since the race began. *Unless he had someone else design the cipher.*

In my peripheral vision, I see Sade pull her white sedan up beside Ollie's window. The rear door still flutters open from when Fletcher exited.

Ugh. What does *she* want, Ollie mumbles as she cranks the passenger window.

Rhett says he's solved the puzzle.

Ollie sighs. *Does he want a cookie, or . . . ?*

We're going to wait for the next opening in the formation and weave in behind the dean's car.

What? Chase leans across Ollie's lap. *There's barely enough room in there for you guys. Plus, the second the dean smacks into your car, it could have a gnarly domino effect.*

That won't happen, Sade replies, her left arm leisurely propped on the car door. *Rhett solved the puzzle. We'll be able to perfectly mirror Dean Mendelsohn's moves and follow him through the fleet of pickup trucks to the other side.*

Chase tilts his head. *The other side . . . ?*

Then it clicks. For all of us. Because the row of pickups is so wide, it practically touches the memory's edges. And the farther away Dean Mendelsohn gets from us, the deeper into the pickup formation he drives, the closer the back side of the memory moves toward us.

Chase gasps. *No, wait—!*

But Sade is speeding ahead. She slips in between two pickups and somehow cuts her way through a second opening, now accelerating side by side with the dean. With Rhett as her copilot, she manages to maneuver in perfect synchronization with Dean Mendelsohn—a flawless dance of two cars wending through and around a sea of trucks—leaving me, Ollie, and Chase to watch, dumbstruck.

I grind my teeth and, without having to glance at the rearview mirror, can sense the ominous edge of the memory scene closing in rapidly.

Ollie folds her arms across her chest and slumps in her seat. *I really wanted to eject on our own terms. Guess Sade did win after all.*

And then we are forcefully yanked from the car in a blink, the jolt so sudden—so violent—that I black out.

36

FLETCHER COHEN

Fletcher jerked awake, breathing in dramatic, sharp breaths. He ripped off the electrode stickers and nearly fell out of his chair. The nurse standing nearby intervened and steadied him.

"Breathe," she instructed, taking him by the hand. *"Breathe."*

Fletcher started trembling and, without realizing it at first, crying. *The crash wasn't real*, he told himself, wiping his eyes with shaky hands. *None of it was real.*

The nurse asked if he was okay, and Fletcher nodded feebly and sank back in his chair. He reached for the glass of water on the tray beside him and took a drink.

Dean Mendelsohn approached, procuring a handkerchief from his pocket and offering it to Fletcher, who declined. "So what happened in there?"

"Your wrecking ball is what happened." Fletcher set down his now-empty glass. "And, well, it worked. Your insane drill scared

Memory Killer right out. Rhett was almost pulled into a memory loop. Happy?"

The dean's face lit up. "And?"

Fletcher nodded. "Sade used Freya's method of recalling a shared memory. Rhett was saved."

Dr. Sanders rushed over, her leather-bound journal in hand. Although her speech sounded normal now, Fletcher couldn't help but notice how bloodshot her eyes looked. "While it's fresh on your mind, walk me through exactly how it happened."

Before he could answer, Freya, Chase, and Ollie began to stir. Soon they were waking up groggily, and only Sade and Rhett remained still, their eyelids fluttering.

"Welcome back to the land of the living," Fletcher whispered to Freya as she batted her eyes open. "How'd you guys get ejected?"

She told him.

"Yikes." Fletcher glanced at Sade's and Rhett's motionless bodies. "She's pretty determined to see the dean's drill through to the end, huh?"

Freya shook her head, pulling the electrode stickers off her forehead slowly. "Whatever. The dean got what he wanted, right?"

"You're the reason Rhett's not in a coma." Fletcher rolled onto his side and lowered his voice. "You know that, right? Sade took what you taught them and implemented it. And just when I thought Rhett was going to be lost forever, he wasn't."

Freya sat up slowly, rubbing her head. "Can we just change out of these jumpsuits already?"

❖ ❖ ❖

Fletcher and his friends tried to block out the scenes from that afternoon's memory knifing as best they could. Over time, it got easier.

Soon the memory they'd knifed became nothing more than a half-remembered event.

The trees on campus got barer with each passing week. The November days grew shorter, which somehow made classes feel even longer. Fletcher and his friends received some relief, though: After learning that Sade had saved Rhett from Memory Killer's clutches, Dr. Grondahl pulled rank and granted Fletcher, Freya, Chase, and Ollie a revised three-days-a-week training schedule. Now they were expected in the facility only Mondays, Wednesdays, and Fridays.

"You've earned it!" he declared. "This defense tactic you've discovered, Freya—which has now successfully been implemented by your peers—is inspired. I'm going to take Dr. Sanders's notes straight to the Capitol. 'Transactive memory' is going to reshape our battle strategy against Memory Killer. Well done!"

Freya forced a smile but said nothing.

Fletcher longed for the California sun, for the cloudless skies and the salty scents of the ocean. Even though he was going to be separated from Freya during their forthcoming break, he found himself excited to return to the coast—particularly to see his mother and get more detailed updates about his father.

But the weekend before Thanksgiving, as he was packing his things for travel, Fletcher's roommate floated an intriguing idea.

"You know," Chase said, pausing his video game and propping his bare feet on the coffee table, "Dr. Sanders and the dean mentioned being in DC all of Thanksgiving break."

"So?" Fletcher zipped up his bulging backpack and tossed it onto the top bunk.

"So . . . methinks *now* would be the best time to sneak into the facility to knife that memory tape we found in your parents' closet."

Fletcher didn't answer right away.

Sensing his roommate was considering it, Chase continued: "I don't leave with Dr. Grondahl and Sade for pilot training until Monday morning. Me, you, and Ol could sneak into the bunker tonight after we drop off Freya."

"I dunno."

"I'll knife with you in case there's a Memory Killer attack while we're under." Chase scooted over on the couch. Fletcher sat down. "Ollie can give us the sedative and be the lookout while we're knifing!"

It might actually be the only chance I'll ever get to see what's on that memory tape. Do I really want to miss my shot, especially if there's something on there that could clear my father's name?

A moment passed between them, then Fletcher bent down and grabbed the hollow book he kept hidden beneath the couch. He tilted the book so the light caught the glossy title: *The Listener, The Scrambler, The Seer, & The Task.*

He opened the cover. Inside, nestled innocently in the cavity, was the memory tape.

"It's probably nothing," Chase said, unpausing his video game. "But at least this way you'd know."

37

FREYA IZQUIERDO

Saturday afternoon, Ollie squeezes me into a firm hug in the campus parking lot. "I can't believe I'm saying this, but your staying with a strange elderly woman over Thanksgiving break actually makes a ton of sense."

We break away and I bat her arm.

"I'm being serious! Okay, well, at first I thought it was a bit random and weird—"

I give her a stare.

"Look, if she can help you . . ." Her tone turns serious, and she takes both of my hands. "I know how badly you want answers, Freya. I hope you find them."

Me too. She steps aside as Fletcher walks to us with the keys to Irene's car in hand. "You ready?"

"Yeah." He picks up my bag and sets it in the back seat. We climb into Irene's black Taurus, which she was kind enough to loan us.

She even left directions in the glove box to my meeting place with Gemma.

Fletcher turns on the car, puts it in gear, and starts to reverse. I watch Chase side-hug Ollie and wave at us. He shouts, "Make good decisions, Freya! We are *so* proud of—!" Ollie jabs him in the ribs before he can finish.

I put my hand on Fletcher's leg as we pull out of campus. "I'm only going to be gone a week. So why does it feel longer?"

Fletcher agrees. "But we don't have to talk about that right now, do we? Let's enjoy this drive."

I nod, then pull the handwritten directions out of the glove box. I help him navigate to a stretch of highway that, per Irene's notes, we're to stay on for nearly thirty miles. Once we're on cruise control, I flip on the radio. Fittingly, "Missing You" by John Waite comes on, midchorus.

"Well, that's just mean," Fletcher says, stifling laughter. I prop my left elbow on the center console and lean my head against his shoulder.

"So then we both agree this *won't* be our song."

"This will not be our song, no."

"Good. What's our song, then?"

I feel Fletcher's cheeks rise into a smile. "Songs trigger memories in ways other things simply can't. They're these powerful gateways into the past. They transport us, make us feel things we've forgotten to feel."

"Look who's gone full-blown poet," I tease.

He laughs uncomfortably, then soldiers on. "When I think about you, two songs come to mind. There's the song that played at the kickoff bonfire the first time I met you. Then there's one song in particular that played on our trip to the mall."

"Yeah . . . Billy Ocean and Bryan Adams. Right?"

"Right."

"For me it's the Mamas & the Papas singing 'California Dreamin',"
I say, thinking back to the dance before fall break. "I remember
watching you under the lights, wondering why you didn't ask me to
the dance."

"Oh, that's easy. Because I'm an idiot." We both laugh. "Okay, so
three contenders."

"Actually, four." I sit up. "On the pier in Long Beach. 'Lovely Day'
came on when—"

"When we had our first kiss," he says, stealing a brief glance my
way. "Yeah. Just hearing Bill Withers's voice in my head takes me
back right now. I can hear the waves too. I can smell the ocean. I can
feel your touch."

I smile. "'Lovely Day' it is."

❖ ❖ ❖

A half hour later, Irene's directions take us down a winding road
peppered with old mailboxes and driveways that snake out of view.
Fletcher clicks on his headlights as twilight approaches.

We sit in silence for a while, until I say, "If they'll let you, you
should go see your dad over Thanksgiving break."

"Oh?" Fletcher shifts his weight in the driver's seat.

"And I don't mean so you can, like, mine him for info about
the Memory Ghosts. You should just go and see him. Just *be* there
with him."

"Yeah."

I consult Irene's map again, having to hold the paper up to my
face in the fading daylight.

Fletcher says, "And your dad?"

I scoff. "What about him?"

"When are you planning to see him?"

I cringe. I walked right into that one. *Sure*, I think, rolling my eyes, *let me drop everything in my life to run to mi papá, who has spent, well, my entire life avoiding me.*

"Soon," I say, and that's that.

We turn down yet *another* side road, and my curiosity really starts to swell. At this point, it's been over an hour since we left Foxtail Academy. Feels like we're off the map.

Fletcher asks, "You sure this is the right street?"

"Mhmm." I look down at Irene's cursive handwriting. LOWELL'S TREE FARM is the next sign we're looking for. "We should see the last turn any second . . . there."

The headlights fall over an ancient-looking sign. Fletcher slows down and turns up the long gravel road.

"Would you look at that." I put Irene's directions away and admire the view. "Tree farm is right."

The expansive field is dotted with Christmas trees, evergreen firs that vary in height. The rows of trees seem endless as they stretch toward the hilly horizon, behind which a radiant half sun is slowly descending. In effect, the sky is dyed with shades of smoky orange.

The road dead-ends at a wall of evergreens. Fletcher parks, we unfasten our seatbelts, and as soon as I open the passenger door, I hear a dog bark in the distance. I glance around and eventually spot a chocolate lab bounding toward the car, its tail wagging happily.

"And who are you?" The dog stands on its hind legs and plants its front paws on Fletcher's chest. I join him on the driver's side, rubbing the dog behind its ears. Its tongue lolls out of the corner of its mouth, smiling the slow-blink smile of dogs.

"Victor!" a familiar voice calls out. The dog drops down onto all fours as Gemma emerges from behind a stand of trees. She wears a heavy wool coat. "Oh, Freya! Fletcher! You made it. And I see you've been greeted by Victor." The labrador returns to her side, his tail wagging even more.

"He's got a lot of energy." I smile as Gemma rubs his back. "Is he a puppy?"

"Ha! He's no more a puppy than I am a teenager. My oh my." She bends over and holds Victor's head in her hands. "You hear that, Vic? They think you're a puppy."

Behind me, I hear Fletcher opening the back door and retrieving my bag.

"You own this property?" I ask, watching Gemma curiously. She produces a small treat from her pocket and feeds it to Victor, who chomps it down in one bite.

"Heavens no." She scans the trees, a sparkle in her eyes. "Sure is beautiful though. No, I'm just staying here for the week. I wanted somewhere close enough to your campus to make your drive manageable but far enough away you'd be free of distractions." She winks at Fletcher after that last part.

He clears his throat. "Er, right. I should be going." He lowers his voice and pulls me toward him. "You need anything before I leave?"

"Just the usual."

He smiles and kisses me, then we hug. "I'll be back in a week."

"I'm counting down the hours," I whisper.

Gemma leads me down a footpath that twists through the evergreens, and I savor the thick scent of pine that hangs in the air. I look past Gemma, wondering when we'll approach the house or cabin, and instead see a white RV parked in a clearing beneath the starry sky. Beside the long vehicle is a small makeshift firepit with two camping chairs. Victor gallops past me eagerly, nudging the door open with his snout and disappearing inside.

"It's not Buckingham Palace, no," Gemma says over her shoulder. "But it's home. I've always dreamed of living out of a Winnebago, and

I stumbled upon this '79 Brave a few years ago. Isn't she a beaut? They stopped making RVs in the '80s, of course. Memory Killer impacted manufacturing in oh so many ways. My oh my." She sighs, then pulls open the door, which has a capital *W* painted on it. "Anyway, this is where we'll be staying for the week."

The Winnebago's interior is more spacious than I expected. There's a tiny kitchen table with booth seating, and across from this a stovetop, a sink, some cabinets, a mini fridge, and a window. To my right is the cab, which is outfitted with two high-back chairs and a center console so wide it could double as another seat. To my left, the "hall" leads past a cramped restroom toward an open door, beyond which I see a full-size bed. Victor lies on top of the floral comforter, panting and looking smug.

"Wow." I set my backpack down on the booth and admire the walls of the RV, which are adorned with countless Polaroid pictures. I see a twentysomething Gemma at the beach, laughing waist-deep in the ocean. A handsome, dark-complected man has his arm around her, smiling so big that his eyes are slits. In another Polaroid, an even younger Gemma balances on vintage skis at the top of a snowy hill. There are pictures of her childhood, scenes at a picnic, Gemma unwrapping a gift, Gemma—

"Pictures matter a great deal, don't they?"

I flinch and meet Gemma's eyes, only they're closed. The wrinkled skin around her mouth creases as she smiles. Then she opens her eyes.

I swallow. "I have a photo album." I look at my backpack, where my photo album is sandwiched between my clothes. I'm not really sure why I brought it. Maybe I didn't want Ollie or the room cleaners to accidentally stumble upon it in my dorm? Maybe for another reason.

"It's been said that a picture says a thousand words." Gemma grabs a Polaroid off the windowsill above the sink. "I suspect whoever said that never encountered Memory Killer." She smiles at the picture, then hands it to me. "In this day and age, a picture tells a thousand *stories.*"

I look down at the picture. A ranch-style house sits in the rain. In the driveway there's a wood-paneled station wagon. Plumes of smoke come out the chimney. The picture is taken from the street.

"This was your house?" I hand her the picture. She takes it back and, without glancing at it again, sticks it back in its place between the others.

"How about some dinner?"

38

FLETCHER COHEN

Fletcher, Chase, and Ollie stalked through the cold, dark woods with their flashlights. Fletcher held the hollow book with his parents' memory tape under his arm. Chase brought a pair of bolt cutters that he had borrowed from the groundskeepers' shed.

Fletcher and his friends waved the wands of light across the uneven ground as they spoke.

"What's my line again?" Ollie asked.

"If someone happens to be in the facility when we get there," Chase replied, sounding offendedly inconvenienced, "you say we're there because you misplaced your backpack."

"That's a dumb lie. They won't believe it." Ollie huffed. "How about something more specific, like I left one of my textbooks there or something."

"Sure. Textbook. That works." If it was possible to hear someone's eyes roll, Fletcher was *sure* he'd just heard Chase's. "The point is that you forgot something and we're there to get it."

"I hate lying."

"You do *not*. And you're really good at it."

"I know. That was a lie."

Fletcher could see her smug expression even in the dark.

"You're exhausting, Ol." Chase shook his head.

"Which is why you love me," she replied sweetly.

They trudged along the familiar path mostly from muscle memory, and before long the stark-white bunker came into view. The uninspired building looked like a massive cinderblock that had been discarded in the woods.

"Before we go cutting padlocks," Fletcher whispered as they darted toward the side of the building, "let's try the back door."

Chase and Ollie agreed, and when they rounded the corner, they found that the lone metal door had a keypad lock. It was polished brass and had twelve squat buttons: numbers zero through nine, an asterisk, and an icon that looked like a key.

"Oh goody." Ollie tried the handle. Locked. "Worth a shot."

Fletcher pressed his ear against the ice-cold door. Before Chase or Ollie could object, he knocked. They waited with bated breath. When no one answered, Fletcher knocked a second time. After a few moments, nothing.

"Anyone got any guesses?" Fletcher shone his flashlight across the doorframe before shining the beam on the keypad. The numbers glittered in the artificial light.

"Knowing Dean M, it could literally be anything." Chase's forefinger hovered over the keypad, then he punched in a six-digit code followed by the key button, which lit up a menacing red.

"What was that?" Fletcher asked.

"My birthday." Chase shrugged. "You never know."

Fletcher rubbed the bridge of his nose with his free hand. "You wasted one of our password attempts on your birthday."

"You got any better ideas?"

"Uh, yeah, I do . . . eliminating our birthdays as a guess!"

"Sure, *now* you say that, after I tried mine and it didn't work."

"Chase, I didn't think you'd be stupid enough to enter your birthday."

"If it had worked, I'd have said, 'Who's the stupid one now?'"

"But it *didn't* work!"

"Guys, shut up." Ollie started pacing. "The adult is thinking right now." She walked away, kicked up a patch of the ground with her heel, then wrote in the dirt with her pinky. When finished, she regarded what she'd written for a moment before returning to the door—gently shoving Fletcher and Chase out of her way.

She sucked in a breath and entered a six-digit code. Fletcher watched as she punched every button with her middle finger: 3–2–6–4–3–5. Lastly, she punched the key button, and they collectively held their breath.

The button lit up green, and they heard the dead bolt slide inward.

Ollie opened the door. "After you."

Fletcher and Chase swapped a look of embarrassment before silently heading inside.

"Why do I feel like she used her middle finger on purpose?" Chase mumbled to Fletcher. After Fletcher flipped on the overhead lights, he checked the bathroom, changing room, and kitchen to make certain they had the place to themselves. Convinced, he joined Chase and Ollie beside the tall Restorey.

"So what was the passcode?" Fletcher set his flashlight down on the floor.

"*Daniel*," Ollie answered, beaming. "His son."

"I . . . what?"

"It's the alphabet, broken down in the same way it is on a dial pad." She cocked her head to the side and squinted at the boys. "You guys act like you've never used a phone before."

"Yeah, well," Chase said distantly. "*Daniel* was gonna be my next guess."

"Mhmm." Ollie took the hollow book from Fletcher, opened it, and grabbed the memory tape. "Now we gotta figure out how to thread this into the Restorey."

Fletcher sighed. "Sounds easy enough."

39

FREYA IZQUIERDO

The small campfire pops and snaps, sending smoke and embers floating toward the darkening, ethereal sky. Past the sounds of the campfire, there's an otherworldly silence, broken up only occasionally by the rustling wind and hooting owls.

I set my half-eaten bowl of soup on the ground beside my camping chair, watching Gemma admire the stars like they're old friends she hasn't seen in years. She chuckles as if they've told her a joke.

"It's important to understand the origin of things." She meets my eyes and smiles. "Only then can we begin to understand true sensitivity."

"You mean . . . how we should treat others?"

"In part, yes." She reaches toward the compact camping stove on a folding table beside her. A teal-blue kettle sits on the two-burner stovetop. Gemma pours herself a steamy cup of coffee in an enamel mug. She offers me a cup; I politely decline. "Let's start with the origin of our abilities.

"The year is 1977. By this point, MeReaders have been in use for a few years, and the practice of artificial recall is quickly spreading throughout the globe. News outlets begin to deify Alexander Lochamire and praise his church, Memory Frontier, which has offered the world spiritual healing. There are dissenters, of course, those who challenge the technology and the ideology behind artificial recall. Alexander and his team dub them Pharisees—radical, close-minded individuals bent on resisting restoration.

"'Artificial recall is our awakening,' Alexander would preach. Unfortunately, for some of us, his neurotechnology awakened something else.

"The MeReaders, you see, created a myriad of unforeseen aftereffects, and Memory Frontier did its best to suppress talk of their severity. In those early days, when you raised your hand and openly discussed your side effects, you were promptly shipped off to the Fold so you could be tested. *You* were the problem, not precious artificial recall. Countless people have been imprisoned under the guise of medical intervention. The Fold isn't just an infirmary; it's a penitentiary.

"Now, those of us with aftereffects know better than to speak up. More importantly, we've decided to redeem the side effects, to reclaim them, to think of them as gifts.

"And we have harnessed our gifts." Gemma pulls the mug up to her face. I watch the steam rise in twin paths around her nose. "It's been said that we only use 10 percent of our brains. As a retired neuroscientist, I can assure you that's a myth. However, it is evident that Alexander Lochamire's MeReader unlocked something in many of us. Though why it happened to only some and not everyone remains a mystery."

I sit back in my chair, stunned. For a long time, I don't say anything. Then, "How many others are there?"

Gemma sighs. "I can't say for sure. No one can. Many keep to the shadows, living in fear."

I think about my brother, Ramon. I have long believed that his untimely death at that Memory Frontier factory was tied to his having learned some truth. Was *this* what he discovered? That certain individuals experience aftereffects from artificial recall? Is this tied to what he witnessed on the bus, the elderly man's fluttering eyelids—the presence of Memory Killer *while* he was hooked up to his Restorey? My mind begins to race.

Gemma's soft, cautious voice draws me back into the moment. "Sensitivity is also akin to a radio's ability to react to an incoming signal."

I consider her words for a moment. So understanding the origin of things leads to understanding sensitivity, which is my capacity for being able to interact with my prophetic gift? I have my visions, and Gemma can read people's thoughts, all because of Alexander Lochamire's neurotech. My ability is some twisted side effect of artificial recall, the very thing Memory Frontier insists is protecting me from Memory Killer.

So now that I know where my ability comes from, I think, organizing my thoughts, *I can start to harness it?*

"Yes."

I look up. Gemma's eyes are closed, but she reopens them slowly. I hold her stare. "Then I'm ready to learn."

She smiles. "Tell me about every vision you've had that you can recall."

40

FLETCHER COHEN

Ollie continued to impress. She located the dean's tape kit behind the Restorey, procured the precision screwdriver, and managed to carefully extract the memory tape from its plastic case. She also found a cleaning kit, complete with cotton swabs and isopropyl alcohol. She gently dabbed the tape as she worked, frequently having to scold Fletcher and Chase for breathing too loudly down her neck as they watched.

Next, Ollie threaded the tape into the Restorey, which proved rather self-explanatory, as the various spools were numbered and guided with arrows.

"It's a good thing I insisted that Ollie come with us," Chase said as he and Fletcher applied the electrode stickers to their temples and foreheads. "See, Fletcher? What'd I tell you?"

"I'm not buying that for a second," Ollie deadpanned, wiping her forehead with her forearm. "Now go and make yourselves useful and locate the sedatives."

Chase saluted her dumbly as he and Fletcher made for the metal cabinet beside the computer stations. Inside, they found a box of unopened syringes, some IV bags, a handful of labeled injection vials, and some IV catheters. They gathered what they needed and returned to the chairs. All six of the chairs were still in their reclined positions.

"What are you guys waiting for?" Ollie asked, hands on her hips. "Roll them sleeves up and lie down!"

They deposited everything onto a metal tray between two of the chairs and then sat, remaining upright.

"Now, Ollie," said Fletcher, feeling his hands start to perspire. "How, um, confident are you with syringes and IV catheters?"

"*Very* confident." She snapped her fingers and gestured for them to lie back.

"Ugh. That was a lie, wasn't it?" Chase groaned, though he obeyed anyway. Fletcher lay back, too, and—for the first time that evening—he started to second-guess this whole plan.

"This is stupid. We're going through all this trouble, and this memory tape is going to be, like, my parents' first dance at their wedding or something."

"Relax, Fletcher," Ollie said calmly, rolling over two IV poles. She had seamlessly assumed the role of nurse, and Fletcher found that it actually helped calm his nerves. A bit. Okay, only a *little* bit. But that was something.

"Yeah, okay. Sorry." Fletcher closed his eyes, listening as Ollie set everything up.

"Ollie, how do you know how to do all of this?" Chase asked, watching as she clipped the IV bags to the poles.

"I dunno." Using her teeth, Ollie tore off the seal to a fresh pack of IV catheters. "I mean, how many times have we all sat back while the nurses prepped us for a memory knife? I'm not the only one who observed them work, am I?"

Fletcher heard Chase snort, which turned into a coughing fit, which turned into Ollie shushing him.

"Now, the only thing I'm not 100 percent on is the exact dosage of this sedative."

Fletcher opened his eyes as Ollie flicked the tiny injection vial.

"That, um, is kind of a big thing to not be 100 percent on, Ollie." Fletcher moved to sit up, but Ollie gently pushed against his chest, halting him.

"I can eyeball it, Fletcher. And I'll err on the side of less, okay? To be safe."

"In this case," Chase said, sounding serious, "I'm thinking *more* might be safer."

❖ ❖ ❖

Fletcher focused on his breathing. By this point, he was so used to having an IV catheter inserted into one of his veins that he'd grown numb to the sensation. The pain was dull, distant, a pain that existed behind a wall in another room in the house.

What he *wasn't* used to, though, was one of his friends digging around for one of his veins with a sterile needle. So he ground his teeth and hissed as Ollie worked on his wrist.

"Oh hush, you big baby." Ollie taped up the catheter when she was finished. "There. All done."

Fletcher blinked his eyes open. He stared at the tube lighting that hung from the tall ceiling until his vision went watery. *This is it*, he thought as Ollie moved to Chase. *No more speculating what's on this memory tape . . .*

Unexpectedly, Fletcher began to drift to sleep. The sedative was working.

"Good luck," Ollie said, her voice far away, and then the neon lights splintered before Fletcher's eyes and drew him up into the memory.

❖ ❖ ❖

It was dark, the swallow-you-up-whole kind of dark. Pure pitch-blackness.

Fletcher worried something was wrong. Had Ollie used too much sedative? Or not enough, as Chase had cautioned against earlier?

Chase? You there?

A long pause.

Chase!

Yo. Chase's voice sounded scratchy, like it was coming through a CB radio. *So, like, you can't see anything either, right?*

Right.

Weeeird. Fletcher could feel Chase standing beside him. *What is this place?*

No idea. Fletcher moved his arms, feeling around in the dark with his hands. *Something is wrong, Chase.*

What gave that away?

Maybe because the memory tape is so old, knifing isn't possible? Remember how Ollie said the tape looked old?

Yeah.

Just as Fletcher's anxiety began to teeter into full-blown panic, a pulsing noise began. The sound was low, bassy, and it emanated from everywhere. There seemed to be no source; Fletcher could feel the beating as much as he could hear it.

Then, light.

The world *scratched* into existence, like an overplayed VHS tape struggling to find a clear picture, and Fletcher found himself in a metro station. Chase was indeed beside him on the platform, looking dizzy. Chase took a step back and managed to steady himself before falling over.

There's my dad! Fletcher said, pointing. Beyond the rush of subway commuters, Fletcher spotted his thirtysomething father standing alone. He wore a cheap-looking suit and held a briefcase, which he set down on the pavement. He scanned his surroundings, looking lost. Not directionless, Fletcher perceived, but disoriented.

C'mon. Fletcher stepped around and through the crowds of people, careful not to bump into anyone. Chase followed, and eventually they reached Fletcher's father, who was rubbing his temples and grimacing. He shut his eyes.

Is he in pain? Chase asked. They slowly circled Fletcher's father, examining him closely, and then the memory informed them what was happening.

Memory Killer, Fletcher said, watching in horror as his father opened his eyes. They were completely gray. *This is the memory of the first time my dad had an attack.*

Fletcher's father began to breathe heavily, then all at once he snatched up his briefcase and marched past Fletcher—bumping into his shoulder and casting him backward a few steps. Fletcher and Chase jogged after him, hopping into the subway car before the doors slid shut. The subway screeched as it departed.

Why would my dad keep this *memory tape, of all memory tapes?* Fletcher whispered to Chase. The two continued to watch Fletcher's father, who now appeared unfazed at having *just* experienced his first bout with Memory Killer. He clasped the handlebar leisurely, yawning as he glanced about the car. The change in his disposition was drastic: before boarding the subway he'd been in visible pain; now he seemed . . . bored? Yes, as the seconds ticked by, Fletcher started to perceive a sense of boredom.

That can't be it. Chase looked around. *Something else is bound to happen, man.*

Yet nothing did. As the subway approached its next stop, Fletcher and Chase could feel the car slowing down, and the memory tape ended and they were ejected.

❖ ❖ ❖

Fletcher coughed nearly to the point of gagging before opening his eyes. Ollie scooped the back of his head with her hands and guided him into a sitting position.

"Whoa, whoa. You good, Fletch?"

He looked around the facility frantically, then found Ollie's eyes. "Yeah, I'm good."

"That was short. Did you guys actually knife the tape?"

"We did," Chase said, removing his electrode stickers and sitting up slowly. "How much sedative did you use, Ol?"

"I eyeballed it, remember? What happened?"

Fletcher said, "We started out in . . . in this dark place. And then there was this delayed glitch, and then we were in the memory."

"Ugh. I'm sorry, guys." Ollie left to fetch them some water from the kitchen.

Chase swung his feet around and sighed. "Why *did* your old man keep the tape of his first Memory Killer attack? And more important, why did it seem to cause him physical pain?"

Fletcher took off his electrode stickers and held them in his lap. Before he could answer, they heard the distinct sound of keys jingling outside the sliding door.

Fletcher and Chase exchanged a panicked look.

"Quick!" Ollie yelped, rushing over to the boys. "You're gonna have to stall whoever that is while I unthread the memory tape!"

Fletcher and Chase stumbled to their feet and then raced toward the bunker's main entrance just as the wide door began to slide open, revealing one of Dr. Sanders's scientists. The shaggy-haired man flinched and nearly dropped his key ring.

"Thank the heavens you're here," Chase blurted out. "See, Fletch? Didn't I say someone would come?"

"Er, yeah, you sure did!" Fletcher gulped, pressing his shoulder against Chase to obscure the scientist's view.

"What on earth are you two doing here?"

"It's Ollie," Chase said, folding his arms across his chest. "Misplaced her backpack. We've turned this place upside down. Haven't we, Fletch?"

"Upside down," Fletcher repeated, resisting the urge to glance over his shoulder at Ollie.

"We were wondering if someone dropped it in the lost and found?"

The man blinked, regarding the two of them with a blank expression. "How'd you even get in here?" He took a step forward, but Chase's answer stalled him.

"The passcode." He rolled his eyes. "You seriously don't remember Dean M giving it to us?"

"There's no way he—"

"I remember where it is!" Ollie slipped in between the boys excitedly, causing the man to flinch a second time. "It's definitely in the library. I'm *so* embarrassed."

The man looked like he was going to reply, but they never gave him the chance. "C'mon Fletch, Ollie—we should skedaddle before the prefects grill us."

Ollie nodded. "Good idea. Thanks anyway, Tobias!"

"My name's not—"

And the three of them were off.

❖ ❖ ❖

They filled the walk back to campus with whispered speculation.

"I'm telling you," Chase said, "we're missing something about that memory . . . some kind of context that would explain why it's such an important memory to your pops."

"Maybe." Fletcher shook his head. "Maybe on that day he was heading to some important meeting."

"It was pretty odd how quickly his demeanor changed."

"What do you mean?" Ollie asked.

They explained how Fletcher's father had switched from disoriented to distressed to disinterested all in a span of a few moments. And, perhaps most interesting of all, how agonizing the experience seemed.

"You're sure it was the first time he had a Memory Killer attack?" Ollie said, balancing her flashlight under her arm so she could button her jacket.

"Oh for sure," Chase responded.

Fletcher explained further. "The memory informed us. Plus, Memory Killer attacks don't hurt once you've grown accustomed to them, right? If not for the gray eyes, we wouldn't know we're having an attack. But my dad was *definitely* in discomfort."

"Such a strange memory tape to keep." Ollie clicked her tongue. Fletcher agreed with her on that point, given that everyone discarded his or her memory tape once the memory was fully restored. Why hold on to a tape after the memories were relearned—and why keep said tape hidden?

Ollie asked, "You're leaving for home tomorrow? Maybe you should ask your dad about it."

Fletcher didn't outright oppose this. He filed away the suggestion and kept quiet as the Foxhole came into view.

"Anyone down for a quick drink before lights-out?" Chase offered.

Ollie checked her watch. "It's almost nine thirty. No way the coffee bar's still open."

"The lights are still on." Chase pointed. "Might as well check. I could *really* go for an overpriced, undercaffeinated cappuccino right now."

❖ ❖ ❖

Fletcher, Chase, and Ollie stood frozen at the top of the stairs, watching with their mouths agape.

Sade was standing on the counter of the coffee bar, banging her head to Def Leppard's "Pour Some Sugar on Me," which blasted from the jukebox. The senior lounge was empty; all the lights were off in the dining hall below too. Only the pendant lights above the cash register were on, throwing Sade into a dramatic makeshift spotlight.

"Just when I think my night can't get any stranger," Fletcher said.

Sade, who finally noticed them, hopped down from the counter and jogged over. "What is up, my friends?" She put her arms around Fletcher and Ollie, laughing. She smelled of cheap, bitter wine. "Been looking all *over* for you!"

"You have?" Ollie asked.

Sade's laughter ratcheted up a notch. "Absolutely!" Her accent was particularly punctuated this evening; it sounded more like "*Ehb*solutely." "C'mon, guys. Let me get you a drink." She sauntered over to the couches by the TV. Fletcher, Chase, and Ollie shared a glance before shrugging and sitting around the wide coffee table.

The wine bottle was half empty, and Sade rationed the rest of it into four plastic cups. "Please accept these liquid reparations on behalf of one Sade van der Merwe. You saved Rhett's life, Fletcher! You deserve to be celebrated!"

He took his cup and sipped it. Sade flopped down onto the couch beside Chase, kicking up her boots on the table. "Cheers!" She took a swig of the last bit of wine from the bottle and set it down on the coffee table with an emphatic *thump!*

"How'd you get in here?" Ollie asked. "I thought they locked up after eight?"

"Rhett." She beamed. "He picked the lock."

"He *what*?" But the next moment, Rhett walked through the swinging kitchen doors behind the cash register with a box of unopened candy bars and a bag of bagels.

He studied his armful of goodies and said, "So how do you feel about Snickers and—Oh!" He looked up and saw everyone seated at the couches, watching him amusedly. "I didn't realize we had company. You guys hungry?"

After snacks were distributed and Rhett had settled into the seat beside Fletcher, Chase commented, "Glad to see you've had a change of heart, Sade. You were just dogging on this place not too long ago. Now you seem to be drinking it all in!"

Rhett tore into his candy. "She just needed a little nudging! I think my near-death experience pushed her over the edge."

Sade shrugged. "After we completed that *mad* knifing of Dean Mendelsohn's drill, I felt a rush such as I've never felt before. I've needed some kind of release ever since. It's like you read my mind, Rhett."

"Dancing on the coffee bar is some kind of release," Ollie said, lifting her cup.

Everyone laughed. The jukebox clicked over to another song, and their conversation ambled along, remaining mostly light and superficial. But Fletcher checked out, nursing his wine and laughing on cue with the others to convince them he was present. His thoughts, however, were the furthest thing from the present. They drifted back to his father's memory. The tape was significant; why else would his father have kept it hidden in a hollow book in his closet for all these years? And speaking of the hollow book, was there some kind of connection between the title and the tape? Now that he and his friends had met Mr. Lear and learned about the Memory

Ghosts' audacious plan to break into the Fold, there was something vaguely familiar about the book's title. *The Listener, The Scrambler, The Seer, & The Task.* But Fletcher couldn't put his finger on it, and the wine wasn't helping.

He finished off his drink, then flinched when he found Rhett watching him, smiling a deep-dimpled smile. "So, guys," he said, keeping his eyes on Fletcher. "What exactly were you up to tonight? You know, before coming here?"

Chase snort-laughed. Fletcher and Ollie glared in his direction.

"Just getting some air." Fletcher sank back into the couch and propped his feet on the table.

Rhett chuckled. "And you didn't invite Freya? I thought you two were inseparable."

Fletcher and Ollie replied at the same time, creating an awkward moment, but then Ollie just nodded for Fletcher to finish. "Yeah, she went back home for the holiday."

"*Back home.*" Rhett's grin dimmed like extinguished firelight. "That sounds . . . nice."

Ollie cleared her throat. "Where, um, where is home for you?"

Rhett's expression grew impassive. He didn't answer for a long time, and Fletcher started to wonder if maybe he hadn't heard Ollie. But when the jukebox clicked over to "Smooth Criminal" by Michael Jackson, he blinked repeatedly as if he'd been stirred from REM sleep.

"I should head to bed." And just like that, Rhett gathered his things and left the senior lounge.

When he was out of earshot, Sade took the drink she'd rationed for Rhett (which had gone untouched) and sipped it. "His grandparents were killed on a bus that was targeted by the Memory Ghosts."

41

FREYA IZQUIERDO

In the morning I'm greeted by the smell of strong coffee and bacon. I sit up from my makeshift bed (the collapsed booth and stacked cushions) and see a small plate on the counter beside a steaming mug. All around me, the many faces of Gemma Morris smile at me from the pinned-up Polaroids. I find it strangely comforting. I yawn, yank off my Reflector receivers, and call out to Gemma.

Nothing.

I glance out the window, expecting to see her and Victor, only instead I see an empty campsite and smoldering firepit.

I get to my feet and find a yellow sticky note beside the plate of bacon. I grab one of the strips, which is burnt to perfection along the edges, and take a bite as I read Gemma's instructions:

Good morning! I hope you found the sleeping arrangements adequate. Your first exercise awaits you in the camping chair.

—G

I cup my mug of coffee in both hands and head outside. The camping chair I sat in last night has a spiral notebook resting on the seat, as well as a capped ballpoint pen. I set my coffee on the grass, pick up the notebook, and turn to the first page. Empty. The second page. Empty. I fan through the rest of the pages with my thumb to find the entire thing is completely empty and devoid of instructions.

"Gemma?" I turn in a circle, scanning the grounds. A mild gust of November wind sways the evergreens, like it's taunting winter to come out and fight. I return to the notebook, slightly annoyed. I pick up my coffee, sit, and take a few sips. *Is this some kind of weird test?* I pull the zipper of my hoodie all the way up to my neck.

I drink my coffee. I wait for Gemma.

After about thirty minutes of this, I pull the notebook into my lap, uncap the pen, and take a deep breath. Gemma's words echo in my head. *It's important to understand the origin of things.*

I write my full name at the top of the first page. *Freya Marie Izquierdo.*

Only then can we begin to understand true sensitivity.

I close my eyes. I start to collect the memories of my childhood, gather them around my feet like eager children vying for my attention. But where to start? How does one actually pinpoint their first memory, and how far back can I actually recall? My life isn't just some book that I can grab off a shelf and flip to chapter one.

I open my eyes and write, *Our apartment on Ackerfield.* I stare at this for a moment before scratching it out.

Think, Freya . . .

I take a drink of my lukewarm coffee, humming to myself, and it hits me. I scrawl *My Definitive Playlist* at the top of the page and circle it a few times.

Music. Songs. Melodies.

This will help me chart a course through my childhood. These sensory landmarks will guide me home, to the beginning, to my origin of all things.

I smile and play back Fletcher's words from yesterday. *Songs trigger memories in ways other things simply can't. They're these powerful gateways into the past. They transport us, make us feel things we've forgotten to feel.*

And so I write.

42

FLETCHER COHEN

At dusk, Chase walked Fletcher across the frigid Foxtail grounds toward the gravel parking lot, where a taxicab waited to take Fletcher to the airport.

They spoke in low voices.

"Hey, so, been thinking." Fletcher kept his eyes fixed on his shoes. The frosted grass crunched beneath his soles. "You know, about Dr. Sanders's theory about why the four of us can memory knife. Well, the four of us and now Sade and Rhett."

"Oh yeah?" Chase's tone was soft, cagey. "Haven't, uh, really thought about it much."

"She theorized that the losses we each experienced makes it possible for us to knife . . ." Fletcher stalled, working through his thoughts. "That our grief is a kind of strength. Remember?"

Chase sighed, though he didn't seem agitated by the probing. *He seems anxious*, Fletcher thought, wondering if this was how *he* had come across to Freya at the mall when she'd asked about his sister.

Unexpectedly, Chase stopped walking. He stood at the border of the parking lot, forcing Fletcher to stop too.

"Chase?"

Chase swore under his breath, his teeth chattering slightly in the cold.

"What's up, man?"

"I don't remember."

Fletcher abandoned his suitcase and rejoined his friend on the frozen grass.

"I'm . . . pretty sure it has to do with my cousin Lyvia." Chase closed his eyes, and just like that, the shivering ceased. He stood there, eyelids clamped shut, breathing steadily. "Yes. Something terrible happened to her, but I don't remember what. I think she and I were close when we were kids. But I see only vague fragments of her in my mind . . . One day she was there, everything was beautifully ordinary, and then the accident disrupted my life. I lost her. My beautiful ordinary was gone."

Chase opened his eyes. They were glassy. "It's because I threw away those memory tapes."

Fletcher cocked his head, confused.

"After my readings," Chase explained. "I couldn't bear to revisit memories of Lyvia through artificial recall. So I disposed of the tapes. Every time. Over the months, the details of the accident faded. And all because I'm a coward . . . a coward who couldn't face his fears. I gave up a part of my life to Memory Killer."

"You're not a coward." Fletcher put his hand on Chase's shoulder. His friend looked embarrassed and ashamed, his eyes bereft of their usual good humor. "And you didn't surrender a thing to Memory Killer."

"Fletch—"

"Loss makes an imprint on our *souls*. When we lose someone, we're changed on the other side. Grief strikes this endless chord inside us. It's a chord that never stops thrumming, something we can't unhear." Fletcher didn't know where the words were coming from, but they spilled out of him. "I bet if you dig deep enough—if you *listen* long enough—you'll recover some of those memories of Lyvia."

Chase shook his head. "That's not how this works, dude. Memory Killer—"

The cabdriver honked.

Fletcher motioned to the driver that he needed one more minute, then said, "I believe there are some things Memory Killer will never claim, and you're living proof."

"What're you talking about?"

"Even though you don't actively remember what happened to your cousin—to your best friend—those memories and the impact of that grief are still lodged somewhere inside you. Otherwise, you couldn't memory knife."

Chase appeared to be processing this theory, but before he could refute his friend, Fletcher jogged off to collect his suitcase. He shouted goodbye over his shoulder, tossed his things into the trunk, and slid into the back seat of the cab.

After buckling himself in, he turned and watched Chase through the rear window. He stood there in the cold, unmoving, likely wondering if there was any truth to what Fletcher said. As the cab pulled away, Fletcher thought about his own grief chord. The loss of his unborn sister reverberated beneath the din of his life, always there, a wonderful sound he couldn't simply unhear.

An endless chord. Fletcher faced forward and then leaned back against the headrest. *Not even Memory Killer can steal that.*

When the cab finally entered the woods between the parking lot and the main road, something gnawed at Fletcher's thoughts: If

223

Chase skipped artificial recall when he threw away those memory tapes of his cousin, had he been struck by withdrawals—those terrifying seizures that assail people when they miss their recall window?

Why hadn't Chase mentioned that?

43

FREYA IZQUIERDO

Songs lead me down the corridors of my childhood. And as I write these memories down, I realize I haven't thought about them in a long, long time . . .

"La Nave del Olvido" by José José plays through someone's boombox. There's a game of tag in the dark alley behind our apartments. The neighborhood kids are feral, suntanned beasts who hiss and growl and laugh. They take this game seriously. I'm, what, maybe eight years old? I can smell carne asada sizzling in someone's skillet as I whip past an open window, the tagger close on my heels.

I've never strayed this far from my and Ramon's apartment, but I can't let this girl tag me. I *will not* be it. I need to prove myself to these wretched animals! I turn a corner, laughing stupidly, and smack right into someone's chest. The impact knocks me onto my haunches, and for the briefest moment I see only stars. When my vision sharpens, I see a tall, masked, armor-clad MACE agent looming over me, blocking out the fiery California sun.

The faceless person breathes steadily.

I feel a warm trickle of blood forming on one of my palms.

The MACE agent lowers to one knee and extends a hand. Their breathing, coming through a voice scrambler, sounds scratchy and artificial. I swallow, then reluctantly offer the agent my hand. Instead of helping me up, they take my wrist and firmly wipe away the droplets of blood with their gauntleted hand. I wince at the pain. Once the agent finishes—once all the blood is wiped from my skin—they stand. And just when I think they are going to say something, a call comes in through their radio pack.

The agent turns down the alley at a sprint, scattering the neighborhood kids to the shadows. And in the shadows they remain, prey startled by a predator.

I glance down. My tiny eight-year-old palm bears the tiny beaded imprints of gravel. I stare at my hand, ignorant of the fact that it will soon bear another scar. Instead of blood, there will be ink. Instead of pain, there will be fear.

Such is the enduring narrative of Memory Killer. It comes for us all eventually, whether we accept its manifest destiny or not.

In this memory I rush home to tell Ramon what has happened. Rather than have sympathy for me, he chastises me for straying too far from our apartment.

I turn to the next page in Gemma's notebook and continue to write . . .

There's another memory, landmarked by another song.

A group of Ramon's friends cover "La Bamba" by Ritchie Valens at a backyard birthday party. Ramon has never dated, or if he does, he keeps it hidden from me, except for this span of a few months when I am seven and he's seeing a girl from Santa Ana whom he met at another birthday party. Anyway. I'm in the driveway with Ramon while this Ritchie Valens cover band is butchering an all-time classic. People are sitting at folding tables, cutting up and drinking cervezas and calling out requests even though the song's not finished.

Rapid gunshots interrupt the party, followed by the sounds of multiple cars gunning it down the street. Everyone screams and scatters. It's a terrifying succession of events—the resounding gunshots . . . the guitars cutting off midstroke . . . the panicked shouts.

But . . .

But now that I think about it, what is *more* terrifying than lying on the pavement with my hands over my head is watching Ramon shield the girl from Santa Ana with his body. I am completely exposed while he covers the girl he barely knows.

I pause writing, biting the cap of the pen idly. This is not where I thought my playlist would take me.

Next, "Retirada" by Javier Solís plays on Ramon's portable Sony radio. He and I are seated on a bench outside a Ralphs, finishing up our ice-cream cones, and I feel like the luckiest, happiest girl in Southern California. I feel like royalty. I think it's . . . 1975? Which means I'm six, and I *think* it's before Memory Killer's arrival. Although now I'm second-guessing the year. Either way, I see us sitting there, I see my feet swinging nearly a foot above the pavement. And then Ramon tells me he has to head back into the store really quick to grab something.

I'm alone on the bench when I hear a soft fluting noise. I stand and follow the strange chirping sound, which leads me around the corner to the east side of the grocery store. A small infant sparrow lies helplessly on its back, one of its wings clearly broken. I can still see the fragile bird in my mind's eye, clear as anything. I slowly bend down, talking to the bird and gently stroking its feathery head. I am so concerned about the injured bird that I let the remainder of my ice cream melt and trickle down my arm in sticky rivulets.

Freya! Ramon shouts, rounding the corner. *You know you can't wander off like that!*

I beg him to let me stay and help the sparrow. The poor creature will bake in the sun! I insist, I wail, and—

My pen stops writing. I look up from the notebook as the rest of the memory plays out in my head: Ramon gets angry. His face changes. It hardens into this hostile, dangerous form. Then he *slaps* me. I watch, stunned, as he grabs a wad of discarded newspaper, scoops up the little sparrow, and tosses her in the nearby dumpster. I scream the whole way back to our apartment.

I feel my hand start to tremble.

I drop the pen, which rolls across the notebook and falls onto the grass.

My chest rises and falls.

Tears lurk beyond the edges of my eyes.

Is that the only time Ramon struck me? What other memories have I avoided? I think back to what I found at Long Beach City Hall, how I discovered my brother's altercation with a coworker. Did Ramon have a history of violence that I completely blocked from my memories?

It's like I never even knew Ramon Izquierdo.

Suddenly, a too-bright whiteness washes over my vision, and my head starts to pound. *No, no . . .* I grind my teeth, preparing for a vision, when—

"Freya."

I almost fall out of the camping chair. Gemma's soft, warm hand gently grabs my shoulder. I steady my breathing and turn toward her voice. She's there, beside me, and so is Victor—lying in the shadow of the RV, panting and proud.

"Hi." I rub my eyes and try to stand, but I'm incredibly light-headed.

"Is everything all right?"

"I . . . yeah. Guess I got carried away with this." I show her the notebook.

"Ah, you've been writing. That's wonderful."

"Wasn't that the whole exercise?"

A smile spreads across her face. "Set the pen and notebook inside the RV. I want to show you something."

44

FLETCHER COHEN

Fletcher's flight didn't depart from Nashville until late Sunday afternoon, which meant he didn't arrive at LAX until around 9:00 p.m. Pacific time. By the time the cab dropped him off at the bottom of his driveway, Fletcher was exhausted. He hung his Walkman headphones around his neck, paid the fare, and trudged up the driveway, lugging his heavy carry-on and fantasizing about his comforter and pillow. He decided he would warm up some dinner, catch up with his mom, get a report on his dad, but keep things brief. His bed was calling, after all.

He yawned, opened the front door, and found his plans instantly dashed.

"Dean Mendelsohn?"

The dean stood at the opposite end of the living room, his back to the door. He was holding a snifter in his hand, looking at one of Lila's framed art pieces. "Ah, Fletcher." He turned slowly. "Your mother said you'd be arriving soon."

Fletcher shut the door but kept hold of his carry-on. "What are you doing in my living room?"

"I came to personally check on your mother." He took a sip and sat down on the couch. Fletcher remained in the foyer. "I've done a poor job of staying in touch with your parents over the years, and I can't imagine what your family's going through. I'm sorry I haven't pulled you aside on campus to check on you."

Sorry? Fletcher could hardly believe his ears. *What kind of sick game are you playing?*

"This complicates things, doesn't it?" The dean crossed his legs. "Your father being tied to the terrorists?"

Aha.

Dean Mendelsohn lowered his voice. "You just let me know if this all becomes too much for you. If you need to withdraw from the knifing of Emilia Vanguard's memory next week, I'll understand."

Fletcher cleared his throat. "I'll let you know."

The dean regarded Fletcher for a moment, then lowered his voice even more: "Now. What delayed you?"

Fletcher tilted his head. "Huh?"

"Your mother said your flight home was originally scheduled for yesterday." Another sip from his snifter. In the dimly lit living room, Fletcher observed Dean Mendelsohn's eyes hardening ever so slightly. "She said you called mere hours before your departure. Said you needed to change your flight. Is everything okay, Fletcher?"

He swallowed, feeling his heart rate climb, but he held the dean's stare. "Yes. Everything's okay. Just needed an extra night of studying. You know, with finals around the corner."

"Finals. Of course."

The living room fell silent. Neither of them spoke, and Fletcher could see Dean Mendelsohn processing, the wheels spinning . . . trying to decide whether Fletcher was telling the truth or he and his friends were up to no good.

Down the hall the toilet flushed, followed by the faucet running. Lila Cohen appeared a moment later. "Fletcher, hon, I didn't hear you come in!" They embraced. "How was your flight?"

"Long."

"Let me warm up some dinner for you." She grabbed his hand and led him to the island. She pulled a small Tupperware out of the fridge and set to work reheating some food. "Rusty here was kind enough to stop by and check on us. I didn't realize he was the acting dean at your school. He and your father go way back, hon. Small world."

"And getting smaller every day." The dean raised his glass and finished off his drink. "I should be going. I have to catch my red-eye to DC."

"Of course, of course." Fletcher's mother fetched him his coat. "Thank you again for stopping by. I'll be sure to let Joshua know; it'll mean so much to him. Support is in short supply these days."

They hugged. Dean Mendelsohn said, "Good night, Fletcher. See you in a week."

Fletcher mustered up the effort to half wave, then swung back toward the kitchen on his stool.

After returning to the kitchen, his mother said, "I'm so glad you're home."

"Me too."

She pulled the plate of steamy pad see ew out of the microwave and slid it across the island. "It's my specialty. Takeout."

Fletcher smiled. "You sure do know the way to your son's heart." He blew on a forkful, then took a bite. "How's Dad?"

"Okay, or as okay as he can be." She set a glass of water beside his plate. "I have good news. Quentin was able to work his magic. Your father's going to be transferred to the Fold next week while he awaits his trial. This is going to buy Quentin a lot of time to build a defense. Plus, your father won't have to be locked up in a federal prison. For now, anyway."

Fletcher nodded, not sure how he felt about his dad—whom he now believed to be virtuous, along with the Memory Ghosts—being hooked up to medical equipment and monitored closely.

"There's just one catch."

"Oh yeah?"

Fletcher's mother sighed. "He's being taken to Nevada. The judge wants him at the Alden hospital."

Fletcher's eyes widened. *The flagship hospital,* he realized. *The one I'm helping Mr. Lear break into.*

"I know, I know," she said, misreading his reaction completely. "But it's only a six-hour drive from here. Not ideal, no, but better than prison. I say this is a win."

"Yeah." He did his best at smiling, then returned to his plate. After a few more bites, he said, "Think I could see him tomorrow?"

Lila reached across the island and cupped Fletcher's hand. "He'd love that. I'll call Quentin in the morning."

Later, Fletcher climbed into his bed, positioned his Reflector receivers, and thought about how badly he wanted to call Freya. He was particularly eager to discuss what he and Chase had discovered on his father's memory tape. Plus, with news of his dad's transfer to Alden, the very place the Memory Ghosts were planning to break into—well, there was a lot he wanted to talk about with her.

He felt a stab in his stomach when he remembered he couldn't just pick up the phone and call her. Freya was off the grid, and he prayed with all his heart that she was safe.

❖ ❖ ❖

Early Monday morning, Fletcher walked into Nolan Correctional Facility in South Los Angeles, where his father was being held under pretrial detention. His mother waited in the parking lot, insisting Fletcher needed this alone time with his father. It was just as well;

he'd decided on the car ride over that he was going to ask his father about the Memory Ghosts as well as the meaning behind his saved memory tape. He just needed to find a way to do this without giving away too much and without piquing the interest of eavesdroppers.

If Fletcher's father knew his only son was getting mixed up in the very things that led to his incarceration, he'd likely insist that Fletcher bow out.

Always better to ask for forgiveness than permission, Fletcher thought as the guard led him into a large circular room. It reminded Fletcher of a school cafeteria; the walls and floors were beige with age, and the whole place reeked of pine-scented cleaning products.

Fletcher's father sat alone at a table underneath a high window, his Restorey in front of him. His eyes were shut and his lips were quivering. Fletcher thanked the guard, who posted up at the door, before crossing the room toward his father.

He sat down on the other side of the table quietly, careful not to disturb his artificial recall. After a few moments, Fletcher's father blinked his eyes open. He gave his son a warm smile, slowly removing the suction receivers from his temples and sliding his Restorey out of the way. Then he interlaced his fingers and rested his shackled hands on the tabletop.

"Hey, Fletch."

Fletcher couldn't even bring himself to say hello. So instead he asked, "What were you recalling?"

"A nearly restored memory from my childhood. It's a long story, maybe for another day?"

Fletcher nodded.

"Tell you what. When I get out of here, it's the first thing I'll tell you. Deal?"

"Okay." Fletcher began fidgeting with his hands in his lap. *Now. Now is your chance to ask him anything you want! Bring up the memory tape, or at least ask him* why *he decided to align with the Memory Ghosts!*

Instead, Fletcher surprised himself by saying, "I really miss Josephina, Dad."

Immediately, his father's smile faded. His face grew impassive, and for a moment Fletcher worried he had upset his father. Until the man's eyes grew misty.

Then, "I miss her too, son," and soon Fletcher felt himself starting to cry as well. Had he ever spoken his sister's name to his father or seen him cry? His mother had lost the only sibling Fletcher had, and yet he couldn't recall talking about her with his father until this very moment.

Fletcher's father slouched forward a bit. "For years I struggled to come to terms with my grief. In a lot of ways, I still haven't. Losing her was so difficult for me . . . I felt like I couldn't feel it, the loss, because I never knew your sister's face. I was numb."

Fletcher nodded; he knew what his dad meant. He discreetly wiped his eyes with his T-shirt.

"But then your mom sent me this poem, and I inscribed it on my heart. Would you like to hear it?"

Fletcher nodded again.

"It reads,

> 'Weightless, learning you're here,
> Giving you your name,
> Dreaming your face,
> Imagining your scent and how you're stretched
> out, kicking in my arms.

> Empty, hearing that you're gone,
> See the blank picture,
> Suppressing the hurt,
> Mourning the could-have-been and
> Your almost-life.

Learning, the lie of not living,
Celebrating your time here,
Embracing the grief,
Confronting the held-in-tension of
Joy and Sorrow, a child so
Loved who was never held.

Until,
Meeting face-to-face when all light
Comes and brings ruin to the dark.

Until,
We're together, two halves made whole.'"

His smile returned. It was deeper this time. "Those words help me manage the more difficult days. They help me know Josephina's face even though I'll never see it in this life."

Fletcher cursed himself as the tears returned, but he somehow managed to choke them back this time. While he found the poem moving, he was more taken by the moment. It was such a contrast to the last few interactions they'd had—namely, the one in their garage. Fletcher played back the scene in his head. His father had essentially threatened him for coming home and witnessing his meeting with Alana Khan.

But this . . . ? Fletcher returned his father's smile. It was the most real, honest, and vulnerable he'd ever seen his father, but more important—it was the most real, honest, and vulnerable *Fletcher* had ever been around his father.

And it took my dad getting locked up, potentially facing a life sentence, to make this happen. Fletcher shook his head and looked away. "That poem . . . it's beautiful."

His father said yeah, it was. "How is your mom holding up?"

"You know Mom. Keeping busy. She's threatening to grill for Thanksgiving."

Fletcher's father chuckled. "What I'd give to see that."

"But yeah. She's good. Strong as ever."

"She's been so patient with me, even when I can't"—he caught himself, then straightened up—"I don't know what I'd do without her. Without either of you."

"Then why'd you do it, Dad?" Fletcher dropped his voice. "Why'd you go and get mixed up with"—a whisper—"with the Memory Ghosts?"

"There's . . . more to the story."

Tell me about it. Fletcher contemplated whether he should tell his dad everything—about how Mr. Lear himself had recruited him and his friends, and they were basically secret operatives for the Ghosts.

Fletcher changed tactics. "What's your plan, then? Mom says you won't disavow the Ghosts, but you're maintaining your innocence. Does that mean the Ghosts *aren't* terrorists?"

"These are things I simply cannot discuss. In time, I hope you'll come to forgive me."

Give him some hint. Fletcher's mind raced. *Tell him you know about Mr. Lear and his big plan to expose Memory Frontier's lies!*

Fletcher glanced at the door. The guards on duty were making small talk and seemed completely uninterested in them. So he leaned forward. "Last month, the pest control company that services our house accidentally sent out a tech twice. Isn't that strange?"

His father perked up. "Huh."

"Yeah, and while I didn't catch him in the act, I'm pretty sure he rummaged through your hidden room in the closet."

"You don't say." He didn't seem worried, or even bothered, really. And why would he be? He had obviously coordinated with Mr. Lear to send Zayne there to retrieve something important. "Was anything stolen?"

"That's where it gets even stranger, Dad. All your stuff was still there, from what I could tell. Even Mom's jewelry."

His father scratched his chin and raised his eyebrows. Fletcher could tell he was trying to keep his responses neutral.

"There was this book too. *The Listener, The Scrambler, The Seer, & The Task.* I guess whoever went through your things knocked it loose from Mom's shoe rack."

Fletcher's father leaned forward, not quite standing but hovering over the table close to his son, his eyes intense. "Did you put it back? The book?"

Fletcher stammered, "Um, y-yeah. Just figured it was s-some antique or heirloom. What's wrong?"

"Nothing can happen to that book." He looked like he wanted to say more, but a guard started to approach their table. Fletcher's father cleared his throat and straightened to his full height. Fletcher followed suit.

"It was great seeing you, son," he said, his voice measured again.

Fletcher, still in slight shock, said, "You too."

They hugged, and before Fletcher could pull away, his father whispered, "Make sure that book is safe."

45

FREYA IZQUIERDO

At midmorning, Gemma and I arrive at the end of a wooded path. Up ahead I see an old rectangular building, its pitched roof sunken in places. Shingles litter the ground and weeds encase the abandoned structure.

"What is it?"

"An old church," Gemma mutters as if not to disturb the sleeping building. "Victor and I stumbled upon it on our walk earlier. There's a cemetery on the south side, and beyond that a winding dirt road. Beautiful, isn't it?"

More like sad, depressing, I think, the word *beautiful* furthest from my mind. Although, as I observe the red door with its chipped paint, the moss-covered stone, the way the whole building appears as old as Earth, I begin to see what she means.

"See those wildflowers?" She points at the sun-facing side of the church, where the ground is coated in luminous pinks and purples.

"They die about a year after they bloom. Imagine being that fearless! Showcasing your electric elegance for the world to bear because you know you only have a year! My oh my."

Victor bounds through the tall, dead grass toward the church.

Gemma smiles and turns to me. "Shall we go inside?"

The church's interior is pure decay. Chunks of the walls are missing, with scraps of drywall strewn about the dusty floors. The pews have long been uprooted and overturned, like someone rushed in here, pried the long benches out of the hardwood, and tried to steal them but was raptured before they could finish the job. I see dust spiraling in the shafts of light, which spills in through the cracked-open roof. And across from me and Gemma, opposite the front door, is a small stage. Above the empty baptismal, someone has messily painted HEBREWS 13:5 in black.

Gemma walks down the aisle, hands clasped behind her back. I remain by the door, worried that too many sudden movements might bring this whole place crashing down. I hear Victor getting into something in the room beyond the stage, and I pray his curiosity doesn't lead to disaster.

I'm about to suggest we leave, because honestly this church is making me *really* uncomfortable, when Gemma says, "Tell me about your family, Freya."

"Oh." I slip my hands into my hoodie pockets. "Where to start?" I give her the high-level stuff, how my mom passed away during childbirth, how my brother, Ramon, was left to raise me when my coward of a father abandoned us. I tell her how Ramon died in a freak factory explosion a couple of years ago, which forced me into the foster system. And then, before I can stop myself, I tell her how I misremembered my brother's identity, how I inexplicably repressed the truth.

Gemma turns on her heels. "Interesting. You conflated their identities in your memories."

"I . . . guess?"

"A defense mechanism, I suspect."

"Are you psychoanalyzing me?"

She walks back up the aisle and joins me by the door. "Deep down, we all idolize our fathers. Indeed, in a patriarchal system like ours, fathers are billed as the heads of the household—the leaders, the ones who have it together. You were starved for that kind of leader, Freya, and so you ascribed the paternal identity to Ramon."

I shrug. I suppose I follow her logic, but I'm suddenly troubled by something.

"What is it?" Gemma asks, watching me.

"Nothing, just . . ." I struggle to articulate what's weighing on my heart. "This morning, when I was journaling, I was mining some memories of my childhood. I guess there were some things about Ramon I had let myself forget."

Gemma nods like she knows what I mean even though I don't elaborate. "How did that make you feel?"

"I guess a little scared, maybe," I reply. "Scared I might let myself remember things about my brother that I don't want to."

Gemma is silent for a moment, then whispers, "What's more terrifying—losing your memories, or confronting difficult ones?"

I tell her I'm not sure.

Over the next couple of days, I settle into a rhythm with Gemma. I spend the morning journaling while drinking coffee, following my thoughts and memories wherever they take me, and then I discuss my writings with Gemma over lunch.

She listens, helps me process, but never inserts an opinion or perspective. I keep waiting for her to unveil some profound insight, but so far she's just doing a lot of hand-holding.

We haven't discussed my visions, or how exactly Gemma means to help me harness my gift.

In the afternoons, Gemma and I take long walks in the woods with Victor. We hardly talk; Gemma is guarded with details of her past, and I don't pry. If she has something to say, she says it. Plus, our walks aren't for small talk. So instead, I practice clearing my head. I figure if I spend the mornings navigating a swath of memories—if I'm dedicating so much head space to recalling and journaling—the afternoons should be a mental reprieve.

In the evenings, we eat around the fire. Gemma's personality comes alive beneath the stars, and she whips out a prepared list of questions for me. Mostly they're about Foxtail Academy, Lochamire's trial, and memory knifing.

"Storytelling is memory preservation," she says, poking the fire with a stick. "And *you* are a fine storyteller."

I laugh, then begin to wonder if her asking me about the last few months is less about her curiosity and more about her helping me cement my memories.

The next day, Thanksgiving, I wake up before the sun. I can hear Gemma softly breathing the tempo of deep sleep in the bedroom. I quietly get dressed and bundle up. Before I sneak out, I hear Victor's tired clacking down the hall. I smile and hold the door open. Outside, he sticks his haunches into the air, stretching, and then we're off.

I'm not really sure where I'm headed. In a few days' time, Gemma and I have explored most of the expansive woods behind the tree farm. I'm guessing we've walked a collective twenty miles by this point. Still, my feet carry me along a familiar path, and in the quiet dawn I think about my brother and my father.

Before this week, I had thought of Ramon only as altruistic—selflessly giving up his dreams to raise me in the wake of tragedy. That tragedy, of course, extends beyond losing our mother. My father abandoned us in the night, and this freshly remembered truth still burns in my stomach like strong liquor. But as I wade through my childhood, my picture-perfect view of Ramon is being challenged. It's clear now he had a temper, one that startled and scared me when it reared its nasty head. He . . . he *struck* me, something I'd repressed.

As I hike through the dead trees, I wonder if it *was* repression.

Did Memory Killer seize these memories of Ramon? And am I starting to regain them because of the Reflector?

Victor and I enter a clearing where the cloud-smothered sunrise wanly spotlights the abandoned church. The old building unsettles me, even in the glittering glow of morning, and I realize it's because it could literally collapse under its own weight at any moment.

So why do I follow Victor inside?

46

FLETCHER COHEN

On Wednesday, the day before Thanksgiving, Fletcher drove his Ducati to Newport Beach and met Ollie for lunch at one of her grandparents' steakhouses. The Royal Crown sat on the water, and the thirty-year-old building was designed to look like an old English inn. Inside, Ollie waved Fletcher over to the dimly lit bar.

Fletcher crossed the "parlor," complete with roaring fireplace and armchairs, and plopped down on the stool beside Ollie.

"Isn't this place nuts?" she asked.

"It smells like the queen of England looks," he joked, admiring the ornate lanterns that hung over his head.

"Ordered us two steak sandwiches." Ollie leaned over the bar and poured two cups of soda. "How's your week been?"

"I dunno. Weird, I guess." Fletcher took a drink. He told her about seeing his father on Monday, and how intense he'd become when Fletcher mentioned the memory tape. "I wish Freya and Chase were here. We could all put our heads together and—"

"What, I'm not good enough?"

"Oh, er, no, I just meant—"

"Shut up, I'm teasing."

The barkeep returned with two plates of food.

"Thanks, Frazier." Ollie tossed a chip into her mouth. "This is my friend Fletcher. He drives a motorcycle too."

Frazier grunted, then picked up a rack of glasses and disappeared toward the kitchen.

"Sweet guy, that Frazier. And he makes a *mean* cocktail." She plucked the toothpick out of her sandwich and dug in. "Got any more theories about that memory tape? Like, why in the world your dad would hold on to it for so long?"

Fletcher swallowed his bite. "I got nothing. It's driving me nuts, Ol. Best I can guess is that it has something to do with a scene *after* the memory tape. Or maybe before? Like maybe where my father was headed or where he was coming from is the important detail."

"And I'm assuming you didn't perceive his destination while you guys were knifing?"

"No, but I'm not surprised by that. I was so struck by his strange change in behavior that it was all I could focus on."

Ollie nodded. She pulled a cocktail napkin over and grabbed a pen from her purse. "What was the name of that hollow book?"

Fletcher told her. She scribbled it down.

"I'm going to swing by the library after lunch and see if I can track it down."

"Perfect. I'll go with you."

"Actually, you should probably head to the grocery store."

"Huh?"

Ollie took another chomp of her savory sandwich. "I need you to grab a dessert for our Thanksgiving dinner. My grandparents are excited to meet you and your mom."

"I . . . what?"

Ollie rolled her eyes. "You and your mom are having Thanksgiving with us."

"We are?"

"Mhmm." Ollie eyed his plate. "Now finish your amazing sandwich before it gets cold."

Fletcher chuckled, dutifully returning to his lunch. After they ate in silence for a few moments, the TV that sat behind the bar showed a troubling news story. Ollie found the remote and turned it up.

". . . And as you can see, authorities *still* have not managed to temper the riots, which began late last night."

According to the newscaster, the shaky, amateur video footage was of downtown Pittsburgh. Throngs of people stormed the streets. Some lifted public waste bins over their heads and threw them; others hurled bricks at storefront windows. One man hoisted a sign into the air that read, OUR MEMORIES, OUR WEAPONS! A small collective of police officers in riot gear stood at the fringes, shouting orders that fell on deaf ears.

The anchor's voice continued over the alarming footage: "We're being told these violent actors are protesting artificial recall and Memory Frontier, which is set to release new technology after their trial completes next year." Fletcher and Ollie swapped a glance. "Earlier, people were seen smashing Restoreys in the street, and many are claiming to have abandoned artificial recall altogether. It sounds like, yes, I'm being told the president is deploying MACE, which means agents should be arriving—"

The TV shut off. Fletcher and Ollie glanced over to find Frazier holding the remote. His scruffy face appeared strained. He tossed the remote onto the bar and started cutting up some limes.

"Do you kids have any idea why the hell I wake up every morning and bartend for rich socialites when the world is ending?" Fletcher set down his half-eaten sandwich, noticing Frazier's two-quarter mark for the first time. "Why do those of us in food, retail, or other thankless jobs keep clocking in? Hmm?"

Ollie stared at her plate; Fletcher took another sip of his soda just to give his hands a task.

"So we don't lose our minds, like them." He gestured toward the tube TV. "Sure, I've thought about how easy it'd be to just give up on artificial recall—to stop letting my life be controlled by a plastic box—but I won't go easy. It's not my way. So I show up for work. And I take pride in it."

Ollie cleared her throat. "You know, Memory Frontier's new tech is gonna change—"

"Why? Because Memory Frontier says so?" Frazier set down his knife and scooped the lime wedges into a container. "Let me guess, they're replacing their plastic boxes with even *smaller* plastic boxes?"

Ollie and Fletcher remained mute.

Frazier sighed and leaned against the bar. "Look, all I'm saying is, my purpose is *my* purpose, and I don't let Memory Killer or Memory Frontier have a say in it. And *that's* why I keep the news off."

Frazier huffed quietly and left for the kitchen again. Eventually, Fletcher and Ollie returned to their sandwiches, but Frazier's sobering words lingered the rest of lunch.

Thanksgiving evening, Fletcher and his mom pulled into Ollie's European cobblestone driveway. The electric gate slid shut behind them as they unfastened their seatbelts.

"You sure you're okay, Mom?" Fletcher put his hand on top of hers. "It's not too late to back out. We could drive through El Pollo Loco and head back to the house."

Lila stifled a laugh. "I'm fine, hon. This'll be good for us. Plus, the gate closed, so it *is* too late to back out." She winked and then got out of the car. Fletcher sighed, grabbed the store-bought pumpkin pie from the back seat, and joined his mother.

They were greeted at the door before they rang the bell.

Ollie's grandparents were bubbly, delightful people who shared Ollie's infectious laughter. They led Fletcher and Lila through the wide foyer, down a set of carpeted steps, and into the vast living room. Fletcher barely had a second to take it all in before Ollie whisked him down the hall toward the kitchen.

"Quick, in here," she whispered. "Before you get dragged along on the official tour."

"Maybe I want the tour." Fletcher handed her the pie. "Maybe I want to see Ollie's room and her secret stash of comic books—"

"*Trust* me, you don't." She took him by the hand and led him through a set of double doors and onto the patio. Various potted flowers hung from the vaulted pergola. Beyond the columns, sweeping out beneath the twilight, ripe, annual vegetables grew in innumerable raised garden beds. Bluish step lights illuminated a stone path, which zigzagged beyond his sight. It reminded Fletcher of the entrance to a labyrinth.

"Your place is incredible, Ol."

She shrugged and collapsed into one of the patio chairs. "Sure, but the property tax is *nuts*. Or so I've heard."

Fletcher chuckled as he sat.

"Well, I'm sure this won't come as a shock, but that hollow book? It's not an actual published book."

Surprise, surprise. Fletcher realized he'd known all along; hearing it confirmed out loud only fed his burgeoning curiosity.

Not wanting to dwell on the defeat, he quickly changed the subject. "How do you think Chase is doing in flight school? Think he'll be ready to manifest a helicopter come Monday?"

Ollie snickered. "He's an inveterate flirter. I think he only volunteered because of Sade."

"It is a smart move, though, on Dr. Grondahl's part. Knifing Emilia's memory tape will be difficult, and if two of us can manifest a helicopter, then at least—"

"Aren't we just gonna throw the mission?"

Fletcher lounged back in his chair, thinking.

Ollie continued, "I mean, you know, we *did* agree to help Mr. Lear and the Ghosts. I just figured we'd only go through the motions of knifing."

"Unless . . ." Fletcher trailed off, staring out at the garden beds.

"Unless *what?*"

"I think we should try to see the mission through, in case we're able to perceive something pertinent about my dad and the Memory Ghosts."

"I'm not following, Fletch."

"We know the dean and Memory Frontier are lying, right? We confirmed that even before Irene connected us with her great-uncle. But Mr. Lear is still keeping some secrets close to the vest. And my dad refuses to elaborate on his involvement with the Ghosts."

Ollie nodded. "Knifing Emilia's memory *could* provide us with some context about the Memory Ghosts. We'll see. I guess if we're going to knife anyway, we might as well use the opportunity to our advantage."

Fletcher sighed. *Feels like all we've been doing is chasing secret after secret.* "Speaking of Irene. Has she tried to contact you?"

Ollie shook her head. "I did talk to her briefly on Saturday while you were dropping off Freya. She said Mr. Lear is nearly finished shoring up his plans, that he might call upon us any week now. Whatever that means."

Fletcher was ready for all of this to be over—for the knifing to end, the truth to be exposed, and his father to be exonerated. *And for Freya to get her answers.* He wondered how she was faring with Gemma. If only he could call her . . .

"Senior year sure is turning out to be unforgettable, huh?" Ollie pulled her feet up into her chair. "And we haven't even made it through one full semester yet."

Fletcher nodded, smiling wryly. "You can say that again. Before I got sent to Foxtail, I was planning on coasting to graduation. Now we're aiding and abetting a corrupt conglomerate *and* we've been recruited by the resistance."

"*The resistance.*" Ollie snorted. "Wow, when you put it like that, it sounds pretty intimidating." She hugged her knees. "I never asked for this. I just wanted to collect my diploma and move out of my grandparents'."

Fletcher felt an unexpected prick of guilt in his chest. "You and Chase have been incredible. Sticking by Freya first, now me. I really don't know what I'd do without you guys."

Ollie stood. "Being an amazing friend is definitely a calling. *Not* for the faint of heart." She winked. "C'mon, let's go eat. I didn't slay this turkey for nothing!"

That evening, as Fletcher sat beside his mother at the dining room table and Mr. and Mrs. Ngo divvied out the Thanksgiving meal while swapping stories about their rambunctious (their word) granddaughter, Fletcher found himself distracted. It was a good distracted, the kind where one is able to leave his troubles at the door—like a coat check—and enjoy a fine-cooked meal with a healthy side of laughter.

Lila, egged on by Ollie and her grandparents, shared stories of Fletcher's childhood. Ordinarily he'd have been mortified, yet Fletcher found himself laughing and correcting his mother when she began to embellish the details. This, in effect, created even *more* laughter at the table. And underneath this joyous raucousness, when he was working through his second helping, Fletcher stole a glance at his mother. They made eye contact briefly, and he spied true peace in her gaze.

Fletcher decided on the spot that they had *both* needed this welcome distraction.

47

FREYA IZQUIERDO

I stand in the center of the church as if I'm frozen mid–altar call. I hear the wind. It enters the building, hissing through the cracked windows and singing a high-octave song. I hear the church's bones creak, joining in the chorus, followed by a dull thumping. A shutter hanging by a broken hinge? The thumping plays an unsteady beat, the blowing wind crescendos, and this erratic hymn surrounds me. I'm *sure* I can feel nature dragging this decrepit building to the ground. And yet, like some biblical miracle, the structure weathers the wind. It remains standing, and so do I.

I steadily breathe through the fear.

This building won't collapse.

I hear Ramon's voice riding the wave of an approaching memory.

And neither will I.

I push through rising anxiety and embrace the memory.

❖ ❖ ❖

Freya, come quick!

I hear Ramon's voice on the other side of the door. I am playing in our shared bedroom in our apartment. Once again, this memory is from when I was six, and as it crystallizes in my mind's eye, I recall that it's just a few days after I found the bird with the broken wing in the parking lot.

It's a few days after Ramon hit me.

Freya, por favor, he pleads. I set down my doll and join him in the hallway. He leads me by the hand toward our lone bathroom, gently swinging the door forward.

Mira, he says, pointing to the wicker basket above the toilet. I see a half-formed bird's nest sitting delicately between rolls of unused toilet paper. The window beside the shower is open. *I forgot to close it last night. Looks like we're getting some roommates!*

Can we keep the window open? So she can finish her nest?

We must, *love!* he says, getting down on one knee and side-hugging me. Then he whisper-shouts into the bathroom, *Oy, little bird! Nuestra casa es su casa.*

I giggle.

The bird returns, of course, and over the span of a few days completes her nest. Then, over the weekend, she lays her eggs.

We can't use the bathroom! We can't use the bathroom! I shout to Ramon as the chirping resounds throughout our entire apartment. The chirping is incessant, and it goes on through the nights and into the mornings. To my brother's credit, he never wavers.

At least not in front of me.

He knocks on our neighbor's door. Explains the situation. And for *days* we use the bathroom next door. While it proves difficult and inconvenient, Ramon stays the course. For me. It matters to him that *I* am happy.

Then one day, the nest is empty.

Just like that.

I leap up and down on the balls of my feet, clapping and shouting, overjoyed that the little birdlings have learned to fly. I feel not an ounce of sadness at their departure. I am proud, because Ramon and I have shared in the responsibility of raising this feathered family.

We save the nest. Display it on the sill above the kitchen sink. And when I pull the stool over to the bathroom window to finally shut it, Ramon gently stops me.

What are you doing?

Finally closing the window!

Ah, but love! He smiles and scoops me up into his arms. *When the little birds grow up, how will they return to lay their eggs if the window's closed?*

I smile bigger than ever. Together, we open the window.

We never shut it again.

❖ ❖ ❖

I don't even try to stop the tears. I let them sail down my face. Ramon was not perfect, no. He made mistakes, yes. I realize now it's more important to see him as a human than a hero. I must accept the good along with the bad. And not just in my brother—in myself too. We are all imperfect creatures hurtling through this life, trying to make the best of the messes we've been handed.

I close my eyes, suck in a mouthful of cold air, then release it through my nose. This act of memory avoidance, of not confronting the flaws in Ramon, was rooted in fear. That fear runs like a thread through my childhood. It's been restraining me—hampering me like shackles—and I didn't even realize it.

I will sever these shackles. I blink open my eyes. *I will confront the flaws. I will love through them.*

Victor appears from behind the stage. He slowly trots over to me, and I see a clump of cobwebs matted to his left ear. I kneel down and wipe his silvery-black fur clean, and together we leave the empty church.

"My oh my." Gemma sets a plate of toaster waffles on the table as I slide into the booth. "That is profound, isn't it? *Memory avoidance.* And you've traced this practice back throughout your childhood?"

I nod and soak my breakfast in maple syrup. Victor forces his way underneath the table, exhaustedly collapsing onto my sneakers. "You said this would help me achieve true sensitivity. Now what? How will this help me with my visions?"

Gemma pours two mugs of coffee and then sits across from me in the booth. "Gifts are received, yes? They're not plundered or looted. So now you wait to receive them."

I was afraid of that.

"Don't worry, Freya." She sips her coffee. "Things will only continue to get clearer."

I skip journaling that morning and instead spend my time in the RV, rereading my writings and eagerly waiting for another vision. *I just hope the last couple of days helps,* I think, turning the page, *that I'll now have some sort of agency over my gift.*

Evening rolls in early, catching me off guard. Feels like the day was just getting warmed up, like an on-deck batter who practice swings but doesn't get the chance to step up to the plate. Gemma cooks bratwursts over the fire in lieu of turkey, and it proves to be the strangest Thanksgiving meal I can recall. I don't complain; the brats pair tastily with the toasted buns and heaping sides of potato salad.

Gemma cycles through her deep catalog of the Beach Boys cassette tapes, and when "Do You Remember?" comes on, she jumps to her feet and starts a youthful dance. Victor yaps at her legs. I can't help but laugh as I watch my elderly friend move and sway beneath the starlight—her trusty life source—starkly silhouetted by our popping firepit.

When the song ends, she falls back into her camping chair beside me. "Laugh all you want." She takes a drink of water. "I used to be able to dance *much* longer than that. My oh my. The inescapable inevitability of time."

She reaches into her coat, sets her clutch purse aside, and pulls a handkerchief out of an inner pocket.

"You always seem to have that on you." I nod toward her clutch purse. Gemma wipes her mouth, puts the handkerchief back, then slowly opens the purse. She pulls out a single Polaroid photograph. The shot is of a framed picture, a smiling woman hugging a toddler. The woman holds a tiny, novelty American flag. The frame sits on a nightstand.

Gemma hands me the Polaroid. "The day my sweet mother got her United States citizenship. I was three."

I study the picture in the Polaroid. It's black-and-white and grainy, and in the toddler I see Gemma's distinct adolescent features beginning to form. Her mother looks as proud as anyone I've ever seen.

"She's beautiful." I hand the Polaroid back. "Why did you take a picture of the picture?"

Gemma considers my question, keeping her eyes fixed on the image. After putting the picture away and snapping her clutch purse shut, she whispers, "I don't want to chance forgetting how I felt when I first saw this photograph. Or how I felt when I learned her story."

❖ ❖ ❖

Gemma pours a bucket of water onto the dwindling campfire. It hisses and smokes. As I stand and collect my things, I hear a distant ringing. At first, I think it's the dying fire, softly screeching in the air, but then the ringing intensifies in my ear. The pitch grows sharper; it pierces like a needle. Strangely, the experience doesn't hurt. Not yet, at least.

"I think it's happening," I say, dropping my plate and cup onto the dead grass. Gemma rushes to me, takes my arm, and guides me back into the chair. Her lips move as if she's asking me a question, but at this point I don't hear anything but the ringing. The sound isn't painful so much as disorienting, like it's coming from all around me, and I expect a pounding headache to follow. The beginning of every vision I've ever had is marked by a headache.

But no such headache comes.

The ringing hits its apex. I blink once, and now I'm standing on the side of the freeway, bathed in late-morning sunlight. I glance around, panicked breaths welling inside me.

Take control, Freya, the voice in my head says. *Receive the gift.*

It's Gemma. She must be whispering into my ear at the campsite. Her words echo through my vision—across the freeway, between the tall trees at my back—and fill me with needed reassurance. *This is only a vision*, I tell myself. *Something that has not come to pass, something I will not fear.*

I take a step forward—I actually move! I can walk, I can move about—I have agency in this vision.

So where am I, and why am I seeing this?

A few highway patrol vehicles whip past me, their sirens blaring. I squint after them, trying to see where they're headed, and then I hear the faint whirring of helicopter blades. I crane my head back and see a pair of helicopters flying through the air toward—

Two bodies fall from one of the cockpits.

I stifle a scream.

They tumble through the air toward the ground, flailing their arms.

And their bodies are fading. They're disintegrating, like Fletcher did in my arms in Malcolm Heckman's memory, and *they* happens to be me and Fletcher. I'm actually witnessing me and him careening earthward while our bodies vaporize into dust.

This can't be happening. That can't be me and Fletcher in that terrifying free fall.

And yet it *is.*

Just before our bodies hit the pavement, a *breath* before the gruesome impact, Fletcher and I dissolve into nothingness.

I'm left standing on the shoulder of the freeway, stunned.

❖ ❖ ❖

"It's over, Freya." Gemma's voice pulls me back into the present.

I open my eyes and nod, still anticipating an agonizing migraine. Instead, I find myself clearheaded and alert. I stand. "In the past, when I've had a vision, I've seen events unfolding through my eyes, like a memory. Just now, I was separated from the event. I saw myself. I saw Fletcher. I wasn't a participant; I was an observer."

Gemma takes my cup, refills it with water from the travel dispenser, and hands it to me.

"It was another warning, like the vision of Fletcher lying in my arms in the snow." I take a drink, playing the scenes over and over again in my head.

"And what did this recent vision show you?"

"Monday, when we're scheduled to knife Emilia Vanguard's memory, there's going to be an accident." My voice remains even. It does not quaver. "Memory Killer will strike both me *and* Fletcher."

Gemma straightens up. "I see."

I finish off the water and hand her the empty cup. "But I'm not going to let that happen."

❖ ❖ ❖

The next day, Friday, I wake before Gemma again. I make coffee. I scramble some eggs. I make her a plate and leave it in the oven to stay warm. Then Victor and I head outside for another predawn walk. As we trek through the woods, as I crunch over the dry leaves and sticks, I make myself a promise: *I will not let anything happen to Fletcher.*

I lost my mother.

I lost my brother.

"I won't lose you too," I say aloud.

Victor, who trotted up ahead, doubles back at the sound of my voice and licks my hand. I smile and give him a good scratch behind the ears in return.

I spend most of the day journaling in the RV, writing down every single detail I observed in my latest vision. Then, when I've exhausted this, I shift my focus to my memories. I pull my photo album out of my backpack for the first time this week and leaf through the crinkly pages, taking my time with each photograph. There are still *so many* untapped moments from my past that I've yet to recall; I know that, eventually, the memories I'm supposed to remember will return. When they do, I'll embrace the happy ones and confront the difficult ones.

Saturday, I pack my things after breakfast. Gemma and I head through the maze of Christmas trees back toward the tree farm's entrance, where Irene is scheduled to pick me up and take me back to Foxtail Academy.

Something occurs to me as we walk in silence. "I didn't see you use your Restorey once this entire week."

Gemma chuckles. "I could've used artificial recall in bed after you retired each night."

"Did you?"

She goes to reply but is cut off by the sound of tires rolling up the gravel. Victor barks merrily at Irene's arrival. And before she gets out of the car, Gemma takes me by the arm and says, "You remember how I said that storytelling is memory preservation?"

"Yeah. Does that mean you've found another defense against Memory Killer?" I tilt my head, confused at her cryptic response. "Oral stories are what help you?"

"A story," she clarifies. "A very complicated story. Only, this one isn't fiction—*this* one is fact. The truth. Our most important weapon in the war with Memory Frontier."

"So this memory—er, *story*—of yours explains why you don't have to use artificial recall?"

"I—"

Irene hops out of her car and waves, cutting Gemma off. I wave back, and then Gemma pulls a small leather-bound journal out of her coat pocket and hands it to me. The journal is held shut by thin twine.

"What's this?"

"An early Christmas gift. I hope you continue to find your writings helpful." She hugs me before I can say anything. "And soon, I *promise* you will hear the complicated story too."

I keep additional questions to myself. It's a long while before we break away.

❖ ❖ ❖

"How was your week with Gemma?" Irene asks after we leave Lowell's Tree Farm.

"Refreshing and helpful," I say distractedly, opening her glove box and fishing out a fast-food napkin. I pull a pen out of my back-pack and start to draw a map. "What do you usually do during third period?"

"Oh, um, shelving. That's a free period for seniors, right? Isn't that when you guys memory kni—?"

"You're going to have to skip shelving on Monday."

"I am? Is everything okay?"

"Yes. It will be. But I'm going to need your help."

48

FLETCHER COHEN

Saturday afternoon, Fletcher walked into his dorm room to find that Chase still had not returned. But Freya was there, and she'd fallen asleep on the couch, waiting for Fletcher to get back.

She shot up when she heard the door click shut. "Hey, you made it."

Fletcher dropped his bag on the floor and sat beside Freya, pulling her against his chest. They sat in the quiet, holding one another and breathing the same rhythm. "I missed you."

"I kinda missed you too."

They pulled away. Fletcher lightly tucked a loose lock of Freya's hair behind her ear. "Tell me about your week."

Freya sighed, then leaned her head in the crook of Fletcher's neck. "It's a lot. You go first."

"Deal."

❖ ❖ ❖

They spent the rest of the afternoon catching each other up on their Thanksgiving break. Freya was impressed that they managed to break into the bunker and knife his father's memory; Fletcher was overjoyed that she had her breakthrough with Gemma.

The hours rushed by, a time lapse of laughter and cuddling and playful banter, and soon it was dusk. Chase arrived shortly before dinner, looking depleted, and Ollie was soon to follow—wearing an oversized *A Christmas Story* sweatshirt with a smiling Ralphie prominently featured on the chest.

As the foursome walked to the Foxhole, they admired the campus's radical transformation. Garland had been wrapped around the light poles. Large fake presents were grouped in threes and fours at the entrances to the library, auditorium, and classrooms. And potted poinsettias lined the sidewalk to the dining hall.

"Bah, humbug," Chase muttered as they entered the Foxhole. The walls were adorned with fanciful red ribbons, and the interior smelled of rich cinnamon apples. "Last Christmas" by Wham! played faintly overhead, nearly drowned out by the dinnertime babble.

"So, what, flight school turned you into the Grinch?" Ollie asked as they got in line.

"I'll have you know I've *always* despised this holiday." Chase served himself a double portion of breaded chicken and mashed sweet potatoes. "I possess a set of consistent pet peeves."

Fletcher smirked. "What's another one of your pet peeves?"

Chase exhaled dramatically. "People asking me what my pet peeves are."

They gathered around a table near the wide stairs that led to the senior lounge. After everyone had taken a few bites, Freya told Chase and Ollie about her time with Gemma. She also shared the startling revelation about MeReaders—how aftereffects of the technology were responsible for Freya's prophetic visions.

Chase pretended to clean out his ears with his spoon. "You mean to tell me that you can see into the future *because of side effects from artificial recall?*"

Freya nodded solemnly. "Gemma said Lochamire's neurotech 'unlocked' something in our brains. It's how she's able to read people's thoughts."

Ollie said, "What other . . . *gifts* . . . are out there?"

"Oh!" Chase snapped his fingers. "Telekinesis? Levitation? Imagine a world where I could just *float* to the john. Man, that'd be something."

"If you could levitate," Fletcher said dryly, "why would you use your gift to glide to the bathroom?"

"Why not?" Chase looked incredulous, but before he could offer a defense for floating to the toilet, Ollie jumped back in.

"This is serious, guys." Her tone was heavy and stern, like a curt teacher's. "Not only is Alexander Lochamire indexing our memories, but his technology is responsible for Freya's condition—and who knows how many others!"

"Keep it down, Ol." Chase gently grabbed her arm, but she jerked it away.

"Screw it. Let's go to the press now. This is unbelievable!"

"Ollie, we can't." Fletcher looked around the dining hall to ensure no one was eavesdropping. "If it was that easy, Mr. Lear would've—"

"I don't care about him, or the Ghosts, or any of it." Ollie's voice was now a low growl, which was far more intense than when she'd yelled. "Lochamire has to pay for what he did to Freya."

"And he will," Freya assured. "He'll pay for all of it. We just have to be smart about this so we don't blow our shot."

Ollie exhaled, reining in her emotions. She eventually returned to her food, and shortly thereafter Irene appeared. She took the seat between Ollie and Chase—her usually earnest expression replaced by a grim one.

"Monday's the big day, huh?"

Everyone nodded seriously.

"You gonna wish us good luck?" Chase ripped his roll into halves and tossed a piece into his mouth.

Irene forced a smile. "Actually, I have good news. I spoke with my great-uncle today." She leaned in, her voice hushed. "This week, they're enacting the first phase of the Task."

Everyone at the table stopped eating. Fletcher cleared his throat. "What day will we be needed?"

"He didn't say. He wants us to be ready this week to leave campus after lights-out. But he wouldn't tell me what day." She made eye contact with Freya, who briefly held her stare and then looked away.

Ollie raised her eyebrows. "Sorry, but how is that *good* news?"

"We do this knife for the dean on Monday, we help Mr. Lear expose Memory Frontier's dirty secrets, and then we get our lives back," Fletcher replied. "After this week, it'll all be over."

Underneath the table, Freya grabbed hold of Fletcher's hand.

"It'll all be over," Chase repeated, raising his soda. "Love the sound of that."

Irene stood. "I should eat. Be on alert this week. I'd pack an overnight bag and leave it by your bedside. I'll collect you guys when it's time." She met Freya's eyes a second time, momentarily, before heading toward the exit.

"Why don't we just skip out on Monday's knifing?" Chase asked as they all settled into their spots on the fallen tree beside Juniper Lake. Even though they were all bundled up to their chins, Fletcher still found the nighttime cold to be punishing. Across the lapping water, the distant Foxhole glowed like a lighthouse.

"You just spent almost an entire week learning how to pilot a helicopter," Ollie deadpanned. "And now you want to skip knifing Emilia's memory?"

Chase sniffed. "All I'm saying is, if we're helping the Ghosts reveal the man behind the curtain, why bother helping the dean?"

Ollie turned toward Chase. "Was that a *Wizard of Oz* reference?"

"It's groundbreaking cinema, Ol. *Groundbreaking.*"

"We should see the dean's last mission through," Fletcher said. He told them about his plan to use Monday's knifing as an opportunity to glean context clues about Mr. Lear, the Memory Ghosts, and his father's connection to all of it.

"Maybe we'll find some hint as to what exactly we're helping Mr. Lear steal from the Fold," Fletcher offered. "Plus, if we back out now, we raise all kinds of red flags. I'm sure Dean Mendelsohn and Dr. Sanders already suspect something's up."

He told them about the dean's surprising visit to his home.

Chase shook his head. "Dean M really leveled up his creepiness, didn't he?"

"Is there a way you could, like, see into the future?" Ollie asked Freya. "Find out what Mr. Lear wants us to help him steal?"

Freya said no, then explained, "Gemma said I can't summon the visions. I have to wait for them. But now I can anticipate them a little better, and when I have another one, I'll be more aware and alert than I have been in the past."

Ollie nodded, then interlocked arms with Freya. "I'm glad she was able to help you."

"Me too."

Chase shifted his weight on the log. "Did anyone else notice how Irene referred to the Ghosts' operation as 'the Task'?"

They nodded, then Ollie perked up. "Fletcher. That's part of the title of your dad's hollow book!"

"*The Listener, The Scrambler, The Seer, & The Task.*" Fletcher's heart beat fast.

"Just how long have they been planning this whole thing?" Chase whistled. "And what's the Task got to do with your old man's memory tape?"

"Yeah . . ." Fletcher's mind raced with questions about the rest of the title's meaning. What were a Listener, a Scrambler, and a Seer?

"Just think," Ollie said, crossing one leg over the other. "This time next year, this will all be behind us. Memory Frontier will have burned to the ground—figuratively and possibly literally. Your dad will be a free man, Fletcher, and we'll all be enrolled at, like, Cal State Fullerton or something."

"By that point, I'll have booked the lead in *at least* two feature films." Chase feigned choking back tears as he continued, "I'll probably even be looking at an Oscar nod."

"Please don't forget about us when you're famous," Freya said dryly. Fletcher and Ollie snickered.

"Hey, I don't control that." Chase held up his hands. "Memory Killer gonna take what Memory Killer gonna take."

Ollie reached across Freya and thumped Chase on the shoulder. "Don't joke about that!"

But Chase's flippant remark gave Fletcher pause. Their decision to help the Memory Ghosts uncover Alexander Lochamire's secrets would come at a cost. *Artificial recall is the only thing keeping hyper memory loss at bay.* He stared out at the rippling lake. *Once Memory Frontier is brought down, who's going to protect us from Memory Killer? Is Lochamire's corporation actually a necessary evil?*

"You good?" Freya whispered.

"Hm? Oh. Yeah."

"Got kinda introspective on me." She winked.

"I'm known for that."

"He's indulging in nostalgia," Chase said, laughing, spreading his arms wide as if to hug Juniper Lake. "This might be the last time we ever hang in this very spot."

Ollie shushed him. "Don't say that."

"He's right," Freya said heavily. "Once we help Mr. Lear steal this mysterious evidence from the Fold, the trial will be shut down. Foxtail Academy will have to close its doors."

Chase's laughter tapered off.

"No Memory Frontier means no artificial recall." Freya leaned against Fletcher. "And that means no more Reflectors, either."

They sat with their thoughts. The reality of their situation robbed them of mirth like a greedy thief.

Eventually, Fletcher asked what they were all thinking: "What happens with Memory Killer after we bring down Memory Frontier?"

❖ ❖ ❖

Monday morning, after Fletcher showered and dressed, he retrieved his *Raiders of the Lost Ark* lunchbox from its hiding place in the closet. While Chase got ready in the bathroom, Fletcher thumbed through his Memory Killer File. The folded pieces of paper contained the many questions he'd considered about artificial recall, Memory Frontier, and—of course—Memory Killer.

One entry caught his attention, something he'd completely forgotten about: the woman in the car at the traffic light, whom Fletcher had witnessed getting besieged by Memory Killer.

He reread his own handwriting, feeling a pins-and-needles sensation swirling in his gut. The experience of reading something he'd written—something he'd witnessed—with no recollection of it was . . . out-of-body, to say the least. He could see the imagery, smell the cigarette smoke and ocean salt on the air, hear the honking horns. And yet that scene didn't feel like a memory. It was like his mind's eye plugged in the details based solely on the words on the page, not from his being able to recall that night. It was similar to reading fiction and dressing the stage—casting the characters—in his head.

Fletcher sighed. He felt lost, as if all he'd managed to do over the past few months was accrue even *more* questions. He went to fold the page when one detail caught his eye.

The woman in the passenger seat removed the Restorey receivers from her temples, having presumably just finished artificial recall, and that's when her eyes grayed over.

Fletcher sat with this, desperately trying to recall what this must have looked like from his vantage point on his motorcycle.

Memory Killer struck after *she finished artificial recall.*

In the case of this woman, it was almost as if Memory Killer was a symptom of artificial recall . . . almost as if artificial recall *caused* the woman's eye discoloration.

Before he could mull this over further, he heard a knock at the door. Fletcher quickly put his Memory Killer File away and stood. Chase poked his head out of the bathroom, his hair dripping wet from the shower.

Fletcher shrugged at his roommate and went to answer the door.

It was Dean Mendelsohn. "Mr. Cohen. May I accompany you to the Foxhole?"

❖ ❖ ❖

"Is everything all right?" Fletcher squeezed his hands beneath his armpits to combat the cold as he and the dean crossed the grounds toward the dining hall.

"I wanted to check in with you ahead of this afternoon's mission." Dean Mendelsohn procured his orange pill bottle from his jacket pocket, popped two capsules, and swallowed. "So. How are we feeling?"

"Um, good, I guess. Just ready to get it over with." *And not just the knifing of Emilia Vanguard's memory,* he added to himself with a shiver.

The dean grunted. Fletcher could feel Dean Mendelsohn struggling to speak, as if his mouth caged his thoughts.

Something's up . . . Is he onto us?

Eventually, the dean spoke with uncharacteristic fragility to his tone. "You know, it wasn't my call to have the memories of you four wiped from the student body and faculty."

Despite the near-freezing temperature, Fletcher's blood boiled. "So it's true. No one remembers us?"

The dean's silence confirmed it. Fletcher swore, then demanded to know why.

"When the administration learned that you and your friends successfully knifed Malcolm Heckman's memory, you effectively became their weapon. I had to fight to keep you enrolled at Foxtail; Dr. Grondahl *insisted* that you be transferred to an offsite military base for testing and further knifing. The administration feared that your absence from school during your training and then sudden return after fall break would draw too much attention. The compromise for keeping you here was twofold: hide your identity from your teachers and peers, and have you train new recruits."

"*Too much attention?*" Fletcher gritted his teeth. "What did you think would happen?" But as he watched the side of Dean Mendelsohn's face, he suddenly understood what the dean wasn't saying.

"You hadn't thought that far ahead," Fletcher whispered. "Because the powers that be didn't actually think memory knifing was possible. Your whole operation in the woods behind campus is a gamble that Alexander Lochamire wasn't sure would pay off."

The dean stiffened. Up ahead, the Foxhole came into view beneath knotty gray clouds. "Once the government got involved, once Dr. Grondahl was appointed to oversee a new phase of operations, everything changed."

Slowly, Fletcher began to see things through the dean's eyes: Alexander Lochamire and Memory Frontier hired him to stop the Memory Ghosts via this great experiment—knifing. The dean's motive was political and personal: help stop supposed terrorists from wreaking havoc on society, *and* potentially find a way to rescue his son, Daniel. Dean Mendelsohn was earnest, albeit tragically misguided.

But Alexander Lochamire had to involve the government, Fletcher realized, *because the lie about the Memory Ghosts being terrorists necessitated federal engagement.* In doing so, though, he'd introduced bureaucratic complications and made things increasingly difficult for Dean Mendelsohn.

The dean was likely further from rescuing Daniel than ever before.

They reached the entrance to the Foxhole, and Dean Mendelsohn cleared his throat. "Dr. Sanders has been installed as Memory Frontier's new chief executive officer. The board approved it over the weekend. Apparently, with Lochamire's waning health, he's no longer of sound mind."

"Wait. Why was *she* promoted to CEO?"

The dean's eyes shrank into slits. "Because she's Lochamire's daughter."

Fletcher's mouth fell open. *What?*

"Understand this, Fletcher." Was that the first time the dean had called him by his first name? "Dr. Sanders is one of the most ambitious individuals I've ever worked with in my twenty-plus-year career."

That was saying something, but why was he telling Fletcher this?

"She has much to prove as the new leader of the globe's largest conglomerate." The dean looked out across campus, the age lines around his eyes deepened by the morning light. "Some will question her qualifications, suggest it was merely nepotism that got her there. And she's out to prove them wrong."

Fletcher nodded, though he was still unsure why the dean felt it necessary to share this.

"Just stay alert, all right?" And then Dean Mendelsohn took his leave. Fletcher's head was spinning as he ducked into the welcoming warmth of the Foxhole.

❖ ❖ ❖

After classes that afternoon, Fletcher and his friends held hands as they trekked in a line through the forest toward Dean Mendelsohn's bunker. Fletcher told them about his pre-breakfast conversation with the dean, and he did his best to field their many questions.

He was just as confused as they were.

They approached the white cinderblock structure. The large sliding door cranked open, and Dr. Sanders stepped outside wearing a hollow smile. Both of her eyes were bloodshot.

"Afternoon, everyone."

No one replied.

"Right. Well, why don't you head inside. We haven't a moment to spare."

Fletcher nodded and led the way. Dr. Sanders reached out and stopped Freya by the arm. "Actually, Freya, would you mind hanging back for a moment?"

"Um, sure." She shrugged. Fletcher, Chase, and Ollie reluctantly went to change into their jumpsuits.

49

FREYA IZQUIERDO

Dr. Sanders holds her hands behind her back and walks away from the bunker, forcing me to follow.

After only a few paces, she turns and faces me. I order myself not to stare at the deep redness in her eyes, but I find it nearly impossible to look away.

She asks, "How is your essay coming along?"

"Oh. Um . . ." Does she really want to talk about assignments right now? "I've written three pages so far. Feeling pretty good, I suppose."

"That's wonderful to hear."

We regard one another for a long moment. My curiosity quickly morphs into anxiety. *Is she baiting me for something?*

"Things have been so busy this quarter I haven't been able to ask you about your half-memory episodes." She reaches out and rubs my arm. Her hand feels stiff with coldness.

"I guess it's good that I haven't had one since the Reflector trial started."

"Is that so?"

I nod.

"You know, in my continued research of the phenomenon you described, I've not been able to locate a single other recorded incident." Dr. Sanders's lips curve into a half smile. "And Memory Frontier keeps extensive data on the MeReaders."

What is she getting at? The anxiety in my chest blossoms into panic. *Does she know about my gift?*

She drops her voice to a whisper, even though no one is within earshot. "But we *do* have other records. Certain individuals have developed peculiar aftereffects. Like, say, visions . . . of the future."

"Huh." *She* is *onto me.* "That's crazy, though. Right? I mean, people can't see into the future."

"Are you *certain* you're okay?" She moves her hand from my arm to my forehead, as if to read my temperature. "You look unwell."

"Just nervous about today, I guess." I swallow. "Ready for all this to be over. Ready for the Memory Ghosts to finally get locked up."

I walk past her and head toward the bunker. She calls out before I step inside. "Freya. How was your Thanksgiving break?"

I turn around and say as confidently as possible, "Great. I had peaceful, dreamless sleep the entire week."

She blinks, then her empty smile widens. "Good. Oh, and don't worry. There's no snow in Emilia Vanguard's memory."

"Um . . . ?" A tingle runs down my spine.

"You know." She steps forward, joining me by the door. "Because a few weeks ago you were worried about knifing a memory with snow in it. You made us promise to tell you if there was snow. Have you forgotten?"

I curse myself inwardly. "No, no. I just . . . I have bad memories of winter."

"It's funny. I didn't think Long Beach got snow."

"I—"

Dean Mendelsohn calls me over. "We're ready for you, Ms. Izquierdo."

I avoid Dr. Sanders's red eyes as I head into the facility.

❖ ❖ ❖

I breathe out slowly through my nose as the nurse finishes attaching my IV catheter. As she starts applying the electrode stickers to my head, Dean Mendelsohn appears beside the Restorey with a clipboard in hand.

"This is it. This is what you've been preparing for for *weeks*." He holds the clipboard behind his back and scans the room. All six chairs recline simultaneously, the gears humming softly. "It's the most pivotal memory knife you'll execute. And hopefully it's the *last* memory knife."

Fletcher and I trade subtle glances.

"We believe you'll arrive seconds before Emilia Vanguard drives her Audi Quattro onto the interstate." The dean turns toward Chase and Sade. "Ms. Van der Merwe, Mr. Hall. Don't dally. Manifest those helicopters as *soon* as you can. You'll then track Emilia from the sky and locate the unmarked helicopter that's waiting at the rendezvous point. Get there quickly. Mr. Villa and Ms. Trang—you two will board Emilia's helicopter and learn the contents of the Ghosts' secret message. Remember: this part is essential to the whole mission. Having two stowaways should increase the probability of successfully intercepting that message, which we believe holds the key to finding the Ghosts."

I perk up. "What about me and Fletcher?"

The dean meets my eyes. "You two will stay back with Mr. Hall and Ms. Van der Merwe respectively. Someone needs to be with them in case Memory Killer strikes."

Oh, right . . .

Dr. Sanders glances at Rhett briefly, then clears her throat. "Any other questions?"

"Yeah," Chase says, chortling. "Where's Doc Grondahl? Figured he'd be here with a party hat and champagne."

The dean opens his mouth, but Dr. Sanders is quicker: "In DC, Mr. Hall. Since we're closing in on the terrorists, he's working closely with the Federal Bureau of Investigation and the Department of Defense. Memory Frontier, and our wonderful staff here, are perfectly capable of overseeing this final mission."

I find that answer troubling. It means that somehow Dr. Sanders has managed to push out the bureaucrats and reclaim control of this knifing. How did she manage to do *that*? How did she convince Dr. Grondahl—a man persistent to a fault—and the administration to back off on the day we've been building toward for *weeks*? I force this question aside as the nurse preps my sedative.

"Good luck, all." Dean Mendelsohn gives the go-ahead nod and queues up Emilia Vanguard's memory tape. I start to feel the warm, prickly sensation of the sedative expanding through my body.

I see Dr. Sanders walk over to Rhett's chair and bend over to whisper something to him, but the last thing I hear are her words from earlier, echoing in my mind in a chilling loop: *Certain individuals have developed peculiar aftereffects . . .*

The brief excursion through the neon lights is a dizzying affair. It's an overwhelming, all-encompassing blur—something I will *never* get used to. All six of us are pulled through the cyclonic colors, through its core, and spit out onto the side of the freeway ramp. We all land unevenly; Ollie and Rhett actually lose their footing.

In the memory, we are greeted by sunlight, a perfect blue sky, and a concentrated dose of Emilia's daring disposition. Her energy permeates the scene. It hangs in the air like humidity but somehow *funnels* into my head, informing me just how determined—just how intrepid—this Emilia Vanguard is. And rather than push against her energy, I *pull* it. I let it empower me.

Look alive, Sade says, pointing. The black Quattro races by with the windows down. A Beastie Boys song roars through the stereo.

Let's see what you got, Chase! Ollie shouts as we all back up and give him and Sade room. They stand with about twenty-five yards between them. Chase closes his eyes and clenches his fists; Sade keeps her eyes open, but she looks like she's working through a breathing exercise. After only a few seconds, we all marvel as huge metallic panels whip through the air and link together on the patch of grass behind Chase and Sade. In no time, two smoke-gray helicopters have formed. The military-grade aircrafts are intimidating, formidable specimens. Vehicular forces to be reckoned with.

Chase and Sade exhale and then clamber into their respective cockpits. Dean Mendelsohn said he wanted me and Fletcher to hang back with Chase and Sade in their helicopters while Rhett and Ollie boarded Emilia's. But given my recent vision, I have no intention of separating from Fletcher while we're knifing. I understand the risk in sticking with him, as it could increase the chances of making my premonition come true.

But I simply can't let him out of my sight. No matter what.

I grab Fletcher's hand and lead him toward Chase's aircraft. Ollie darts toward Sade's. Overhead, the blades begin to rotate—whirring louder and louder with increased velocity. After boarding, I click my double seatbelt into place as Chase turns over his shoulder to check on us, a pair of beige aviation headphones materializing on his ears. Fletcher gives him the thumbs-up, and at the last second Rhett boards our aircraft too.

Fletcher and I swap a glance. Before we can say anything, we slowly rise into the air beside Sade's helicopter.

You guys impressed yet? Chase asks, reaching his desired elevation and then moving us forward over the stretch of interstate. Because we perceive rather than hear his words, his jovial voice is clear beneath the deafening helicopter blades and rushing wind.

I'm just waiting for you to play Wagner's "Ride of the Valkyries," Rhett jokes from across the cab, looking out. The tops of trees and rolling hills expand toward the edges of the glitching memory scene.

I know this isn't real, I know we're in someone's memory, but vertigo still seizes me. My stomach lurches when Chase gradually angles the helicopter east. I spy Emilia's black car below, darting recklessly across the freeway.

You good? Fletcher reaches across the seat and takes my hand.

I nod, then catch Rhett watching us, his expression unreadable. He swallows, then looks away.

Fletcher, I say, trying to whisper. *Look at me.*

His eyes are still a vibrant green. No sign of Memory Killer yet.

What's wrong?

I hold his face. *Nothing, I just . . .* I glance at Rhett; he seems distracted by something outside. *Are you picking up on anything yet—anything about the Ghosts or their mission?*

Fletcher closes his eyes. *It's hard . . . most of Emilia's memory has to do with her determination. Her mind hasn't seemed to wander yet.*

Fletcher, listen to me closely.

He opens his eyes. I know Rhett can hear what I'm saying, but the stakes are too high—I need to warn Fletcher.

At some point, we're both going to get struck by Memory Killer during this knife.

Wait . . . what?

I'm not sure when it happens, but it will, so we need to remain alert.

Why didn't you say something sooner? His breathing turns to quick, sharp pants. *What happens if we can't anchor each other?*

I have a plan, I tell him earnestly. *We needed to go through with this knife. It's like you said: if we'd have skipped out, Dr. Sanders and the dean—*

Rhett starts to gag, cutting me off midthought. His eyes roll back violently, and somehow he manages to unfasten his seatbelt. He collapses onto all fours, dry-heaving.

What the hell? Fletcher yanks off his own seatbelt and gets onto the floor of the cab, gingerly placing his hand on Rhett's back. *Breathe, Rhett, breathe.*

Yo, everything okay back there? Chase asks, keeping his eyes straight ahead.

Before Fletcher can reply, before I can get out of my seat and see if he needs my help, the unthinkable happens: Rhett lurches up, grabs Fletcher by the collar of his jumpsuit, and throws him out of the helicopter.

50

FLETCHER COHEN

Everything happened so quickly, so unexpectedly, that Fletcher never saw it coming. He was rolling out of the cab and into the air. In a scrambled, frantic move, he threw his hands out in front of him at the last possible second, somehow managing to grab hold of the helicopter's landing skid.

He clung to the metal bar, the world rushing beneath his feet from a nauseating height.

Fletcher!

Freya's head appeared a second later. She completely disregarded that Rhett was still at her back as she bent over the lip of the cab with an outstretched hand.

Fletcher shouted when Rhett kicked Freya in the ribs.

She tumbled, feet over head, but was able to grab hold of the bar beside Fletcher before it was too late.

They dangled in the air, refusing to look down as the fear inside them swelled.

Guys! Chase screamed. *Someone tell me what's going on!*

These two are traitors, Rhett said, getting down on one knee, the wind tousling his red hair. *That's what's going on.*

You're insane! Fletcher bellowed, boring his eyes into Rhett's. *Pull us back up now!*

Chase's panicked voice grew louder. *That's it, I'm landing.*

Fletcher, don't let the fear overtake you. None of this is real! Freya pleaded. *I think this is how Memory Killer grabs hold of us . . . this fear of falling draws it—*

She gasped. Fletcher knew what that meant. His eyes had turned gray. His body was slowly beginning to deteriorate, like dimming starlight at dawn.

And so was Freya's.

You two should guard your thoughts better, Rhett said coldly, hardening his gaze at Fletcher. *Otherwise, someone might overhear you thinking about your allegiance to the Ghosts.*

Fletcher understood immediately: that night he and Chase and Ollie had snuck into the senior lounge after hours, Rhett had been sitting next to him on the couch as Fletcher was deep in thought, ruminating on Mr. Lear, the hollow book, and—

You can read our thoughts? Freya asked through gritted teeth, the metal bar slipping from her fingers with each passing breath.

You think you're the only one who's been endowed with a gift? Rhett shook his head. *What a myopic view of the world! Oh well. It's all moot now that you'll both be stuck inside this memory forever.*

And then, as the last bits of Fletcher's and Freya's hands faded, they slipped from the landing skid. They raced toward the ground in a terrifying free fall. The world careened top over bottom, top over bottom.

Fletcher tried to scream as he clawed through the air for Freya's body, but he had no voice. Next, he lost his vision. Then his hearing.

There was only falling.

Deep within the memory that wasn't *his* memory, Fletcher lost all his physical faculties. The treacherous dive toward earth wrought an unbearable fear that rendered him helpless. In an instant, the fear of hitting the ground was swallowed up by the even greater fear of imprisonment—of being trapped inside a memory loop.

It's over. We lost. We're lost forever . . .

51

FREYA IZQUIERDO

I jerk my eyes open.

My chest rises with distressed gasps.

I'm on the side of the freeway, at the memory's start, standing on the small embankment. Fletcher and everyone else materialize around me.

No . . . My mind is spinning out of control. *It's happened . . .*

Beside me, Ollie shouts, *Let's see what you got, Chase!*

I mean to scream. To shout to the others and explain what's happening. But I'm frozen in shock.

Fletcher turns to me, his gray eyes bulging. *We can find a way out of this, Freya. We just have to think!*

I mean to nod, to tell him he's right.

The words never make it off my tongue.

C'mon, Fletcher says, taking my hand. *I have an idea!*

He pulls me along with the others toward the newly formed

helicopters. Chase and Sade are already in their respective cockpits. Just like the first time, Ollie climbs into Sade's, and Fletcher and I board Chase's aircraft with Rhett on our heels.

Our helicopter begins its ascension, and once we're nearly twenty feet off the ground, Fletcher leaps to his feet. He pulls off Rhett's seatbelt in a mad dash and then casts him out of the cab.

I stifle a scream as I watch Rhett's body tumble earthward, where he will smack into the ground and be promptly ejected from Emilia Vanguard's memory.

Or so I think . . .

Instead of Rhett vanishing, the world around us *tips* . . . everything spins upside down and turns inside out, like some black hole is sucking us *into* ourselves.

The next thing I know I'm standing on the side of the freeway.

Emilia Vanguard's black Audi Quattro whips by, the smell of burning gasoline trailing in its wake.

Let's see what you got, Chase! Ollie shouts, her hands cupped around her mouth.

Beside me, Fletcher curses. *Okay, so that didn't work. Got any ideas?*

Why don't we just try the original method of anchoring? I whisper, my hands shaking uncontrollably. Fletcher says that's a good idea, and once Chase and Sade manifest their helicopters and we board, we immediately set to work recalling the same memory.

The pier, I tell him, pressing my forehead against his. *Our first kiss.*

We leave our eyes open so we can keep Rhett in our peripheral vision.

After a while, Fletcher speaks. *I'm there. Right now. I can smell the ocean.*

Me too.

We take control of our panting, drawing in measured breaths together. In this moment of sharing the same oxygen, of sharing the same memory from the Belmont Veterans Memorial Pier, nothing happens.

Absolutely nothing.

Except that Rhett slowly begins to remove his seatbelt. Fletcher sets his jaw and leaps to his feet.

Fletcher, wait—!

It's too late. He wrestles Rhett to the floor of the cab and pummels him. I throw myself on top of Fletcher, trying with all my strength to pry him off of Rhett.

What's going on back there? Chase shouts, chancing a glance over his shoulder. When he does this, his hands lightly pull on the cyclic control.

The effect is immediate. Fletcher, Rhett, and I roll over one another haphazardly and fall out of the cab, plummeting helplessly toward—

❖ ❖ ❖

The side of the freeway.

Emilia Vanguard's Audi Quattro whizzes by.

Fletcher pulls at his hair and shrieks.

Okay, okay . . . His gray eyes look crazed and desperate, like he's on the verge of accepting our doom. I have to admit, everything's looking bleak.

How about this, I offer, jogging toward Ollie.

Let's see what you—!

I cut her off and pull her toward me and Fletcher. I tell her the situation.

No . . . She looks like she wants to cry; her bottom lip quivers and her eyes mist. *Does that mean . . . am I stuck too? And Chase?*

I don't think so, I say, piecing my theory together as I go: *I think you're just, like, an echo of the real Ollie. Fletcher and I have already reset three times, and both times before now you just repeated your actions.*

Behind her, Chase and Sade manifest their helicopters.

Come with us, I say. *I have an idea.* We race toward Chase's helicopter and I push Rhett aside. Fletcher, Ollie, and I hop into the cab.

What are you doing? Rhett demands, adjusting his glasses.

Change of plans. I point toward Sade. *You ride with her.*

Rhett flushes. Before he can argue, Sade's shouting at him—urging him to just come aboard before they waste more time. He fumes but dashes toward her helicopter nonetheless.

Ol, check it out, I'm piloting a helicopter! Chase raises us off the ground with the cyclic control, where we hover for a few seconds before taking off after Emilia's black Quattro.

What are you thinking, Freya? Fletcher bounces his hands on his knees, more tense than I've ever seen him.

The three of us. I grab one of Ollie's hands and one of Fletcher's. *We need to try to share a memory.*

They both nod their heads eagerly.

Ollie says, *Chase's dance routine. At the Foxy Ladies dance.*

We close our eyes while holding hands, likely looking like we're performing some kind of seance in the back of the helicopter.

Fletcher chuckles nervously. *He was so into his routine.* In his cracking voice, I hear him tempering his tears—sobs that threaten to burst forth from a weakening dam.

Ollie agrees. *His bell-bottoms were ridiculous. It's like he had two balloons under there.*

We all snicker, and I play back the memory of Chase dancing in the Foxhole over and over again until—

I hear a loud *whoosh!* in my ears, great gusts of wind rushing past me, and when I open my eyes I find myself standing on the side of the freeway yet again.

Fletcher screams into his hands until a vein bulges in his neck.

The memory must reset at the exact *time Rhett first threw us out of the cab,* he guesses, pacing on the grass in front of me. *That means we only get like five or six minutes before the memory resets. Freya . . . what do we do?*

Behind him, Ollie shouts, *Let's see what you got, Chase!* and then he and Sade set to work manifesting the helicopters.

I plop down on the ground and hug my knees. *I don't know, Fletcher. Is this it? Are Fletcher and I forever trapped in this endless, torturous cycle?*

He bends down and hugs me, weeping quietly into my shoulder.

I hold him, gripping so tightly I can feel the tips of my fingers digging into his back. Only it's not *actually* his back. The real Fletcher Cohen is lying in Dean Mendelsohn's bunker, unconscious and vulnerable. A prisoner in his own mind.

Just like me.

Guys, let's go! Chase shouts from the cockpit of his helicopter. The rotor blades begin to spin. *Now's not really the time to stare into each other's eyes dreamily!*

Fletcher pulls away. *I can't stand the thought of us dreaming this nightmare on repeat . . .*

My breath stalls in my throat. *Wait.*

I'm serious, you two! We need to move! Chase presses us. But I ignore him.

It's something Ramon used to say, I explain to Fletcher, getting to my feet. *In a world where memories are like currency, dreams can be a complicated business.*

That's . . . cryptic. We sprint toward the helicopter and pull ourselves into the cab.

He always talked about his problems with the MeReaders, how it wasn't clear how the technology parsed dreams from memories.

What does that have to do with—?

Give me your hands. He obeys without question. I glance at

Rhett. He fastens his seatbelt, watching us with an inquisitive stare. *Fletcher . . . think about a dream of yours.*

I . . . what?

A dream! Something you've thought about for a long, long—

But, Freya, how can you recall something I've dreamed if you never dreamed it? And vice versa?

I shake my head.

No . . . not something you've dreamed while sleeping. I squeeze his hands firmly. *I mean a dream . . . like an aspiration.*

52

FLETCHER COHEN

Fletcher had no idea where to start. What Freya was asking felt incredibly far-fetched. Yet given how grim things were, what did he have to lose?

So Fletcher acquiesced.

I . . . I just want to leave this place, Freya. His voice quavered considerably, tears threatening to reemerge. *I want to wake up beside you in the facility and hold you, for real.*

I want that too. They heard Rhett shifting his weight in his seat. The seconds were ticking by and soon he would attack Fletcher—again. *And . . . and I want you to take me to prom, like a normal high school couple.*

He laughed softly, letting loose fresh tears. Even though he was only crying in his head, Fletcher felt the sensation of warm teardrops running over his cheekbones and onto his hands. *Yeah, prom. But we ditch the dance early with Ollie and Chase, and—*

Head to our secret spot wearing our dresses and tuxes. Now Freya was crying too. But it was a gentle conflict of weeping and laughing. The laughter-tears of being reunited with someone who was lost. Fletcher pulled her closer, their eyes remaining shut. He could feel his rapid pulse stabilizing.

They heard Rhett unclicking his seatbelt.

I take you by the hand, Fletcher said, almost meekly. *We go to the water's edge.*

We slow dance. And since prom is in the spring, maybe the fireflies are back.

Yeah, maybe they are.

They heard Rhett getting to his feet.

I love you, Fletcher. Her words permeated the scene: they filled the cab, they drowned out the roaring helicopter blades, they filled his chest with a sunlit warmth that triggered gooseflesh. Fletcher was certain the goose bumps were there—even on his *actual* body in Dean Mendelsohn's bunker.

He swallowed, trying to compose himself. Because in truth, the words had been there for weeks . . . possibly months. But he'd been too nervous to utter them before this moment.

Now the words passed over his lips in a softly exhaled reply, like he was providing harmony for a whispered duet. *I love you, Freya Izquierdo.*

53

FREYA IZQUIERDO

Those five words are the last thing I hear before a blast of hot, colorful light penetrates my closed eyelids.

Everything that happens next is frantic and frenzied. I bat my eyes open. It takes a second for my vision to acclimate to my surroundings, but I'm in the bunker. Two nurses scramble toward me as I wheeze and writhe awake. Fletcher is rousing from the memory loop, too, and he starts to rip off his electrode stickers with trembling hands. Chase is already awake and standing beside his chair. He's being held back by two men and screaming and pointing at Rhett, who is still lying motionless in his chair—his eyelids faintly fluttering. It appears that Ollie and Sade are still knifing too.

The fear that I experienced in the memory loop, the one that had crushed me into submission, is gone.

I scan the facility as the nurses remove my IV. I try to spot either Dean Mendelsohn or Dr. Sanders, but before I can locate them in the pandemonium, a loud explosion throws us to the ground, and we cower under our chairs.

An imposing armored vehicle has rammed through the sliding door. Huge chunks of cinderblock and bits of wood spray across the floor; the sliding door, now crumpled and bent, lies on the ground like a drawbridge over a moat.

A high-pitched Klaxon shrieks.

All of the adults scatter.

Dust and fractured light settle over the room.

The Restorey continues to hum beneath the bedlam.

Zayne Olson and Alana Khan emerge from the vehicle, racing toward us like firefighters storming a burning building.

I scramble to my feet as Alana locates Ollie. Alana whips out a small device from her trench coat and unspools a cable from it. Next, she connects a single electrode sticker to Ollie's forehead and works the black gadget, which looks like a Restorey that's undergone custom modifications.

Beyond her, I watch Zayne peel off a huge wraparound sticker that encased the armored vehicle. Underneath this are the distinct red, orange, and white decals of an ambulance. There are even LED light panels and blue Star of Life stickers.

While Zayne works to transform the vehicle from battering ram to ambulance, he urges the three of us to head into the back of the vehicle. Instead, Fletcher stumbles toward me and throws his arms around my neck. His face, hair, and shoulders are coated in white drywall dust. On his cheeks I see small lines over the grit where he's been crying.

I pull him against me tightly. "We did it."

"Yeah, but we're not out of the woods yet."

We pull away as Alana presses a button on her device. Zayne nods and cautiously removes the electrode stickers that were connecting Ollie to the dean's giant Restorey. Then he scoops Ollie up.

She remains still and unconscious in his arms as he whisks her away from the chair. We follow them at a sprint. Alana flings open the armored vehicle's back doors and then heads for the driver's seat. Before I enter the van, I chance a glance at Sade, whose eyes are still sealed shut as she lies in the knifing chair. I say a quick prayer on her behalf and then climb inside.

In no time, Chase has helped Zayne load Ollie into the vehicle. They gently lay her down on the floor as Fletcher swings the doors shut. The armored vehicle lurches, then reverses out of the facility. I hear heavy pieces of debris spilling off the roof as we move.

"Is she going to be okay?" Chase asks, brushing some hair out of Ollie's face.

"I . . . hope so." Zayne whips out an inhaler and takes a shot of the medicine. He finishes his thought with his stomach sucked in. "We've never pulled someone out of a knifing before. This device"—he gestures toward the small tech that Ollie is connected to—"is an Interceptor, but it's just a prototype and—"

"You *hope* so?" Chase's face reddens. "What happens if she isn't?"

Before Zayne can reply, we hear a round of erratic gunshots outside the vehicle. Alana swerves, and Fletcher, Chase, and I drop to our stomachs. Zayne gets to his feet, unboxes a stethoscope from an emergency first-aid kit, and begins to check Ollie's vitals.

More gunshots.

More wild driving. The ride turns considerably bumpy, and I picture Alana racing through the woods toward civilization while narrowly avoiding gunfire. I hear a loud *clack!* and figure Alana just clipped her side mirror on a tree.

"How did you know where to find us?" Fletcher asks after the gunshots taper off.

"Freya here gave Irene a map." Zayne moves on to Chase, checking his pulse and heart rate.

Fletcher gives me a reproachful look. "Oh, she did?"

"I had a vision of us getting attacked by Memory Killer," I explain to him and Chase as I climb back into a sitting position. "I had this feeling I couldn't shake . . . like something bad was going down."

"I guess it's good you tipped off Irene then." Chase wipes the sweat from his brow with his hands. "Could it have hurt to tip us off too?"

"I didn't want to spook anyone. We needed to go through the motions of knifing and not let Dr. Sanders think that—"

"*Freya.*" Fletcher scoots next to me and hugs me again. "I trust you."

"Yeah, well." Chase sighs. "It appears your instincts were right. There's no telling what Dr. Sanders would've done with your unconscious bodies once the knifing mission was complete. How do you guys think she got Dr. Grondahl off her back?"

"I suspect she lied to him about the date of the mission." Zayne pulls a pager out of his pocket and glances at the display. "She knows we're closing in on Memory Frontier. She's trying to take back control."

We all nod. I watch Ollie, who still hasn't so much as stirred this entire car ride. I try not to panic—I try to convince myself she'll be fine.

"What happened after Rhett pushed us out of the helicopter?" Fletcher asks.

I'm not sure I want the answer.

Chase curses. "Rhett manifested a knife and held it to my throat. Told me to pull the helicopter up beside the one waiting for Emilia. So I did. Only, after Rhett leapt into the other cab, I backed up my helicopter and tried to sabotage the whole mission by crashing into Emilia's helicopter."

I trade a glance with Fletcher.

"Yeah, well, I wasn't thinking rationally!" Chase continues. "Obviously, the results were disastrous. Emilia's aircraft didn't budge a hair. But the impact sent me catapulting backward, where I crashed into a stand of trees in a fiery blaze of glory. Last thing I saw before I was ejected was Emilia scaling the rope ladder as her ride glided toward the horizon."

We sit in silence for a moment. Zayne punches a few buttons on the device that's hooked up to Ollie.

"The worst part," Chase says ruefully, "is if I had just called Rhett's bluff and let him 'kill' me, we'd have *both* been ejected from the memory tape after I crashed. I should've just hovered in place . . . let the edges of the memory scene claim us both. Instead, Rhett's still in there, doing Dr. Sanders's dirty work." He shakes his head, then swears again—louder this time.

Fletcher asks, "What happened next?"

"I came to. Saw that you two hadn't woken up, which told me you were stuck in a memory loop. I'd seen you fall toward the freeway. I charged after Rhett, but Dr. Sanders had her staffers restrain me. Then she got a call, and she and the dean disappeared outside. It was around that time you guys started waking up."

I hear the vehicle's sirens start to blare. Then the drive levels out, and I can tell we're on a paved road now.

"Where are we headed?" I ask Zayne.

"Colorado. Though where *in* Colorado I can't say for sure. But Alana knows."

Chase rolls his eyes. "You guys make a game of withholding details from one another?"

"It's for everyone's protection." Zayne unzips a duffel and divvies out water bottles to everyone. "Our memories are precious, vulnerable things. We must take precautions."

I take a long swig of lukewarm water. "What's in Colorado?"

"Our halfway point." Zayne stands and stretches. "We'll regroup with Mr. Lear before traveling to Alden to complete the Task."

"Yay." Chase reclines, careful not to accidentally nudge Ollie.

After a few moments of smooth driving, we feel the armored vehicle slow to a stop. Zayne checks his digital wristwatch, then cocks an eyebrow—clearly confused. A second later the back doors fling open. Alana stands on the road, panting and bleeding from her left shoulder.

I gasp, watching as Zayne leaps into action.

"It looks worse than it is," she tells us once Zayne sets to work with the alcohol and gauze. She peels back the torn fabric on her shirt, fully exposing the bloody injury. "It was just a graze." She grimaces as Zayne cleans her wound with steady hands. I watch, unable to look away—feeling the cool, stinging burn of the antiseptic as it washes over Alana's gash.

"Who was shooting at us?" Chase asks, paling at the sight of all the blood.

"Dr. Sanders's staff." Alana gnaws on her lip as Zayne finishes. "Apparently, she armed her scientists. If they'd been properly trained to use a firearm, I'd have been killed in moments."

I swallow a quarter-sized knot.

"I should drive." Zayne starts to climb out of the vehicle, but Alana holds him back with her good arm.

"I'm fine. Just get me the Tylenol. We need to keep moving, and I'm the only one who knows our destination."

An hour or so later, Ollie stirs from her unconscious state. She's a little dizzy, confused, and ravenous. Zayne immediately fetches her water, and while she drinks, he rechecks her vitals. Fletcher, Chase, and I take turns filling her in.

When we finish, I ask her, "What did *you* see in Emilia Vanguard's memory?"

Ollie rubs her temples. "I definitely didn't see you guys getting thrown out of Chase's cab! Sade got her helicopter pretty close to the one that was waiting for Emilia, and when I jumped into the cab . . ." She turns to Zayne. "I saw Malcolm Heckman in there, waiting."

Zayne nods. He pulls a handful of snack bars out of his duffel and passes them out while he explains. "Transference is like delivering a message during a relay. Think of the messages like a baton. Mr. Lear needed to get information to an important recipient, so it was handed off to multiple runners before eventually reaching its destination."

"You guys went through a lot of trouble, and it was all for naught." Ollie rips open her snack. "Memory Frontier still intercepted your message. Once Rhett joined me in the cab, he pushed me aside and started to memorize the contents of the note. He's probably waking up right now and relaying it to—"

"Alexander Lochamire is too late." Zayne zips up his bag. "The Task is in full motion."

"First order of business when we arrive in Colorado?" Chase finishes off the last bite of his snack bar and tosses the wrapper into the corner. "Burning these jumpsuits."

"While I love that idea," Fletcher says, holding up his water bottle, "these are the only clothes we have with us."

"Actually." Zayne points to the bench Fletcher and I are sitting on. We stand so he can flip open the seat, revealing a storage compartment. I see our overnight bags and my leaden heart lifts. In my backpack, I stored my brother's keepsakes, along with my photo album and the journal Gemma gifted to me. And I'm glad to see that Ollie and the boys took Irene seriously when she told us to have our things ready to go at a moment's notice.

"Irene collected these for you," Zayne explains as Ollie and Chase rush over and gratefully gather their bags. We all take inventory of our things, and for a while, no one speaks. The only sound comes from the scratching of pen to paper as Zayne writes something down in a tiny notebook.

"I still can't believe that Rhett could read our minds this whole time." Fletcher clutches his backpack in his lap and leans his head against the wall. "Makes you wonder what else he *overheard*."

I shake my head, teeth gritted. "I just . . . *why* would he help Dr. Sanders?"

Chase sits up, but his expression's dark. "Because his family was killed in a terrorist attack."

"*What?*"

Fletcher nods. "Sade told us they were on a bus that was bombed. And who do you think the news pinned the attack on?"

The Memory Ghosts. I bring my knees up to my chest and hug my trembling legs. "So Dr. Sanders asks Rhett to spy on us, and when one of us *thinks* something incriminating, he runs off and tells her." I swear softly. I did this. I gave us away to Dr. Sanders when I mentioned my half-memory dreams—when I panicked to her about my vision in the snow. I'm about to bare this to my friends, when—

"The abandoned storefront." Fletcher balls his hand into a fist and punches his backpack. "*Of course.* That guy who was on surveillance detail the day you and I went poking around! Remember, Freya? I'll bet word got back to Dr. Sanders that we investigated the address."

Ollie raises her eyebrows. "And once she found out that we knew the truth about the address—that it's not a MACE field office—she figured out we were onto her and the dean."

Zayne shuts his notebook and pockets it. "Ah, yes. That storefront was one of Mr. Lear's designated safe houses for the Ghosts. I've since learned that there's a windowless room in the back, a place he intended for us to meet. Of course, when Mr. Lear found out that location was compromised, we never stepped foot in there."

So this information that Memory Frontier is having us knife has to do with specific meeting locations for the Ghosts.

"It would seem that Dr. Sanders is building her own army." Zayne stares off musingly. "She's training memory knifers. She's recruiting Listeners. She's—"

"*Listeners?*" Fletcher perks up.

"Mhmm. What Gemma and Rhett are." He says this conversationally, almost nonchalantly, but I'm starting to connect the dots.

"You're a Scrambler." I point at Zayne, who yawns idly and then opens one of the crates, tending to busywork. "Which means I'm a Seer?"

Zayne doesn't answer. But I don't need him to; his silence says I'm right.

"*The Listener, The Scrambler, The Seer, & The Task,*" Fletcher whispers, citing the title of his father's hollow book. He stands, his feet wobbling with the swaying vehicle. "My father has a hollow book with that title. What does he, and the memory tape he keeps hidden inside, have to do with the Memory Ghosts?"

Zayne shuts the crate and turns, holding the wall to keep himself balanced. I can guess what he's going to say before he even opens his mouth. "In due time."

"We didn't even give Foxtail Academy a proper goodbye." Ollie leans against Chase on the bench across from me and Fletcher. Chase hangs his arm around her and squeezes. The back of the vehicle is windowless. There's no telling what time of day it is, though it feels like we've been driving for hours already. I wish I had the ability to turn off my thoughts and succumb to exhaustion's snare. What I'd give to be able to just curl up on the floor and nap.

"Even though the trial was just a front for Memory Frontier," Ollie adds, "I'm really going to miss that place."

"Juniper Lake, the Foxhole, our spot." Fletcher sighs. He picks at the white drywall dust burrowed beneath his fingernails. "Yeah. I'm gonna miss it too."

Our conversation turns nostalgic. We list the specific things we'll miss, like Herschel Jones's Southern cooking and Ollie and me whipping the boys in foosball in the senior lounge. Strangely, reflecting on these moments from campus brightens my spirits like one of Gemma's crackling campfires, even though I abhor Alexander Lochamire's sham institution.

Foxtail Academy was created to cover up Alexander Lochamire's secret knifing operation. But that doesn't mean Memory Frontier has claim over the memories we created while we were there. They'll never take those away from us. We'll share those together until we die.

"Where's Irene now?" I ask Zayne, who is still busying himself. Using his notebook, he's moving among the crates and taking inventory of their contents.

"Well, since she got a head start, I imagine she's already in Colorado with her great-uncle." He doesn't look up while he writes. Watching him stand under the low light, his feet spread apart to help with balance, makes me feel seasick. "Since we're accelerating the Task, her employment at Foxtail has come to an end."

Ollie leans forward. "What do you think is going to happen to the school?"

Zayne shuts his notebook, looking irritated. "I imagine Alexander Lochamire's camp will spin up some outrageous headlines for the media. Something like, 'Terrorists storm school, kidnap students, and endanger others.' You know, especially *delicious* stuff."

I curse inwardly. I'm so tired of Memory Frontier controlling the narrative. I guess after we help Mr. Lear with the Task, we won't have to worry about that anymore.

Assuming, of course, that we don't fail.

"Get some rest. We won't be making a pit stop for another couple of hours." Zayne returns to his busywork. "I need you as rested as possible before we reach our destination."

Chase leans his head against the wall. "I guess we're not gonna waste time kicking off this elaborate Task of yours, huh?"

Zayne jots something down in his notebook and mutters, "The Task began when we extricated you from Foxtail Academy."

54

FLETCHER COHEN

Westcliffe was a remote town in south-central Colorado. Established in 1887, it nestled at the base of the Sangre de Cristo Mountains in the way an anthill sits beside a chateau. Indeed, the mountains were godlike, reigning over awestruck mortals with benevolence and grace.

The population of Westcliffe was around five hundred, a number that barely constituted a town. The people preferred it that way, thank you very much. They had their ranches and their cattle, and the mountains safeguarded their splendor from the outside world and its greedy hands.

Westcliffe was also the darkest town in Colorado, so named because its community had worked diligently to protect the visibility of their night skies from light pollution. This unified effort was a sacrifice of sorts; in return, the Sangre de Cristo Mountains seemed to shelter the Westcliffeans from evil.

Gazing at a star-dotted sky unblemished by city lights was a religious experience, like worship.

"You see, Mr. Lear is suspicious of staying the night in a place where he can't look skyward and see the stars." Alana Khan shut the back doors of the vehicle once everyone filed out. Fletcher and the gang moaned as they stretched, and it wasn't long before the cold mountain air seeped into their bones. Everyone's teeth were chattering within seconds.

"Think I'll wait in the car," Chase said weakly.

Alana ignored the remark. "This way." She led the four of them down a stone footpath that wound toward a single-story house. Fletcher turned in a circle as they marched single file—drinking in the view of the enormous, snowcapped mountains and extensive stars.

"Gemma loves the stars too," Freya said, hanging back and waiting for Fletcher to catch up. "Wonder if that's a prerequisite for joining the Ghosts."

Blessedly, their walk was brief, and soon they were stepping across the threshold, greeted by the wood-burned heat of a roaring fireplace. The spacious home smelled of evergreen sap and old leather. As soon as Alana shut and deadbolted the door, Irene came bounding around the corner.

Her face lit up like a lantern in the woods. "You made it!" She hugged Freya first, then went down the line. "Where's Zayne?"

"Unloading some stuff." Alana took off her trench coat and hung it on the rack beside the door. "Where's Mr. Lear?"

"In the great room. You guys look exhausted."

"Do we also look hungry?" Ollie dropped her bag at her feet as Alana excused herself.

"Dinner! Of course." Irene chuckled. "I hope you like flank steak sliders?"

Fletcher's stomach roared at the mention of beef. "Kindly lead us to the promised land, Irene Porter."

❖ ❖ ❖

Once they'd eaten their fill in the kitchen, Fletcher, Freya, and the others took turns showering. For his part, Fletcher considered the shower a cleanse. He stood beneath the metal faucet, engulfed in the steam—hot water running down his head, shoulders, and back. He pictured the filth of the bunker, the grime that represented Memory Frontier's facility in the woods, washing off his body and spiraling down the drain.

It was one of the best showers he'd had in months.

He felt restored and mostly whole again.

After everyone was dressed and sleeping arrangements were made, they gathered in the great room. The space was wide and open with tall windows that faced west. The panes of glass were so clean that they gave the illusion of no windows—just open, rectangular portals that led to the snowy beyond.

Mr. Lear stood near the hearth while Fletcher, his friends, and Irene sat on the couches. Zayne and Alana were in the other room, and Fletcher could hear one of them talking on the phone.

Mr. Lear took off his fedora and set it on the mantel. "Tell me everything."

And so they did.

When they finished, Mr. Lear settled into the armchair next to the fireside tools. He picked up the wrought-iron poker and idly nudged the logs. One of them snapped and spilled embers out of its guts.

He eventually spoke. "Memory Frontier never should have put you in danger like that." He turned to Fletcher and Freya, who sat nearest him. Freya was wrapped in a blanket; Fletcher was leaning forward, his fingers interwoven. "I am *so* sorry, and I'm glad you two found a way out of Emilia's memory."

Fletcher received the words of consolation with a forced smile, even if it didn't make him feel any less angry. Now more than ever, he wanted to help the Memory Ghosts dismantle Memory Frontier. Fletcher wanted Alexander Lochamire and his daughter to personally pay for what they'd done.

If not for Freya, they would still be stuck in that endless, horrifying loop.

"How interesting, though." Mr. Lear stroked his chin with his free hand. "A shared memory was your escape during a knife; a shared *dream* was your escape during a loop."

"Why do you suspect that is?" Freya tucked her feet underneath her haunches.

"I'm not sure." Mr. Lear put the fire poker back. "We know that Memory Killer devours our past—bit by bit, memory by memory. An aspiration, though, is something newly formed, something that hasn't transpired yet."

Fletcher perked up. "You're thinking our past might be vulnerable but looking to the future isn't?"

Mr. Lear smiled weakly. "Indeed. I will ruminate on this. It's all very interesting."

Freya cleared her throat. "So when do we get started?"

Mr. Lear nodded and rose to his feet. "Tomorrow. Right now, it's time for your briefing."

At 6:00 a.m. they would travel to Alden, Nevada. It was a nine-and-a-half-hour drive from Westcliffe, which would put them at the Fold around three or four Pacific time if they stopped for fuel only twice.

"We have requisitioned a MACE transport vehicle," Zayne said, setting up an easel beside the fireplace. The easel displayed a large printed map that had been glued to a poster board. "Every weekday evening between five and six, the Fold admits new low-risk patients via its south entrance. That's here." Zayne placed a red tack at the indicated spot on the map. "Once we get past the guard shack and enter, there are two more security checkpoints before we can get inside. Here"—a second red tack—"and here"—a third red tack. "Alana and I will be clad in MACE gear, and we'll be transporting you four inside."

"Straight into the belly of the beast," Ollie said from the floor, sipping the hot cocoa Irene had prepared for everyone.

Alana and Mr. Lear traded glances. "This is an incredibly risky endeavor." He took off his reading glasses, handed Alana the document he was reviewing, and stood. "I can only imagine the emotional toll you endured, Ms. Trang, when you were admitted to the Fold at sixteen."

Ollie set her mug down but remained seated. "That was nearly two years ago. I'll be . . . fine."

Mr. Lear sighed but acquiesced. "Thank you, Ms. Trang. You truly are special."

"Now," Zayne said, drawing their attention back to the map. "When we're inside, we follow this corridor *here* toward the back corner of the first floor, where a hospital coordinator is stationed. They're responsible for processing new patients. That's you."

"From jumpsuits to hospital gowns." Chase moaned. "Oh well. And don't be surprised when you guys find out I'm nude under there. I fully commit to my roles."

Ollie rubbed the bridge of her nose. "I really wish you were kidding, but I know better."

Chase smiled at her wolfishly.

"Right. Anyway." Zayne glared at Mr. Lear as if to say, *You're putting the future of the world on* their *shoulders?* "Since there are more than three of you, this will require the attention of the senior resident nurse. On this shift, that will be Brandon Maddox." Alana handed Zayne a large photograph, which he showed to the room. The picture was a still frame pulled from security camera footage: the man, presumably Brandon Maddox, walked down a square-tiled hallway. He was broad-shouldered and tall. He wore a lab coat and held a clipboard, though he looked like he should have been lining up on a football field. Two MACE agents flanked him.

Zayne continued: "Alana and I will escort you to Mr. Maddox's office, where he will conduct the standard check-in process for groups larger than three. I will disrupt and disorient him using some good ol'-fashioned scrambling. Once that's complete, he'll accompany us to the nearest elevators, here." Zayne placed another red tack. "And using Mr. Maddox's credentials, we'll be able to take the elevators to the basement, where the archives are."

Fletcher cleared his throat. "I'm sorry, what's the scrambling part you mentioned?"

Zayne beamed. He clasped his hands behind his back and rolled onto the balls of his feet. "Well, now, where's the fun in spoiling *that* surprise?"

Alana rolled her eyes.

"What about a map of the basement?" Freya looked from Zayne, to Alana, and lastly to Mr. Lear.

"We don't possess a map of the basement, I'm afraid." His voice was thick and wistful. "We almost retrieved a copy but were unsuccessful."

Zayne and Alana gave each other a quick sideways glance. They seemed embarrassed. A failed mission of theirs?

"It's no matter, though." Mr. Lear tried sounding optimistic. "First, we worry about getting you four down into the basement. Then we worry about locating the archives."

Alana took over. "We'll have a change of clothes for you all in the elevators. Additional MACE outfits and gear. When the six of us exit the elevator, it'll be time for a shift change for the basement agents."

"That's right." Zayne nods. "The team we relieve will board the elevator, but a maintenance malfunction will stall them halfway up to the main floor."

"A *maintenance malfunction*?" Chase repeated, raising his eyebrows. "Nicely done."

Zayne's chest puffed out, though all he said was, "Thanks."

"How much time do we have down there?" Fletcher asked, worried what the answer might be.

"Not long," Alana said.

"Ten minutes, maybe fifteen." Zayne looked back at his map, analyzing it with a tilted head.

"Okay, so"—Fletcher leaned forward—"we find the archives, we locate the right memory tape, then we knife it. Then what? We just walk out of there with stolen information?"

"That's where Gemma Morris comes in." Mr. Lear returned to his armchair. "She checked herself into the Fold yesterday, and—"

"Gemma's there?" Freya shot to her feet. "At the Fold? As a *prisoner*?"

Mr. Lear clearly hadn't expected this response; his face paled and his eyes widened. "Yes, of her own accord, Freya. She knows what she's doing. And she's essential to your being able to get out of there alive tomorrow. Trust me when I say she insisted on helping in this way."

Fletcher took Freya's wrist gently. "Hey." But she said nothing back. Instead, she swallowed and returned to her spot on the couch beside him. She pulled the blanket around her shoulders and remained still.

After an uncomfortable moment passed, Ollie said, "You're wrong about the time."

Everyone turned to face her. She looked forlorn, withdrawn into herself. "I remember once, when I was there . . . I was riding the elevator up to meet my psychiatrist. There was a malfunction. Within *minutes* a maintenance crew appeared through an emergency hatch. They got the elevator working in no time."

"Whoa, Ol." Chase put his arm around her.

"Yeah." She smiled wanly. "They really don't want you being by yourself for too long in that place."

"Not because you're a threat to yourself." Mr. Lear gripped the armrests of his chair, and in the firelight, Fletcher saw the man's face harden. He looked downright enraged. "It's because if you're alone with your thoughts too long, you might become a threat to *them*."

After the particulars were sorted, a few questions remained: (1) How were Fletcher and his friends going to memory knife in the basement without Dean Mendelsohn's Restorey? (2) How exactly was Gemma going to assist in their escape? (3) Just what *were* they expected to knife from the memory tape in the archives?

More intriguing questions popped up in Fletcher's head, though he didn't articulate them: *Whose* memory would they be knifing? And how would it take down Memory Frontier?

But he and the others didn't press Mr. Lear for more details. Tomorrow on the road they'd shore up the final pieces. Tonight they'd rest.

By the time the clock struck ten, everyone collected their Reflectors and dragged themselves to their designated guest bedrooms. Mr. Lear bid them good night, and then he, Zayne, and Alana went into the kitchen for further planning.

A half hour later, Fletcher and Freya found themselves back in the great room. They sat on the couch in front of the dying fire.

"Been thinking about my visions." Freya curled up beside him, leaning her head against his bicep. "And how I only get them when I'm away from you."

"I . . . is that true?" Fletcher lazed back on the couch, agog.

"Mhmm." She yawned. "I had a vision on the airplane, when I first arrived in Tennessee; in the woods with Ollie the day we found our secret spot; on the pier when I was by myself, after our trip to the mall; the night Dean Mendelsohn took me to meet my father; and—"

"The vision you had when you were staying with Gemma." He stared at the fire. The remaining log began to disintegrate, succumbing to the merciless flames. "Does that mean I'm holding you back?"

Freya giggled drowsily. "I took it to mean that you're my lucky charm."

"I'll take that."

She leaned her head back, and they kissed as if they were on the pier in Long Beach again—enraptured in one another, absorbing the moment, the sounds, the feel of each other's warm lips.

"That's twice now you've saved me from a memory loop, by the way." Fletcher put his arm around her after they pulled away.

Freya patted his chest. "You're gonna have to step up and start to do some of the saving."

"Ain't that the truth." He pressed his cheek against the top of her head, taking in the tropical scent of her coconut shampoo. "Was that a vision you had in Emilia's memory loop? The one of us at prom, dancing by Juniper Lake?"

He heard her smile. "If it was, it's one of the few visions I've had that I actually pray comes true."

Fletcher tried to arrange his thoughts in an attempt to say this next part delicately. "There's still the vision you had of me . . . in the snow outside that mansion."

He could feel her body stiffen. "I know."

"The memory tape we're going to knife at the Fold." Fletcher heard his voice grow fragile. "Is that when it happens?"

"I don't know." Freya leaned in closer, like she was trying to tether herself to him. "But I'm not going to let anything happen to you."

He believed her. When the last of the fire seemed to crackle away, when only smoke danced in the fireplace, Fletcher whispered, "During one of our knifings—in the in-between with all the neon lights—I saw you."

Freya remained still.

"You seemed at peace. But how can that be? That journey through the lights is anything but peaceful."

She gave a frail shrug. "I don't know. Maybe my premonitions have desensitized me to that aspect of knifing?"

"Maybe." *Whatever the case*, Fletcher thought, sighing inwardly, *I'll be glad when we never have to access another memory that isn't our own again.*

55

FREYA IZQUIERDO

At dawn, Zayne rouses us from our sleep. Ollie and I get out of our cots and groggily gather our things. I'm so tired that I forget to remove my Reflector receivers at first; the small device rolls off me and smacks onto the carpeted floor with a *thump*.

I curse under my breath, scoop up my Reflector, and finish packing.

Outside, the metallic sky is stained with splotches of orange and yellow. A certain smell hangs in the air—something almost minty I can't place—and it seems to warn of approaching snowfall.

A MACE transport vehicle idles on the dirt road. It's longer than the armored vehicle we rode in yesterday, solid black, and looks like an amalgam of a military truck and an eighteen-wheeler.

I can't believe this is what MACE uses to transfer innocent people to the Fold, I think, walking to the back of the vehicle. The all-terrain tires, bulky frame, diesel engine—this looks like a type of warcraft, not an ambulance.

True to their word, Alana and Zayne are decked out in full MACE gear—complete with steel-toed boots, knee and shoulder padding, and matte-black masks that cover their faces. Even though I know who's behind the menacing helmets, the hairs on my neck stand up.

Alana slides up her visor and divvies out freshly laundered hospital gowns. "No need to change into these until we're about half an hour out."

Everyone grunts appreciatively and starts to clamber into the back. I loiter on the road.

"Everything okay, Freya?" Alana asks, folding her arms.

"Yeah, it's just . . ." I set my backpack on the ground and pull out my journal. "I'd kinda like to be alone with my thoughts. Or as alone as one can be while traveling with five other people."

Fletcher pops his head out of the back of the vehicle. "You coming?"

"I'm kidnapping Ms. Izquierdo." Alana pats my shoulder. "She's going to ride up front with me for the first half of our drive."

"She is?" Zayne walks up beside us. "That mean you expect me to ride with *them*?" He glances into the back of the vehicle, where Chase is holding the hospital gown up to his torso—his pinkies in the air—and muttering, "I think it really brings out my eyes!"

Zayne flips his visor down and curses behind his mask.

Fletcher hops out of the vehicle. "You good?"

"Yeah, just need to unburden myself." I wave my journal.

"I've been known to be an effective unburden-er . . ." He leans in for a kiss, but I slide my journal between our lips at the last second. He laughs. "Fine."

We hug, then I pick up my backpack and head for the passenger side. I climb the two steps into the cab and scoot into the seat, feeling instant relief from the heater. I go to close the door, but Mr. Lear catches me before I shut it.

"Freya, might I steal a quick word?" His eyes are alive and lightning-like.

"Sure."

"Irene tells me that you were developing a close relationship with Alexander's daughter?"

"I . . . *what?*"

"Dr. Sanders." He says this like it's common knowledge, but when I just stare back open-mouthed, he understands. "Oh, yes. Well. She's Alexander Lochamire's daughter."

"I had no idea."

"I assumed she would've mentioned it on the first day of class, at least in passing." Mr. Lear strokes his chin. "That's interesting, her decision to withhold that information from the student body."

"I asked for her support back when I thought my visions were just flashbacks." I curse loudly.

"It's okay, Freya. You didn't know who you were dealing with." But Mr. Lear now looks troubled. I can read it in the way he gazes out at the distant mountains with an equally distant look in his eyes.

Zayne and Alana are carrying a few items to the back of the vehicle, where I can hear the muted chatter of my friends. A thought occurs to me. "Mr. Lear, did you know my brother? Ramon Izquierdo?"

He processes this. I say, "He worked at one of the factories that built MeReaders for Memory Frontier, but he died in a freak explosion a couple of years ago."

"But you don't think it was a coincidence, do you?"

I draw my lips into a straight line. I hear Alana and Zayne bantering, and then the back doors of the vehicle shut. I continue, "That morning, before he died, he called me from a payphone. Said he'd seen someone using artificial recall, only the old man's eyes were fluttering open while he was hooked up to his Restorey, and my brother said his eyes were solid gray. Why is that significant? We now know that if Memory Killer strikes during a knifing, it traps you in a memory loop. But what happens when Memory Killer strikes during artificial recall?"

I think back to Fletcher's Memory Killer File—his cataloged questions about rapid memory loss and how details of artificial recall have long been painted in shades of gray.

Mr. Lear appears conflicted. He conveys a myriad of emotions with his tired eyes but says nothing.

Alana hops into the driver's seat and fires up the engine. I reluctantly close the door but roll down the window so I can give him a proper goodbye.

"I never knew your brother, Freya, but he was getting close to the truth." His tone is sorrowful. "Memory Frontier takes drastic measures to ensure their secrets remain hidden. If not for the risk of your memories being stolen by Alexander, I'd tell you everything right now. But that would jeopardize our hard work with us *so close* to completing the Task. Rest assured that the answers are coming. In a way, you're finishing what your brother started."

I never thought of it that way, and I appreciate Mr. Lear saying this. It helps me reframe his death, to think of it as not in vain.

I'm getting the answers to the questions he asked.

"Where will you go?"

Mr. Lear takes off his fedora and holds it over his heart. "To see an old friend." He winks and puts his hat back on. Then he stalks back toward the sunlit house, where Irene is standing on the threshold, waving as our vehicle departs.

For the first hour of the drive, I journal while the flat snow-covered world rushes past. Weak sunlight hangs over the mountaintops like warm LEDs low on battery. Alana navigates the growling vessel with unblinking focus, her black helmet resting on the seat between us.

I set down my pencil. "You ever have a vision while driving?"

Alana arches an eyebrow. "Mr. Lear told you I'm a Seer, too, huh?"

I shrug. "Process of elimination. Gemma's a Listener. Zayne's a Scrambler. So unless you're like, I dunno, a Thinker, I just figured you're the Seer of the group."

"Touché." She sighs through her nose. "No, I've never had a vision while driving. Although I've gotten much better at hearing them before they approach. If that did happen, I would just pull to the side of the road until the vision passed."

I nod. "When did your visions start?"

"Five years ago." Her eyes fix on the barren road. "The same day I had my first MeReader scan, I had my first vision."

I watch the side of her face carefully. While I don't want to pry, I never thought I'd be sitting beside someone who has had to deal with the exact same thing as me—and for twice as long. Alana is a wealth of knowledge when it comes to these prophetic visions. But I need to be sensitive.

"Why didn't your parents admit you to the Fold?"

"I never told them. They both worked so hard to provide for me and my sisters, and I didn't want to burden them with even more." She loosens her grip on the steering wheel. "I knew what I was dealing with was unnatural. You know those headaches? Those piercing, skull-crushing migraines?"

I nod again. I can feel a phantom headache coming on just at the mention of them.

"They got worse my freshman year of college. One night, in the dorms, I hit my breaking point. It felt like my head was caving in, like I was a rod in the middle of an electric storm. And the vision that followed was nightmarish.

"My roommate, the only person I ever talked to about my visions, insisted that I see Professor Morris. She took me under her care, helped me reframe my visions—claim them as a gift, not a curse."

"Professor Morris? As in . . . *Gemma?*"

"Retired neuroscientist turned tenured professor." Alana smiles for the first time on the drive. "I owe her my life, Freya. That next year, she introduced me to Mr. Lear, who—at the time—was in the early stages of drafting plans for the Task."

It should come as no surprise to me that Gemma spent time teaching in higher education. The way she challenged me to exhume and confront half-remembered memories, and to write about them . . . well, it's a method only a teacher could have conceived of.

I owe Gemma my life too, I realize.

"Is there anyone who keeps your visions at bay?"

"What do you mean?" Alana asks, visibly intrigued.

"It's just that . . ." I quickly contemplate how to say this next part without sounding like a naive, head-over-heels-in-love teenager. "When I'm with Fletcher, I don't get any visions. When we're separated, I do. Is that common?"

Alana chuckles, though—thankfully—it doesn't sound condescending. "None of this is common, I'm afraid. Those of us with neurotech-wrought abilities are a minority. I don't know if what you're describing is common, but I can say that hasn't been the case for me. Guess I need to find a partner, huh?"

We both laugh softly. I turn my attention to something else she said: *neurotech-wrought abilities.* "You ever wonder what other abilities people might've developed after being subjected to a MeReader? I mean, besides mind reading and seeing visions of the future?"

Alana's playful expression melts away. For almost an entire minute, she doesn't reply. Then, "All the time."

❖ ❖ ❖

The second hour passes more quickly than the first.

I write some more.

In my mind's eye, I see this foggy memory of Ramon in our apartment. I'm fourteen or fifteen at the time, sitting on the couch in our living room and listening to my brother's record player. I'm holding the VHS tape of the sports documentary we're supposed to watch later, but the title of the film escapes me. Anyway, I set the VHS down when the vinyl scratches to the end.

I get up to go to the bathroom but stall in the hallway.

Ramon is seated at our rickety kitchen table.

He's lit a prayer candle, something I've never seen him do. He's writing on a piece of lined paper—also a first, at least to my knowledge—with a blank envelope resting on the tabletop.

He looks up when he feels me watching.

His eyes are solid gray.

"Everything okay, love?"

I avert my eyes. Seeing Memory Killer wreak havoc on someone's mind is something you *never* get used to. Getting used to seeing the gravestone of a loved one would be easier.

That day, Ramon's eyes are gravestone gray.

I clear my throat. "Going to the baño. Ready to watch our movie?"

"Just finishing up. Gimme another sec."

I never ask him who he is writing to, and he never tells me.

❖ ❖ ❖

"Gemma get you that journal?"

I finish my thought and then glance up. Alana gestures toward my journal, driving with one hand on the wheel. As the hours tick by, her posture's loosening.

"Yeah. I'm journaling about . . ." I stop myself, not sure if I'm ready to discuss my—

"Memories that you've suppressed?" She gives me a knowing look and then chuckles. "I have so many journals that I stopped counting after fifty."

Oddly, I find that comforting. I close my journal with the twine but keep both hands on it, like I'm shielding it from harsh rainfall. "It's strange how much it's helped me, even in just a week."

"It's important to understand the origin of things," she replies, quoting Gemma. She even slightly mimics her slow, pleasant accent.

I mean to finish the saying for Alana, but the familiar ringing sound echoes in my head—growing sharper by the second.

I give Alana a look.

She understands.

I close my eyes once the ringing hits its sharpest note. When I open them, I'm standing on rubble in the middle of a street beneath a black sky. Purple lightning illuminates the darkness, cracking like gunshots.

I'm surrounded by a city in ruins.

Buildings are toppled. Plumes of smoke and smog drift skyward. There's a low rumbling in the distance—thunder or warfare. Perhaps both.

I sit on my haunches and slide down the mound toward the scorched pavement. When I reach the bottom, I see the bodies. Hundreds and hundreds of motionless bodies, lying as if thrown back by a powerful blast. I see mostly one- and two-quarter marks tattooed on their hands.

No recollectors in sight.

And there's this woman in the distance. Standing with her arms outstretched. Wearing a peculiar-looking mask.

Is that . . . ?

I move among the bodies, careful not to disturb the dead. As I get closer, I see that the woman has nearly a dozen electrode stickers on her head: on her cheeks, on her forehead, on her temples. The wires drape the front of her body like tendrils, running across the broken street and disappearing behind her.

It's Dr. Sanders.

She opens her eyes. They're the grayest eyes I've ever seen. Two bottomless pits, where dreams go to be annihilated.

I stifle a scream and I'm back in the cab with Alana.

"Breathe, Freya," she tells me calmly, and I realize I've been gasping like my lungs have forgotten how to work. "Breathe."

Once I reclaim some air, I tell her what I saw.

Wordlessly, she pulls the vehicle over to the side of the road. She forgets to turn on her hazards, and a couple of cars whiz by honking irritably.

"What's the matter?" I ask, my voice small.

"I've had the same vision."

56

FLETCHER COHEN

"Guess I managed to dodge that college meeting with Mr. Williams after all." Fletcher lazed on the floor of the vehicle, his back against the wall. Chase and Ollie sat on either side of him, using their folded-up hospital gowns like pillows. Zayne was seated on one of the two benches, his legs crossed, reviewing something on a clipboard. His MACE helmet sat at his feet.

"You're not out of the woods yet," Ollie said, yawning. She added playfully, "Once we finish the Chore, who's to say we won't just transfer back to our high schools to finish up senior year?"

Zayne grumbled, "It's the *Task*."

Chase snickered. "Ollie's right, Fletch. After the Memory Phantoms relieve us of our duties, we're getting our old lives back."

Zayne closed his eyes momentarily, shook his head, then went back to reading. As opposed to the previous armored vehicle they'd ridden in, this one had back-door windows, for which everyone was immensely grateful. Fletcher, Chase, and Ollie spent the first couple of hours of the drive halfheartedly playing I Spy, which got old pretty quickly since the only things they could see were the tops of distant mountains and the purpling morning sky.

Still, the game managed to lighten the tense mood. Something about the innocence and youthfulness of it all put Fletcher at ease.

I need this. He gazed out the rectangular windowpanes at the Colorado mountains. *Feels like we're soldiers on a boat, getting ready to storm Omaha Beach on D-day.*

The vehicle jerked and then slammed to a halt.

Fletcher and his friends froze. Zayne put his helmet on and ordered them to stay put. He opened one of the doors and got out, and Fletcher followed. They found Freya standing on the side of the road, hugging herself.

Even though the sun was out, the wind chill was aggressive. She was shivering.

"Hey, hey." Fletcher walked up beside her and pulled her into a hug. Zayne walked around the front of the vehicle to consult with Alana.

"What's going on, Freya?"

She told him about her vision.

Fletcher pulled away and tilted her chin up. "Just because you saw that vision doesn't mean it's going to come true." He reminded Freya of her vision with Ollie, where they'd spotted Dean Mendelsohn in the woods overseeing the transfer of Malcolm Heckman. In that vision, the dean caught them. In real life, Freya had avoided getting caught.

Freya shook her head slowly. "If we fail today, I'm afraid it *will* come true."

❖ ❖ ❖

When the cold became unbearable for Freya, Fletcher helped her into the back of the vehicle. Zayne rode up front with Alana. Chase and Ollie, sensing that their friend was troubled, refrained from assailing her with questions. Ollie draped her hospital gown over Freya's legs, a makeshift blanket, then sat on the bench with Chase across from her and Fletcher.

For nearly an hour, no one spoke.

❖ ❖ ❖

Lunch consisted of gas station sandwiches and stale chips.

"What I'd do for Herschel Jones's barbecue right now." Chase screwed up his face after swallowing the last bite of his BLT.

"Foxtail Academy employed a genius for a cook," Ollie added, but she quickly turned to Chase. "Hold on, though. I'm curious. What *would* you do for some of Herschel Jones's barbecue?"

Chase grinned deviously, picking up on her game. "I'd . . ." He glanced about the back of the vehicle like a dog trying to locate a fly. "Oh! I'd cut my hair like Fletcher's to get my paws on that savory barbecue goodness." He kissed his own fingers like a pleased chef.

"What's wrong with my hair?" Fletcher deadpanned. Freya and Ollie busted a gut.

"Me next, me next!" Ollie exclaimed, bouncing up and down in her seat. "For Herschel Jones's barbecue, I'd skinny-dip in Juniper Lake."

"*Pfft.*" Chase flipped his hand. "That's nothing. Pick something—"

"*In the dead of winter,*" Ollie finished. Freya and Fletcher oohed and aahed.

"Well played, good sir." Chase tipped an imaginary hat.

"Why thank you, good sir." Ollie bowed back.

"Okay, let's see," Fletcher said, rubbing his chin. "I'd shave all my body hair—yes, mullet included."

Ollie's eyes widened. "Whoa."

"Respect." Chase looked winded.

Freya leaned back on the bench, tapping her cheek in thought. "Okay, so for Herschel Jones's barbecue, I'd spend an entire week doing nothing but listening to Ms. Schneck's algebra lectures."

Chase pretended to faint. Ollie stood and applauded.

"You're *sick*," Fletcher teased, throwing his arm around her.

"No, wait!" Freya snapped her fingers. "For some of Herschel Jones's magical barbecue, I'd knife one of my thirteen-year-old foster brother's memory tapes."

Ollie faux gagged. "Only God above knows what kind of memories thirteen-year-old boys possess," she said with theatrical bravado. "But for heavenly barbecue over soggy turkey clubs, it'd be worth it."

"*So* worth it," Freya agreed.

The back of the vehicle fell quiet for a moment. The four of them swayed slightly with the driving motion, and occasionally they hit a soft bump in the road.

Eventually, Freya spoke. "Thank you, guys."

Chase snorted. "For what?"

"Keeping me distracted."

Fletcher leaned against her head, thinking back to his Thanksgiving dinner last week with Ollie's grandparents.

Distractions are more important than we give them credit for, he mused.

"All right!" Chase rolled up his sleeves. "For a piece of Jones's chess pie, I'd . . ."

❖ ❖ ❖

They crossed the Colorado-Nevada border in the early afternoon. Soon they were only an hour away from the Fold.

With their backs to one another, Fletcher and his friends changed into their hospital gowns. Then, as instructed, they put their civilian clothes into one of the storage bins underneath a bench. Their knifing jumpsuits were stowed in a large black duffel, along with the MACE outfits they'd be changing into once they got inside the elevator.

At one point during the drive, Zayne slid open the small square window from the cab and turned up the radio so they could hear what he and Alana were listening to:

". . . which officials claim they did not foresee, despite tell-tale signs in Pittsburgh, Chicago, and Boston." The male reporter sounded as if he was choking down fear. "The riots are now spreading across the West Coast and are unquestionably coordinated as men and women set repositories and Memory Frontier fulfillment centers ablaze. Experts believe the Reflector, Alexander Lochamire's latest innovation in artificial recall, was the breaking point. The technology has been veiled in mystery as minors trial it at Foxtail Academy, a remote institution in rural Tennessee. In response to the sweeping riots, the president has mandated curfews in all major cities, effective—"

Alana turned the radio knob, switching stations. Michael Jackson's "Beat It" blared through the cab speakers midverse. She glanced at Fletcher and his friends through the rearview mirror and flipped her visor down to hide her eyes. "Get ready. We're approaching Alden."

Alana let the song finish before shutting off the radio.

57

FREYA IZQUIERDO

"Guys, listen."

I stand up from the bench and walk to the doors, peering through the windows. Sun-beaten desert terrain stretches as far as I can see, expanding toward far-off mountain ranges. Fletcher and the others join me, pressing their faces against the panes.

"I hear something," Ollie says, her breath fogging up the glass. "But I don't see anything."

"What is that?" Chase tilts his head toward the roof of the vehicle. "It sounds like . . . a swarm. A swarm of bees?"

We crowd around the tiny window separating us from the cab and look over Alana's and Zayne's shoulders and through the windshield.

My heart batters my ribs as I see our destination looming in the distance.

The Fold consists of four bone-white buildings surrounded

by razor-wire fencing. The buildings themselves are nine, maybe ten stories tall and completely windowless. They look like massive obelisks—enormous, polished, sterile monoliths that defy the Nevada sand and heat.

I spy three or four guard towers outfitted with gun turrets within the compound. This place instantly reminds me of those state penitentiaries I've seen on TV, complete with surveillance cameras and armed guards.

Only the guards here are helmeted MACE agents wielding semi-automatic rifles.

"There, look." Fletcher points as we crest a hill: at the base of the razor-wire fencing, hordes of people are gathered—civilians holding signs and chanting something unintelligible. "That explains the noise."

There are hundreds of protesters. And while they don't appear to be doing anything illegal at the moment, dozens of MACE agents stand on the other side of the fence with riot shields at the ready. This place could become a war zone at any moment.

The four buildings seem to get taller the closer we approach.

"It's game time, guys." Zayne flips down his visor and pulls two lanyards holding forged credentials out of the glove box. "Get into position."

Silently, we move away from the cab window and take our seats: me and Fletcher on one bench, Chase and Ollie across from us on the other one.

The yelling and chanting and shouting grow louder.

Soon Alana is slowing down the vehicle, and I picture us crawling toward the electric gate.

I wipe my sweaty palm on my hospital gown and grab Fletcher's hand. I take my other hand, my right one, and hold up my cognition wheel. The three-quarter mark is baked into my skin as if I were born with it. But these are marks, *brandings*, that have reduced humanity to cattle. I wasn't born like this; it's not natural. Alexander Lochamire and his Memory Frontier have the world convinced that artificial recall is the only path to salvation.

MeReaders. Restoreys. Now Reflectors. These are his tools, his chisels, and with them he's carved out a fear-based world—his monument to monitored memories. This is Alexander Lochamire's way. Resist, fall out of line, and suffer the hellish consequences.

But there's more than one way to defeat Memory Killer. I think of Gemma, how during the entire week I spent with her I didn't see her use a Restorey once. I think of Malcolm Heckman's and Emilia Vanguard's memories, how both times that Memory Killer attacked we managed to burst free from its clutches. *Together*, working as *one*.

As I reflect on all of this, I see my foster sister Nicole's face. Nicole, who has been skipping artificial recall windows. Though she described having increased spells of eye discoloration, she made no mention of seizing or convulsing—the horrifying effects of recall withdrawals.

I've seen that there's another way, one that doesn't involve artificial recall.

And so today begins the resistance.

Today we resist Lochamire's way.

Today we reject it, we defy it.

The world will learn the truth about memory indexing. The world will learn about the troubling aftereffects caused by MeReaders. The world will learn the unsettling secret buried within the memory tape we're about to knife. We will be responsible for ending the old way and, hopefully, forging a new one for the future.

Chase looks up and meets my eyes. "Forgotten."

Ollie smiles. "But."

"Not," Fletcher whispers.

"Forgetful." I take a deep breath, really fill my lungs with as much oxygen as they'll hold, and think, *Because to forget is to die.*

❖ ❖ ❖

As we inch closer to the gate, the transport vehicle begins to sway. The protesters are pounding and slapping and shoving the back of the vehicle. Faces appear on the other side of the window—angry, desperate men and women who scream things I can't understand through the bulletproof doors.

Abruptly, a blast of water fans the protesters back, and then we're lurching forward. I gasp, watching through the water-soaked windows as men and women topple backward from the force of the hose. After a few beats, the electric gate grinds to a close behind us. We're sealed in.

The next instant, the back doors fling open, letting in a burst of harsh sunbeams. We all shield our eyes. A silhouetted MACE agent, either Alana or Zayne, orders us to get to our feet and file outside.

"One at a time," they bark, their voices electronically scrambled through the masks. Fletcher goes first, then me, Chase, and Ollie last.

I hop to the ground, and when my eyes adjust, I scan my surroundings. The only thing I see are MACE agents patrolling the grounds and talking into handheld receivers. The sunlight glints off their shiny helmets, giving them an alien quality.

I don't see any "patients" around, which tells me they aren't allowed outside.

This is worse than a prison, I realize with a chill. *This is like an internment camp. We are prisoners of war.*

The second agent is Alana; I can tell because of her chest and smaller frame. She climbs into the back of the vehicle, retrieves the long duffel, then rejoins us beneath the shadows of the Fold.

"This way," Zayne grunts, shoving Fletcher and Chase. We follow Alana single file, with Zayne at the rear. As we approach the first security checkpoint, a squat guard shack nearly fifty yards away, three MACE agents on patrol stop to watch us pass.

Don't give them the pleasure of seeing your fear, I think, setting my jaw.

We amble past the agents, who shake their helmeted heads before resuming their march.

"Wait here." Zayne strides toward the MACE agent posted at the guard shack, and the two begin conversing inaudibly.

Behind me, I hear Ollie's breathing quicken. I'm sure she's having flashbacks to that summer when she was sixteen, when she spent time at the Fold so doctors could recalibrate the MeReaders and prevent her from artificially recalling painful memories of her father.

Ollie is the bravest one here. I wish I could hold her.

The desert heat is dry and tolerable, but I'm guessing that's because it's November. I can't imagine what this place is like during the summer, or how these armored agents fare in the blistering sunlight.

"In the movie *Dune*," Chase says behind me, "there are these things called *stillsuits*. They help to preserve the body's moisture on the desert-planet Arrakis. You think these guys have stillsuit tech in their pants?"

Fletcher releases a nervous-sounding chuckle. I can tell he's grateful for our friend's levity.

Zayne waves us over, and we're off again, silently moving to the second checkpoint. This one is located just outside the entrance to one of the four buildings. As we get closer, I marvel at the walls. They look like they're made of marble, some kind of heavy and fine-aged material.

The MACE agent stationed at the entrance opens the door but leaves it cracked and holds up his hand. "Just a second."

We all freeze. I can see both Zayne and Alana tense up.

"You got four patients here."

"That's correct," Zayne says.

"You'll have to get 'em processed with Brandon Maddox."

"We're aware."

The guard glances at me and my friends. He flips his visor up, squinting his beady eyes and scrutinizing each one of us.

He flips his visor back down and turns to Alana. "What's in the duffel?"

"Their clothes."

"Those usually come in individual bags."

Alana straightens. "We consolidated."

The guard folds his arms across his broad chest. "I'm going to need to check."

"Of course." Even through Alana's distorted voice, I can hear her unease. Slowly, she breaks rank and walks over to the guard, taking her time removing the duffel from her shoulder and setting it onto the ground.

No, no. I glance at the others worriedly. *He can't see what's in that bag!*

The guard pulls off his gauntlets, sets them on the ground, and puts on a pair of latex gloves.

We have to stop him!

Fletcher steals a look at me over his shoulder, his green eyes panic-stricken.

The guard bends over, pinches the zipper with his thumb and index finger, and starts to pull the duffel open when—

A guttural shriek hits our ears.

We all flinch and turn, watching as a man in a tattered hospital gown barrels into three guards and falls. He scrambles back to his feet, tossing erratic haymakers. He lands a few hits. Beyond him, the protesters chant and howl on the other side of the fence.

The violent scene stills me and my friends.

And there's something strikingly familiar about the man creating the ruckus.

The guard curses. "Stay with them!" he shouts to Zayne and Alana, abandoning the half-opened duffel and racing toward the scene. The patient looks absolutely *wild* as he throws punches and jabs, kicking up dirt clouds with his bare feet. A handful of MACE agents form a loose circle around him. The guard with the latex gloves eventually corners him, pouncing on him with predatory precision.

I watch as the patient struggles on the ground beneath the guard's bulky weight. He manages to slip one of his arms free and elbow the mask. The guard's head snaps back from the impact, then he forcibly grinds the side of the patient's face into the red dirt. I can see the man choking and spitting as he inhales the sandy air, and that's when I recognize him.

Malcolm Heckman. The Memory Ghosts' first runner, whose memory tape we knifed.

As he's wrestled into submission, I feel as if I can *taste* the dirt he's gagging on. I can *smell* the sweat and grime and blood dripping down his face. I can *hear* his heart drumming in his ears. The sheer hopelessness of his situation steals my breath like a blow to the stomach.

I step forward, but Fletcher grabs my forearm.

Another MACE agent steps in to help the guard subdue Malcolm's writhing form. Despite being outnumbered, he's making life very difficult for them. The guard cranes his head toward us and yells, "Just get those four inside already so we can deal with this one!"

My mouth goes drier than the ground I'm standing on. What does he mean *deal*?

"C'mon." Zayne shoves me and Fletcher forward, and before I can throw Malcolm Heckman one last look of gratitude, we're crossing the threshold into the Fold.

58

FLETCHER COHEN

The long white corridor was cold, and the cold air smelled of antiseptics. The chemicals seemed to singe Fletcher's nose. While he was grateful to be away from the MACE agents and their faceless stares, he found the quiet and sterile interior more unsettling.

They marched along, passing unmarked door after unmarked door.

Zayne was at the head now, and he led them down the hall with confidence in his gait. *Zayne must've spent all night memorizing the map,* Fletcher thought as they turned a corner.

A woman in a lab coat passed them going the opposite direction. She spoke into a boxy cell phone, not so much as glancing at Fletcher and his friends.

They turned another corner.

And another.

Finally, they approached a curved desk, behind which sat a young woman in scrubs and a hairnet. She wore a device on her head that looked similar to headphones, except the round speakers sat on her temples.

She flashed a *Stepford Wives* smile. "Good evening! Nonurgent patients?"

Zayne nodded once. "That's correct." He handed the woman his and Alana's credentials, which she scanned with a handheld device, not once looking down at what she was doing. She only continued to smile at the group, her eyes hollow and deep.

The scanner beeped and lit up green with each reading.

"Wonderful." She handed the lanyards back to Zayne. Next, she stood, walked around the desk, and went down the line—scanning everyone's cognition wheel. Each time she did, she repeated their name, and the handheld scanner spit out a wristband with a unique barcode. The woman whistled to herself as she attached everyone's wristbands with practiced hands; each had to recite their name and birthday before she moved on to the next person.

Freya was last, and the woman squealed with delight after taking a reading of her three-quarter mark. "Oh! A newly minted recollector! How lovely."

Freya blinked.

Once everyone was tagged, the woman said, "Take this corridor to the fifth door on your left. The senior resident nurse, Brandon Maddox, will check in our new patients." She turned her attention to Fletcher and his friends. "I sure hope you four get to feeling better soon. We promise to heal your ability to remember, and in a holistic way!"

Sure you do, Fletcher thought as he shuffled along with the others down the hallway.

When they reached the fifth door, Zayne knocked once.

"Enter." The man's voice somehow sounded bored *and* brusque. Zayne led them inside the wide, circular room. Brandon Maddox stood behind a standing desk reviewing a ledger. He seemed much taller—and thicker—than in the picture Zayne had shown them yesterday. He had a device on his head similar to the one worn by the nurse who affixed their wristbands, though his had two wires that connected to some unseen transponder inside his lab coat. On the desktop sat three things: a framed photograph of a family, a clay vessel holding blue pens, and a small octahedron sculpture.

Mr. Maddox set down his square reading glasses and pointed to the far wall where there was a row of ten metal stools. Obediently, Fletcher and the others sat down. Zayne and Alana remained by the desk while Mr. Maddox took the device off his head, unclipped the wires, and set these beside his reading glasses. Then he grabbed a clipboard and set to work processing his patients.

He began with Ollie, his back to Zayne and Alana. "Name."

"Hoa Trang."

"Symptoms?"

"My vision's extremely blurry after using artificial recall." She rubbed her forehead for good measure.

Mr. Maddox mumbled as he jotted this down on his clipboard. He took a step to his left. "Name."

"Christopher Hall. But you can call me Chase."

"Symptoms?"

"I get dizzy spells before and after my monthly MeReader scans." More mumbling. More scribbling.

"Name."

"Freya Izquierdo."

"Symptoms?"

"I . . ." Fletcher could tell she was debating whether or not to just mention her visions. At this point, why not? She looked up and met Mr. Maddox's eyes. "I'm getting these flashes in my mind's eye. Like, flashes of the future. It started a couple of days ago."

Mr. Maddox didn't even skip a beat: "I see." He wrote down a very long note. "We'll have to admit you to the fourth floor to run some tests. I'm afraid your stay with us will be an extended one."

Fletcher clenched his fists at his sides. *Like hell it will . . .*

Mr. Maddox moved in front of Fletcher last. "Name."

"Fletcher—"

A soft, low hissing came from Zayne's direction. Mr. Maddox turned toward it. "Is that . . . did you hear that?"

Zayne and Alana looked at each other, then shook their heads. But Fletcher noticed that Zayne's gloved hands were behind his back as he stood at attention. The hissing sound ended abruptly, and Mr. Maddox's eyes fell on his desk. Slowly, he moved away from Fletcher, his mouth slightly agape.

His desktop had been rearranged: the framed photograph was of a younger Brandon Maddox holding his college degree; the pens in the clay vessel were red; the octahedron sculpture had been replaced with a stainless-steel spinning top.

"How did this . . . ?" Mr. Maddox dropped his clipboard, which clanked when it hit the ground. He rushed to the desk and picked up the picture frame. "Did you mess with my things?"

Fletcher marveled as Alana approached the nurse, obstructing Mr. Maddox's view of Zayne, who—in one fluid move—scooped down to pick up the clipboard while replacing Mr. Maddox's handwritten notes with an official-looking document.

Alana asked, "Are you feeling okay?"

Zayne approached the desk and set down the clipboard. "You dropped this."

Mr. Maddox kept his eyes on the picture. "My family. Where's the picture of my—"

Now that Zayne's back was to Fletcher and his friends, he could see Zayne holding a thumb-sized clicker, which he pressed. The low hissing returned for a moment, then vanished.

"Mr. Maddox, you truly look unwell." Alana adjusted the large duffel over her shoulder. "Are you misremembering something? We should get the on-call doctor in here at once."

"*No.*" Mr. Maddox set down the frame. He looked pale and disoriented. "I . . . it's not . . ." He picked up his clipboard and studied the paper.

Zayne tilted his head. "You were just getting ready to escort these patients to the basement for indexing."

"I was?" Mr. Maddox reached for his reading glasses and flinched when he realized the frames were round, not square. He set down the glasses instead of putting them on. "Right, um. This way then."

Fletcher shook his head in disbelief before rising to his feet and following the others back into the hallway.

59

FREYA IZQUIERDO

As we march down the corridor toward the elevator, I think of Malcolm Heckman. I don't want to picture what he's going through right now, so I just try to remind myself that this will all be over quickly. He'll be set free soon, along with the rest of the prisoners who are wrongly incarcerated around the country—and the world.

Stay focused. We're so close to the end.

The brass elevator doors come into view. *This is it. Just get inside the elevator.*

Mr. Maddox appears flighty as he walks between Zayne and Alana; he keeps glancing over his shoulder at me, Fletcher, Ollie, and Chase as if we're going to violently ambush him.

Just a few feet from the elevators, he stops in his tracks. Mr. Maddox looks from us, to Zayne, to Alana, then back to us. "This isn't right. This *can't* be right."

My heart rate feels like it's spiking.

Alana asks, "What are you talking about, Mr. Maddox?"

Before he can reply, four MACE agents round the corner, each wielding long nightsticks. They're escorting a tired-looking prisoner with a five-o'clock shadow and shaggy hair. He looks up at us as they pass by.

Joshua Cohen. *Fletcher's father.*

Beside me, Fletcher stifles a gasp. Joshua's face flashes with understanding. He somehow discerns the urgency of our situation, as if seeing his son in a hospital gown with three other teenagers and two MACE agents, one of whom carries a very large duffel, makes it all click for him.

His son has taken the baton from him. He's seeking to complete the Task.

Joshua nods at Fletcher, then mouths, *I love you.*

The next instant, Fletcher's father throws his body into two of the agents, tackling them awkwardly. He screams and punches and thrashes about, and his escorts flog him on the back—occasionally striking their fellow agents.

The scene is pure chaos.

Mr. Maddox flattens himself against the wall, watching in shock. Zayne discreetly unclips Mr. Maddox's ID from his hip and gestures for us to follow. I grab Fletcher's hand and yank him toward me. I can tell he's conflicted, and for the briefest moment it appears he's going to intervene, but he pulls himself away and we're off.

I don't catch my breath until the elevator doors seal shut.

Zayne puts one foot on the railing and hoists himself up toward the security camera in the corner. He takes a travel-size cannister out of his back pocket and sprays a foamy substance on the lens, completely encasing it. While he does this, Alana punches the button for the basement and then uses Mr. Maddox's credentials to grant us access. The square reader glows a deep green, and then we're descending, just like that.

I pull Fletcher into a hug. "He's going to be okay. This will all be over soon."

He nods into my neck.

"We don't have much time." Alana tosses the duffel onto the floor and unzips it. "Jumpsuits first, then MACE outfits."

Alana and Zayne turn their backs toward us, and the four of us scramble to change as quickly as possible in the cramped elevator.

"How were you able to manipulate Mr. Maddox so fast?" Chase pulls his arms through his jumpsuit sleeves and then zips himself up.

"Scrambling is all about making the target second-guess their ability to remember." I hear Zayne set a timer on his wristwatch. "The differences in their surroundings have to be subtle but noticeable enough to give them pause. Scrambling doesn't work in a world without artificial recall." He then opens a Velcro pocket on his thigh and pulls out all of the things he swiped from Mr. Maddox's desk—the blue pens, circular reading glasses, and octahedron sculpture—and tosses them into the duffel.

"Where's the picture of his family?" I put on the black MACE gloves and tighten them at the wrists with the drawstring.

"Still in the frame, behind his graduation photo." Zayne gathers our hospital gowns off the floor, stuffs them in the duffel, and closes it.

While I finish getting dressed, I think about that statement. *Scrambling doesn't work in a world without artificial recall.* Mr. Maddox seemed frightened at the possibility of a doctor being summoned to examine him. He knows firsthand what will happen if he's accused of misremembering.

Fear extends to Alexander Lochamire's staff. No one is immune to it.

As the elevator slows, the four of us pull our MACE helmets over our heads, click them into place, and flick on the voice scramblers. Zayne stands on the railing again, pops out one of the tiles, and stores the duffel in the ceiling. When he hops back down, I notice him carrying a smaller, nondescript bag—one that had been stored in the duffel along with everything else. He clips this bag to his utility belt behind his back.

What we'll need for knifing, I realize, feeling myself sweat underneath my MACE gear.

The elevator dings. The doors open. And before we can step into the lowlit hall, we're greeted by Dr. Sanders and a small company of armed guards.

My breath catches in my throat.

Dr. Sanders blinks her bloodshot, deep-sunken eyes. "Welcome."

60

FLETCHER COHEN

The words *It's over* rang in Fletcher's head as he and the others were escorted down the winding hallway. Their hands were bound behind their backs and their helmets had been removed. As they silently marched, they passed a set of double doors marked ARCHIVES.

We were so close, Fletcher thought bitterly, furling his hands into fists.

Dr. Sanders led them into a long room. There was only one door—one way in, one way out. Bulky chairs lined the gray walls. They reminded Fletcher of the hooded hair-dryer chairs at salons; heavy-duty domes hovered above each chair with black cables snaking out of the tops of the domes. The cables ran along the baseboards toward the wall opposite the door, and Fletcher saw a massive, movie theater–sized screen. Currently, it was filled with the snowy picture of a lost signal.

It cast the room in a flickering, hypnotic half-light.

Wordlessly, the guards took Fletcher, his friends, Zayne, and Alana to the chairs. Dr. Sanders watched, her shadowed face impassive, as Fletcher and the others were unbound and seated. Freya was stationed across from Fletcher, as well as Alana and Zayne, while Chase and Ollie were set up on either side of Fletcher.

No one resisted, no one struggled. A palpable sense of defeat hung in the air, and Fletcher couldn't even bring himself to look his friends in the eyes.

Once his wrists were shackled to the armrests, the dome hummed softly as it lowered onto his head. It clicked into place above his nose, cutting his line of sight in half.

Dr. Sanders walked over to his chair, her hands clasped behind her back.

"I must thank you for tipping me off, Fletcher." Her voice was low and scratchy, as if she'd been nursing a cough. "Rhett Villa overheard you thinking about—how did you put it?—the Memory Ghosts' 'audacious plan to break into the Fold.' This little plan might've actually worked if not for you."

Fletcher closed his eyes, his bottom lip trembling. *She knew we were coming. She let us get this far on purpose so she could ensnare us.*

"Let them go," Alana demanded. "They're just kids. You have us, and—"

"Don't speak unless spoken to!" Dr. Sanders thundered, her words echoing in the room. Fletcher's eyes shot back open. He sank into the chair, startled by her explosive response. She fell into a coughing fit as she paced among the six of them, then regained her voice. "Don't worry. I shall be releasing *all* of you once the indexing is complete."

The hairs on Fletcher's arms stood.

"This will all be over soon." Dr. Sanders turned and stood with her back to the flickering screen. Her outline glowed a ghostly white. "After your memories have been deleted, you'll be reborn. Think of this as a fresh start, a new beginning."

The room fell quiet as the implications of Dr. Sanders's words hit them.

Fletcher couldn't believe it was actually over, that everything leading up to this moment had been for naught. And every important memory he'd formed thus far, every question he'd had and secret he'd learned, was about to be stolen from him.

And Freya? Would he lose all memories of her too? The idea sent him into a rage. He thrashed about—kicking at the air and pulling his hands against the shackles. The cold metal dug into his skin, burning his wrists. He screamed. He tugged. He threw all his weight back into the chair over and over and over again, rattling the dome that encased his head.

It was no use. Eventually, he sagged forward, panting and humiliated.

Dr. Sanders cleared her throat. "If you're done, Mr. Cohen, we'll begin now."

On her command, the screen behind her filled with vertical color bars. The domes above everyone's heads lit up a dark purple. The chairs began to rattle subtly.

And Dr. Sanders and her guards exited the room and locked the door.

61

FREYA IZQUIERDO

At first, it's just a tingle, a dull sensation that spreads across the crown of my head. But the tingling swiftly turns to burning, a white-hot pain that seems to set my mind ablaze.

My head is on fire! I breathe unsteadily. It's actually *on fire!*

Even with my eyes clamped shut, dancing colors from the large screen bleed through my eyelids. I'm in far too much discomfort to open my eyes, but I picture flashes of our memories filling the screen as they're identified and deleted.

I hear Ollie and Chase moan.

The headache intensifies.

And the experience somehow becomes *more* unnatural. This . . . this forced forgetting is like seeing a picture in my mind's eye—an image right up close to my face—that slowly fades into wispy shadows. Then, with a gasp, I lose complete recollection of the image. The disorientation is so terrifying! It's something akin to feeling lost, to finding myself in an unfamiliar place and having no memory of what brought me there or why I'm there.

The cycle continues.

A picture. A face. A moment. *An emotion.*

Then it's gone.

"Freya . . ." Fletcher's voice is shaky and small. At first, I believe it to be coming from within a fading memory. But then I realize he's trying to call out to me from across the room. "If . . . if we forget one another . . . I promise to find my way back to you."

My throat tightens as another image appears in my mind's eye: I see me and my friends, laughing at our secret spot on the shore of Juniper Lake. I see the crepe myrtle, the white tree that shines in the forest. I claw at this scene with my mind, try to hold on to it with everything I have.

But the images drift toward the darkness, toward the unseen hole that's pulling them away.

Before the memory vanishes, I say, "I will find you too, Fletch—"

The pain abruptly stops. The chairs stop rattling. The overhead lights flick on.

And a familiar voice calls out to us.

62

FLETCHER COHEN

Dean Mendelsohn raced across the room, unshackling Freya and Ollie first, then Fletcher and everyone else.

"Wh-what's going on?" Fletcher managed to ask as he slid out of the chair and landed on all fours. Before the dean could reply, Chase retched a few times before ultimately throwing up. Zayne stumbled over to Chase and helped him to his feet.

"What's going on is that you're running out of time," the dean said, cracking open the door and peering into the hallway. "All security personnel have been drawn outside, where the protesters are—"

"Why are you helping us?" Alana asked, taking Freya and Ollie by the hand and slowly guiding them up.

Dean Mendelsohn's eyes grew soft. "I couldn't sit by after I learned what Dr. Sanders intended to do to you. I've always been a pawn in Memory Frontier's game. I know that now. And I'm ready for the game to be over."

Fletcher found his way over to Freya and his friends, and they loosely held one another in a hug. They broke away as the dean said, "I don't know what you planned, but if it means taking away Dr. Sanders's and Memory Frontier's power, I want to help."

"How did you manage to get inside Fort Knox?" Chase asked, rubbing his forehead.

Dean Mendelsohn blinked. "I walked in through the front door." He held up his lanyard and ID badge.

"Oh, right. Duh."

The dean handed Alana the small bag that Zayne had brought off the elevator. She took it, nodded once, and the dean opened the door all the way and stepped aside.

"Let's move," Dean Mendelsohn whispered.

In a mad dash, everyone stumbled down the corridor toward the set of double doors labeled ARCHIVES. The dean led the way, and when he reached the square reader mounted on the wall, he flashed his credentials.

Fletcher held his breath.

The lighting seemed dimmest on this side of the corridor.

After a soft, barely audible *ding*, Dean Mendelsohn threw open the doors. "Go! I'll stay in the hall and guard the entrance."

63

FREYA IZQUIERDO

At the center of the massive room is an open reel-to-reel tape machine. It's a tall Restorey, nearly three times as big as the one in Dean Mendelsohn's bunker.

There's a single reclined chair beside the Restorey.

The huge, eight-foot walls that surround us are nothing but square filing drawers. Hundreds, maybe thousands of them, ordered with some kind of numeric system.

Bluish light bathes the entire place.

Behind me, Zayne slams the door shut, unfastens his belt, and ties the two knobs together with an intricate knot. I hope that between this and Dean Mendelsohn out in the hall, it's enough to stall anyone who tries to get inside.

Fletcher, Ollie, Chase, and I strip to our jumpsuits while Alana races toward the Restorey. She spills the contents of the small bag onto the pavement.

Electrode stickers.

A single syringe.

IV bags of fluid and plastic catheters.

A vial of sedative.

We roll up our sleeves, plopping down in a half circle around Alana. Zayne, meanwhile, jogs alongside the filing drawers, mumbling to himself. Sooner than I expect, he halts and hunches over, saying a number sequence out loud.

"This is it!" He pulls open the drawer. It extends nearly six feet, like one of those cadaver trays in a morgue, and he starts searching for the memory tape in question.

"Freya, it's your turn." I turn back to Alana, then give her consent to insert my IV catheter. My adrenaline is pumping so much that I don't even feel it pinch. I use this brief moment to take inventory of my memories. I focus on what I can recall and try not to feel anxious about what I cannot.

The problem with forgetting is that you don't know what you forgot.

But I remember Fletcher and my friends. Foxtail Academy. Our spot in the woods, our time together on campus. I know there are now gaps, moments that were forcibly taken from me, but I home in on what I remember.

I glance at Fletcher, Ollie, and Chase. All three of them are applying their own electrode stickers to their heads and reclining on the floor.

Alana preps the sedative and is inserting the tip of the syringe into the vial when Zayne bellows, "It's not here!"

"What?" Alana almost drops her things. "What are you talking about?"

"The memory tape. It's miss—"

Urgent, muted voices approach on the other side of the double doors. We hear a scuffle. Shouting.

Oh no . . . the dean.

After a second or two, whoever is outside starts jerking the door handles and demanding entrance. I picture Dean Mendelsohn being restrained, unable to do anything but watch as everything unfolds.

Zayne slams the filing drawer shut and races toward the doors. He braces them with his back.

The reality of our dire situation washes over me.

And then things get worse.

"I imagine you're looking for the memory tape that's already queued up." Dr. Sanders's ice-cold voice sends gooseflesh up my arms.

You have got to be kidding me.

She appears from behind the Restorey holding a sleek black handgun at her side. The Restorey is so massive that we never saw her hiding behind it.

She pulls the hammer back and points the gun at Alana's chest. "I'm alerted every time a visitor signs in at the front desk. At first, I thought it strange Dean Mendelsohn was paying us a visit. Apparently, he felt it necessary to meddle in my affairs. He should not have done that.

"Now, don't let me stop you. These four were about to knife a very important memory."

The banging on the doors heightens with a low thudding sound. They're using a battering ram. But Zayne holds his ground, grinding his teeth.

Why is she doing this? Why not just shoot us on the spot!

Beside me, Alana grits her teeth. "How did you find out about this memory?"

Dr. Sanders turns to me. "For that, I have Ms. Izquierdo to thank." She winks one of her bloodshot eyes at me. "You and Mr. Cohen sure are a pair, aren't you? You've made this all too easy for me. You see, if you hadn't expressed such distress about snow, I might've never made the connection. Your visions aren't of your past, are they? You can see into the future, which means you saw yourself knifing *this*." She points at the tall Restorey with her free hand, and for the first time I notice there's already a tape threaded in the reels.

My hands begin to tremble. My eyes start to mist. *No, no, no.*

The slamming against the door gets louder.

Beside me, Fletcher, Ollie, and Chase are petrified; the only part of them that moves is their chests as they suck in quiet gasps of air.

"*Now.*" Dr. Sanders narrows her eyes at Alana. "Kindly finish prepping our memory knifers. There's no point in them not getting what they came for, right?"

I can tell Alana knows it's a trap, but she visibly weighs her options: resist and get shot, then have Dr. Sanders tether us to the Restorey herself, or just skip the getting shot part.

Either way, we're at Dr. Sanders's mercy.

Alana swears under her breath but cautiously rises to her feet and connects our wires to four inputs on the Restorey. Dr. Sanders keeps her gun trained on Alana's back. Next, Alana slowly stalks back to us and picks up the syringe.

As she kneels beside Ollie to apply the sedative, Dr. Sanders says to me, "I guess you didn't foresee any of this happening, did you?"

Zayne screams something at Dr. Sanders, but I'm too flustered— too shell-shocked—to make sense of his obscenities.

Dr. Sanders laughs wryly at him. "I'd get out of the way. One way or another, those MACE agents are getting inside."

"Why are you doing this?" I ask as Alana moves on to Chase. "Why not just kill us all?"

She glares at me, her red eyes blazing with hate. "Because the only thing worse than not knowing the truth is knowing the truth— and not being able to do *a thing* about it."

Alana finishes up with Fletcher and then inserts the tip of the syringe into my IV catheter.

Just as my vision starts to cloud, I see Fletcher getting to his feet.

"After we knife this memory tape, we'll just find another way to get the truth out there!"

Dr. Sanders's tone is chilling in its nonchalance. "Not if you never wake up."

The last things I see before I'm pulled into the memory: Dr. Sanders walks to the Restorey and flips a switch; a mini explosion blows the doors open and sends Zayne sliding across the floor; and the blast knocks Fletcher off his feet.

He smacks into the reclined chair and then tumbles onto the pavement headfirst.

I try to scream, but my voice barely croaks, and then the neon lights slingshot me into the memory.

I fall onto the snow.

Ollie appears next, followed by Chase.

He jumps up and helps me and Ollie to our feet.

Then I see him. *Fletcher!* I trudge across the thick snow toward his unmoving form. He lies on the white powder, one arm twisted behind his back in an unnatural way. Just like in my vision, his left eye is bruised and swollen.

I pull him toward me, sobbing and screaming for him to wake up.

Fletcher just lies there in my lap, looking colder than the snow.

Chase and Ollie stand over me, and I don't have to look up at them to know they're crying too.

Guys. My voice sounds like a whimper. *Why won't he just wake up?*

64

FLETCHER COHEN

Fletcher's eyes blinked open.

He stood on his feet in the basement of the Fold, though he expected to find himself thrown from the blast.

But he was still standing.

And something was . . . off.

The world was moving with significant delay: Zayne was rolling across the ground from the explosion in slow motion; Dr. Sanders stood at the Restorey, her hand on the lever; Alana was attempting to shield her head, but her hands were barely to her cheekbones, moving at a snail's pace toward her clamped-shut eyes; Freya, Chase, and Ollie were lying on the pavement, their eyes closed.

And . . .

And there was a floating mass—an assemblage of countless particles that formed what *looked* like a body—lying between Chase and Freya, where Fletcher should have been.

65

FREYA IZQUIERDO

Let me carry him, Chase offers lightly.

No! I hug Fletcher's limp body against mine. *I'm waiting here until the memory ejects us!*

I don't think it's that simple. Ollie points. In the twilight, we see two forms trudging up a snowy embankment toward the mansion. That's when I perceive something unique about this memory: it doesn't belong to just one person; it belongs to two.

We're knifing a shared memory—Alexander Lochamire's and Philip Lear's. Somehow, this is a fusion of *both* of their memories from the same evening.

I glance around. There's no edge, no visible dome that marks the perimeter of this memory. That must mean shared memory tapes are much stronger—much stabler.

C'mon. Chase bends down and scoops Fletcher into his arms, cradling him while Ollie pulls me to my feet. We scamper off toward

Alexander and Mr. Lear, and when I glance behind me, I see no foot-prints in the snow.

We jog through a frozen garden toward the mansion's patio entrance. Alexander opens the door and we slip in before he closes it.

The memory informs me that this is one of Alexander's many homes. Inside, a college-aged and unmarried Brenda Lochamire is gathering some books off the coffee table in the living room. She says hello to Mr. Lear and bids her father good night. Seeing Dr. Sanders enrages me; even though I know it's just a memory of her, I'd give anything to charge at her.

"Here, let me take that." Alexander grabs Mr. Lear's wool coat and scarf. He hangs these, along with his own coat, near the door and then joins Mr. Lear by the fireplace. Chase gently sets Fletcher on the oriental rug. I get on the floor and place his head in my lap. In the firelight, I can see that Fletcher is breathing, albeit very weakly.

Ollie comes over to my left side, placing a soft hand on my upper back.

He's going to be okay, she whispers. *We'll find a way out of this.*

Alexander crosses his legs. His face is gaunt, his eyes sunken, and the shadows from the fire only obscure his features more. In that moment, the memory informs me that his dementia has accelerated, that the only thing preserving his agency is artificial recall.

"Now, old friend." Alexander makes a temple with his fingers. "What was it you needed to discuss?"

66

FLETCHER COHEN

Do something, Fletcher!

He looked around frantically as the scene continued to transpire in slow motion. Through the blazing blast—through the settling debris—he could see MACE agents positioned behind riot shields.

By this point, Alana had shielded her face and dropped to a half crouch. Zayne had stopped rolling and lay unmoving on the floor. Dr. Sanders remained by the Restorey, though she had turned around now. Bits and shards of metal were tumbling toward Freya, Chase, and Ollie. Fletcher reached out to bat the raining rubble away.

He gasped.

The debris reacted to his hand. It changed trajectory midair, its course now avoiding his friends.

I'm here for a reason, Fletcher realized. *So do something!*

67

FREYA IZQUIERDO

We need to discuss the side effects of your MeReader, Alexander. Mr. Lear leans forward in his chair, absently flattening his paisley tie.

It's under control, I assure you. Alexander sighs, then calls for his attendant to bring them some drinks.

Thank the heavens. Mr. Lear sags into a seat. *So you've made the necessary alterations to the design? Or are you stalling the release so it can remain in beta until we fix its flaws?*

I said it was under control, didn't I?

Mr. Lear looks anxious again. *What have you done?*

I glance nervously at Chase and Ollie.

Philip, what's the one thing you and I discovered when we founded Hart Industries? A woman appears. She sets two chilled glasses of water on the table and leaves. *That businesses and consumers will sometimes purchase things they want, but they'll adopt and embrace a product when they believe they need it. Do you remember? People first must feel this burning need, this necessity, before they can embrace a product. They must believe they can't live without it.*

Alexander . . .

I'm choosing to view these aftereffects as an opportunity. Alexander takes a drink of his water. *Imagine it, Philip. What if our MeReaders didn't cause eye discoloration? What if they weren't responsible for the other aftereffects we've seen in testing, like spells of memory loss or—*

One of our volunteers has succumbed to terrifying fits of hallucination. He claims he can see the future!

Alexander flips his hand. *There will be some whose minds reject my neurotech more than others. That's unavoidable. But those are rare cases, Philip. Exceptions, not the rule. We'll just have them committed to a hospital so they can be monitored.*

Mr. Lear grips his armrests as if he's about to leap out of his chair. *Any neuroscientist worth his salt will immediately see that the patients' symptoms are caused by your MeReaders!*

Then we'll establish our own hospitals. Private institutions fully staffed by our scientists and doctors.

As everything starts to become clear, I feel my mouth falling open. Beside me, Chase and Ollie are starting to tremble.

Just what are you proposing?

It's simple. Alexander leans forward and wipes away the condensation ring on the table with his bony hand. *Our MeReaders don't cause memory loss; they're needed tools in our fight against memory loss. But this memory loss is sweeping the globe with the ferocity of a pandemic. Artificial recall becomes a necessity, not a commodity. And that's it. That's our story.*

But that is a lie. How on earth will you sell what is clearly a lie to the entire world?

Memory indexing presents a unique opportunity for world leaders. Alexander sets down his water and smiles crookedly. *Think about it. We have billed this entire project as a means for people to safeguard their most precious memories. Our name alone, Memory Frontier, evokes a sense of exploration into cognitive territory that we, as a species, have never trod before!*

Only you're not safeguarding people's "precious memories" at all, are you? Mr. Lear's jaw begins to twitch. In this shared memory, I perceive dueling emotions: Alexander is filled with dark ambition; Mr. Lear is angry and troubled. *You would secretly catalog memory tapes and make them available to the highest bidder?*

Well, now, that sounds rather crass when you put it like that. Think of this as a way for a government and its law enforcement to more effectively protect the public! What if terrorists', rapists', and murderers' deepest and darkest secrets were available to district attorneys, supreme courts, and—

Mr. Lear stands. *This is wrong. And it will never work.*

All it takes is the first memory tape.

The living room falls eerily quiet. Snow drums against the windows, though it barely registers a sound. Behind a wrought-iron screen, the logs snap and pop in the fireplace. In my lap, Fletcher stirs, though his eyes remain shut and his breathing erratic.

Mr. Lear takes a step forward. *What are you talking about?*

The fiction of memory loss will be written into everyone's first memory tape. Alexander crosses his legs with much effort, like the simple movement takes all the wind out of him. *We will call it Memory Killer, the great enemy of the mind. But this pandemic won't divide us; it will unite us around artificial recall.*

No . . . you can't . . .

I have, old friend. It's done. Now that the MeReaders have buy-in from nearly twenty countries, it's only a matter of time before its adoption spreads throughout the rest of the globe.

All color has drained from Mr. Lear's face. I perceive great distress on his part, and that distress extends to me, Ollie, and Chase. Ollie is shaking her head; Chase runs his hands through his hair, looking on the cusp of sobbing; I feel numb.

Memory Killer is a *side effect* of the MeReaders. As are the gray

eyes, the accelerated memory loss, and the "unlocking" of unprecedented cognitive abilities such as mind reading, premonitions, and
whatever else is out there.

This is why Fletcher's father preserved his first memory tape.
Mr. Lear recruited him and the others, told them the truth, and found
their first memory tapes to supply the proof. That's what was so
strange about Fletcher's father's behavior in that tape! When Fletcher
and Chase knifed that memory, they witnessed the exact moment
Joshua Cohen was implanted with the lie about Memory Killer . . .

Now we know the truth.

*You would lay bare everyone's memories under the guise of granting
them agency over their lives.* Mr. Lear walks over to the door and gathers his jacket and scarf. *You won't get away with this.*

Be careful, Philip. Alexander pushes himself up shakily and stands.
You've a vested interest in all this too. Or have you forgotten?

That last question is a cruel joke, because at this moment the
memory informs me that Mr. Lear's wife died of Alzheimer's. It
happened shortly before they sold Hart Industries. The fatal disease
claimed her life slowly, over the span of a terrible year, and Mr. Lear
is still racked with trauma and grief.

Both of these men have been impacted by the terrible effects of
dementia and Alzheimer's. In a way, Memory Frontier has been their
joint crusade. It's given them each a path to healing.

Although Alexander's path clearly took a disastrous detour.

Our MeReaders will offer memory preservation. Alexander slips his
hands into his pockets. *But they'll also empower us to locate and destroy
the harmful ones.*

Mr. Lear says nothing as he puts his jacket back on, then his scarf.

*Just remember, Philip. People will always inject medication into their
systems despite side effects because the reward of healing outweighs the risk.
Memory Killer is just another side effect.*

Goodbye, Alexander. And then Mr. Lear is gone.

Nothing happens.

We're not ejected from the memory tape.

Instead, the memory continues to play out. Alexander sighs, walks over to the end table beside his couch, and retrieves a hardback book. He sits and, after putting on a pair of reading glasses, begins to read as the fire dies. He eventually clicks on a tabletop lamp.

That Restorey in the archives. Ollie turns to me, her eyes flickering with fear. *It was . . . big. Much bigger than the one Dean Mendelsohn uses.*

Chase finishes her thought. *Meaning there's no telling just how long this memory tape goes.*

This scene that we just witnessed must have happened, what, ten years ago? Maybe eleven or twelve? Is it possible that Dr. Sanders sent us into a memory tape that spans years?

The sedative Alana gave us has to run out eventually, right?

I don't know. I glance at the door that Mr. Lear exited through, and a thought occurs to me. *Here, take Fletcher.* I gently transfer his head onto Ollie's lap and leap to my feet.

Freya! Where are you going? Chase sounds scared, not curious.

To test a theory.

❖ ❖ ❖

Outside in the dark snowfall, I spot Mr. Lear traipsing across the grounds toward an idling car at the end of a winding driveway. I run at full speed, and the closer I get to him, the more I feel the memory beginning to split from a shared one to an individual one.

But oddly, it's not Mr. Lear's.

As he approaches the car, a younger Gemma steps out of the driver's side. The memory informs me it belongs to Gemma now.

How strange . . .

She leaves the door open, jogs to the passenger side, and gets in. I seize this brief window and slip into the car before Mr. Lear does. I fumble over the center console and collapse into the back as Mr. Lear shuts the door.

Well? Gemma asks.

It's just as we feared. Mr. Lear pulls his scarf off and rubs his hands to warm them. *We must go to the press immediately.*

Which publication? Doesn't Lochamire own several?

Mr. Lear swears.

And what will you say? How will you prove that his neurotechnology isn't sound? Gemma grabs the handlebar above the window. I perceive a faint wave of anxiety creeping in. *Can we obtain documents or some kind of physical proof? Otherwise, it's just your word over his.*

Mr. Lear pauses for a moment, then his mouth forms a circle as an idea forms. *This memory.*

What?

This memory—my conversation tonight with Alexander—is proof. We use artificial recall against him.

My oh my. Gemma gazes out the windshield. *But how will you extract that memory and show it to the world? I don't imagine you'll be subjecting yourself to a MeReader anytime soon now that we know about its flaws.*

I must, in order for this to work. Mr. Lear pulls a notepad out of the glove box and starts scribbling something. *Alexander is archiving all of his memories, so what if there was a way to merge two memories— from two separate individuals—of the exact moment or scene from the past?*

Your memory of tonight plus his memory of tonight fused into one *tape.* Gemma clicks her tongue. *It would contain a rich amount of detail to be sure. I'm not even certain a memory tape could hold that much data.*

But it's possible. Now, I'd have to have a change of heart. Mr. Lear keeps writing. *Convince Alexander I'm still committed to Memory Frontier so I could experiment with this hypothesis in secret.*

Won't he just have his memory erased, or at the very least avoid imprinting it onto a tape? Something tells me Alexander isn't the type to leave his tracks uncovered.

Mr. Lear stops writing. *You're aware of hyperthymesia, yes?*

Of course—one's ability to recall an unprecedented number of details with ease.

Alexander strives for more than that . . . This is no longer just about his battle with dementia. He believes he'll achieve an awakening if he can recall every single memory from his past.

In the back seat, I shiver at that. Why would someone want to be able to remember *every single thing* in their life? Not only does it sound impossible, it sounds . . . crazy, self-absorbed, and kind of harmful. If Alexander spends all his time remembering, when does he spend time living . . . forming *new* memories? I can't imagine a life spent endlessly scrolling through one's own history, playing back memory tape after memory tape.

Alexander Lochamire is crazier than I thought. Gemma's tone is filled with pity. *Okay, so you imprint your memory from tonight onto a tape and then try to find some way to merge it with Alexander's. How in the world will you do that? It could take years before his technology catches up with your intent!*

I have to try.

And suppose you succeed. What happens when the MeReader locates the memory of our conversation in this very car? Aren't you worried Alexander will be flagged?

Mr. Lear writes down something else. For a moment, it's just him fleshing out his thoughts and Gemma watching expectantly.

Then, *I'll need your help.*

Well, I've gathered that. Be more specific.

I need you to imprint this memory onto a tape. Then I can try to find a way to erase it from my consciousness.

Gemma stares back, breathless. *You want me to use a MeReader?*

In fact, I'll erase everything from today except for my conversation with

Alexander. Then I'll take your *memory from our conversation in this car and tack it onto the fused memory of my conversation with—*

But why, Philip? Say we go through all this work and you actually man-age to archive Alexander's lies onto a single memory tape . . . what then?

Mr. Lear sets down his pen. *Then someone will artificially recall the memory and show the world the truth.*

I sit with all this information, my head spinning. Mr. Lear knew that the only way to expose Memory Frontier's dark secrets was by using this memory against Alexander. He also knew that in order for this to work, he'd have to wipe his own memories of the secret plan in case he was ever caught—in case Alexander wised up to him.

So after the evidence was successfully preserved, he and Gemma went into hiding. Mr. Lear couldn't risk getting caught and having his mind scanned by Memory Frontier and their ever-advancing MeReaders. This meant he'd never be able to step foot near the Fold.

To Alexander Lochamire, he became a wanted man.

And Mr. Lear had to find someone else to artificially recall this memory for him.

In fact, I wouldn't be surprised if he has absolutely no recollection of what he initially intended for us to do with all this information.

In the window beside me, I expect to see my reflection. But of course, I don't; I wasn't present when Gemma formed this memory. Instead, through the snow-coated gloaming, I see the edges of her memory begin to close in.

Philip . . . is it even possible to access someone else's memories? As a scientist in this field, you'll have to trust me when I say I think that's impossible.

Of course. At the time of this conversation, knifing hadn't been achieved yet.

We must try. Alexander's words from this evening cannot be forgotten. To forget is to die.

I connect the dots. *This* is Gemma's complicated story, the one she alluded to when we said goodbye: the truth about MeReaders and artificial recall. I think of Fletcher's Memory Killer File, how he was obsessed with discovering whether it was possible for Memory Killer to strike during recall. Now I understand . . . Memory Killer is a *symptom* of artificial recall.

Yet it doesn't matter that I know the complicated story now too. None of it matters while we're trapped in here.

Gemma's memory ends. Ordinarily, I'd have been ejected. Only this time, when I close my eyes and brace for the jerking momentum, I hear Ollie's soft words in my ear. *Hey, what happened?*

I open my eyes. I'm back in Alexander's mansion, sitting near the hearth with Ollie, Chase, and Fletcher, who still hasn't regained consciousness. When Gemma's memory from this evening elapsed, I must've been pulled back into Alexander's. With Gemma's memory severed, we remain inside only Lochamire's. And speaking of Alexander, he is still on the couch with a book in his lap. He slowly turns a page and adjusts his posture.

I mean to suggest memory ejecting—for one of us to leave the mansion and charge the memory's edges to see if we'll simply be ejected. Yet I can't bring myself to move or talk.

Freya? Chase scoots closer to me. I hear Dr. Sanders's words reverberating in my head in an endless loop: *The only thing worse than not knowing the truth is knowing the truth—and not being able to do a thing about it.*

I stroke Fletcher's face with the back of my hand. The *real* Fletcher feels miles and miles away. This version of Fletcher is just a projection, like Chase and Ollie.

Like myself.

This version of us is all we have right now. It may be all we ever have again.

I pull Ollie and Chase into a hug. We sit there, huddled around Fletcher's unmoving form, slowly accepting that up there in the archives—where Dr. Sanders is, where her MACE agents are flooding the basement and likely dragging Zayne, Alana, and Dean Mendelsohn off—the situation is as bleak as it is down here, in Alexander Lochamire's decades-spanning memory tape.

And in this memory that's not my memory—this mental prison—I feel myself growing weak with defeat. Whatever hopes and dreams I had for the future will die right here, in the past.

For all the energy and attention I poured into my premonitions, it ended up not mattering a single bit. I never could have foreseen this end. I never could have prevented it.

I'm so sorry I broke my promise, I whisper to Fletcher, hoping he can hear me but deep down knowing that he likely cannot. *I never wanted you to get hurt. I just wanted to—*

Fletcher's eyes flash open and he screams, *Hang on!*

68

FLETCHER COHEN

Fletcher rushed to the Restorey. He threw his entire weight into Dr. Sanders, who slowly flew backward through the air after the awkward impact—her face gradually contorting into one of utter surprise. He watched her lose her footing and stumble, moving as if she were underwater.

He grabbed hold of the lever she'd pulled.

The MACE agents were getting closer, creeping into the wide room like an oil leak filling a crack in pavement.

He wrapped his fingers around the lever tightly.

"Hang on!" And he flipped it to the OFF position.

The Restorey's lightboard began to flicker from green to blue. Fletcher spun and sprinted toward the particles that hung suspended above the ground. Then he lay *into* the glowing form—filling the space with his body and—

Darkness . . .

. . . muted, far-off sounds . . .

. . . shouts and slamming and gunfire . . .

69

FREYA IZQUIERDO

I gag on warm, smoke-filled air. My head is fuzzy, and I blink through my unfocused vision. We're back in the archives. There's shouting and gunfire.

Chase's head appears over me. "C'mon!"

He helps me into a sitting position, then we crawl across the cold pavement toward Ollie and Fletcher, whose eyes are still sealed shut. Ollie holds him like I held him in the memory tape.

Once my vision fully returns, I see that protesters are overwhelming the MACE agents who blew down the door. Somehow, the men and women burst through the fence and have made their way down here, where it's pure anarchy.

As we four huddle underneath the knifing chair, I try to spot Dr. Sanders. She's nowhere to be seen. Alana, meanwhile, has the presence of mind to unthread the memory tape from the Restorey. She wisely shed her MACE gear and wears only a tank top and joggers.

Zayne, who is bleeding from one of his ears, helps Alana transfer the tape to a case.

Another round of gunshots rings out.

Chase shields us with his body.

I glance down at Fletcher, and my heart soars to great heights. He's blinking his eyes open.

"Wh-what's going on?"

I graze his bruise with the tips of my fingers. I'm so grateful for this bruise. This minor injury that will heal in a week or two. Fletcher winces at my touch.

"I think you saved us," I whisper.

We rush down the crowded hall toward the elevators. The deafening disorder makes it nearly impossible to navigate corridors, yet we find our way toward one of the walls and move along the outskirts of the rioting. Fletcher has one arm around Chase and the other around Zayne; Alana leads the way, with me and Ollie at the rear.

"Okay, so *now* what?" Chase shouts. Crashing noises sound on higher floors. This place is getting overwhelmed. I pray we can make it out in one piece.

Instead of taking us to the elevators, Alana takes us to a single door that's several feet away. Zayne procures Mr. Maddox's credentials from his pocket and tosses them to Alana, which she uses to get us access. She flings open the door and we spill into the maintenance stairwell.

"Stairs?" Chase rattles off some colorful expletives.

"Gotta move." Alana flies, taking the stairs two steps at a time. When she reaches the first-floor landing, she consults the rectangular map that's hanging on the door. "Third floor. Okay. So. Everyone *has* to think about the third floor right now!"

Everyone's panting, trying to catch their breath. "I . . . what?"

"Just do it!" Zayne urges. So we all stop and loiter on the landing, and I think, *Third floor . . . third floor . . . this is me thinking about the third floor.*

"Good. That should do the trick." Alana continues to bolt up the stairs. "Follow me, guys!"

Confused but adrenaline-filled, we all climb the stairs as fast as we can. Fletcher even manages to regain his faculties, now using the railing to guide his steps.

We reach the third floor and Alana rams the door open with her shoulder. It's loud and hectic in the white corridor. Men and women in lab coats run about, shouting to one another. Phones ring off the hook. An alarm sounds overhead.

In the sea of confusion, a familiar face emerges.

"My oh my." Gemma wears a hospital gown, and she's tagged with a barcoded wristband. "How's *this* for a change of plans?"

I run past Alana and hug Gemma. I don't really know why I do it, I just feel compelled to. She chuckles softly, but in that soft and scratchy voice I hear brief shock turn to gratitude.

"Well, it's good to see you too, Freya."

"Is it here?" Alana asks once we break away.

"Yes," another voice says. "It's on the far end of the hall." A young woman, also clad in a hospital gown, emerges. Her eyes are tired, her skin pasty white.

Alana's and Zayne's faces fill with color. *"Emilia!"*

"Wasn't sure we'd see you again." Alana clasps her forearm.

"That makes two of us." Emilia Vanguard regards me and my friends. "You enlisted the help of *kids?*"

"Don't underestimate these four." Gemma winks at me. "They just single-handedly saved the world."

❖ ❖ ❖

We cut through the chaos unnoticed. Beneath our feet, I hear more gunshots rattling off. We're on the fringes of a battlefield.

Emilia takes us to a door at the end of the hallway. The door plate bears a numeric sequence similar to the ones on the filing drawers in the archives.

She pulls down on the handle. It's unlocked. And we walk into the room single file.

Alana flips on the light and shuts the door, deadbolting it immediately. The only thing in the room is a large mechanical device that looks similar to both a film projector and a transmitter. The body is square and boxy, and four reels are mounted to the top at staggered heights. Near the base, there's a long display panel with rounded edges. Right now, the screen is black.

Gemma steps aside as Alana and Zayne rush toward the device and set to work threading Alexander Lochamire's memory tape into the big reels.

Fletcher, Ollie, Chase, and I collapse onto the ground, absolutely spent.

Ollie points halfheartedly. "What is that thing?"

"Oh, that?" Gemma smiles. "It's Alexander's very own memory network. You see, in his old age, he's not able to travel much. So R&D developed a way to send Alexander his memories across a unique, undetectable frequency. This way Alexander can just artificially recall any tape in the archives from the warm comfort of his bed."

Zayne opens a small panel on the side of the body and begins to redirect some wires.

"Tell me, what happened down there?" Gemma asks us while her fellow Memory Ghosts race against the clock. Emilia remains stationed near the exit, her ear to the door.

We take turns filling her in, and when we get to the part about Fletcher, she snaps her fingers.

"You have no recollection of what happened after you blacked out, Mr. Cohen?"

Fletcher shakes his head and looks away, embarrassed.

"Yet someone stopped the memory tape!" Gemma turns to Alana, who has her tongue clamped between her teeth while she works. "And what did you see?"

"I dunno," Alana replies absently, trying to focus on the last reel. "Dr. Sanders just . . . stumbled backward, but it was *after* the blast. I remember thinking how odd that was. And then the lever just flipped . . . and they started to wake up."

Gemma snaps again. "My oh my. Fletcher, have you ever heard of astral projection?"

Chase snickers. "What kinda projection is that?"

"An out-of-body experience," Gemma explains. "One in which the projected subject can actually interact with our reality. My oh my. How *fascinating.*"

Fletcher cocks his eyebrows. "You're saying that while I was unconscious I . . . projected a part of myself, er, *outside* my body?"

"So you have a gift too!" Ollie smacks him in the chest, and I chuckle despite myself. "Why didn't you tell us?"

"I don't remember projecting!" Fletcher turns to Gemma. "If that actually happened, why can't I remember it?"

Gemma taps her chin, thinking. Before she can respond, though, Alana finishes threading the last reel. She punches the air with accomplishment, pulls over a rolling stool, and sits down.

Zayne gives her a thumbs-up.

She flips on the device.

We all watch with rapt attention as the memory tape we just knifed begins to play on the small monitor. The picture quality is poor, but I'm guessing that's because the display can't fully handle all the detail of the scene.

And yet there are Mr. Lear and Alexander. Sitting by the fireplace in heated discussion.

Alana begins to cry. Zayne falls to his knees and hobbles over to her, pulling her into a hug. Behind us, I hear Emilia sniffing.

"What's happening?" I hazard, turning to Gemma.

"Zayne, he . . ." Gemma composes herself. "He was able to change the frequency. This clip, this memory tape, is broadcasting all over the airwaves on repeat."

"You're . . . you're serious?"

She nods, her tired eyes swelling with fresh tears. "And none of this would've been possible if you hadn't located this *exact* moment in Lochamire's long memory."

Except that Dr. Sanders is the one who queued up this memory tape on the Restorey, I think, realizing that she sealed her own fate.

"Still," Gemma says, replying to my thoughts. "Someone needed to knife the tape to confirm it was the correct memory before it was extracted from the archives. You did it, Freya. You guys actually did it."

Zayne and Alana join us by the door and we all get to our feet. Alana wipes her eyes with the hem of her tank top. "We should try to leave now. We can celebrate later. I suspect the National Guard is en route, so our best chance at getting out of here is—"

A loud gunshot resounds on the other side of the door. Everyone flinches and then ducks.

Everyone but Alana.

I peek up at her through my fingers. I see a perfect red circle expanding over her belly button. She looks down at her own blood, her eyes misting.

No, no . . .

Zayne and Emilia jump up and catch Alana together, shouting and yelling as they tear her away from the door. Whoever pulled the trigger took an intentional shot. This was no stray bullet.

Gemma, who's in the corner, looks back and forth between the projector and the door.

No, don't.

She turns her attention to me, smiling weakly. And then she stands, rushes to the door, opens it, and disappears.

There's a second gunshot.

70

FLETCHER COHEN

Without wasting a breath, Fletcher rushed into the hall and found Gemma pinning Dr. Sanders to the wall. A mass of bright-red blood spread between Gemma's shoulder blades.

Fletcher dove.

He smacked into them, Dr. Sanders lost her footing, and the three of them tumbled to the ground. Fletcher heard the loud distinct *clack* of her pistol hitting the linoleum as it slid away. Freya, Chase, Ollie, and Emilia rushed into the hall.

Before Dr. Sanders could roll Gemma's body off of herself, Chase located the gun and scooped it up. He trained the barrel on Dr. Sanders's head while Freya and Ollie gently removed Gemma and laid her on her back.

Zayne rushed past them, screaming for a medic. Emilia seemed in shock, unable to focus on either Gemma or Alana.

Freya slowly knelt beside Gemma's head. The woman's perfect

caramel-colored eyes stared at the ceiling, unblinking. Fletcher lowered himself to the floor, wincing, and placed his hand on Freya's trembling arm. Beside them, Dr. Sanders shouted, spittle spraying from her mouth. But her words were drowned out. The only thing Fletcher paid attention to were Gemma's doll eyes.

There wasn't a trace of gray in them.

INTERLUDE

The mansion sat atop the hill, despondent. It was the only building for miles. When Alexander Lochamire had commissioned it years ago, it was intended to be his retreat. His sanctuary.

It feels like a morgue in here, Mr. Lear reflected after he'd been shown in through the front door. The nurse led him down the familiar corridor to Alexander's rooms. Mr. Lear knocked twice.

The hoarse voice on the other side bid him welcome.

"I've been told I overuse the word *special*," Mr. Lear said after sitting beside the four-poster bed. Alexander lay under the covers, his frail body covered up to his neck and his bloodshot eyes half opened. Electrode stickers covered his bald head, and from these stickers sprang red and white wires that connected to a tabletop device. The open reel-to-reel tape machine hummed softly as the reels spun.

"The truth is," Mr. Lear continued, removing his fedora, "after Alzheimer's took Nora from me, I wasn't sure I'd ever find anyone special again. And yet life surprised me. The journey to this moment has been marked by the support of special individuals."

Mr. Lear grabbed the remote on the nightstand and clicked on the television across the room. The news came on, midbroadcast. Images flashed of the National Guard descending on the

Fold. Armed men and women divided MACE agents from the violent protesters. Smoke spiraled toward the sky. Bodies, debris, and bullet casings covered the desert floor.

And then the broadcast switched to the scene the Memory Ghosts had knifed. The footage was scratchy and crude, and it vacillated from color to black-and-white like an overplayed VHS tape. Yet there sat Philip Lear and Alexander Lochamire, openly discussing the secret about Memory Killer—that artificial recall actually causes memory loss.

"If you're just joining us, we have been playing this back all evening," the newscaster said over the footage, her voice quiet and quivery. "We're trying to verify the legitimacy of this clip, which shows Memory Frontier cofounders discussing artificial recall."

"The fiction of memory loss will be written into everyone's first memory tape," Alexander's voice said in the clip. "We will call it Memory Killer, the great enemy of the mind. But this pandemic won't divide us; it will unite us around artificial recall."

Mr. Lear clicked off the TV. "I suspect the authorities are on their way now to arrest us. It's over, old friend."

Alexander drew his hand up from beneath the covers and coughed into it. "No. Brenda will fix this. She possesses many of my memories now, and she'll know what to do."

"She's already in custody," Mr. Lear said firmly, putting his hat back on. "Wait. What do you mean she *possesses* your memories?"

Alexander's eyes fell shut. "I've been having her recall some of my memory tapes." Another cough. "With my time coming to an end, I needed to download details from my past somewhere safe to ensure—"

"That could kill her." Mr. Lear sighed, watching as Alexander opened his eyes. The redness from burst blood vessels gave his gaze a frightening quality.

Before Alexander could reply, sirens resounded in the distance.

Mr. Lear rose to his feet. He crossed the room but hesitated near the door when Alexander whispered, "You're guilty in all this too, Philip. You knew the truth about Memory Killer for over a decade and did nothing!"

"And I will atone for my sins." Mr. Lear stood beside the door, pocketing his hands. "We both will."

Urgent footfalls echoed down the corridor on the other side of the door. Before the police stormed the room, the open reel-to-reel tape deck on Alexander's nightstand stopped spinning.

71

FREYA IZQUIERDO

SIX MONTHS LATER

My friend Gemma Morris once said that storytelling is memory preservation. Some stories are fiction; some are innocent and help to pass the time; others hold the key to the truth. And just as everyone deserves to hear a good story, everyone deserves the truth.

In the months that followed the completion of the Task, the truth spread like daybreak's light—no corner of the land left untouched by its reach. That light, that reassurance, promised a better way.

At the Fold that fateful night, the National Guard descended on the buildings shortly after we lost Gemma Morris and Alana Khan. When the fighting was finally subdued, the MACE agents laid down their weapons. The mobs were corralled and led away in handcuffs, though they remained vocal all the while. The number of casualties was great; the Red Cross arrived and tended to the wounded.

Through it all, the Memory Frontier staff fully cooperated.

It's no wonder: In under an hour, the memory we broadcast made waves across the country. Alexander Lochamire's great lie about Memory Killer had been exposed. Memory Frontier stock plummeted. Employees around the world abandoned their posts. There were public burnings of MeReaders and Restoreys that very evening. There were even calls for Alexander Lochamire to be burned at the stake.

I half expected the nation to implode.

But more often than not, people are resilient. They find a way to persevere.

What other choice do we have?

We quickly found a way to ween off artificial recall. For some, the process was painless. Others experienced intense withdrawals and even more intense aftereffects. But soon our dependency on artificial recall waned, and the rebuilding began in earnest.

❖ ❖ ❖

"I can't believe you're still living here." Nicole hops onto her bed and pulls a book off her nightstand.

"What's that supposed to mean?"

"Dude. You turned eighteen in February. You can live literally *anywhere* but here!"

"Sounds like you just want this room to yourself."

"Be that as it may . . ." She cracks open her book, then shoots me a smirk.

I finish tying my Chuck Taylors and grab my hoodie off the closet-door hook. "Where would I even stay?"

Nicole shrugs. "I dunno. Figured you and your *beau* would have moved in together at this point."

I roll my eyes. "I'm still in high school, you know. At least for another two weeks."

"Speaking of Señor Cohen . . . you going to see him now?"

"Actually, no."

"Oh?"

"My father's picking me up."

Nicole lowers her book and gives me a soft-eyed smile. "Awesome."

"You know," I say, grabbing the door. "Last year, when you started skipping artificial recall, you didn't experience any of the intense withdrawals that Memory Frontier warned about. Did you?"

She shakes her head and returns to her book. "Nope."

It's crazy how evidence of the truth can exist all around us. But if we're not looking for it, if we're just wrapped up in someone's lie, we're as good as blind.

Alexander Lochamire blinded us all.

Thankfully, miracles actually happen.

❖ ❖ ❖

My father drives a clunker, a beat-up El Camino that's been through the wringer. Twice. We drive around Long Beach at twilight, neither of us saying much. Around Christmas last year, I decided to call him. I wasn't ready for full-blown reconciliation and healing. Not yet. But I was ready to try.

I *am* ready to try.

So we drive and don't talk much.

We sit in each other's silences, learning the unspoken things about one another, like how he rubs his mustache with his bottom lip at every red light. Or how I constantly fidget with my seatbelt strap, tracing my fingernails across the nylon.

Tonight he pulls into a parking lot outside a baseball park. He gets out of the car without saying anything, walks a few paces, and stares out at the lights standing tall over the field. "Eye of the Tiger" by Survivor plays scratchily over the loudspeakers.

My father just stands there, drinking it all in, so I get out of the car and join him. As I watch the side of his face, I can't help but marvel at how much he resembles Ramon—at least from this angle.

Just when I think he won't speak, he does. "Your brother sure knew how to swing a baseball bat."

I smile. "I wish I'd gotten to see him play, even once."

"It was a thing of beauty, *mija*."

"I bet."

He turns to face me. "I'll never forgive myself for what I did . . . leaving you two after your mamá died."

My hands perspire. I'm not prepared to get into this now.

"I know no amount of apologizing will ever make up for my sins." He chews on the inside of his mouth, trying but failing to stave off some tears. "I wrote to your brother every week, you know. To check on you."

"You did?"

"*Sí*." He wipes his eyes. "He only wrote back once." Then he fishes into his front pocket and procures an envelope that's folded three times. He hands it to me. "You should have it."

I say thank you and take the crumpled envelope.

"Your brother loved you very much, Freya."

I stare at the smeared-ink handwriting on the envelope. "I love him very much too."

❖ ❖ ❖

It would have been prom week. But after Foxtail Academy shut down and the world was shaken by the truth about Memory Killer, public schools the world over paused while leaders and decision makers debated the best course of action.

Suffice it to say, Fletcher, Chase, Ollie, and I are *still* high school–less.

So we throw our own prom in Ollie's backyard garden.

"Fletcher, I'm hurt," Chase says as Ollie pins his boutonnière to his black tuxedo. "We agreed to wear matching tuxes, and here you are wearing Calvin Klein."

Ollie giggles. "What I'd give to see these two in matching tuxedos."

"For the record, I never agreed to that," Fletcher says, rolling his eyes.

"Hold still." I bat his shoulder so I can pin his boutonnière too.

He leans in close, his warm breath running down my hand as I work. His cologne smells like birch and firewood. "Is this still enough?"

"I'm holding a sharp object, Fletcher."

He laughs.

"Hang on, hang on," Chase snaps. "Let's go back to that, Ollie. What *would* you give to see us in matching tuxes? Hmm?"

"*No*, not that again." Ollie pulls up the hem of her dress and crosses the yard to the patio table where the boombox is. She turns up the radio. "You'll give us PTSD, Chase."

Fletcher takes my hand and raises it toward his mouth, sniffing my wrist corsage. "You have good taste."

I giggle despite myself. "Now if only I had good taste in boys."

He leads me underneath the pergola. The next song that plays is a slower one, and we naturally gravitate toward each other.

I ask, "How are your parents doing?"

"Better. They're talking about selling the house when the market's right, whenever that'll be."

"Oh yeah?"

"Dad says he wants to go back to school. Maybe start teaching."

"Wow, big life change."

"There's a lot of that happening right now."

I nod into his neck. "I saw my father earlier this week. We're taking it slow."

"Good, that's good." Fletcher takes a step back and twirls me to the beat. After he pulls me back toward him, we kiss.

"Hey, what do you think is going to happen to the Foxtail Academy campus now that the school's shut down?" Chase asks as he and Ollie dance beside us. The strings of lights overhead glint against the sky. They're not fireflies, but they'll do.

"We should all go back and see for ourselves," Fletcher offers.

I smirk. "Oh yeah?"

"Yeah. The campus borders a national park. And if you'll recall, I'm supposed to be taking you on a tour of my favorite national parks. Land Between the Lakes is a new addition to my list."

I smile and tell Fletcher that sounds great.

❖ ❖ ❖

A few days after our "prom," we get our chance to return to Foxtail Academy. On the news, we learn that the former faculty and student body have been invited to return to collect our belongings. Memory Frontier's downfall was so quick and profound, they couldn't even afford to mail us our things.

"I ain't complaining," Ollie says, sucking in the spring air and admiring the campus as the four of us head toward the dorms. "Strangely, it feels really good being back here."

"That is strange, Ol." Chase shakes his head in mild disapproval. "Look at this place!"

"It's postapocalyptic around here," Fletcher adds, chuckling.

Indeed, with no groundskeepers on salary, vicious weeds and overgrown bushes run amok. The library—the glass structure that separates the girls' and boys' dormitories—is boarded up, with multiple panes of glass busted out. In the distance, the Foxhole emanates an air of emptiness and depression. It's as if Herschel Jones's cooking was keeping that building alive.

This all makes me wonder if Foxtail Academy was looted, if any of our personal effects were taken.

We pass a few groups of former students who mill about with their parents, moving boxes clasped in their hands. Everyone seems to carry this mixture of grief and relief. It's a heavy kind of look, but we all seem to carry the load with our chins up.

When Ollie and I separate from the boys and head into our old dorm room, I'm struck by unexpected nostalgia. I pause in the doorway and glance about the room. Dust has accumulated on all the surfaces, but everything is mostly as we left it. My clothes are still balled up in a laundry basket beside the dresser and TV. My textbooks are strewn about the coffee table. Our beds are unmade.

I cross the room toward the closet and see a flashback, clear as water in a glass, of Ollie and me standing in this very spot, hours before the kickoff bonfire. Wordlessly, I dig through the hangers and manage to find the denim jacket she lent me that night.

I put it on slowly, the memories from that evening rushing back.

Ollie smiles up at me from the floor, where she's gathering her cassette tapes. "Wow, you still kill in that."

"I remember that night last year so vividly." I sit on the edge of the couch, interlacing my fingers. "Meeting the boys, eating that barbecue, the music at the bonfire, heading out into the woods after dark."

Ollie's smile widens. "Me too. And we don't even need the help of artificial recall."

I sigh through my nose. *Because we never did . . .*

❖ ❖ ❖

On the walk to our secret hang spot, Ollie and I pass Mr. Williams. He drags a rolling suitcase, merrily whistling to himself.

He perks up when he sees us. "Ah, hello, ladies!"

"Hey, Mr. Williams," we reply. He takes off his aviators, and my heart lurches at the sight of his eyes. *Gray.* Both of them.

Reading our reactions, he chuckles and slides his sunglasses back on. "Er, sorry about that, y'all. Keep forgettin', no pun intended. Apparently, those of us who need to ween off artificial recall will be stuck with the gray eyes for a while. Hopin' I get my color back soon."

I try to give him a look of encouragement. "It really is good to see you, Mr. Williams."

"Yeah." He chuckles. "And you're . . . Ollie? Which means you're"—he points at Ollie—"Freya. Right?"

My expression falls, but then he bursts into laughter. "Only foolin'!"

Ollie rolls her eyes but laughs all the same. "So . . . you're starting to remember us, then?"

"Sure am. They said it'll take a lot of time for me to reclaim *everything* that was taken from me." He grabs his suitcase and then tips an imaginary hat. "But here's the good news: I've got all the time in the world now."

The woods are coming alive again. The trees are sprouting leaves. Wildflowers and ankle-high weeds dot our path toward the water's edge. Ollie and I approach the edge of Juniper Lake, and I feel that sense of wonder again—that sense of seeing the expansive water for the first time and marveling at its picturesque beauty. It fills my chest with a burgeoning warmth that spreads down to my stomach.

Up ahead, as we near our secret spot beside the fallen tree, I spot the crepe myrtle. The tree isn't in bloom yet—apparently, that won't happen until summer. But seeing her there, standing tall and proud in the shadows of the evergreens, takes me back to that moment in Malcolm Heckman's memory. I'd almost lost Fletcher to a memory loop, but when he and I recalled the memory of this crepe myrtle together, it drew him back to me like a life preserver.

This tree saved his life just by *being*, and she'll never even realize it. But that's okay; she shouldn't have to know. She's just a tree. A beautiful, stoic *anchor* of a tree.

"You okay?" Ollie's soft voice pulls me from my thoughts.

I wipe my eyes. "Yeah, it's just . . . it's great to see this place again."

"Hear! Hear!" Chase bellows. We turn and see him and Fletcher marching to meet us. Together we stride to the fallen tree, sit down in our usual spots, and quietly survey the water. I keep waiting for Ollie or Chase to make some joke—to offer some levity to the moment. Honestly, that'd be welcome. It's hard to think that this will be the last time we'll ever sit in this spot.

But maybe it doesn't have to be the last time.

Maybe we'll make this an annual thing, revisiting our safe haven where we formed so many memories in an age of memory indexing.

After a while, Fletcher suggests returning to the bunker one last time.

"You out of your mind?" Chase scowls in his direction. "I never wanna go within ten feet of—"

"I dunno," I say, warming up to the idea. "It might be good. One last time. For closure."

Chase's mouth hangs open, but when Ollie nods in agreement, he shrugs. "What the hell? For closure."

72

FLETCHER COHEN

The bunker was mostly barren. The tables had been stripped of their computers. The metal filing cabinets had been cleared out. Chairs were overturned. The large Restorey had been cracked open. Much like Foxtail's campus, Dean Mendelsohn's bunker was abandoned and bereft of purpose.

Fletcher and the gang paused in the doorway when they spotted him standing in the midst of the desolation, slouching, carrying the weight of Memory Frontier's thwarted plans on his shoulders.

He, too, seemed to lack purpose.

The dean turned when he sensed the foursome loitering. His left arm was in a sling. "I wondered if you four would find yourselves back in this place . . . where it all started."

Fletcher and his friends exchanged a look. The Restorey, which once stood over seven feet tall, was busted in several spots, and bits of plastic, metal, and wiring littered the pavement. A shaft of light spilled into the facility from the open back door, ricocheting off the broken technology and spotlighting the crowbar at Dean Mendelsohn's feet.

Freya approached him. "Alexander Lochamire manipulated you into helping him, just like you manipulated me." Her words were whispers. "Your son, Daniel, really was in a car accident while using artificial recall. *That's* how he got stuck in a memory loop. And Lochamire promised to help your son if you helped him."

Dean Mendelsohn's face softened. "Before you four proved that knifing was possible, the theory of it enticed Alexander Lochamire and his Memory Frontier shareholders. At first, I was just consulting part-time for his R&D division. And once my team began to posit that young people were the only ones capable of knifing, I . . . I actually contemplated using Daniel as a test subject."

Fletcher thought back to when he'd first learned how to manifest within a memory. Fletcher and Freya had perceived then that Dean Mendelsohn was pondering using his son as a subject for the experiment.

The dean cursed. "The car accident happened while I was away, and sometimes I wonder if Daniel's stuck in that memory loop because of me—if God's punishing me because I considered subjecting my own child to something as heinous as knifing."

"Instead, you subjected someone else's kids to it." Chase walked up beside Freya. Fletcher and Ollie fell into line too. They stood there just as they had on that night in the bunker nearly a year ago when they'd first discovered Memory Frontier's secrets.

Dean Mendelsohn was about to reply, but Chase continued, "Look, you were only helping Memory Frontier because of Lochamire's empty promises. You were trying to help your son. But it's over now."

"Maybe for you it is." The dean pocketed his good hand, regarding the demolished Restorey with eyes of contempt. "Daniel may never wake up. I ran out of time."

"Actually . . ." Ollie tilted her head, lost in thought for a moment. "The Memory Ghosts used a device to pull me out of a knifing mission. Remember, guys?"

"*Interceptor,*" Fletcher replied. "That's what Zayne called it."

Dean Mendelsohn's face filled with color. "You were still knifing when they whisked you away from here?"

Ollie nodded.

"They said the tech was a prototype," Freya explained. "But it worked. Instead of ripping the electrode stickers off Ollie and risk damaging her consciousness, they used this Interceptor to safely draw her out of the knifing."

The dean's eyes filled with tears. "That's . . . remarkable. I would very much like to try this with my son."

Fletcher and his friends smiled, and they told the dean they'd find a way to get him in touch with Zayne Olson.

"What happened to Sade and Rhett?" Chase asked.

"They're safe." Dean Mendelsohn's head dropped slightly. "And while Rhett may have aided Dr. Sanders, he's still a minor with plausible deniability when it comes to Memory Frontier's true intentions. He and Sade were both manipulated, just like the rest of us, and I suspect they'll be dealing with the fallout for quite some time."

Won't we all, Fletcher thought.

Eventually, they said their goodbyes, but as they turned to leave, something occurred to Fletcher. He stalled inside the bunker as his friends went ahead.

"What do you mean you *ran out of time?*" he asked.

The dean sighed. Slowly, he procured an orange pill bottle from his front pocket.

The bottle was empty.

"Memory Frontier was supplying me with this medication."

The dean shook his head, then tossed the bottle onto the pavement. "It was the only thing staving off the memory particles. And with Memory Frontier now in total ruin, it's only a matter of time before the vasospasms return to claim my life."

Fletcher understood at once. That morning after he and his friends had memory knifed for the first time, the dean explained why teenagers were the only ones who should perform a knifing.

Adults with fully developed brains who artificially recall someone else's past will wake up after knifing and find their consciousness tearing, Dean Mendelsohn had said. *They cannot separate their memories from the ones they've knifed. Lingering aspects of the foreign memory—memory particles, as it were—bleed into their subconscious, creating the illusion of two pasts. It drives them mad.*

The dean, it appeared, had learned this lesson the hard way.

"There has to be a way to get you more of that medication," Fletcher said, his voice rising. "We just need to find the doctors who were on staff and—"

"That process could take months, Fletcher." The dean smiled despite the seemingly hopeless situation. "Every former Memory Frontier staffer is being deposed in the midst of a sprawling investigation into Lochamire's company. The only reason I've not been summoned yet is because I was a contract employee. It's only a matter of weeks before my number is called. By then, I could be long—"

"*Stop.*" Fletcher surprised himself with how firm he sounded. "There's still a way . . . We'll find a way."

The dean's smile expanded. "Perhaps. But right now, my priority is my son. And yours is to—" He stopped midsentence, staring past Fletcher, who turned and saw Freya standing in the entryway.

"Go, Fletcher," the dean urged softly.

With much effort, Fletcher managed to pull himself away and join Freya outside. As they walked away, he glanced over his shoulder and saw Dean Mendelsohn turning in a slow circle—likely taking it all in one last time.

He may be saying goodbye to the bunker, Fletcher mused, clasping Freya's hand. *But that wasn't goodbye for us.*

73

FREYA IZQUIERDO

Fletcher slows his Ducati to a stop on the street. In the distance, the abandoned remains of the Memory Frontier factory sit beneath gathering clouds. Evening draws near, and there's a chill in the Long Beach air.

"You good?" Fletcher asks, dismounting.

I tell him yes, I am, and then I get off the motorcycle. We jog across the street toward the structure that looks as if it's been crumbling for years.

"I've been rewatching the footage all week," I tell Fletcher as we identify a loose portion of the chain-link fence. He pulls it up and I crawl inside first. I continue once he's on the other side: "The footage I captured when I snuck in here last August. I've been desperately trying to find any clue in the ruins."

We slowly move toward what remains of the large factory, and I find myself at complete peace.

"And?"

"And then I realized this whole place is the clue."

"What do you mean?"

Together we walk through the busted doorframe where the entrance to the factory once stood. Inside, the place is awash in fading sunlight. The mounds of trash. The graffiti. The rubble. Everything's painted in the dim orange tones of diffused sunbeams.

Before, I demanded answers of this place.

Now I see that this place *is* the answer.

"If Memory Frontier bombed their own facility to cover up their secrets," I explain, "then why keep the crime scene intact all these years later? Why not flatten the place and erect a new factory?"

Fletcher scans the factory's interior, and I see him piecing it together. "Memory Frontier quarantined this place because *they* were trying to find out who bombed it."

"I don't think this was ever about what my brother witnessed on the bus. I think it's about the altercation he got into with his co-worker." I pull a folded envelope out of my pocket.

"What is that?"

"A letter from Ramon. My dad gave it to me, and he said it's the only time my brother ever wrote to him."

Fletcher puts a steady hand on my arm.

I continue, "It's postmarked one week before he died."

"And you haven't read it yet."

I shake my head. "I think I'm ready to, though. But I'd very much like to read it with you."

He brushes the hair out of my face and plants a kiss on my forehead. Then he stands at my side as I open the envelope and extract the letter. We both laugh.

It's written in Spanish.

"I'll just give you the CliffsNotes," I tell him, my eyes flying across Ramon's sloppy handwriting. I start to pace, mumbling summaries to Fletcher: "He says that while he's sorry he hasn't written back, he's not ready to forgive Dad for abandoning us after Mom died. That he understands how distraught Dad is after losing her, but did he consider how distraught *Ramon* is after losing both of them? He says . . ." I feel a knot forming at the back of my throat. It tightens as I read each word. "That I make him very proud . . . that Dad's crazy for leaving after the best thing that's ever happened to our family arrived . . . me, *su hija.* He says that while he's a far cry from a perfect guardian, he's doing his best to raise me. And that—"

I reread the next few sentences a couple of times.

"What is it?" Fletcher asks delicately.

I look up from the letter, hot tears filling my eyes. "It's a confession. He says he knew one of his coworkers had radicalized and was planning to blow up the factory with homemade explosives. Ramon says he confronted his coworker about it . . . that his coworker attacked him when he threatened to go to the police, but . . ."

I glance back down at the letter. "But Ramon confesses that he never told authorities about the bomb. He says that when the police took his statement after the altercation with the coworker, he couldn't bring himself to tell them *why* they'd gotten into a fight—that a bomb was hidden somewhere in the factory—because Ramon had begun to wonder if an attack on a Memory Frontier factory was a necessary evil."

I stop pacing and wipe the tears off my face with the back of my wrist. I fold the letter and slip it back into its envelope. My heart sinks as I walk back over to Fletcher. "He ended the letter by telling Dad he was working up the courage to do the right thing . . . that he was going to tell his bosses about the bomb."

He waited too long, I think with a chill. *Somehow, the bomb detonated before Ramon could speak up.*

His silence resulted in his death—along with the deaths of many others.

I remember asking Ramon why he didn't just quit and go work somewhere else. He'd said it was too late for that, which confused me at the time. And while he didn't elaborate on what he meant by "too late," I know now. He was struggling with guilt and shame over knowing the truth about the bomb and doing nothing about it.

"He had a change of heart," Fletcher says, pulling me into a soft hug. "Your brother's not the bad guy here."

"He was complicit, though. By remaining quiet, he became an accomplice."

"It's not black-and-white. Should he have said something immediately? *Absolutely.* But your brother loved you very much, and he knew in his heart he couldn't continue to sit by if it meant he'd be taken away from you—if it meant innocent people would die."

And yet in the end, both things happened. I sigh into Fletcher's chest. "During my time with Gemma, I came to peace with Ramon's imperfections. I decided it's more important to see him as a human than a hero, that I have to accept the good along with the bad. This new discovery challenges my resolve, Fletcher. Why can't it just be black-and-white?"

He smiles into my head. "Because rarely is life black-and-white. Rarely is it perfectly binary. On this colorful planet we inhabit, gray is ubiquitous, which is to say gray areas are *all* areas."

I know he's right, but I'm not ready to accept that.

I hope to one day.

❖ ❖ ❖

After we mount his motorcycle, Fletcher asks me if I've had any more premonitions. I tell him no, that they stopped months ago, around the time we stopped using Reflectors and MeReaders.

"It's for the best," I tell him, fastening my helmet into place. "We were never meant to see into the future. It robs us of memory-making in the present."

"*Memory-making.* I like how that sounds." Fletcher puts on his helmet too. "C'mon. Chase and Ollie probably grabbed us a table already."

And then he fires up the engine and zips toward the PCH. I glance at the factory in the side mirror. The battered building gets smaller and smaller before vanishing altogether in the twilight. I pull myself against Fletcher's back, watching as gray buildings whip by. Eventually, the coast comes into view, where the faintest bit of color still hangs in the sky.

I close my eyes and commit this moment to memory.

STREAM THE AUTHOR'S PLAYLIST

Every song referenced in *The Recall Paradox* has been compiled by the author in this exclusive playlist to enhance your experience with the book. Novels are wonderfully immersive, and the author hopes that your immersion is amplified by the book's playlist.

"Time to Forget"—Bootpack (feat. Joel Porter)
"Gimme! Gimme! Gimme! (A Man After Midnight)"—ABBA
"Jane"—Jefferson Starship
"Vacation"—The Go-Go's
"It's My Life"—Talk Talk
"Higher Love"—Steve Winwood
"Manic Monday"—The Bangles
"Dreamtime"—Daryl Hall
"Monster Mash"—Bobby "Boris" Picket & The
        Crypt-Kickers
"Africa"—Toto
"Missing You"—John Waite
"Pour Some Sugar On Me"—Def Leppard

AUTHOR'S PLAYLIST

"Smooth Criminal"—Michael Jackson

"La Nave del Olvido"—José José

"La Bamba"—Ritche Valens

"Retirada (Bolero)"—Javier Solís

"Do You Remember?"—The Beach Boys

"Last Christmas"—Wham!

"Beat It"—Michael Jackson

"Eye of the Tiger"—Survivor

ACKNOWLEDGMENTS

Once again, I find myself overwhelmed by the support and encouragement of so many remarkable people. Even though I face crippling anxiety over missing someone, I must still endeavor to be exhaustive (knowing that I will surely fail)!

First, I want to thank the Vaca family—my dad's brothers, sister, my cousins, my abuela Estella and my late abuelo Ramon, every in-law and "outlaw." My Californian/Mexican tribe. Our history and heritage are preserved, in large part, in memories.

To the incredible world-class team at HarperCollins—namely, publicists Margaret Kercher and Taylor Ward; marketing director Kerri Potts; associate publisher Becky Monds; and of course a *massive* thanks to the brilliant, incomparable Laura Wheeler. Not only is she the sharpest editor in the biz, but I'm convinced she's the most patient one too. Thanks for elevating both me and this book, Laura!

Even though I stepped into the wild, wonderful world of publishing unagented, I can now declare with gratitude and joy that I'm repped by the magnificent Nat Kimber of The Rights

Factory. I owe a lot to my new team: Sam Hiyate, Milly Ruggiero, and Karmen Wells. We're just getting started.

Huge thanks to all my friends and beta readers, specifically Justin and Jessica Brown, Challice Parker, Megan Haggerty, Renée Olson, and Larry Rutledge. A special thank-you to Chris Gouker, a contender for my biggest cheerleader, and lifelong brothers Jeremy Grondahl and Rusty Shipp for showing me constant grace and humility.

I cannot thank my dear friends Chris Haggerty and Phil Earnest enough for selflessly serving me (and many others) with their talents. I'm forever indebted to friends Wes and Kailey Langdon and Joel and Megan Porter for tirelessly supporting me and . . . well, for being amazing. To Chris and Eileen Canady, for opening their beautiful home to me when I needed a writing retreat; to Thann Bennett and his beautiful, warm family—you greatly inspire me.

I'd better wrap this up before they play me off the stage. To Megan Morano, for agreeing to help me with my crazy book launch for *The Memory Index* and exceeding my wildest expectations. On that note, I cannot thank Nate Underwood, Leslie Eiler Thompson, Rachel Matar, and everyone at the Rabbit Room enough for a truly memorable night. And the music of Jack Settle, Spencer Miller, Jessie Villa, and Stephen Keech (with coordination by Ashton Myers) . . . just *wow.*

I'm forever grateful to my Soundstripe family—to every single person who purchased this book or cheered me on. Thanks to Joelle at The Bookshop, Rae Ann at Parnassus, and Deezy at Novelette. Nashville has *the* best bookstores in the country. Grateful to fellow writers Lauren Thoman, Francesca Flores, Nathan Elias, Claire Gibson, Sara Wigal, Lindsey Frazier, Rob Rufus, David Arnold, and Jeff Zentner!

gasps for air

A special *special* thank-you to my new friends Joe Clemons and Holley Maher, creative trailblazers in Nashville and beyond. To my

ACKNOWLEDGMENTS

writing community at the Porch—the vital work of Susannah and Katie is far-reaching and important.

And to my loving, supportive wife, Katie: thank you for believing in me when I don't—which, admittedly, is often. To each of my kiddos—Lane, Luna, Lennox, Lyvia, and Lincoln—I love you all so much. Gracias to my eternally encouraging parents, sisters, brothers-in-law, nephews, and nieces. For all the love and support from my Forney family.

Most importantly, thank you, Jesus, for saving me. You give me the words.

DISCUSSION QUESTIONS

1. Freya navigates complicated memories of her brother, Ramon. What's your response to the question posed by Gemma: "What's more terrifying—losing your memories, or confronting difficult ones?"

2. When Fletcher and his mother, Lila, have Thanksgiving with Ollie's family, Fletcher concludes that he and his mother needed the "welcome distraction." What are some welcome distractions in your life when navigating difficult seasons?

3. Freya concludes that it's important to remember her brother as a human, not a hero. Do you agree with this in your own life regarding people in your community? Why or why not?

4. Gemma keeps a picture of a picture because she doesn't want to lose the feeling she felt when she first saw the photograph. What do you think she means by this?

5. It's been said that even villains are the heroes in their own story. What do you think is the driving factor

behind the decisions Dr. Sanders makes—particularly in the closing chapters of the book?

6. As Freya and the gang are driving to Alden, Nevada, Freya has a terrible premonition. How do you interpret the chilling vision?

7. Do you agree with Freya when she says, "We were never meant to see into the future. It robs us of memory-making in the present"?

8. After everything the foursome went through, they decided to return to Foxtail Academy for closure. Would you have done the same? Why or why not?

From the Publisher

GREAT BOOKS

ARE EVEN BETTER WHEN THEY'RE SHARED!

Help other readers find this one:

- Post a review at your favorite online bookseller

- Post a picture on a social media account and share why you enjoyed it

- Send a note to a friend who would also love it—or better yet, give them a copy

Thanks for reading!

ABOUT THE AUTHOR

Chris J. Haggerty (@ChrisHaggertyDP)

Julian R. Vaca has been a creative writer for over a decade. He was a staff writer on PBS's *Reconnecting Roots*, a nationally broadcast show that drew in millions of viewers over its first two seasons. He's also the co-writer of *Pencil Test*, a feature-length documentary that's being executive produced by Disney animation legend Tom Bancroft (Earnest Films, 2023). Julian lives in Nashville with his family.

Connect with him at JulianRayVaca.com
Instagram: @JulianRayVaca
Twitter: @JulianRVaca
Facebook: @JulianRVaca